Lisa started her career teaching English and Drama, and when she had her family, combined all three to write novels about family drama. Originally from Yorkshire, she now lives in a London suburb with her husband and two teenage daughters, so expects there's plenty more drama to come.

T0190582

Her Daughter's Secret

LISA TIMONEY

avon.

Published by AVON
A division of HarperCollins*Publishers*
1 London Bridge Street
London SE1 9GF

www.harpercollins.co.uk

HarperCollins*Publishers*
1st Floor, Watermarque Building, Ringsend Road
Dublin 4, Ireland

A Paperback Original 2022
2

First published in Great Britain by HarperCollins*Publishers* 2022

A catalogue copy of this book is available from the British Library.

ISBN: 978-0-00-855315-9

Typeset in Sabon by Palimpsest Book Production Ltd, Falkirk, Stirlingshire
Printed and bound in the UK using 100% renewable electricity
at CPI Group (UK) Ltd

To my mum, Bronwen, for everything x

NOW

Chapter One

Bea didn't fit in here. For a start, it was a long time since she'd had egg-shaped buttocks like the other mothers in the playground. Hers probably looked like two hot cross buns squashed at the bottom of a carrier bag. She tugged down her sleeves to warm her hands, her gaze fixed on the double doors, trying not to imagine how Phoebe must feel when she watched all her classmates skip towards their mothers. Eventually, Phoebe appeared, flanked by the classroom assistant, Kelly. Bea rushed to greet her.

'Aunty Bea!' Her niece held out her arms and Bea crouched down, wrapping her in a hug. 'I didn't know you were coming today.'

Bea pulled back, looking into Phoebe's face. The birthmark covering most of her right cheek and eyelid was livid against the rest of her pale skin. She wondered if Phoebe was tired or cold since it was a darker red than usual. 'I'm doing early shifts this week, so I can pick you up.' Planting a kiss on Phoebe's dark hair, she stood, feeling her knees creak with the effort. She smiled at Kelly. 'All okay today?'

1

'There was a bit of unpleasantness, but we dealt with it, didn't we?' Kelly rubbed the top of Phoebe's head, seemingly oblivious to the little girl's grimace. Phoebe reached up to flatten her hair.

Bea stiffened. 'Anything I need to tell her dad?'

'It's fine.' Phoebe flapped a dismissive arm and set off across the playground.

'We're on it,' Kelly said, touching Bea lightly on the wrist before turning and heading back inside.

By the time they reached Bea's old Yaris, the car park was almost empty of the SUVs and sports cars that usually jostled for space.

'Blimey, what did you have for lunch? Lead weights?' Bea groaned as she lifted Phoebe into the passenger seat and the little girl giggled, stopping when Bea leaned over to pull the seatbelt across.

'I can do it,' she said, a note of defiance in her voice.

Bea smoothed down the maroon tunic she hadn't changed out of since her shift at Sweetingdale and stood back, listening for the click. The memory of a passenger in another car where the seatbelt hadn't been done up made her wonder if she'd ever see Phoebe in a car without the ghost of her mother coming along for the ride.

* * *

When they arrived at Phoebe's home, Bea switched off the alarm, standing aside to let her niece skip past the glass-encased staircase, which would have a permanent mosaic of sticky fingerprints if Bea didn't know how to wield a microfibre cloth. She kicked off her trainers, popping them into the cupboard hidden under the stairs. The temptation to abandon them on the polished wood floor was strong. It would be funny to watch the consternation on Ewan's face when he came home to a house that didn't look like something from an interior design magazine.

'Homework,' said Bea, with a mock stern voice, following Phoebe to the kitchen. She deliberately slapped the satchel onto the white table and made Phoebe jump. The little girl sniggered.

'It's smellings today, isn't it?' She remembered Immy at the same age as Phoebe, giggling when she told Bea she'd accidentally called spellings *smellings* in front of her teacher. The memory stung the back of her eyes for a moment before she blinked it away.

She opened the kitchen drawer where Ewan kept the stationery. It was neater than any in Bea's house; the pens, pencils and felt tips all segregated like knives and forks in a cutlery drawer. Plucking out a sharp pencil, she pointed at one of the emerald velvet dining chairs.

'Come on.'

Phoebe clambered onto the chair and opened a page with a list of ten printed words glued in. 'These smellings are easy,' she said. 'I can do all of them with my eyes shut.'

'Let's see if you can.' Bea could still recall the distress on her husband Oli's face when Ewan called to tell them why his beautiful baby had started having seizures. A brain scan had revealed that the birthmarks covering much of the right side of Phoebe's face and upper body were also on the occipital lobe of her brain. She shoved the memory back, concentrating on the bright, funny girl at the table.

Taking her scarf from the bottom of her bag, she picked off the sweet wrappers that were stuck to it and gently blindfolded Phoebe, who squealed in delight. She wrote the words with her eyes closed, then said them out loud

3

before Bea relented and put the book back in the bag. Placing the pencil back into the slot with the felt tips, she slid the drawer closed.

'Want to help make dinner?'

'What are we having?'

'Your daddy asked me to make fish pie and salad.' She lowered her voice. 'But I'm not allowed to add any chilli to the dressing because we don't want to . . .' She let the sentence hang, watching Phoebe's eyes dance as they both said, 'Blow Grandma's head off!' and laughed at the familiar joke. She doubted Joyce would find it funny. What would her mother-in-law find funny? Maybe next door's cat being run over so it couldn't crap on her lawn?

Opening the fridge, she felt her smile chill in the cold air. In the last year she had gone from occasionally picking Phoebe up from school and making her something to eat, to frequently making dinner for Ewan, too. Recently his texts asked if she'd mind making enough for Joyce and taking it down to her house. *If it wasn't too much trouble.*

* * *

Phoebe's chatter was like soothing music as she nibbled on the fish pie. This was the highlight of Bea's day. When she finished her last mouthful, Bea leaned her elbows on the table and yawned.

'Am I keeping you up?' Phoebe asked. It was as though her grandmother's words were coming out of the six-year-old's mouth.

'Ha, ha. I'm a bit tired. I was in the shower by five this morning. Then I did an eight-hour shift before collecting you from school.'

Phoebe's eyebrows dipped in the middle. 'Does that mean you won't come and get me anymore?'

4

Bea sat up straight, forcing her eyes wide. 'Don't be daft. I want to pick you up. It's my favourite thing to do. I'd only be at home on my own if I wasn't here and that would be no fun, would it?'

'I like it when you say daft like that.'

'Well, it's not daaarft, is it? There's no "*r*" in it. You sound like Immy, taking the Mickey out of my accent.'

Phoebe's gaze dropped to the floor. Bea froze, then busied herself plating up two meals for Ewan and Joyce. She made sure three quarters of Joyce's plate was made up of salad, with the merest gloss of light vinaigrette. Heaven forbid the woman should be exposed to too many carbohydrates. They were for people with poor self-control, apparently.

She covered the plate and prepared to take it outside, down the gravel drive, past the two neighbouring houses and into the beautiful Arts and Crafts house her husband grew up in and which her mother-in-law still presided over like Queen of The bloody Crescent.

As she bent to slide on her shoes, her eyes rested on the photograph on the hall table. Any feelings of resentment about how much help she was expected to give to this family melted away when she saw a three-year-old Phoebe, wrapped in the arms of a stunning young woman who shared the same bright eyes and blunt brown fringe as the little girl. Gemma's chin rested on Phoebe's tiny shoulder. Her creamy cheek nestled against the bright red of her daughter's as they smiled identical, beautiful smiles.

Bea stood and hugged Phoebe tightly to her.

'What's that for?' Phoebe's voice was muffled against her tunic.

Softening her hold, Bea took her niece's face in her hands. 'I just love you, that's all.'

But that wasn't all. That wasn't nearly half of it, but she couldn't say how sorry she was; how much she wished she'd been a better mother to Immy. If she had been, she was sure things would have turned out differently. She lifted the plate and trudged down the road to make one of a million amends that would never amount to enough.

Chapter Two

The plate was too hot to hold comfortably. Bea swapped it to her other hand as she and Phoebe waited on Joyce's doorstep in the miserable autumn drizzle. Joyce opened her front door and smiled. Or, at least, gave her version of a smile, which was a minute drawing back of her ruby lips and the narrowing of her blue-lidded eyes. Joyce had worn the same style of make-up for the twenty-seven years Bea had known her. Now eighty, the black kohl along her upper lid was sometimes shaky, and the red lipstick bled into the lines around her mouth, but with the tight plait wound around her head – grey where once it was chestnut brown – it was still a strong look.

A strong look for a strong woman.

'Fish pie?' she asked, nodding towards the plate as Bea and Phoebe stepped into the wood-panelled hallway. 'How nice.'

Bea rolled her eyes at this pretence at surprise and wondered why Joyce bothered. They both knew Bea would follow orders. She was like a broken-in horse, keeping her kick firmly under control. She never deviated from what

Ewan *suggested* in his texts. She never reared up and showed her teeth. This was her penance for what had happened three years ago. She knew it was the least she could do.

Joyce's march was slower than usual, her gait uneven as they wiped their feet then followed her past the grandfather clock into the kitchen.

'Your leg alright? Are you limping?'

'I'm perfectly fine.' Joyce's back straightened.

Bea put the plate on a slate mat that sat, lonely, on the table.

'Would you like us to sit with you while you eat?' She took the cellophane from the plate, the delicious smell of the pie wafting up with the steam.

'No, thank you. I'm used to my own company.' Joyce peered at the plate. 'Prawns?'

'It's nice, Grandma,' said Phoebe. 'I ate all mine, didn't I, Aunty Bea?'

Bea touched her niece's head, wondering how Joyce could resist scooping her into a hug whenever she saw her. She remembered Joyce telling her to leave Immy to cry when she woke in the night as a baby, and her saying how Bea had spoiled her by picking her up when she raised her pudgy arms towards her as a toddler. Guilt crept over her skull as she remembered how sometimes, when they visited Joyce, she'd fought her instincts and let her child cry. She wondered if the wails of her infant daughter had been absorbed by the wood lining these walls. Maybe that was why she hated being here so much. Or at least partly why.

She rested her arm around Phoebe's shoulders. 'You did really well, poppet.'

'Prawns have no place in a fish pie.' Joyce scraped the

curled pink creature to the side of the plate and dug under the potato, examining the creamy filling.

'I think they add something,' said Bea, grabbing the prawn and popping it into her mouth, not looking at Joyce. A small moment of rebellion before she returned to her stall. She picked up yesterday's clean plate from next to the porcelain sink and gestured to Phoebe to follow her back out to the hall. 'Enjoy your dinner.'

'Can you take the rubbish out with you, Beatrice?' called Joyce. 'It's behind the door.'

Bea widened her eyes at her niece and Phoebe covered her mouth with her hand to stop her giggles as Bea said, 'No problem.' She dipped back into the kitchen and grabbed the black sack.

She swerved around the side of the house and dumped the bag in the wheelie bin, jumping out of the way of the rainwater sloshing off the lid. She peered up at the dormer window above the garage, feeling a familiar twinge of longing; imagining Oli's face at the window after he came back from travelling, when, to save falling back into the old patterns of doing whatever his mother dictated, he'd moved into the room above the garage while he did his post-graduate teaching course.

It was the first place Bea had stayed with him in Belmoat. She'd travelled down from Yorkshire to meet his family and stayed in that chilly room as he tried to persuade her his mother did like her, that her snootiness was just a façade.

If that was so, it was a heavily fortified façade. Bea had only ever seen through it when she'd interrupted Joyce playing with Immy as a young girl. But as soon as Immy stopped being compliant and golden, the barriers went back up. Years later, even Phoebe couldn't get past them.

As she walked back to the front of the house, she clocked Phoebe's screwed-up face, as though she was grappling with a difficult decision. In response to Bea's questioning look, she said, 'I've found something in my craft box. Do you want to see when we get home?'

'What is it?'

'Some writing in a book.' Phoebe sounded hesitant. 'Stories, I think.'

'I like stories.'

'Mummy wrote them.'

Hearing Phoebe say 'mummy' caused Bea's knees to weaken. She stumbled. Phoebe grabbed her hand and Bea bit back tears. Phoebe shouldn't be taking care of her – not when she was to blame for everything. She squeezed Phoebe's hand and steered her to the inside of the pavement, avoiding the puddles dappled orange by the streetlights. 'I've got to clear up after dinner, then you need a bath. Maybe another day, okay?' She wasn't strong enough to read stories Gemma had written for her daughter. Not yet. She didn't know if she ever would be.

Phoebe paused to tap her shoe in a shallow pool of water and Bea waited, tense.

'Okay.' Then, as though the thoughts were a sequence, she asked, 'How does Grandma know she doesn't like fish pie with prawns in it?'

Bea exhaled with relief at the change of subject. 'I don't know.' They ambled back up The Crescent, towards Ewan's square, modern house. 'Perhaps she's had it before?'

'But she hasn't had your one before. She might like that one.'

Bea nodded. 'It's easy to get stuck in your ways, to think how you've always done things is the right way.'

'But then you might miss out on something new, and

that new thing might be better.' She turned her head towards Bea and Bea's heart melted.

'You are very wise, Phoebe James. Do you know that?'

'Yes,' said Phoebe confidently, 'I do.'

I'm sorry you had to grow up before your time, thought Bea, and held Phoebe's hand a little tighter.

* * *

When Bea pushed open her front door that evening, white envelopes slid across the faded *'Welcome'* on the mat. Bending to pick up the paper, she realised she was tired to her bones. She was tempted to lie down right there in the narrow hallway, which still had the patches of paint she and Oli had daubed on the wall. Smears of what might have been.

She flopped down next to the mat. There was nobody to notice if she slept there. She could nod off looking at the different patches of green on the wall and remember laughing with her husband as they wrote the names of each colour underneath in faint pencil. Who thought that *Lichen* was a good name for a paint? She read Oli's pencil marks *Ball Green,* hearing the ghost of his voice say that sounded like a matter for the doctor, not a painter and decorator.

They'd never got around to painting the hallway, of course. She pushed her hands against the carpet, heaving herself up to standing. She wandered through to the kitchen, knowing she shouldn't be shoving unopened bills into the drawer. *But we don't always do what we should, do we?* She slammed the drawer closed, made a cup of strong tea, and opened her laptop for her evening ritual of scrolling the internet, scrutinising the missing persons websites and social media groups.

For months, when Immy first went missing, she'd toured the streets on her bike, scouring the faces of strangers, dismounting, heart thudding, if she saw a dark-haired girl curled in a doorway, or a slim figure in a sleeping bag. Soon, hostel workers knew her voice at the end of the phone line. They were kind, but eventually, they asked her not to ring, that they wouldn't be able to tell her if Immy was there. She'd left her number anyway.

The small pile of postcards stacked on the windowsill caught her eye. One arrived every so often from random cities across the country. They were always blank, the address in block capitals, no signature, not even a hint that they were from Immy. But Bea chose to see them as a sign that her daughter was still alive and still thinking of her. Despite everything.

She lifted one from the top of the pile. It was from Morecambe and had a picture of The Midland Hotel on the front. She pinned it on the fridge with a magnet in the shape of The Tower of London, which they'd bought on a trip for Bea's fortieth birthday, just before Ewan and Gemma's wedding. Seven years, and another lifetime ago. She viewed it for a minute before snatching the magnet away and dropping the card back on the windowsill. It hurt too much to see it there, as if it were a postcard from a family holiday. Anyway, Ewan or Joyce might see it and ask who it was from. Then she'd have to tell them how much she hoped it was from Immy, and they'd all feel her betrayal.

She gave a humourless snort. As if Joyce or Ewan would ever deign to call here. If you lived on The Crescent, people came to you.

Scrolling through her emails and texts, the residue of hope that Immy might have messaged lingered. Emails from utility companies had ugly blue dots at the side telling her they wanted to be opened. She closed the page.

Typing 'Harley Davidson Fatboy 2001 sale price', she scrolled through the results, assessing whether selling the motorbike could solve some of the financial mess she'd amassed in the last four years. It could. But the thought of a space in the garage with just the oil stain on the floor, instead of the bike they'd ridden on, her arms wrapped around Oli's waist, or his around hers, the muted sound of the engine rumbling through the helmet, was too much to bear.

The letters in the drawer with the mortgage company's logo in the corner taunted her as well. The house, the bike, they were all she had left of the life she'd had before, when she'd been a wife and a mother. When they'd been happy.

She couldn't lose anything else. She'd find a way through this. She had to.

Chapter Three

In the staffroom at Sweetingdale, Jan unbuttoned the bottom of her tunic and groaned. 'Our Ciara made a Victoria sponge last night and it's gone already.' She sat on the chair next to Bea.

'Oh yeah?' Bea nodded at Jan's gaping buttons. 'I suppose you had nothing to do with that?'

Jan's mouth opened in mock indignation, her chin disappearing into the roll of soft flesh below. 'Me? They're like bloody gannets, that lot. You know the scene in *The Birds*? It was like that. As soon as she smeared the last bit of jam and slapped the top on it, they swooped in. Didn't even wait for her to sprinkle the icing sugar on.' She made a beak shape with her hands, pecking at Bea's neck.

Bea batted her away. 'Get off.'

Jan pointed at Bea's hair. 'Did you come on the bike today, or is that a Kate Bush look gone wrong?'

'Rude!' Bea scooped her hair off her neck, trying to tame it into a ponytail. 'You're right, though, I came on the bike. The childminder's picking Phoebe up today, so I thought I'd give it a run.' She didn't add that she was trying to squeeze as much freedom and joy from it as she could, in case she couldn't cling on to it. She pulled the hairband from her wrist and gathered her hair in an untidy bunch.

'So, you're not on duty at Lord Ewan's this aft?'

When she'd first met Oli's little brother as a jumped-up student studying business at Durham, she'd given Ewan that nickname. Jan was one of the few people she'd shared it with. 'Free as a bird.' As she said it, the thought of going home at two with the rest of the day ahead of her made her stomach flip. Still, she tried to keep her voice light.

'Fancy a brew and a catch-up at yours? We could do mine, but there's no cake left. and Ciara's given up college again, so she'll be hanging around like an eggy smell.'

'Yeah, that'd be good.' Bea could have kissed her friend. It would be bloody brilliant. 'Are you stressed about Ciara?' She tried to imagine how she'd have reacted if Immy had given up on a series of courses the way Jan's eldest seemed to. But she could hardly talk. Immy hadn't exactly taken the route she and Oli had planned for her. Joyce had always banged on about how important it was for Immy to get into a top university, but by the time Immy was applying her interests could be listed as underage drinking and a bit of light shoplifting. Maybe Bea should have tried harder to explain Immy's increasingly wild behaviour to Oli's mother, but how could she when she hadn't really understood it herself? Maybe Joyce was privately satisfied her predictions about Bea's parenting had come true. She shook the thought away. Even her mother-in-law wouldn't be that malevolent.

'Nah. She'll find her way eventually. I mean, look at me.' Jan gestured to herself, puffing out her chest. 'I didn't

15

know I wanted to be plumping up pillows for loaded nannas when I was seventeen, did I? But here I am, living the dream.'

A loud sniff came from the doorway. They both jumped and turned to see Lynn standing with her hands on her wide hips. Bea wondered if the woman hovered instead of walking, she moved around so quietly. She imagined her sticking felt to the soles of her sturdy shoes so that no one ever heard her coming.

'I hope you're not being disparaging about the residents, Jan? They deserve our respect as well as our care.'

Jan slumped back in her chair. 'Would I ever?'

'Make sure you don't.' Lynn crossed the room and clicked the kettle on. Bea tried not to giggle as Jan stuck up two fingers behind her back and danced her hand up and down, dropping them just in time when Lynn turned around sharply. 'Kenny's reported a theft.'

Bea's heart sank. This spate of thefts was getting worse, and it always seemed to happen when she was on shift.

'He said a hundred pounds in cash has gone missing from his locker. He said it was there last night but when he looked an hour ago it had gone.'

'What was he doing with a ton in his locker?' asked Jan.

'That's not really the question, is it?' Lynn cocked her head to the side. 'We need to ask where it's gone.'

'Where do you think it's gone?' Jan's tunic rustled as her shoulders shifted. Bea wanted to put her hand on her friend's arm to calm her but couldn't risk antagonising Lynn.

'Is he absolutely sure it's gone missing?' she said, in her most soothing voice.

'You were on that corridor this morning, so perhaps

16

you should check with him,' Lynn said to Bea, dipping a teabag into the hot water twice before dropping it in the bin.

'We've *all* been here this morning,' Jan said pointedly.

Lynn blew into her steaming mug. 'I've tried to placate him, but since it isn't the first time this has happened on Primrose corridor, we need to be extra vigilant. I have my suspicions, but if you see anything out of the ordinary, or if you suspect one of your co-workers, you need to come straight to me.'

Lynn gave Bea a prolonged gaze before gliding out of the room.

* * *

Jan's Fiat was parked outside Bea's 1930s semi when she pulled the bike into the driveway and turned off the engine. Her friend waited patiently by the front door while Bea dragged off the helmet, blowing at the hair stuck to her face.

'With you in a minute.' In the garage, Bea breathed in the smell of the engine oil, allowing the memories it conjured to settle before heading to the house.

More white envelopes sat on the mat. Bea opened the door wide for Jan to pass through before bending to pick them up. She hung her leather jacket on the banister and followed Jan into the kitchen.

'You haven't washed up your breakfast bowl. I'd have something to say if you left that out in my house.' Jan tutted. 'Slippery slope.' She raised her eyebrows and peeked over her glasses.

'Need to have something to do when I get home.'

Jan laughed at what she clearly thought was a joke, and Bea smiled along with her. But what was the point in clearing up straight away when you lived alone? She opened the drawer, dropping the envelopes on top of the others.

'You not going to open those?'

Bea's jaw tightened. 'Did you just come to have a go at me? Because I've got enough people in my life who do that, thanks.'

Jan's face fell. 'Sorry. God, sorry. I'm so used to bickering at my lot, it's hard to get out of the habit.'

Bea dropped into a chair. 'Ignore me. I'm in a funny mood.'

'Anything to do with those unopened envelopes?'

'They're not helping.'

'Anything I can do?'

'Have you won the lottery?'

'Would I be cutting pensioners' toenails three days a week if I had?'

Bea hoisted herself from her chair and walked over to the drawer. She trusted Jan. Jan was good with money. Maybe she could help her find a solution because the envelopes and the unopened emails were making her brain too heavy in her head.

She dropped the pile on the table. 'I've made a mess of everything.'

'Nothing is unfixable.' Jan reached for her hand across the table.

But she was talking as a woman with a husband and four kids at home. Maybe it *was* possible to fix things when people were still there. But Oli was gone and Immy was gone, and the mortgage company wanted to take back her home. So, Jan was wrong. Some things couldn't be fixed.

Chapter Four

Ewan was working longer hours than usual, and Bea felt increasingly resentful on Phoebe's behalf as she waited in the school playground, her hand shielding her eyes from the weak October sun. She knew he would never get these precious years back. Phoebe would grow up despite him. Soon, she'd have a boyfriend, start drinking, and he would lose whatever power he had to keep her safe.

She reined her thoughts back in as Phoebe bounced towards her. She was six. She wasn't Immy. Bea wasn't her mother.

'Alex has got a baby in her tummy.' Phoebe waved at children she passed, each one studiously ignoring her. Bea glowered at the mothers who were oblivious to their children turning their heads away from the little girl, avoiding her eyes, or running in the other direction when she shouted their names.

Focusing all of her attention on Phoebe, she plastered a smile on her face. 'Has she? That's exciting, isn't it?'

'Babies take up a lot of time, so, she won't be able to look after me when it comes out.'

'Is that right?'

Watching Phoebe nod vigorously, the muscles in Bea's shoulders tightened. If Alex was pregnant, who would be Phoebe's childminder first thing in the morning and after school? Alex was perfect. She lived on the estate around the corner and could fit working with Phoebe around her shifts at the local pub. And it took time to understand Phoebe's epilepsy medication. A random babysitter couldn't just take over.

'Bye, Sydney!' Phoebe waved at a child with long blonde hair who walked alongside an older woman who must be her grandma.

When Sydney ignored Phoebe, the woman nudged her. 'That little girl spoke to you, Sydney. Where's your manners?'

The girl stared at her feet and said, 'Bye,' quietly.

The woman fell in step with Bea, peering down at Phoebe. 'That looks sore.' She pointed at Phoebe's face. 'Did you burn yourself?'

Bea tensed. 'No. That's just one of your birthmarks, isn't it, poppet?'

'It's not sore.' Phoebe poked at her cheek. 'Look.' She rubbed her hand up and down the port-wine stain, beaming up at the woman, whose brow formed an ugly V.

'Bless you, poor thing,' she said.

Bea wanted to slap her. A thousand words gathered in her throat but before she could find any appropriate to say in front of small children, Sydney ran off towards another girl with glowing, pale skin. The woman scurried after her calling for her to be careful not to fall.

Phoebe squinted up at Bea, her eyes narrowed against the bright sky. 'They don't hurt.'

'I know, sweetheart.'

20

'They might do, after I've had the thingy, though.'

Bea crouched down, her face level with Phoebe's. 'You mean the laser treatment at the hospital?'

Phoebe nodded. 'Daddy said it might hurt a bit.'

'It wasn't too bad last time, was it?' Bea remembered rubbing moisturiser into the bruised skin under Phoebe's chin two years ago, after the laser treatment to lighten the colour of the port-wine stain on her face and neck.

'Not too bad.' Her face broke into a smile. 'Daddy let me have ice cream and watch the iPad in bed.'

'Wow.' That didn't sound like Ewan at all. It broke Bea's heart that after Gemma died, he struggled to show Phoebe the kind of love a three-year-old who has lost their mother needs.

She nodded towards Sydney, who was playing a complicated clapping game with another child. Phoebe made the same motions with her hands as she walked along, playing with an invisible partner.

'Do you play with her?'

'Yes,' said Phoebe, seriously. 'She's my friend. But she doesn't want to play with me.'

Bea's heart pumped faster. 'Why not, if she's your friend?'

'Some of the girls are my friends, but they don't want to touch me. They're scared they'll catch my birthmarks.'

Forcing herself to carry on walking, Bea resisted the compulsion to turn around and march straight into the Headteacher's office. She'd thought the bullying was getting better. Phoebe no longer came out of school crying because the children called her names or picked on her. This felt worse. She was still being excluded by these entitled brats, but they were clever enough to dress it up as fear rather than nastiness.

'Did you tell them you can't catch birthmarks?'

'Yes, but I'm not sure they believe me because they still run away.'

Bea held Phoebe's hand, avoiding looking at any of the mothers in case she lost control and told them some home truths about their little angels. They shouldn't allow their children to behave like that.

Bea's heart lurched as she replayed that thought. *What kind of mother brings up a child who can cause so much pain?* A mother like her. That's who.

* * *

Bea started as she heard the slam of the front door. Ewan was early. The office must have burned down or something equally dramatic to get him home in time to eat with his daughter.

'Daddy!' Phoebe jumped down from the table, abandoning her five times table, and ran into the hall.

Bea looked at her watch. She hadn't thought about dinner yet and realised she hadn't received the customary text from Ewan today. She closed her eyes and exhaled, remembering there was nothing that would constitute a meal in her fridge at home. The thought of calling in at the shops to get a ready meal for one made her tired bones ache.

'I didn't know you were coming home early today,' she said, as Ewan strolled in, dropping his suit jacket on the back of a chair, the pink lining clashing with the green velvet.

'Sorry. Forgot to message. Thought we could have a family dinner for a change.'

Bea felt her chin retract. 'What were you planning for dinner? There's not much in.' She mentally scanned the

22

contents of the fridge, wondering if she could rustle up a Spanish omelette. That's the inside of two fridges she'd pictured in her mind's eye in the last minute. Add the fridge she kept her sandwiches in at Sweetingdale and there was the metaphor for her life: Cold, dark, and generally ignored until somebody wants something.

'I thought we might get a takeaway. Quattradicci?'

Phoebe wiggled her bottom in an excited dance. 'Can I get pizza?'

'They don't do pizza, but you could have lasagne?' Ewan pinched his daughter's chin.

Bea lifted an eyebrow. 'Posh.'

'Mother's coming over, so it's the only place I could think of ordering from.'

'You don't think she'd fancy a vindaloo?'

Ewan ran his fingers through his hair, pushing the grey-streaked waves back in place. 'Very funny.'

Bea sat at the table watching Ewan flick through his phone to find the menu. 'What's all this in aid of?'

'Sorry? What?' He glimpsed up and she recognised his feigned misunderstanding. Joyce's genes were strong in this one.

'Don't pretend this is spontaneous. What's going on?'

He let the phone hang in his hand. 'Alright. I want to ask you something. But wait until Mum's here, okay?'

She wrinkled her nose. 'I'll have the rib-eye steak and chips, then, if you're ordering.'

'Right-ho.' He lifted the screen up again. 'And would you mind giving Phoebe a quick bath before the food comes? It will give us more time to talk afterwards. Thanks, Bea. What would we do without you?'

'What indeed?' He didn't look up to see her shake her head then gesture to the little girl to follow her from the room. Even though he was home early, he still didn't see it as an opportunity to spend time with his daughter. Bea might be getting steak tonight, but not before she'd sung for her supper. She checked herself. She was only doing Phoebe's bath because her own mother wasn't there to do it. It was only right she did everything she could to lessen the impact of that, given her own role in it.

* * *

Joyce arrived at the same time as the food. She was dressed in a Chinese-style silk jacket.

'I wish I'd had some notice before this dinner.' Bea tugged at the bottom of her maroon tunic. 'I feel under-dressed.'

They didn't reply. Ewan was busy dancing around his mother, settling her in her chair as though she were a visiting dignitary, so Bea dished up the food from the various containers onto matching crockery and set it on the table, feeling like the hired help. Maybe her uniform was the right outfit after all.

When they were all seated, Bea felt reassured to see Joyce poke at the ridiculously expensive food from the Italian restaurant in the same way she examined the food she cooked for her. She thought privately Joyce may have missed her calling as a crime scene investigator. She'd spent her life being judge and jury instead. Bea shoved another chip in her mouth and chewed, making sure her lips remained closed, and she didn't speak until her mouth was empty.

'How's everything at Sweetingdale?' Ewan glanced up from his food, then back at his plate.

Bea took a moment to take the question in. Was Ewan genuinely interested in her work-life? This had never

24

happened before. A piece of gristle refused to be severed by her teeth so she swallowed it down, hoping she wouldn't choke. 'Not too bad, I suppose.' She coughed, trying to dislodge the meat from her throat. 'There's been a few suspected thefts recently, so everyone is behaving a bit oddly.'

'Oddly?' The way Joyce sat with a straight back, head swivelling, reminded Bea of a meerkat.

'Until we find out who the culprit is, everyone's a bit suspicious. I suppose it's only natural, but it's not the ideal working environment.'

'Are you under suspicion?' Joyce's voice was clipped.

'Don't be silly, Grandma,' said Phoebe. 'Aunty Bea wouldn't take anyone else's things.'

'I didn't ask if she were culpable, I asked if anyone else thought she might be.' Joyce's head twisted to Phoebe, who looked confused.

Bea shrugged, wondering if using words a six-year-old wouldn't understand made Joyce feel superior. 'I suppose I'm as much under suspicion as anyone else.' She turned to Phoebe with widened eyes. 'Let's hope the burglar makes a bungle soon and we can cart them off to jail.' She ignored the rumbling feeling that she seemed to be the only person at Sweetingdale Lynn was watching closely.

'Well, that's hardly likely, is it, with the policing system stretched to capacity and the leniency of namby-pamby judges these days? They'd probably get a warning or something equally ineffectual.'

Bea checked Joyce was looking away and made a face at Phoebe, who grinned back.

'How's the bike running?'

Another question from Ewan that didn't include her schedule for looking after Phoebe. He was clearly having some kind of episode. Should she call a doctor? 'Good, although I suspect the head gasket is spraying. I smelled burning oil last time I took it out, so I'll have to get that looked at.'

'Sounds expensive.'

Bea sighed. 'I've been thinking about selling it.' She glanced around the table and noticed Ewan staring at her as though he actually saw her, not just *the help*. It was quite unnerving. She started to backtrack. 'I know Oli loved that bike. So do I, but since I'm picking Phoebe up more and there's the insurance and maintenance even when I'm not riding it . . .' She trailed off.

Ewan turned to Phoebe and her empty plate. 'All finished? Good girl. Upstairs to do your teeth and get into your pyjamas.'

Bea put down her knife and fork. 'I'll give you a hand, poppet.'

'The child is old enough to brush her own teeth,' said Joyce. She turned to watch Phoebe climb off her chair. 'Come down to say goodnight when you've finished.'

Phoebe looked as if she were about to complain. Bea gave a tiny shake of her head and her shoulders dropped. She sloped from the room.

Bea was aware of Ewan and Joyce's eyes on her, and her neck grew warm under her hair.

'Are you selling the bike because you can't afford to keep it?' asked Joyce.

Bea bristled. If Joyce was concerned about her financial affairs, she could have offered to help back when all the trouble started. Not that Oli would have accepted anything from his mother. He felt he had to prove his independence after Joyce was so critical when he decided to become a history teacher at a comprehensive, instead of a city banker like his father and brother. The stubborn genes hadn't skipped a generation, however different he felt to the rest of the family.

'As I said, it's just sitting in the garage most of the time. It seems wasteful to spend money on it.'

'But you'd prefer to keep it?' Ewan's gaze was still fixed on her.

'Well . . .' She felt a stab of irritation, which melted into sadness. Of course she'd prefer to keep it. It was one of the few links to Oli she had left.

'Are you keeping up with the mortgage?' Joyce asked. Her lipstick had worn to show pale pink skin where her lips met.

Bea sat back in her chair, crossing her arms. 'What's going on?'

Ewan turned back to his plate and attacked the remains of his steak with his knife and fork. 'Nothing. We're showing an interest.'

Bea shook her head. 'No. You arrive home early, order a fancy takeaway, then you two start interrogating me on my financial affairs. What's all this about?'

Their heads turned as they heard Phoebe's footsteps bounce down the stairs. She appeared in the kitchen doorway, opening her mouth wide and showing off her tiny teeth with a gap where one at the front was missing. 'All done.'

'Good girl. Say goodnight to everyone and up we go.' Ewan rose from his seat.

'Can Aunty Bea read my story?'

Ewan flopped back in the chair. 'Bea?'

'Course I can.' She stood and watched Phoebe reach her small arms around Joyce's neck while the old woman sat stiffly, patting Phoebe's back over her pink pyjamas.

Bea remembered Joyce pulling Immy onto her knee at this age, smothering her face in kisses. She had been like a different woman when Immy was small. She was cold to Phoebe in comparison and the unfairness was another needle in Bea's conscience. Joyce had allowed Immy into her heart and Immy broke it. Now, Phoebe suffered the consequences.

Snuggled next to Phoebe in her bed, Bea decided she'd far rather be up here than downstairs with Ewan and Joyce. She tucked her arm under her niece's small body, breathed in the scent of toothpaste and strawberry shampoo, and gave her a tight hug. Kissing the top of her head, Bea opened the cover of *My Naughty Little Sister* and started to read.

* * *

'Bea!'

Her eyes snapped open and she blinked at the whispered sound of her name.

'Beatrice.'

She'd fallen asleep next to Phoebe. Grimacing, she mouthed *sorry* to Ewan, who put his fingers to his down-turned lips and tiptoed out of the room.

Wiping drool from the corners of her mouth, she shuffled downstairs, finding Ewan and Joyce on the sofa and armchair at the far end of the kitchen. They both watched her as she entered. It was so unusual to be the centre of their attention she felt she should do a high kick and a bit of a twirl to make it worth their while. All she could muster was a yawn.

'Must've dropped off. Sorry about that. These early shifts are a killer.'

She watched Joyce take in her words but knew she

would never be able to understand. She'd never had a job. Her grandfather was a wealthy architect who designed the house she lived in and the other older houses on The Crescent. Her father worked in the city, and she'd married young and stayed at home with her boys. No five o'clock starts for her. No Lynn looking at her watch, no mortgage to pay every bloody month. She yawned again, remembering too late to cover her mouth.

'Join us,' said Ewan. 'We have a proposition for you.' His suit trousers rustled as he crossed one leg over the other.

'Right.' Bea drew the word out as she exhaled and perched on the edge of the sofa cushion. She'd been correct in thinking they were up to something, then.

Ewan licked his lips and flicked a glance at his mother before he spoke. 'Since you're having difficulties at work and experiencing financial problems—'

'Hold on,' Bea cut him off. 'That's not what I said.' She thought of Oli and his refusal to be defined by his family and their expectations. She wasn't about to start taking handouts from them now.

'Please. Hear him out.' Joyce's voice was warmer than usual, a request rather than an instruction.

'Okay. Go on.' She crossed her arms and sat back.

'The owner of my fund wants me to relocate to New York.'

Bea squinted from him to Joyce. 'But, Phoebe? She's got her treatment coming up. You can't move her now.'

'Yes. Phoebe is the problem.'

Bea felt a surge of rage. 'The *problem*?'

Ewan put his palms up. 'That's not what I meant. It's—'

'Oh, for goodness sake.' Joyce's voice was exasperated. 'You never could articulate.'

29

Ewan seemed to shrink into the chair.

'What he's trying to say is that we could work together to solve all our difficulties collectively. This is a brilliant opportunity for Ewan. A prestigious position. I only wish his father had been offered such a lucrative package. It will set him up for life.'

She smiled as though she'd made everything clear. Bea shook her head. 'I still have no idea what you're saying to me.'

Ewan cleared his throat. 'We're asking if you'd consider leaving your job and coming to live here. To take care of Phoebe . . . and help out with Mother while I work abroad. The job I've been offered is a big promotion. It will mean I can afford to slow down and spend more time with Phoebe when I come back. In two years.'

'Two years?'

Joyce nodded. 'A mere twenty-four months.'

Bea laughed. She looked from Ewan to Joyce and back again, but they weren't even smiling. 'Are you on drugs?' It came out before she could stop it.

Joyce's face turned to stone. 'I think you'll find that kind of behaviour doesn't run through our side of the family.'

Winded, Bea stared at Joyce in disbelief at her cruelty. She opened her mouth to bite back, but the icy glare from her mother-in-law silenced her. What could she say, anyway? She had no choice but to listen to Ewan, who was still speaking as though he were in a board meeting suggesting a company takeover. That's what it felt like, an ambush to take over her life.

'The timing works well because Alex is expecting a baby, so she's leaving anyway.'

How convenient. They had it all worked out. 'When would the job in New York start?'

'I'm leaving in a month. The fund manager wants to make sure everything's set up correctly and I'm the only man he trusts to get it right.'

Bea gaped at him. 'You're leaving? You've already accepted the job?' This was looking more like a hostile takeover.

His chest deflated, and she felt a flash of anger. Had he expected her to congratulate him on being the big man? 'Yes. In four weeks.'

'You want me to give up my home, and my job?' Bea blew out her cheeks. She didn't add that they made up her entire life because that sounded sad, even to her. She owed them, but surely they could see how much they were asking of her. 'And if I say no?'

'Why would you?' Joyce rubbed a polished fingernail under the collar of her jacket. 'In two years' time you could be in a much better position. Ewan would pay you well. Yours is the kind of job you can simply slot back into, isn't it? You could see it as an opportunity, rather than a sacrifice.'

She opened her mouth to argue, but they'd had time to plan what they were going to say and she was on the back foot. Words formed in her mind, but she didn't seem to be able to mould them into a cohesive sentence. How could she explain to these two, who valued money and status above all things, how much her job and her home meant to her? How she loved the residents at Sweetingdale, how her house bound her to the people she'd lost. The fact Ewan and Joyce could ask her to give up so much showed how little they appreciated the life she'd been left with. It might be small, but at least it was hers.

More words formed in her throat. She wanted to explain that she'd always planned to get her diploma and move

31

into management after Immy started senior school, but she hadn't factored in how time-consuming living with a teenager could be. The management of her emotional upheaval was a full-time job. Then there was the ferrying her around to show rehearsals and friends' houses. There never seemed to be any time left, even before everything went so horribly wrong. She shook her head. They would never understand.

Ewan's eyes flicked between the two women. He licked his lips again, like a lizard assessing its prey. 'Phoebe—'

'Phoebe has her operation in seven weeks. And there's always a risk her seizures could start again.' Bea glowered at him.

'I'm aware of that, which is why she needs to be with someone she loves and trusts.'

'Like her father.'

'Well, it can't be her mother, can it?' Joyce's words were like acid. Bea felt them burn – as Joyce had meant them to.

'I need a drink.' Bea pushed herself off the sofa and walked to the sink, feeling their eyes on her back as she ran the tap, holding her hand under the water until it was ice cold. She took gulps from the glass once she'd filled it, trying to find a way through her thoughts. Eventually, she turned, leaning her back against the porcelain.

'What if Immy comes back?'

The muscles in Joyce's jaw bulged. 'It's been three years.'

'But what if she did?' Blood pulsed in Bea's ears.

Ewan shook his head. 'I will not have that girl near my home or my child.'

Bea let out a breath. Of course, she knew that was what he'd say. She couldn't really blame him. 'Then you'll understand why I have to say no.'

Joyce raised her hands then let them fall back in her lap. 'She's not coming back, Beatrice.'

Bea blinked away tears and looked at the darkening sky through the bifold doors. Refocusing her eyes on the blurred reflections of Ewan and Joyce, she saw their heads turned in her direction.

Ewan leaned forwards. 'Think about it, Bea. You'd have a beautiful home, no money worries. I'll pay more than you make now. You'll have no mortgage or bills. It's a two-year contract, and when I come back from the States, I'll help you out with a deposit on a flat. You could keep the bike in the garage . . .' He seemed to be running out of steam.

'You'd have a little girl to look after again.' Joyce viewed her through lowered lids, fully aware of the impact of her words. 'Another chance.'

To get it right this time? Bea wanted to say, but her throat felt clogged.

'Think about it,' said Ewan. 'Let me know by the end of the week.'

Bea nodded and without another word, she gathered her things and made for the door.

Chapter Five

After her shift the following day, Bea drove to Jan's. Her shoulders loosened when she saw her Fiat parked on the drive. She squeezed past it and knocked on the side door.

'Christ on a bike!' said Jan when Bea finished telling her what Ewan had proposed. 'Did he tuck fivers in your tunic while he talked?'

Bea spluttered, halfway through a sip of tea, wiping liquid off her chin before it dripped onto her chest. 'By past performance, I think if he wanted a lap dance, he'd go for someone a bit younger than me.'

'Ooh, lap-dancing!' Jan's eldest daughter, Ciara, came into the kitchen, plucking a biscuit from the packet on the table. 'That's an idea.'

Jan slapped her bottom, laughing. 'With that backside? You'd starve.'

'Body-shaming? *Rude.*' Ciara started winding her hips, the ring in her belly button glinting in the glow of the fluorescent strip light as she raised her arms. 'I think I'd be a good lap-dancer.'

Bea watched Jan guffaw, imagining her own reaction if

Immy had suggested erotic dancing as a career choice. God, Immy might be working as a stripper right now. The thought made her stomach ball.

'I thought you were going to catering college?' Jan said, serious now.

Ciara dropped her arms and stilled. 'Yeah. Actually, I think I'm too feminist to be a lap-dancer.'

'That's your only issue?' Jan lifted her eyebrows.

'And I like making cakes more than getting leered at by dirty old men.' She bit into the biscuit and sauntered from the room.

'Do you worry that she's not settled at anything?' Bea asked as the sound of the TV started up in the sitting room.

'Not really.' Jan took her third biscuit and chomped down. 'Look at her dad. Started off as a butcher's apprentice, now he's a landscape gardener.' She laughed. 'At least that's what the business cards he got done at the service station say. It can take some people a while to work out what they want to do. What makes them happy.' She stood to close the kitchen door, muffling the noise coming from the other room. 'It's more unusual for people to have one job for life these days. Your Oli and Ewan are the odd ones. We're normal.' At that she roared, her double chin wobbling.

Bea leaned her forearms on the table, wrapping her fingers around her mug. 'I know you think I'm weird, but I really love my job. Vera and the others feel like family. I don't know what I'd do without Sweetingdale, to be honest. I've been there that long it's like a home from home. What would you do if you were me?'

'God knows. There's a lot to think about before you even consider handing in your notice. Looking after

Phoebe's one thing but being at Her Ladyship's beck and call is another thing altogether.'

'You're the only one who knows how much money I owe,' Bea said quietly.

'They must have an idea, or they wouldn't have suggested you move in. Let's look at what your house is worth.' She took her phone from where it was charging on the worktop, clicking onto Rightmove. When she tapped in the postcode, house details appeared on the screen. 'That one's almost identical to yours, isn't it?' She pointed a thick finger at a 1930s semi, which could have been Bea's house but for the red front door.

'Yep. I know that one. It's only a minute from ours. From mine.'

Jan pointed at the figure underneath. 'If you got that for it, you'd be able to clear the debts.'

'I know, but—'

Jan put her hand on Bea's arm. 'Sweetheart, the last letter said the mortgage company would start eviction proceedings if you missed another payment. You might not be given a choice. I don't want to be a doom-monger, but when my cousin was evicted, the lenders sold her house at auction. When it didn't cover what she owed, she ended up with no house and a massive debt.'

A headache pumped at the front of Bea's skull. 'I don't know what to do.'

'I know you don't want to leave Sweetingdale. I don't want you to, either. But wouldn't looking after little Phoebe in a fancy house be a step up from clocking on at five to watch old boys like Kenny dribble cornflakes down their chins?'

Bea smiled weakly. 'But what about Immy? It would feel like I'm choosing Phoebe over her.'

Jan closed her eyes and nodded. 'You can't sit around waiting forever, though.'

I can, she thought, *if that's what it takes.*

*   *   *

Back home, Bea didn't bother picking up the white envelopes from the mat. She kicked off her trainers and climbed the stairs. Standing in front of the door to her daughter's bedroom, she replayed scenes in her head: her tiptoeing in while Immy slept, craving another look at her peaceful face before tiptoeing out again and snuggling in bed next to Oli.

The scenes got uglier after that, but she couldn't stop them looping. She heard the ghost sound of the door slamming, even when she'd asked Immy to keep it open the first time she took Zach to her bedroom. She saw the figure of Immy asleep under the duvet when she should have been at sixth form and remembered the vicious arguments that followed.

Pushing the door wide, she stepped inside. She tried to detect the Stella McCartney perfume Immy used to wear, but the room smelled like the rest of the house: empty.

An envelope sat on the bed where she'd found it on the day of Gemma's inquest. It glared white against the navy covers. Maybe that's why she hated white envelopes; she never found anything good inside. She sat on the bed and leaned back on the shocking pink cushions stacked against the headboard. She took the envelope in her fingers, opened the torn lip, pulling out the well-worn sheet of A4 paper. Unfolding it, she started to read:

Mum

I wish I could start this letter with 'Mum and Dad'. If Dad was still here, maybe things would be different. Maybe I wouldn't be writing it at all.

37

I thought about saying this in person, but I'm not sure you'd even hear me if I did. I don't feel like anyone's heard a word I've said for a very long time. That's not meant to be an excuse. I just wanted to put the way I feel on paper, to make it real.

I know you think I'm spoiled and selfish, but I've grown up a lot in the last few years. I've had to. I want you to know I do take responsibility for my part in what happened. I know why you'll never forgive me. I won't forgive myself.

I haven't made anyone happy for as long as I can remember. I'm leaving so you can move on. I hope you'll find remembering Dad easier if I'm not here like a shadow of him – all the dark bits and none of the sunshine.

You'll think I'm just being dramatic and attention-seeking, I can hear you saying it, but I mean this: please don't come looking for me. I've been thinking about this for a long time, even before what happened, and I have thought it through. I've saved some money and I've got a plan, so don't imagine me sleeping on doorsteps or anything awful happening to me. I'll be okay.

Give Phoebe a kiss from me. I'm sorry.
If you still love me at all, don't look for me.
Immy x

It was the *if you still love me at all* that broke Bea. Every time.

* * *

Downstairs, she scrolled through listings for private investigators on her laptop yet again. The websites she'd visited before came up in purple type instead of blue. She'd clicked each one at some point over the last three years. She'd even got quotes from a few, but she only had meagre details about where Immy could be, so the research alone could cost thousands and she might still have no idea where her daughter was. She didn't have thousands. She didn't even have hundreds.

Immy had left her phone, taken everything from her bank account and closed it. She'd taken her passport, but when Bea checked with the police, they'd told her that because Immy was eighteen and left of her own free will, they had no grounds to investigate. She wondered if Immy's caution for shoplifting booze from Tesco had anything to do with that.

The image of Zach appeared in her mind, tall and cocky, self-proclaimed King of the Universe. He often polluted her memories when she thought about the last few months Immy was at home. She shuddered at the thought of his hands on her little girl. What happened to him was awful – his poor parents – but she couldn't forgive him for what he did. If only Immy had never met him. If only . . . She closed the laptop down.

Her mobile buzzed on the table with an unknown number. She picked it up and pressed the green icon to accept the call. 'Beatrice James?' said the voice on the other end. 'It's Sharon calling from HSBC. Can I go through some security questions with you before we discuss your account?'

Bea pulled the phone away from her ear and glared at it. Her finger sprang up as though it had a mind of its own and pressed the red button to end the call. Her tears fell, blurring the screensaver of Phoebe's gappy smile.

Chapter Six

When Bea went into Vera's room at the start of her shift the following morning, Vera was sitting in her armchair waving a sheet of pink notepaper. 'It's from Gordon,' she said, her voice giddy with excitement. 'He's sent a picture of the children, too. Look at those beautiful babies.'

She lifted a photograph from the table with her other hand, her eyes bright.

'Let's have a look then.' Bea crossed the room and took the photograph from Vera. She smiled at the grinning faces. 'Tyger's bonnie, isn't she?'

'If you mean gloriously chubby, then yes.' Vera held out her hand for the picture and Bea passed it back. 'I have no idea why they chose such a silly name. Perhaps it's a normal name in Australia. Like Vera?'

She peered up through the lenses of her glasses, a crease appearing between her eyebrows.

'I'm not sure there's many babies called Vera these days, my love.'

Vera's eyes twinkled. 'You're right. It would be a cruelty!'

Bea remembered how her name had stood out amongst

the Louises and Tracys on the register at her school in York. She'd hated it, and she and Oli had tried to choose something pretty and timeless for Imogen. But Immy hated her name, too. Another thing Bea had failed at.

'Any news from down under?' She gestured to the pink notepaper.

'Lots, but the most exciting thing of all . . .' Vera paused, energy vibrating from her. 'They're planning a trip to England in the New Year!'

'Oh, Vera. I'm delighted for you.' Bea watched as Vera scrunched her thick-knuckled hands into fists and beamed. 'That's fair cheered me up.'

Vera became still and raised a finger in the air. 'Would you do something for me? Can you get me a calendar?' She put both hands onto the arms of the chair and levered herself from the seat. 'I'm not usually interested in what day it is – it doesn't make much difference – but I want to start marking off the weeks. That will be a lovely thing to do, won't it, to see the time they arrive getting closer?'

Bea cupped Vera's elbow with her hand and helped steady her on her feet. 'I will. Do you want one with cats on, or one of those with sexy firemen with their pecs all slathered in baby oil?'

Vera viewed her with mischievous eyes. 'Definitely the latter.' She giggled as she passed Bea, limping at first, then walking more confidently to the wardrobe. She opened the door and pulled a handbag from one of the shelves. Turning, she placed it on the bed, unclasped the top and pulled out a purse as big as a notebook.

'I'll give you the money now, whilst I remember.' She opened the purse and her fingers moved over the top, flicking the divider in the middle from side to side. 'That's peculiar.' Her lips tightened, and she sighed. 'Oh dear.'

41

Bea crossed the room, her pulse starting to race. 'What's up?'

Vera handed her purse to Bea, and she examined the inside. A five-pound note was folded neatly in one compartment, but other than that, it was empty. Bea looked at Vera's face, her heart pounding. 'Was there more in there last time you looked?'

Vera sighed again. 'Seventy-five pounds.'

'Not five?'

Vera took the purse from Bea and threw it in her open bag. 'Definitely not five. I might not be quick on my feet, but I did the accounts for my husband's business long enough to know the difference between seventy-five and five pounds.'

'Sorry, I didn't—'

Vera raised her arm to stop her. 'I know. Sorry. My ire isn't directed at you. Whoever the culprit is has chosen the wrong victim this time, though. I am no sitting duck.'

'I'll get Lynn,' said Bea. 'We need to get to the bottom of this.'

Vera snorted. 'Her? She won't do anything.'

'She's the manager. I have to report it to her.'

Vera took slow steps back to the chair by the patio door. 'She'd like us all to think we're just forgetful old fools. I know her game.' She sat down with a grunt.

'What is her game?'

'She's in it for what she can get, that one. She's replaced all the toiletries with cheap rubbish. The hand soaps are like water, but I bet she's still claiming to pay for the luxury stuff we were promised when we moved in here. The food's gone downhill too, and the portions are smaller.'

'I had noticed all the toiletries are different brands. You think she's creaming off the top? Fiddling the budget?'

'I'm sure of it. I think she'd like us all to stay in our rooms and keep our mouths shut. She's not interested in any complaints we make.'

'I'm sure she is.' Bea looked away, sure that the shame of briefly thinking about how handy it would be to have an extra seventy pounds in her own purse would show on her face.

'This place isn't the same since she came. This was a care home when I moved in, with the emphasis on *care*. Now there's only you and Jan left who seem to care at all. All the others are agency staff or about twelve years old. They shout when they speak to me. I'm not deaf, but they haven't taken the time to find that out.'

Bea sat on the bed and took Vera's hand. 'I'm sorry you've been made to feel like that. I'll do my best to find out what's happened to your money, and I'll look into the other stuff. But I've got to tell Lynn, okay?'

'Alright.' Vera looked like a different woman to the one who waved the letter at Bea five minutes ago. 'If you must.' She raised a smile. 'What would I do without you, Beatrice?'

Bea patted the back of her hand, swallowing the acid working its way up her throat.

* * *

Bea always sat next to Jan in staff meetings so they could jab each other in the ribs when Lynn was being boorish or unreasonable. Today, Lynn presided over them in her navy polyester trouser suit, with a cream blouse tucked in. Bea could almost hear the static electricity crackling in her armpits.

'Unfortunately, money has been reported stolen from Primrose corridor.' Lynn drew back her chin and it

43

disappeared in the creases in her skinny neck. 'Seventy pounds has gone missing,' she paused, 'according to Vera.'

Bea didn't like her tone. 'She was very upset. She knows how much she had in her purse,' she said, and Lynn turned her coal-black eyes on her.

'I never implied she didn't.' She cocked her head. 'You were on Primrose this morning, Bea.' She didn't move her eyes from Bea's face. 'Did you notice anything unusual?'

Heat spread across Bea's chest and made its way up her neck. 'Vera didn't say it went missing this morning, did she? She said she only left her room for any length of time last night, when I wasn't on shift.'

'You're very defensive.'

Bea tensed. 'I'm not, I'm just saying.' She wished she could be swallowed up by the chair cushion.

'Saying what?'

Jan's hand squeezed gently under her forearm. 'Nothing. I'm not saying anything.'

'What did the police have to say about it?' Jan said, and everyone seemed to take a collective breath.

Lynn crossed her arms. 'I haven't called them yet. As you are aware' – she regarded everyone in the room in turn – 'this is a business that relies on its reputation. If it gets out that the belongings of our community here at Sweetingdale are not safe, or that the staff can't be trusted' – her eyes stopped on Bea – 'then our reputation as a safe and caring home is in jeopardy.'

She blinked and shifted her gaze and Bea felt as though she'd been released from a witch's spell. Where was a flying house when you needed one? She imagined Lynn's thick ankles and sensible shoes sticking out from under some brickwork and felt a little better.

'So, I'm hoping we can put a stop to this ugly pilfering

before I have to get the police involved. Keep your eyes peeled, everyone. I'm sorry to say somebody in this room knows where that money has gone. It breaks my heart to think of our residents suffering at the hands of one of our own. Be vigilant, and let's hope we don't have to take this any further.'

She dismissed the meeting with a nod of her head and the murmuring group shuffled from the room, followed by Lynn, trotting officiously as though she had patients to save in the ICU, instead of budget toilet roll to order.

'Was she looking at me, or was I imagining it?' said Bea, flopping back in her chair.

Jan shifted heavily to face her, leaning her elbow on the back of the seat. She spoke quietly, 'It seems our esteemed leader has got it in for you.'

'What's her problem?'

'I don't know.' Jan rolled her bottom lip between her teeth. 'It could be because they all like you. The residents, I mean.'

'They all like you, but she's not practically pointing in your face when she's talking about grand larceny.'

'I think you'll find it's *ugly pilfering*.' Jan's impression of Lynn almost made Bea smile. 'I only do about half as many shifts as you, so I'm not as much of a threat.'

'I'm not a threat.'

Jan leaned in closer. 'You know she's shagging that slimy bloke from the recruitment agency?'

Bea shuddered. 'Creepy Dave?'

'That's him. I wonder if she's trying to get rid of you so she can get more agency staff in. He'll get commission if she does, and I wouldn't put it past her to get a cut.'

'Vera said something about her ordering cheaper supplies and maybe fiddling the budget. Have you noticed

45

the new brand of toiletries is a bit rubbish? You can barely raise a lather with the soap. Do you think she's on the make?'

She waited for Jan's shocked expression, but instead she just lifted an eyebrow. 'Without a doubt.'

'How is she getting away with all of this? Why hasn't she been sacked?'

Jan shrugged and lifted herself from the chair. 'This is the smallest place the company owns, so they probably don't keep a close eye on her as long as she doesn't go over budget or kill all the nannas. I'm sure she makes it look kosher.'

'Kill all the nannas?' Bea tutted. 'You're as bad as her sometimes.' She checked the door to make sure Lynn hadn't hovered back in. 'I feel like I'm being framed.' She felt silly saying it. The words sounded like something from a cop drama, not the staffroom of Sweetingdale.

Jan inspected her seriously. 'Honestly? I think you might be right. But what can we do about it? Do you want to take on Lynn and Creepy Dave and face a police investigation after all that other business, or—?'

Bea closed her eyes and shook away the memories of blue flashing lights outside her window and the sickening sound of the knock at the door. Jan put her hand on her arm and carried on. 'Or, you could live, rent-free, in a posh house, with no debt, no five a.m. starts and no Lynn breathing down your neck about stuff you've got nothing to do with.'

Jan pinched Bea's cheek and looked her directly in the eye. 'I know which I'd choose.'

Bea tried to smile, but what Jan wasn't factoring in was how much Bea loved her job and her house. She felt like she needed them to carry on existing. Other than Phoebe and the bike, they were the only things that made life worth living.

* * *

Bea was about mount her bike at the end of her shift when she saw Lynn crossing the car park towards her. Lynn stopped opposite her and glanced around before speaking in hushed tones. 'You know I've always liked you, Bea. That's why I'm giving you the opportunity to do the right thing before I get the police involved.'

'Do the right thing? I had nothing to do with—'

'I have a witness.'

Bea gripped the helmet tighter. 'You can't have.'

'Dave saw you.'

Bea almost laughed. 'Your *boyfriend* Dave?'

Lynn blinked. 'He's not my . . .' She pulled back her shoulders. 'He's a supplier, actually.'

'Pull the other one.'

'Do I need to remind you who's the manager here?'

Bea fixed Lynn with a stare, but when she didn't flinch, Bea looked away. She didn't want Lynn to see the distress in her eyes. A leaf fluttered off a branch from the tree behind them and Bea watched it float to the ground, joining the pile of red, brown and green on the tarmac. She wanted to lie down right there with the fallen leaves.

She raised her eyes to Lynn's. 'You know what? Forget it.' Bea was out of energy, too tired to fight. She shook her head wearily. 'Sod it all. I'll leave at the end of the week. I did not steal anything, which I suspect you already know.' Pointing a finger in Lynn's face, she summoned the last of her strength. 'If I find out you're suggesting other-wise to the residents or the rest of the staff, I'll get the police involved myself and fight to the death to clear my name.' She jabbed her finger and Lynn stepped backwards. 'I can see you're looking for a scapegoat and I'm not going to waste my time trying to work out why that is. But, unlike you, I've got options, so I'll take the one that gets me as far away from you as possible.'

She pulled the helmet over her head, started the bike, and roared out of the car park. She waited until she was out of view of Sweetingdale to stop the bike, lift the visor and wipe the angry tears from her eyes.

Chapter Seven

There was no benefit to standing in the gloomy weather with no one to talk to at school pick-up, so now Bea sat in her Yaris in the car park, watching the time tick by on the dashboard clock until the minute before Phoebe was due to be released from lessons. Looking out of the dirty window, she tried not to compare her knackered old car with the shiny SUVs and sports cars. She decided she wouldn't want to fit one of those in the tiny parking spaces at Aldi, so, really, she was better off in her little rust-heap.

At 3:29, she scurried along the path and into the pen of the playground, avoiding eye contact with the waiting parents. She noticed the bottom button of her shirt had come undone and buttoned it back up, but then it looked too tight, stretched across her hips, so she released it again. She'd changed into black trousers and a shirt because she didn't want the other kids to have more reasons to pick on Phoebe, but it felt like putting on a cocktail dress for the school run, since she only ever wore jeans and fleeces when she wasn't in her uniform these days.

She knew how cruel kids could be and imagined them

asking why the woman picking her up wore a uniform from an old people's home. The wind blew her hair into her eyes. She scraped it back, blinking, trying to find Phoebe in the stream of children now emerging from the door at the far end of the playground.

One by one, the parents and their offspring trickled away until Bea was standing in the chilly air on her own. She pulled her phone from her pocket to see if Ewan had messaged to say Phoebe had gone home early. There was nothing but the screensaver and big, glaring numbers shouting that the time was 3:45.

As she walked towards the building, the door opened and Kelly stepped out, followed by a whimpering Phoebe. Bea sped towards her. 'Oh, poppet. What's happened?' She wrapped Phoebe in her arms and glared at Kelly, who looked close to tears herself.

'Phoebe's had a rotten day, I'm afraid. Do you mind going in and having a word with Mrs Andrews? I'll take Phoebe to the playground, and we can have a little play on the slide.'

Bea crouched down so she was face to face with Phoebe. 'Is that alright with you? If I go and talk to your teacher while you play with Kelly?' She wiped the tears from Phoebe's red cheek and kissed the wet skin.

Phoebe sniffed and nodded.

'I won't be long and we'll get an ice cream on the way home. Alright?'

She watched Kelly lead Phoebe across the tarmac and steeled herself before entering the building.

Mrs Andrews stood when she spotted Bea through the glass window at the top of the door to her classroom. She hurried forwards and held out her hand as Bea entered the bright room that smelled of sugar paper and cast-iron radiators.

'Thank you for coming in, Mrs—'

'Mrs James, I'm Phoebe's Aunty. Bea. Call me Bea.' The teacher's hand was warm against her freezing fingers.

'Please, take a seat.' Mrs Andrews gestured to one of the tiny chairs at the table nearest the door and Bea wasn't sure if she was serious until she drew one out herself and sat, gingerly, tucking her skirt underneath her thighs. Bea sat, hoping the chair legs wouldn't buckle under her. Her knees seemed unnaturally high. She wrapped her hands around them and viewed the woman sitting opposite her, who seemed no more comfortable in this position than she was.

'I take it you saw Phoebe before you came in?'

'Yes. She was very upset. What happened?'

What did the little bastards do this time and where do they live?

'We had games last lesson and there was an incident in the changing rooms.'

'What kind of incident?'

Mrs Andrews shifted in her seat. Her hand fluttered around the silk scarf tied at her neck. 'I wasn't actually there, so I can't be . . .'

'What kind of incident?' Bea knew she was speaking through gritted teeth, and Mrs Andrew's nervous blinking wasn't enough to calm her.

'From what I can gather, when Phoebe took off her school shirt, the other girls appear to have . . . run away from her.'

Bea's jaw unclenched, dropping open in horror. 'Run away? Why?'

'Kelly heard some screaming and went in to find the other girls huddled in a corner.'

Bea could see the picture in her head and her chin puckered. She took a deep breath. 'Why was that?'

51

Mrs Andrews stared down at the table. 'Apparently, because it was cold today, the birthmarks on Phoebe's arm turned a blueish, purple colour.'

'They do that.' Bea was used to assessing how Phoebe was feeling by the colour of the birthmarks on her right arm. If all was well, they were pale pink, barely noticeable. If she was cold, tired, or ill, they became much darker and changed to the purple colour Mrs Andrews was describing.

'I'm afraid the children are only used to seeing the darker red of the birthmark on Phoebe's face and neck. When she took off her shirt, the girls thought they were spreading and that led to them believing it might transfer to them if they went near her. I'm afraid it escalated from there, as these things can sometimes do with young girls.'

Bea dropped her head to her knees and tried to suppress the urge to swear. When she looked back up, Mrs Andrews' eyes were wet.

'They were cowering. From little Phoebe?'

Mrs Andrews visibly swallowed. 'Yes. I'm sorry.'

'Like she was some kind of monster? Something to be scared of?'

Mrs Andrews stood and turned her back, and Bea watched her shoulders rise and fall and heard her take quick breaths before turning back. 'Sorry, Mrs James. It's unprofessional of me to get emotional in front of you, but both myself and Kelly were shocked and saddened by what Phoebe went through today. The Head has been informed, and we will do everything we can to make Phoebe's time at school a—'

'A safe one? A happy one?' Bea asked. 'Can you imagine how she's feeling right now?'

Mrs Andrews ran the end of her scarf through her fingers but didn't reply.

'We need to do something about those girls.'

'I agree, but we need to tread carefully. The difficulty is that they say they were scared. While that sounds ridiculous and cruel to us, and their reaction was hysterical to say the least, I can't accuse them of bullying Phoebe when they maintain they responded out of fear.'

'Of what? Skin?'

'I know. Unfortunately, they remember the few times she's had seizures in class, too. I think that's added to their . . .' She shook her head. 'I wanted to speak to Phoebe's father about what happened, and what he thinks is the most appropriate way forward, but I couldn't get hold of him.'

The acid in Bea's stomach sloshed. 'You called him, and he didn't ring back?'

'Not yet. I hope it's okay to talk to you about this though. You're on the approved contacts list.'

'Yes. I'll talk to him. Don't worry about that.' She stood, feeling like a giant next to the tiny chair. 'Thank you for your time. I can see you care about what happened. That means a lot.'

Mrs Andrews smiled sadly.

'But this can't happen again. You know that, don't you?' Bea held her gaze.

'I do.'

Bea left the classroom and marched across the playground and down the path to where Kelly was waiting for Phoebe at the bottom of a shallow slide.

'Thanks, Kelly,' she said. 'I've got her.'

When Phoebe slid down the plastic, Bea scooped her up and she wrapped thin legs around Bea's waist as she held her tight. She cupped the back of Phoebe's head with her hand and held it in the crook of her neck, pressing their heads close.

'You alright, poppet?' She felt a little nod under her hand. 'I think today is a two-scoop day.'

Phoebe's head bobbed back, and her face appeared next to Bea's. 'Three scoops!' she said and grinned.

Bea carried her back to the path, Phoebe's body warm against her chest. She didn't ask to be put down to walk, and Bea didn't know if she'd be able to let her go if she did.

* * *

Ewan's face was white by the time Bea finished telling him what had happened in the changing room. Phoebe was safely tucked into bed with her Koala Beanie Boo. She hadn't mentioned school and Bea didn't know whether to bring it up or not. She was so different to Immy at this age. Everything that happened in six-year-old Immy's head had spilled out of her mouth in a torrent of thoughts and feelings, and Bea and Oli had drunk them in. At least, she'd thought they had.

Phoebe was more reserved. Bea put it down to spending so much time with Ewan and Joyce, who both thought *because I said so* was the definition of good parenting. Maybe they were right. Immy's words dried up when she got older, and as a teenager, they were lucky to get a grunt out of her.

'Where was the bloody teacher? They're six years old. They shouldn't be left unsupervised.' He ran his fingers through his hair and paced from the sofa to the dining table.

'Apparently, Kelly left something she needed in the classroom, so she nipped back to get it.'

'She should be sacked.'

Bea rolled her eyes. 'Phoebe loves Kelly. Anyway, that's not going to solve anything, is it?'

'What is?' He stopped pacing and focused on her, and for a fleeting moment his resemblance to Oli weakened her knees.

'I don't know.'

'Does she need to change schools?'

She pulled out a chair and sat. 'I don't think there's a practical solution to this.' She pointed at another chair, and he dutifully lowered himself onto it. 'Sacking people and changing schools is, I don't know . . .' She searched for the right word. 'External.'

His face scrunched. 'What else can we do? We can't force the mothers to do a better job of parenting their little shits.'

And fathers, she thought, but she wasn't brave enough to say it after everything she'd put this family through. 'We need to make sure Phoebe feels secure enough in herself to cope with the' – she made air quotes with her fingers – 'little shits.'

He sat back and crossed his arms, and she could tell he thought his way was better. *Bloody Ewan.*

'You can't fix things by telling everyone else what to do, who to sack, how to parent.' Bea hoped he didn't realise it was her turn for irony. Ewan might be a crap parent, but she'd been worse. Her palm tingled with the memory of that slap to Immy's face. It was the blind leading the blind here. She pointed to the ceiling. 'This is about Phoebe, isn't it? We've got to step up, find ways to make her feel safe and, I don't know . . . special. Remember what the doctor at the birthmark clinic told you? Phoebe's self-esteem is the most important thing in all this.'

'Those kids haven't exactly helped with that, have they?'

'No, but we can.' She hoped her voice sounded more certain about this than she felt.

He took his head in his hands and she watched, confused by this uncharacteristic show of emotion. 'I signed the contract today.'

'Jesus, Ewan.'

His hands dropped onto the table, and she examined his long fingers, with their neat, square nails. She imagined them confidently holding an expensive pen and signing his name with a flourish on the contract that would take him away from his own daughter for two years. She stood and walked to the sink to stop herself from slamming her fist onto his fingers.

'You'll have to unsign it. She needs you.'

'I know she does. I know you don't see it this way, but I'm doing this for her. I want her to have the very best future I can provide. You know as well as I do that the epilepsy might not always be easy to control. I'm painfully aware of how that might impact her future.'

The torn look on his face stopped Bea asking how much money he thought one person needed. She remembered how her own life had pivoted and spun out of her control when Oli left them. She wouldn't wish that on anyone.

'Could you ask for your old job back? Tell them it's not a good time?'

'It's too late. My job here doesn't exist anymore. The office is being closed. The whole operation is moving to New York and I'm heading it up.'

'Ah.'

'Yep.'

'There are other jobs.'

Ewan's fists closed and she watched his knuckles turn white. 'If Gemma was alive, this wouldn't be a problem.'

Bea stepped back and grasped the edge of the sink. He may as well have punched her. The air left her body, and it was all she could do not to crumple. 'I think we're all well aware of that, Ewan.' He had played his strongest card and she couldn't argue. She didn't even want to. 'Okay,' she said, shakily. 'I'll leave Sweetingdale and move here.' She walked towards the door, touching the wall to steady herself as the blood rushed to her head. 'We're both doing this for Phoebe, right?'

Ewan nodded, but she'd known him too long to be convinced. This was her chance to finally atone, so even if he didn't mean it with all of his heart, she did. The trouble was, so much of her heart belonged to her own girl – which was why it was breaking in two.

Chapter Eight

Bea found Vera sitting on the bench outside her patio doors on the pink cushion she kept in a carrier bag on the door handle, ready to grab as soon as the sun came out. She stepped carefully over the threshold and into the triangle of autumn sunshine that seemed to mark the bench out for special treatment.

'There you are.'

Vera looked up and shielded her eyes with her hand. 'Ah, you're a sight for sore eyes.' She patted the bench next to her. 'Sit down. I'm afraid I only have one cushion, but we won't be here long. The sun's weaker than it looks.'

'I've got something for you.' Bea reached into her bag and pulled out a calendar. 'Ta da!'

Vere's eyes sparkled. She held out her hand and took the calendar from Bea, her top dentures closing over her bottom lip and her shoulders bouncing. She lifted the first page, then closed it again, chortling.

'Goodness. They didn't make them like that in my day,' she said, opening the page again and turning it around so Bea could see the man with a naked torso, shining with oil, a fireman's helmet pushed back on his head as he held his face up to the sun.

'Good Lord,' said Bea. 'I hope that's suntan oil he's slathered in, or he'll burn something rotten.'

'That was my first thought too,' said Vera, still giggling. 'Or maybe my second.'

'Cheeky.' They turned over the pages, pretending to only be interested in the settings, never mentioning the models posturing in their firemen costumes, their huge biceps dripping in sweat, or stretched out, half-dressed on a bunk, making eyes at the camera.

'That's a very shiny pole,' said Vera, finger pointing at the metal, not the semi-naked man wrapped around it. Bea sniggered, then noticed the goosebumps on Vera's arm.

'Just a sec.' She dipped back inside to collect the knitted blanket that hung over Vera's armchair. She laid the pink and white wool across both their knees. Vera put the calendar down and stroked the fabric, smiling. 'Gordon sent this last Christmas.'

'It's very pretty.'

'Warm as a hug,' said Vera. 'Well, nearly.'

Bea laid her arm around Vera's narrow shoulders and gave her a squeeze. She suspected she needed the hug more than Vera.

'You're good to me,' said Vera, peering into her face over her glasses.

Bea closed her eyes and held her a little closer, breathing in the smell of setting lotion in her hair. 'Vera.' She lifted her arm and placed it in her lap, worrying at the cuticle on her thumb. 'I've a bit of news.'

A magpie bounced around the neat lawn in front of them then flew up to the top of the laurel bush, balancing for a moment before launching itself into the sky.

'You're leaving, aren't you?' Vera's voice was quiet.

'I am, lovey.'

They sat and watched the magpie land back on the lawn. Bea searched the sky and the laurel for another thinking, *come on, two for joy* but the lone magpie pecked at the grass and flew away.

After a minute Bea said, 'I need to look after Phoebe, so I'm going to live with her. Her dad's moving to the States.' She watched Vera carefully. 'I told you that, didn't I?'

Vera nodded. 'He's leaving that precious girl behind.'

Bea shrugged. 'It's not far, these days; New York. He can fly home in seven hours.'

'Not every night though.' Vera pursed her lips. 'What is he thinking? A child needs its parents.'

'I pick her up most days now and she's ready for bed by the time he gets home. It probably won't be much different. For her, anyway.'

'What about you? Could you work here part time?'

'Afraid not. Phoebe's school seems to be on holiday every other week. Seems the more you pay, the less they go in.'

Vera was quiet for a moment before asking, 'Are you getting a tenant in your house?'

Bea looked away. 'It's going on the market. Can't be doing with all the fuss of renting, you know.'

Vera pulled away so she could look directly at her. 'Tread carefully, Bea. You might get swallowed whole. You do enough for that lot already.'

'I owe them, Vera. If I worked for free for the rest of my life, I couldn't make up for . . .' The images of that night rushed across the back of her eyes. 'I owe them so much.'

Vera gripped her hand with a strength Bea didn't know she had. 'Listen to me. You are allowed to put yourself first. I know Phoebe needs looking after, but you'll still be her aunt if you say no to this.'

She felt Vera's thick knuckles hard against her own. 'It's a chance to do something to make it all a bit easier, for me as much as anybody else. If I could lessen the guilt I carry around every day, that would be something, wouldn't it? And it's another chance to do right by a little girl who needs me. Somebody's got to put that child first and it's only right that I step up.'

Vera released her grip and rubbed her hands together, the skin sounding like sheets of paper sliding against one another. 'You have nothing to feel guilty about.' She sighed. 'But I can't make you see that, can I?'

Bea laid her head on Vera's shoulder. She pretended to cough to cover the sob rising in her throat. 'I'll come and visit.'

'You'd better. Make sure Lynn doesn't sell my old bones to the glue factory. I wouldn't put it past her.' Vera smiled thinly and patted her hand and they watched the magpie land back on the grass, closer than before, and fix them with a glassy black eye.

* * *

'This is a great family home.' The small, pale woman, who had introduced herself as Molly, smiled insincerely at Bea as they trudged upstairs, followed by a photographer who she hadn't bothered to introduce. 'We'll have no problem selling this in the current market. It's got a good school nearby. That's always a big tick in the box.'

I know, thought Bea. *My daughter went there.*

It felt like a betrayal, letting the chirpy woman and the

scruffy man with a camera into Immy's bedroom. Bea had hidden the letter under the pillow, but it still called out to her from where she stood in the doorway as the woman tapped notes onto her iPad and pointed out angles to the photographer.

'Flown the nest?' she asked, but didn't seem to need a reply. 'Houses can feel big when they've gone, can't they?'

She had no idea.

'You downsizing? I've got some lovely flats listed.'

Bea stepped back onto the landing to make way for Molly and the man to bustle through to her bedroom.

'Take this room from the doorway,' Molly instructed the photographer, as though this was nothing more than a collection of boxes to be pictured and advertised, not the empty space Oli's breath had filled; where Immy's giggles rang out, then her shouts, then silence. Bea could hear all of them while the cameraman clicked away. Especially the silence.

'You're alright.' She watched as Molly popped her head into the box room, nodding as though it met her hard-won approval. 'I'm moving to The Crescent.'

Molly's head swivelled and it took a moment for her body to catch up. '*The* Crescent?' She emphasised the first word, as though the road was an Oscar-winning actor. Bea knew from Oli, and from living in Belmoat long enough, how desirable houses on the road his great-grandfather designed were, but she wasn't prepared for how wide Molly's eyes grew.

'*The* Crescent,' Bea confirmed.

Molly looked her up and down, obviously reassessing her. 'I didn't know any of the houses were on the market. We usually get an alert.'

'I'm moving in with family,' she said. 'They own a couple of houses on there.'

She didn't know why she said that. She and Oli always shook their heads at people who were impressed by the Arts and Crafts splendour of Joyce's home, or the obvious affluence of Ewan's more modern house. They'd prided themselves on having a different value system, but here she was, showing her hand to impress this woman. It wasn't even her hand. In this game, she'd be the croupier.

'Alright for some!' Molly started back down the stairs.

'I'd like to move quickly. Sell quickly, I mean.'

Molly narrowed her eyes, clearly trying to work out why someone related to people on The Crescent would need a quick sale.

'Okay?'

'Of course. I've got a few families on my books who'll bite my hand off. Don't you worry about that, Mrs James. One open house should be all it needs. I wouldn't be surprised if it went to bidding wars.' She reached the hallway and Bea became very conscious of the splodges of paint on the wall. Molly followed her gaze and said, 'That's not a problem. Anyone buying this place will want to make their mark on it. A few paint samples aren't going to put them off.' She slapped the cover of the iPad closed and held out her hand.

Bea took it and shook to agree the marketing of her home. The house with the paint next to the door. The paint she and Oli had planned to choose from when they thought their little family had a future in that house. When they thought they had a future at all.

Chapter Nine

The removal men shoved the last of her boxes across the thick carpet and stood back to let her survey the room.

'That's the last of it,' said Rory, the squat man in charge. 'You've got the key card for the storage unit?'

She'd been surprised how much was left after she'd pared down her belongings. Every kitchen utensil had been held by Oli and Immy. The cushions probably still had their DNA deep in their fibres. There was no way she could let them go. She reasoned she'd have her own place again in two years, so she'd need most things anyway, and the cost of the storage was nowhere near the cost of the mortgage.

She tapped her pocket and tried to smile at Rory. 'Got it, thanks.'

Rory nodded. 'We'll be off then. If you could fill in the review form when they email it and say we didn't smash any of your priceless heirlooms, that'd be grand.' He rolled his eyes. 'Used to be able to drop pianos and say *whoops* in the good old days. Now you can't even break a mug without being sued.' He gave a throaty laugh and she joined in as best she could.

Rummaging in her bag, she found the envelope she'd prepared with a tip. 'Buy the lads a pint.'

He took it and dipped his head in thanks. 'That's very kind.' He glanced around the bedroom. 'I hope you'll be very happy here. I know I would be.' He laughed again. 'We'll see ourselves out.'

She listened to their footsteps on the carpet, muffled by the blue plastic covers over their boots, and wondered what they made of the woman who'd packed up a three-bed-semi, stored its contents and moved into one of the most expensive houses in the neighbourhood. They probably thought she was staff. But then, she supposed she was.

She sat on the bed and the memory foam mattress melted under her bottom as she took out her phone and clicked onto her banking app to check the balance of her account. Ewan had transferred the housekeeping budget to her and the figure on the screen made her giddy. She'd been worried about money for so long that her balance now looked like a lottery win. She'd laughed when he told her how much he was allowing for the running of the house, on top of her salary.

'It'll never be that much,' she told him. 'Surely the bills and council tax come out of your account by direct debit?'

'That money's for food and sundries,' he told her. 'For Phoebe's clothes and extra-curricular activities. Things like that.'

'Unless we're eating Marks and Sparks ready meals and Phoebe's planning to dress head to toe in Burberry, that's far too much.'

'Then buy yourself a latte now and again.' Ewan looked at her as though she were mad. 'Honestly, it's fine. This new job pays more than enough, even for Marks and Spencer.

You could get yourself some clothes, too, if you wanted.'
She'd felt her cheeks redden and he hesitated, clearly thinking
he'd overstepped the mark. 'It's just that since you won't be
wearing your uniform anymore, I thought . . .' He trailed
off before adding, 'I wouldn't be able to do the job if you
hadn't agreed to move in. See it as a perk.'

How nice to be able to see money as a perk, she'd
thought. It didn't sit well, taking money from family, but
she didn't have much choice. She looked at the balance
again. It all felt very different to three months ago when
going a penny over five pounds at the petrol pump gave
her palpitations. Maybe she *would* buy the odd latte. She
might even have one of those almond biscotti biscuits on
the side. She knew she wouldn't – they were too hard to
bite – but her new options were dizzying.

She scanned the room; the beige chaise longue with
cream spots under the sash window, the open door off to
the right, leading to the ensuite with its stand-alone shower
and claw-foot bath. Her hand dropped to the silky material of the throw folded on the end of the bed and she
wondered what Oli would make of her move. Selling out?
Survival? Betrayal?

Offering a silent apology, she opened her favourite
picture of him on her phone and studied his round face
and kind eyes. He was leaning against a wall with Tower
Bridge in the background. Immy took it on that weekend
trip to London and he was grinning so wide all of his
straight teeth were on show. He'd shunned this life in
favour of following his own path and Bea had fully
supported that. She'd never had much interest in material
things, until she couldn't afford to pay the mortgage. Then
it didn't seem materialistic to want a roof over their heads.
Her head, she corrected herself.

Ewan and Phoebe would be back in an hour, so she needed to get moving. When she stood up, she turned to see the mattress slowly fill out the dip where her backside had been. That would take some getting used to.

She walked to the smallest packing box, opened the lid and pulled out a picture of Immy in a silver frame with a teddy bear peeking up from the bottom corner. She was two, toddling on the pebble beach at Whitstable with an ice cream in her hand. Chubby legs sprouted from frilly white pants, a pink sun hat matched her rosy cheeks. Bea trailed her finger over the dark waves escaping from the hat and could almost feel the silkiness of Immy's hair.

The next photo was in a dark wood frame, and she was struck, as always, by how beautiful Immy looked. It was taken just before the last dance show she performed in, before she'd had to give up because when things got rough with Oli they couldn't always drive her to rehearsals, and she was missing too much to keep up with the complex choreography. By then she'd said the classes were 'lame' anyway, but Bea suspected it was another reason Immy concluded nobody cared about her anymore.

Bea stared into Immy's green eyes and found her beautiful daughter there; the one who danced and sang and laughed. The one who would sit next to her on the sofa eating Doritos and squeal with laughter at *Gogglebox*. Not the sullen girl who blamed everyone and everything for her misery. She missed her girl to aching.

Next, she pulled Immy's pillow from the box, slid her hand inside the pillowcase and touched the envelope. She resisted the temptation to drag it out and torture herself by reading it again. Phoebe would be home soon and excited to see her. She didn't want to meet her with a tear-stained face on the first day of the long sleepover they'd talked about. Instead, she walked to the fitted wardrobes and stood in front of the middle panel with the full-length mirror on the front, opened the door, laid the photos on a shelf and stuffed the pillow in front, blocking them from view.

She heard the scrunching of gravel under tyres on the driveway and knelt on the chaise to peer down at Ewan's black Range Rover dwarf her Toyota as it parked alongside it. She was sure Ewan's head gave a brief shake when he stepped from the driver's seat and saw her old car. Bloody snob.

Her mood lifted as soon as Phoebe jumped from the passenger side, tiny next to the hulking 4x4. She skipped towards the house and Bea leaped from the chaise and rushed down the stairs to meet her.

* * *

'Grandma's coming for dinner,' whispered Phoebe, after she'd been given a tour of Bea's bedroom. Bea hadn't opened the mirrored wardrobe door, even though she was sure the pillow covered the pictures. 'Do you think she'll come every night now?'

'Are you worried you'll always have to swallow your mouthful before you speak?' Bea teased.

'And wait until she's finished to get down from the table. She takes forever to eat her dinner.'

Like her niece, Bea was in no hurry to endure mealtimes with Joyce every day. When it was just her and Phoebe they could be as casual as they liked. Joyce liked a properly set table and manners to match.

'When people get older, they don't have the same appetite,' said Bea, wondering how long she'd be able to keep up the niceties now she was here full time.

Joyce's shrill voice shouted upstairs, 'Phoebe. I'm here!'

The little girl jumped to her feet and left the room and Bea resisted the urge to do the same. This was her home now. She wasn't a guest, so she didn't have to leap to attention every time Joyce glanced in her direction.

She heard Jan's voice in her head. *Set boundaries,* she'd told her. *Make sure she knows from the start that you're not her servant.* She gave one more look around the room, flicked her hair over her shoulder, raised her chin, and headed for the stairs.

Joyce sat on the sofa, back as straight as a ballerina, in a red cashmere cardigan and silky black skirt, her gold drop earrings dangling to her shoulders. On anyone else the outfit might look daring. On Joyce, it simply looked expensive.

'There you are,' she said when Bea entered the kitchen. Bea felt her eyes assess her leggings and hoodie and find them lacking. 'You appear to have settled in?'

Her things were unpacked, so she supposed she must have.

There was a popping sound at the other end of the room, and she turned to see Ewan wielding a bottle of champagne. 'Thought we'd celebrate.'

'I can't,' said Bea. 'I've got to dr . . .' She trailed off. 'I don't have to drive, do I?' She watched Ewan grin and shake his head and bit the inside of her lip to stop herself from saying, *because I'm never going home.*

* * *

Ewan, Joyce and Phoebe sat at the table while she delivered the bowls of salad, chicken and potatoes to the mats in the centre then leaned over Phoebe to help her cut her chicken breast into pieces.

'Surely you can do that yourself?' Joyce said to Phoebe, her voice icy.

'She's learning,' said Bea, avoiding Joyce's eye. 'It's a bit tough, isn't it, poppet?'

'It is a touch dry,' said Joyce. 'Better to steam it next time.' She took a tiny piece of meat on her fork and inspected it before moving it to her mouth. She chewed for an age before saying, 'Could you pop over tomorrow morning? I have a few errands I need you to run.'

Boundaries, Bea said to herself. 'I'm busy in the morning. I could come after lunch.' For a moment she felt triumphant, but the feeling passed swiftly. Was that the best she could do? Acquiesce, but just later in the day? Now she'd have to think up something to do in the morning. Maybe she'd paint her toenails. Is that what people with time on their hands did? Joyce was the only person she knew who'd never had a job outside the home and she wasn't about to ask her.

Joyce's eyes narrowed, but she didn't say a word.

The sky lit up outside the bifold doors and they all turned to see little flowers of red and gold blossom and spread across the dark sky before falling and fading. Next there was a series of bangs like gunshot and Bea put her hand on Phoebe's when she jumped. Ewan and Joyce turned back to the table without commenting on the fireworks. It was a firm rule that Phoebe wasn't allowed to go to any of the Guy Fawkes night displays in case the flashing and banging triggered her epilepsy but, surely, ignoring the fifth of November spectacle they could all clearly see was peculiar. That's what the James family did, though; ignore things that didn't suit them.

More colours burst in the blackness, popping then filling

the sky with a thousand pinpoints of light. 'Aren't they beautiful?' asked Bea gently.

Phoebe looked up briefly and nodded. Poor child. She was clearly too nervous to watch the display, even from a distance. Bea's heart broke for her.

'I've been meaning to talk to you about how you'll get on when I'm away, Mum.' Ewan's voice had the obsequious tone it always had when he talked to his mother, as though he were a wheedling schoolboy, not a city high-flyer.

'Get on?' Joyce turned, hawk-like, to him. 'I shall *get on* just fine.'

Ewan's lips moved, as though trying to find the right words. He cleared his throat. 'I wanted to make sure you were properly cared for when I'm abroad.'

'Cared for? I'm not an invalid. And if I were, Bea's here now, and that's what she used to do for a living; care for the elderly.'

Ewan dabbed at the corner of his mouth with a napkin. 'But she doesn't anymore.' He looked at Bea and relief flooded her, allowing the muscles in her neck to relax. 'Bea only agreed to look after Phoebe.'

Joyce's head snapped around to Bea. 'I'm sure you won't mind doing the odd job for your mother-in-law, will you?'

'I have someone coming tomorrow to assess whether you need any extra help,' Ewan continued, ignoring his mother's comment.

Bea gasped. She had never felt like kissing Ewan before, but she did now. Although the thought made her shudder.

'Assessing?' Joyce's voice was almost a screech.

'It's a social worker from a private company. They specialise in helping people of your . . . of your age, stay in their homes.'

'I have no intention of being anywhere other than my

home. What are you planning?' Ewan put his palms up, but Joyce was in no mood to be placated. 'Are you plotting to take my house? What are you up to? Explain yourself.'

Phoebe's forehead furrowed and Bea reached out and took her hand, wondering how they thought this was appropriate to discuss in front of her.

'Don't be hysterical, Mother.'

Bea grimaced. She could have told Ewan this was not the right phrase to use. She gripped Phoebe's hand and waited for the explosion.

'How dare you?' Joyce stood, throwing her napkin onto the table. 'Don't you think I've lost enough, without losing my home, too?'

The irony was not lost on Bea. She herself had lost more than any of them, and they'd pushed her to sell her home as though it was just a dress that didn't fit anymore.

'Sit down. Please. Nobody wants to take the house – as I say, I'm trying to keep you *in* there. I'm only thinking of what's best for you.'

Phoebe snuffled and they all turned to see her bottom lip trembling.

'It's alright, Phoebe. No need for blubbing.' Joyce tucked the silk of her skirt under her and patted the back of her granddaughter's hand in a rare gesture of comfort as she sat. She took a deep breath and turned to Ewan and said calmly, 'Explain what you mean. Clearly, this time.'

'I'm trying to make life easier for you. I know you suffer with your arthritis, so I wanted to see if there was anything that could be done around the house to make things more comfortable. Like one of those chair lifts for the stairs or a seat in the shower. That sort of thing.'

'Heaven help me,' said Joyce, her eyes raised to the ceiling. 'Has it come to that?'

'Can we have one of those?' Phoebe said. 'I'd like that.'

'Well, I wouldn't,' said Joyce.

'Nobody is going to make you do anything you don't want. I just thought it was a good idea to get an expert in to see what could be done if you wanted it.'

'And you didn't think of asking me first?'

'Would you have agreed?' He rose, but before he turned, Bea caught a look of fear on his face. It was costing him to stand up to Joyce. This was probably the first time he'd ever tried. He opened a kitchen drawer and pulled out some papers. 'It would also help us all a great deal if you would sign these forms consenting to myself and Bea being involved in any care you might need in future.' He placed the papers on the table and presented her with a pen, giving her a pleading look. 'You wanted me to take on this new job, so help me make things as easy as possible while I'm away.'

Joyce glared at her son and pinched her red lips together. She might not be impressed with him, but Bea was delighted. It seemed he had the forethought – and the mettle – to act without consulting Her Ladyship. Even if it was a cynical ploy to keep Bea onside, it was a welcome one.

Perhaps this move wouldn't be a disaster after all.

Chapter Ten

Bea woke at five o'clock. She lay in bed watching the frilled shadow under the curtain brighten and spread light into the room until it was time to wake Phoebe.

She could hear Ewan moving around the kitchen and felt awkward about going downstairs. She wasn't sure what to wear when she did. She looked at the dressing gown hanging on the back of the door and thought about showering and dressing before leaving her room. What was the protocol for moving around your brother-in-law's mansion first thing in the morning? Certainly not over-washed, battleship-grey knickers and a t-shirt like she would have done at home. She rolled over, trying to dislodge the pang of longing for her own bedroom. No good could come of letting those thoughts fester.

At last, the front door clicked closed and she crossed the room in time to see the Range Rover indicating at the end of the drive and pulling out. Dressing in leggings and a hoodie, she dragged a brush through her tangled hair and wound a band around a messy ponytail then walked along the corridor to Phoebe's room. It was dark and quiet inside, and the little girl was still asleep. Bea tiptoed over to the bed, holding her breath so she had the best chance of watching her sleep.

When Immy was a teenager and Bea could no longer exhale without being told she was doing it wrong, she would creep into Immy's room in the early hours of the morning. She would look at her beautiful face and, if she ignored the nose ring and the smudges of yesterday's mascara, she could still see her little girl – the one she'd had before she became an angry and distant stranger.

Phoebe looked so like Immy now. Her button nose starting to lengthen, her lips slightly parted to show the gap in her top teeth, just like the one Immy had at about the same age. Bea kneeled beside the bed and put her hand on Phoebe's arm. 'Morning, poppet. Time to wake up.'

Phoebe opened her eyes and smiled. 'Aunty Bea. That's nicer than when Alex wakes me up. She yells and opens the curtains.'

Bea leaned over and kissed Phoebe's red cheek. 'That sounds like a rude awakening.'

'I like it better now you're here.'

'I like it better with you, too,' said Bea, getting to her feet, watching Phoebe yawn and stretch. She wasn't lying about that part at least.

* * *

After the school run, Bea lay on her bed with the uneasy feeling she had forgotten to do something important. She picked up her phone and scrolled through clothes on a shopping app, trying to imagine if any of the jumpers and dresses would suit her. She'd never gone in for fashion, but Ewan was right, she didn't have many clothes since she always wore her uniform or what she imagined he'd term 'loungewear'. Since she hadn't been able to afford new clothes, she'd never thought about them. Now she should probably buy a few bits, but the choice was bamboozling.

Her phone rang, making her jump. She accepted the call.

'Hello.'

'Mrs James?' asked the voice of a young woman. 'It's Molly, from Carthing Estates.'

Bea felt suddenly cold. 'Hi.'

'I've got some good news.' Molly's voice was bright and Bea suddenly felt like she was in the dentist's chair, waiting for the needle to pierce her gum. 'We've got a proceedable buyer, no chain, and they're offering full asking price!'

The sting made Bea's eyes water. Her house. Her family's home. After a pause in which Bea could imagine Molly's gleeful smile fading, she said, 'Thanks. That's great, but . . . can I think about it?'

Molly's voice dropped an octave. 'It's a fantastic offer. Exactly what we'd hoped for.' Bea heard the emphasis on *we'd*. She had put her house on the market. It selling shouldn't come as a shock. But it did.

The temptation to end the call, shove the phone under a pillow and pretend this wasn't happening was almost overwhelming. 'What's the timescale if I accept the offer?'

'If you accept the *asking price* offer,' said Molly, pointedly, 'we could exchange pretty soon. The buyers want to move quickly. Which is good, right?'

Bea looked around the luxurious room. Her room. She remembered how relieved she'd felt when she saw the new balance of her bank account. Scrunching her eyes tight she forced herself to say, 'Yes. Okay. Please accept the offer. Thanks.' She closed the call before Molly said anything else and fell backwards onto the bed. She felt a tear roll down her cheek and into her ear.

As she lay still, she noticed an unfamiliar sound buzzing on the drive. She dragged herself up and peeked out of her bedroom window to see the top of a metallic blue helmet, some broad shoulders and long, narrow thighs, but she couldn't see what was underneath. The body flung one leg up and dismounted, revealing a tiny red and white Lambretta scooter. She looked at the height of the man walking towards the front door, then back at the minuscule scooter with incredulity before heading downstairs.

When she opened the door, the man went to offer his hand, but he had his bike helmet in one and the keys in the other. He frowned, dropped the keys inside the helmet, wiping his hand on his jeans before sticking it out towards her again. 'Eddie Lorimar, from Goldfinch Social Care.'

She drew her eyes away from his short, spiky fringe and long grey sideburns. Who had he come as, Paul Weller? The rising urge to snigger at her own joke subsided at the sight of his serious face.

His handshake felt firm and assured. That was good, at least; he'd need all the confidence he could muster if he was going to win Joyce over. He looked around the hallway as if making an assessment, and by the look of his face, the house didn't impress him. Bea was surprised by a surge of self-consciousness. She wanted to tell him that she hadn't chosen to live in a big, fancy place on this overpriced crescent. 'Come in.'

'Am I right in thinking Mrs James lives in a neighbouring property?'

Bea nodded. 'She's two doors down. This is her son's house. I'm Bea, her daughter-in-law.'

'Right.' He held her eye for a moment then looked away. 'Your husband said you'd be able to go through some of the information before we go to Mrs James' home.' He shook a rucksack from his shoulders and hooked it in the crook of his elbow.

It took Bea a moment to understand what he meant, then she laughed. 'Oh, Ewan's not my husband. I just live here.'

Eddie tugged at one of his bizarre sideburns and looked irritated. 'But you're Mrs James' daughter-in-law?'

'Yes.'

'So, Mr James is your partner?'

Bea gestured for him to follow her through to the kitchen. 'No. He's my brother-in-law.'

She paused. 'I hadn't thought about how complicated this must sound. Tea, coffee?'

'Tea, please. Milk, no sugar. Complicated?'

Bea glanced around and saw he'd taken a seat at the table without being asked. 'Yes.'

'How?'

She wondered if all social workers were so direct. He spoke as though he had a right to know all of her business. Remembering why he was here she felt a twinge of sympathy for Joyce. They'd invited this man to go into her home and assess whether she needed help just to exist in her own space. She made the tea as she answered his question.

'I was married to Ewan's brother, but he's not around anymore.'

'Right.'

She stopped momentarily, the chill from the open fridge making her shiver. She took out the milk and closed the door, sploshed milk into the cup, then offered it to Eddie.

'A bit more milk, please.'

She poured a drop more, then stirred, thinking how unusual it was for someone to be at home enough in themselves to ask for more milk in their tea. She always accepted whatever was offered, even if it was the colour of dishwater.

'But you live here?' His voice was perfunctory.

She sighed. She would give him enough to make her situation make sense, no more. 'Ewan's wife isn't around anymore either.'

'Right.'

Abrupt, she thought, taking a sip of tea. Most social workers she'd met were all about the warm words and kaftans, not blunt mods who looked like extras from *Quadrophenia.* 'Now Ewan's got a job in New York, and someone needs to be here to look after Phoebe, because she's only six.' She joined him at the table. 'So, here I am.'

'Right.'

Bea clamped her mouth shut. This man seemed an odd choice for a caring profession.

'And Mrs James?' He examined a printout he took from his rucksack. 'Joyce James.' His eyebrow raised minutely.

'Yep. Don't mention the name. She'll turn you to ashes.' When he gave her a blank look, she flushed and hurried to explain. 'Having the back-to-front name of an Irish novelist made her the butt of a lot of jokes at school, apparently. She'd have been alright at my school. Nobody'd heard of James Joyce.' There she was again, giving her life story.

'Received and understood.' He scanned the paper again. 'She's signed to say she consents to me discussing her care with you and Mr James, but from what he said, she's a reluctant participant in this assessment?'

'That's one word for it.'

'Is there a better one?'

Bea bristled. If she'd known she was going to be quizzed on her vocabulary, she'd have read the dictionary over breakfast instead of scrolling the internet for pictures of animals who looked like celebrities. 'She's reluctant.'

'Is she managing, in your opinion?'

Bea shrugged. 'She's sure she can look after herself. But Ewan's worried she might be struggling but covering it up.'

'That wouldn't be unusual.'

'Good luck trying to get her to admit it,' Bea said. 'Needing help is a sign of weakness in her eyes.'

'Stiff upper lip, eh?' Eddie smiled, lifting the deep lines around his thin mouth. Bea wondered where he'd got such pronounced laughter lines. Not at work, from today's performance.

'Something like that.' She didn't know why she said that. It was exactly like that, and she was being vague and inarticulate again. She felt heat rising up her neck and she stood, turning away. 'Biscuit?'

'No, thank you.'

Bea shoved a whole custard cream into her mouth and chewed furiously, trying to swallow it down before she turned back.

* * *

After another painful fifteen minutes of functional discussion, they'd been through the forms and were ready to visit Joyce. On the driveway, Bea stopped next to Eddie's scooter. 'You don't see many of these around. This the 200CC? You wouldn't be able to go up hill otherwise.'

'It does the job.'

'I'm more of a Harley fan.' She watched interest grow on Eddie's face.

'You've got one?'

'In the garage.'

He paused and Bea waited for him to say more, but he gave a brief nod and set off down the drive towards Joyce's house. She followed, feeling that she'd made a fool of herself but not quite sure why.

When she answered the door, Joyce's rigid back and sour expression suggested she was not pleased to see them. Her tightly wound plait appeared immovable, and she was wearing her favourite Chinese silk jacket. Bea had to admit, she looked like she was coping perfectly well – as she had probably intended.

Joyce looked Eddie up and down, failing to disguise her judgement of his unusual hairstyle, Fred Perry polo-shirt and bomber jacket. She'd probably expected a man in a suit. Or, more likely, a woman.

'You can go after you've made us a warm drink, Beatrice. Mr Lorimar and I can manage, thank you.'

'Call me Eddie, and I'm fine, thanks. I had a cup at Bea's.'

Joyce narrowed her eyes. 'Ewan's.' She peered at Bea. 'You've already discussed me, then?'

Bea opened her mouth to speak, but Eddie jumped in first. 'With your signed consent.'

Bea watched Joyce's eyes flit between her and Eddie, suspicion tightening her already taut features.

'Thank you for your help,' Eddie said as he turned to Bea, and she knew she was being dismissed.

* * *

81

She was surprised when he knocked on the door again half an hour later. She left him on the doorstep this time instead of inviting him in. 'What can I help you with?'

'It's usual to tell the primary contact how the first client meeting went.'

Primary contact? Client meeting? This was about as personal as talking to Ewan about investment banking.

'How did it go?'

'I get the impression she's scared,' he said. 'Getting older can be terrifying, especially if you're used to being in control. Change is hard for everyone. We get used to seeing ourselves a certain way and when something comes along to challenge that, we get defensive. It doesn't matter if what we believe about ourselves is right or not. It's what we're used to. I think that frostiness might be a front for someone who's not coping as well as they'd like.'

'It's a bloody good front,' said Bea, 'and one she's kept up for a quarter of a century, to my knowledge.'

'No chinks of . . .'

'Humanity?' Bea offered.

His face remained blank. 'I didn't say that.'

Bea thought back to how Joyce was when Immy was little; the gentle voice she used when she read to her, the way she stroked the hair back from her face. 'She had her moments, I suppose.'

'It took a while to persuade her to show me how she manages the stairs, and I'm pretty sure she was hiding how difficult she finds it with arthritic hips and knees.'

'Can you even put a stair lift in a house like that? That banister's original Arts and Crafts.'

Eddie sighed. 'That's what she said. The fact that it twists like that makes it difficult so I suggested she might want to install a lift, or convert one of the rooms down-stairs into her bedroom if the stairs became unmanageable.'

'How did that go down?'

'I think you can imagine.' His eyes rested on hers. 'You're looking after the whole family?'

'Ewan will be abroad soon and Phoebe's a pleasure. She's no work at all.'

'Joyce said she's got an operation coming up?'

'She let you call her Joyce, not Mrs James?'

'I didn't ask her. I think if you're working in someone's home, first names seem appropriate.'

'Right.' Bea was impressed. 'Phoebe's having laser treatment on her birthmarks. She has something called Sturge-Weber syndrome, which means, as well as the port-wine stains, she's got some abnormal blood vessels on her brain, kind of like the birthmarks on her face, but it makes her have seizures. The epilepsy's well controlled, though, and the redness on her face will probably be much lighter when she's had another couple of rounds of lasering.' She didn't know why she was telling him all this. He must be using some social worker superpowers on her. It certainly wasn't down to the warmth of his personality.

'Must be a worry?'

'Yeah. But she's a strong little thing. She'll manage.'

'I meant for you.' He didn't move his eyes from hers. 'It's part of my job to make sure the carers are looking after themselves. You can't look after other people if you're not taking care of yourself.'

'Oh, I'm fine.' Her neck felt warm under her hair, and she shifted her eyes from his. 'I'm used to it.'

'Good.' His tone was clipped again, and he stepped backwards into the drive. She felt foolish for misinter-preting his professional advice for . . . for what? As if anyone was going to be attracted to her. God, this fancy house was giving her notions.

He glanced at his watch. 'Better get on to my next appointment.' The gravel scrunched under his biker boots. 'See ya.'

He shouldered his rucksack and took his helmet from where it was hooked on the scooter's handlebars, pulled it over his head and fastened the clasp. He started the engine and pulled away, and she was still staring into the road even when the buzz of the engine had faded.

Chapter Eleven

Ewan stood in the kitchen with his computer bag at his feet, ready to say his goodbyes. Bea had offered to help when his other bags were being carried to the car by a driver. Ewan hadn't.

The first time Bea heard the term *driver* was when she came to visit Oli, and his parents took them to the city for dinner. Joyce shouted up to the room above the garage, which she called *the annexe,* 'The driver will be here in five minutes. Please be ready.'

'Does she mean the taxi?' Bea asked Oli.

'They call them *drivers* when they're employed by the bank. They're like chauffeurs, but they can be booked by anyone above a certain pay scale.'

'Different world,' Bea said, adding, 'My uncle's a driver. A bus driver.'

'It's all a load of elitist bollocks. They think turning up in a Merc with blacked-out windows makes them look monied, when it actually makes them look like drug dealers,' said Oli. 'Anyway, at least your uncle is doing some good for the community and the environment.'

'Might not mention that tonight though,' said Bea. 'The drug dealers or the bus.' She wondered if the denim mini-dress she was wearing was the right kind of thing for this evening. She tugged at the hem, trying to make it reach her mid-thigh, keen not to feel any more out of place than she already did.

'Mention whatever you like,' said Oli, pulling her towards him and kissing her neck. 'It's not you who lives an odd life. It's them.'

She thought about that now, the way Oli had always positioned it as 'us against them'. Her relationship with this family had begun as a battle, and now here she was, in league with the enemy.

'Come and give your old dad a cuddle.' Ewan opened his arms and Phoebe ran into him, burying her head in his stomach. He kneeled and took her face in his hands. 'I'm going to FaceTime you every day, okay?'

She nodded as tears dripped into his palms and Bea could see he was swallowing back his own tears. That was twice he'd shown emotion in the last couple of days. At this rate, he might upgrade from robot to fully-fledged human by Christmas.

'Daddy will be back to visit in a couple of weeks,' she said, and took Phoebe's hand as Ewan got to his feet, blinking hard.

'You'll have a lovely time with Aunty Bea. She's much more fun than I am.'

Bea couldn't argue with that. She wiped Phoebe's wet cheek with her hand. 'And you've got Sydney's party this afternoon. So, when Daddy's set off, we can choose an outfit and do your hair.' She pretended to whisper, 'And I might have accidentally bought a strawberry-flavoured lip gloss you can try out. But don't tell your dad.'

Phoebe's brown eyes twinkled.

'Don't lead my little angel astray, you,' said Ewan, leaning forward and giving Bea a peck. 'I'll message when I get there and call tonight.' He gave Phoebe another squeeze. 'Love you, Phoebs.' He dotted his forefinger on her tiny nose. 'Be good for Aunty Bea.'

They followed him to the door and waved as the huge black car rolled out of the drive and disappeared behind the laurels.

* * *

In the queue for the soft play centre, the combined smell of fried food and feet was almost as overpowering as the sound of children's shrieks. Phoebe gripped her hand and Bea could feel her excitement building as she jumped from foot to foot.

'There's Sydney!' Phoebe said and pointed, shouting Sydney's name. Sydney glanced around and gave a quick wave then sped away with another little blonde girl, disappearing through a red flap onto a padded apparatus.

Bea gave Phoebe's name to the girl on reception whose ponytail was so tight and high it dragged her hairline skywards, taking her heavily dyed eyebrows with it. She ticked her off a printed list then released the gate lock, and they stepped into the play zone, where the sound of children squalling from every angle was even more disorienting than in the queue.

'Can you see your friends?' asked Bea, scanning the room for faces she recognised.

Phoebe's arm flew out and she pulled Bea by the hand towards a seated group of women dressed in expensive-looking leisurewear. Small girls in sparkly leggings buzzed around them like designer-clad wasps. Bea followed, trying not to trip on the children who crossed in front at knee-level, carrying the present she'd bought from the list emailed to her by Sydney's mother, along with the party invitation. There was nothing on the list costing less than twenty-five pounds. She had been glad of Ewan's generous budget as she clicked the link to buy a doll in a skimpy sundress, whose face was painted in more make-up than a drag queen.

The mothers looked up as she approached and tight-skinned faces smiled as she hovered next to Sydney's mum's chair, holding out the wrapped box.

'Aww, thank you,' she said. 'You're Phoebe's aunty, ain't you?'

Bea nodded, surprised her accent wasn't as posh as she'd expected. 'Yes. I'm Bea.' She held out her hand and Sydney's mum shook it. Bea noticed the false tan was darker on her knuckles and bled up the inside of her wrist to her palm.

The woman turned to Phoebe. 'Hello, darling. Don't you look pretty?'

Phoebe grinned and tugged proudly at the hem of her blue sequinned top.

'Why don't you go and find Sydney? She's in there somewhere.'

Phoebe stared up at Bea and shook her head.

'Go on, Poppet. It looks like fun in there.' It didn't, it looked like Dante's inferno, but she supposed she wasn't the target audience. She scanned the table and realised she wasn't even the same generation as the other mothers. This was going to be torturous. But Phoebe needed a distraction after this morning, and it might help her make more friends.

Phoebe beckoned Bea to come down so she could whisper in her ear, 'Can you come in with me?'

Inside the swarming innards of the frame, children clambered over each other, dangling from poles, chasing each other up slides. It looked like a monkey enclosure. She'd rather take her chance with a bunch of chimpanzees. 'I can't see any grown-ups in there. I think it's just for kids.'

She followed Phoebe's eyes to the slide, where one boy was holding on to the back of another's t-shirt as he tried to drag him to the top and she instinctively pulled her closer to her side.

'Go and play, Phoebe. Come back and get some squash when you get hot,' said Sydney's mum and Bea loosened her grip on Phoebe's hand in an attempt at encouragement. Phoebe glanced up, then took a couple of tentative steps, gradually disappearing through the red plastic drapes.

'They get so hot, running around, don't they? I'm Lavinia by the way,' said Sydney's mum and Bea dragged her eyes away from where she'd been trying to follow Phoebe's progress through the maze of bodies. 'I don't often get to pick-up because I'm at the salon, but I think you know my mum.' She nodded across to the woman who'd been irritatingly sympathetic about Phoebe's birthmarks. Bea smiled a hello. 'Sit down.' Lavinia pulled a plastic chair from a neighbouring table and Bea worried for her talon-long nails. 'I wanted to talk to you about something.'

Bea took off her coat and hung it on the back of the chair, glad she'd ordered some semi-fashionable jeans and a Breton striped t-shirt, so she didn't look too out of place. She searched the apparatus with her eyes, but Phoebe was nowhere to be seen. Lavinia put a hand on hers and was about to speak when there was an ear-splitting scream from somewhere inside the frame.

All the heads lifted and swivelled, and a couple of the

89

women started to kick off their shoes, ready to clamber inside the equipment, when Sydney appeared, leading Phoebe by the hand. Phoebe's chin was puckered, and her breath came in jagged sobs.

Bea leaped to her feet, followed by Lavinia. 'What happened, poppet. Are you hurt?' Bea scanned Phoebe for bumps or bruises as the little girl shook her head.

Sydney was still holding Phoebe's hand and said indignantly, 'William was mean because he doesn't know all about birthmarks like we do because he's not in our school, so he screamed and said Phoebe was covered in blood like somebody had shot her and I said she wasn't, and Phoebe cried.'

Phoebe let out a distressed splutter. 'The boy said I'd been shot,' she said.

Bea's heart broke for her. She lifted her up and cuddled her tightly. 'I'm sorry he was unkind,' she said. 'Thanks for bringing her back, Sydney.' Sydney's face was serious, but her eyes kept darting back to the soft play. 'Why don't you go back and play with your friends?' The little girl looked at her mum for approval then sprang back inside.

'I'll get William to apologise. He was in our baby group so I had to invite him, but he can be a right little sod,' said Lavinia and turned to search the multi-coloured frame.

'It's alright,' said Phoebe, her head lifting from Bea's shoulder. 'I don't think he meant to hurt my feelings. He just hasn't seen me before, so he didn't know about my birthmarks.'

'Do you want to sit with me for a bit?' said Bea. She set Phoebe's feet on the carpet.

Phoebe's eyes skipped from the table to the apparatus, and she ran her hand over her eyes, wiping away the remaining tears. 'I want to carry on playing,' she said.

'That's my girl,' said Lavinia, high-fiving Phoebe as Bea watched her face break into a grin. 'If anyone else is unkind, bring 'em to me and I'll actually shoot 'em.'

Bea grinned in spite of herself. Watching Phoebe climb onto the first padded ledge with a smile on her face was worth any murderous threat.

'They're little shits, aren't they?' said Lavinia when they sat back down, accepting lattes delivered by the girl on reception. 'Sydney told me what happened at school, and I gave her a talking to. It sounded like something from *The Crucible*. Have you read that, or seen the play? Arthur Miller?'

Bea had read it and chastised herself for being surprised Lavinia had, too. 'Yes. It did sound like a scene from that.'

'Poor little thing. Anyway, I've put Sydney straight, and I showed her that model – you know, the gorgeous one with the birthmarks? She was impressed by that. Thinks Phoebe's going to be a supermodel now. What's she like?' She laughed, then her face became serious. 'But to be honest, she's surrounded all day by' – she glanced around to make sure none of the other mothers were listening – 'entitled little princesses. Some of the things she comes out with, I worry she's getting as bad as the rest of 'em. Honestly, I don't think these private schools are all that. I'm working all day, waxing mimsies, to pay for my kid to turn into someone who doesn't know right from wrong. What's that all about?'

Bea could have kissed her, but before she could reply, Phoebe emerged again with her bottom lip trembling.

'Was that William again?' said Lavinia. 'I'll kill him.'

Phoebe shook her head vigorously. 'No. I didn't know the boy, but he was pointing at my face and whispering to his friend.' She blinked up at Bea. 'Can we go home now? I'm tired.'

Bea jumped to her feet. 'Course we can, poppet.' She wrapped Phoebe up in a hug, then pulled her coat from the back of the chair.

'Come over to reception and I'll get your party bag,' Lavinia said, mouthing *sorry* to Bea. Bea shook her head and helped Phoebe fasten her shoes then followed Lavinia to the counter.

'Here you go, lovely.' She handed a pink sparkly party bag to Phoebe. 'Hold on.' She turned to where a huge cake with a number seven in shocking pink icing sat on a silver board. She took the knife that lay behind it and cut an enormous triangular slice and wrapped it in a napkin. 'The least you deserve for putting up with idiots,' she said, offering the cake to Phoebe who had to hold it with both hands.

Lavinia crouched down to Phoebe's level. 'I'm in the beauty business, so I want you to listen very carefully to what I'm about to say, because I am fully qualified.'

Phoebe nodded gravely.

'You are beautiful. You have big brown eyes, a cute button nose and plump, pink lips. But that's not the important part.' She paused. 'Are you still listening?' When Phoebe nodded again, she continued, 'The important thing is you're *more* beautiful than the others. Do you know why?'

Phoebe shook her head.

'Because you're beautiful in here.' Lavinia poked a pointed nail at Phoebe's chest and the little girl followed it with her eyes. 'The others might catch up and grow beautiful in there too, but you're already there. I can see it shining out of you. And you've got your beautiful Aunty Bea looking after you and helping you stay pretty.' She nodded towards the soft play. 'Some of those little girls haven't got someone to help them be pretty on the inside. I feel sorry for them. Don't you?'

Phoebe nodded and Bea bit back tears of her own.

Lavinia stretched back to full height and high-fived Phoebe again. 'Stay pretty, my friend.'

'Thank you,' Bea said, her voice cracking.

'No problem.' She rubbed Bea's arm. 'Take care.' And she walked back into the tangle of colour and kids like the boss she was.

Chapter Twelve

Bea leaned against the front door as Eddie dismounted his scooter and took off his helmet. He nodded hello, smoothing down the long hairs in front of his ears. His fringe was even shorter than last time he'd visited, and it reminded her of the time she'd cut her doll's hair when she was little and it ended up with scrubby blonde spikes over its forehead. She couldn't deny it suited him though. He hadn't gone down the standard middle-aged man in chinos and checked shirt route and she grudgingly admitted to herself that he would be attractive if he wasn't so churlish. How a man could take himself so seriously with that hairdo was a mystery to her.

She nodded in return. 'You didn't have to come over with those leaflets. I only messaged because I was wondering about meal deliveries for Joyce. I'm not even sure she'll go for it. It could have waited until the next appointment.'

'It's my job,' said Eddie.

She swallowed. 'Come in.' However snippy he was, she was too polite to leave him on the doorstep again. 'Tea?'

'Thanks.' He followed her through and sat at the table while she made the drinks.

'That enough milk?' She held the mug in front of him.

'You remembered.'

She smiled despite herself.

'Where are those—?' He rummaged in his rucksack and pulled out a ream of papers. 'That's not it.' He put a pile of booklets on the table and carried on digging in his bag.

Bea picked up the top one and read the title. 'Diplomas?' She opened the cover and scanned the contents page.

'Yeah, one of my clients wants to do a course, so I'm taking these for her to have a look at.'

'I thought your company only did geriatric care?'

'We do. She's in her seventies.'

'Wow.'

Eddie lifted his head briefly. 'Some people need a purpose. It's good for mental health.'

He was clearly making a point. An indignant breath caught at the base of Bea's throat. So, that's what he thought of her; she was a little woman living in a big house. He'd made his judgement and come up with a conclusion so far away from the truth it was astonishing.

She kept her eyes on the contents page and they came to rest on number ten on the list: Diploma in Elderly Care Management. She tapped her nail on the page. 'Do you have another copy of this?'

'Why?'

'I've been thinking of doing a course myself.'

He leaned back in his chair and narrowed his eyes. 'Really?'

She frowned. No, she was lying. She was actually a hoarder of shiny paper and this one had the added bonus of staples. 'Really.'

'You can keep it. I've got more at the office.'

He looked at the page Bea held open and the smell of his aftershave took her back thirty years. She breathed in. 'Are you wearing Kouros?'

'Yep.' His lips tweaked upwards. 'I started wearing it as a kid and I've never found anything I like more.'

'You smell like sixteen-year-old snogs!' She clapped her hand over her mouth, but it was too late. The words were already out there.

Eddie guffawed with a throaty sound she couldn't have imagined him making. The grin completely changed his face, and Bea smiled, too.

'That's a new one.' He laughed again.

'I'm so sorry.' Bea felt her colour rise. 'That was very unprofessional. I'm so sorry.'

The word *unprofessional* seemed to flatten Eddie's lips back into a stern line. He shoved his hand back into the bag and found the paper he was looking for. 'I'll leave these leaflets about the food options with you. Let me know if Joyce is interested.' He repacked his bag and stood, looking awkward, and before Bea could think of anything else to say he turned away from her and said, 'I'll see myself out.'

After he left, Bea breathed in again. The smell of the aftershave lingered. It reminded her of the sixth-form common room, where she would sit with her friends, all with identical curly perms and baggy jumpers, Monkey Boots up on the table, talking about the lives they would lead. She and her friends smelled of Impulse body spray and listened to The Smiths. They watched boys who reeked of Kouros and Paco Rabanne flirt with pretty girls who wore Anaïs Anaïs and danced to Kylie Minogue.

She was sure Eddie knew she was an Impulse girl. She imagined him dancing at seventeen, jumping from foot to foot to 'A Town Called Malice', then taking an Anaïs Anaïs girl home on the back of his scooter. He'd probably always been cool. He had that air.

Oli hadn't heard of Impulse. She'd tried to describe it to him when they first met in the south of France, but he was a private school boy who wouldn't have been caught dead wearing any of the perfumes or aftershaves she mentioned. He'd looked at her like she was mad when she told him he was probably more suited to a girl who wore Obsession. He shut her up by kissing her and then thoughts were colours and feelings and all theories of who should be wearing what had disappeared.

She forced her mind to come back from Oli and the beach in Cannes the summer she'd turned nineteen, and read through the booklet. It wasn't long until the application deadline. Was she kidding herself that she could take on a new qualification at her age? She thought about the woman who the booklet was intended for and the look on Eddie's face when he talked about purpose. Sod it. She would apply. And she'd get a bloody distinction, too. That would wipe the judgemental look off Eddie's face.

Not that it mattered what he thought of her. Obviously.

* * *

Bea regretted inviting Joyce for dinner the evening before Phoebe's treatment as soon as the woman scrutinised the food on her plate. Ewan's pixilated face was falsely cheery as he joined them via video call from Bea's laptop screen.

'It looks like your head is on a plate, Daddy,' said Phoebe.

'We just need to stick an apple in your mouth.' Bea was only half joking.

'Very funny,' said Ewan, his voice distorted and a second

behind the movement of his lips. 'How was your lunch delivery, Mother?'

Bea could detect a more wheedling tone when he spoke to Joyce, even through the laptop's tinny speakers.

'Passable.' Joyce lifted the fish finger's breaded coating with her knife, her lip curling. 'At least it was fit for adult consumption.'

Bea rolled her eyes without trying to hide it for once. She felt the chill from Joyce's icy glare and tried not to shrivel back into her seat.

'This is my favourite,' said Phoebe, picking up a fat chip with her fork and nibbling the end. 'Would you like some ketchup?'

Joyce shuddered. 'No, thank you.' She peered at the computer screen. 'I had bouillabaisse and crusty bread. It was too salty, but better than . . .' She flapped her hand over her plate, the bangles on her thin wrist jangling.

'It's what Phoebe chose for her—' Bea stopped as the words *last supper* died on her lips. Why had that occurred to her? She swallowed and looked down at her plate, the beans oozing into the orange fish fingers making her stomach roil.

'I'd kill for that right now,' said Ewan. Bea felt a stab of annoyance. Why was everything about death? 'I'm ravenous. I'm going for lunch after I've spoken to you. Weird that it's lunchtime here and dinnertime there, isn't it?'

They nodded.

'Time for dessert!' said Phoebe, wiping a chip around her plate to collect the last of the ketchup. 'We've got ice cream.'

'Have you now?'

Bea stood and took Phoebe's empty plate and her almost full one across to the kitchen counter, bravely trying to ignore Joyce's open-mouthed disdain that she'd left the table before everyone finished eating. She hated herself for still caring about Joyce's judgement. She needed to grow a backbone if she was going to survive the next two years.

'We need to eat up because it's nearly time for Phoebe's bath.' She turned to Phoebe. 'We're going to put lots of bubbles in tonight, aren't we, because there'll be no bubble bath for a few weeks after you've been zapped.'

Joyce put her knife and fork down and offered her plate to Bea, as though she were a waitress in an inexpensive restaurant. Bea took it with a sigh and put it on the counter with the others, wondering how much she should have earned in tips over the last few years. Her phone buzzed and she picked it up and glanced at the screen.

Good news! All on course to exchange on the house tomorrow. Congratulations!

'That's a message from the Estate Agent. My house is exchanging tomorrow,' she said. Dread slipped through her. She knew this was happening, but it still hit her in the gut. It was too real. Too final.

'Good,' said Joyce.

'That must be a relief,' said Ewan.

In that moment, Bea felt more alone than ever. The urge to rush upstairs and pull Immy's pillow from the cupboard and hold it almost overwhelmed her. Their home was gone. Her husband and daughter were gone. It was too much.

Instead, she took a deep, calming breath. She pulled out two tubs of ice cream from the freezer and placed them on the table in front of Phoebe. 'Strawberry or chocolate?'

'Both?'

Bea looked at the screen for approval. Ewan nodded. 'Okay. Both it is.'

'I'm sure Phoebe is old enough to bathe herself,' said Joyce. 'Whilst she's upstairs, I'd like to talk to you about a few jobs I need you to do.'

An image of Phoebe floating, lifeless, in the bath flashed across Bea's vision. Her eyes were closed, and the water lapped over her face, distorting her features. Bea took a deep breath. 'I'm sure it can wait until after Phoebe's treatment.' Joyce's eyebrows furrowed at the sharp note in her voice.

'But—'

'You could talk to me while Phoebe and Bea are upstairs?' Ewan sounded wheedling.

'You are in a different country,' snapped Joyce. 'I need practical help, here.'

'I'll ask Eddie to call around tomorrow. He's more than happy to arrange whatever you need. I'm going to spend the rest of this evening with Phoebe,' said Bea, through clenched teeth. Today wasn't about Ewan and his fancy meals out in a far-off country, or Joyce and her endless list of demands. She watched Phoebe lick a mixture of brown and pink ice cream from her spoon.

The heavy feeling at her core was worse than usual tonight. It had crept through her body slowly since that awful incident in the changing rooms. It began with an intangible unease that made her fingers need to be busy all the time. Now it sat like an unexploded bomb with its taper lit, solid and fizzy in her abdomen. Every so often it gave off a spark that brought images like the one of Phoebe drowning in the bath.

She was sure she'd feel better after Phoebe's operation. She hoped so, anyway, because the bomb felt like it was getting ready to explode.

Chapter Thirteen

'Could you stop the car?' Bea shouted to Geoff, the driver Ewan had arranged to take them to the hospital the following morning. She pressed the button for the electric window. The whoosh of cold air on her face didn't stop the thick saliva collecting in her mouth.

The car lurched to a halt. Bea unclicked her seatbelt and flung the door open, staggering towards the back wheel in the morning half-light, then retching out the content of her stomach onto the ground.

'You alright?' asked Geoff, scratching at his scalp under his cap. 'Maybe you shouldn't be going to the hospital if you've got a bug?'

She straightened her back and rolled her head from side to side, assessing how she felt. 'I don't think it's a bug. It came on suddenly. Weird.' She rubbed her tummy, trying to massage away the unease.

The rising sun formed a yellow halo in the sky beyond the field and Bea watched the day dawn, trying to manage the rolling inside her. Suddenly, her brain threw her a picture of Phoebe being sick during the procedure and nobody realising, and her mind's eye watched as she choked on her vomit as the laser blasted on, oblivious.

Her insides flipped again, and she doubled over, waiting for what was left of her morning coffee to re-emerge.

'Aunty Bea?' Phoebe's voice was tiny and scared.

Bea pulled herself upright and swilled her mouth out with the water Geoff gave to her. 'Coming, poppet. I was a bit car sick, but I'm alright now.' She nodded at Geoff and they both climbed back into the car and carried on to the hospital as the sun rose in the sky.

* * *

When they arrived at the theatre suite, they were shown into a small room with a child-sized bed and a chair by a nurse.

'Dev, at your service.' Strands of dark hair escaped from his hairnet onto his forehead as he dipped his head in greeting. 'I'll be with you for the whole time you're here, even when you're asleep,' he said. 'I'm here to make sure you have nothing to worry about.'

Easy for you to say, thought Bea, her fingers furling and unfurling repeatedly behind her back. She wished there was someone else here with her. A proper grown-up who could take full responsibility for Phoebe without puking or feeling the urge to run from this room that smelled of disinfectant. Her husband, ideally. She pushed the thought away.

Phoebe looked under her fringe at Dev as though he were a God. Bea wished he was. She needed someone with superhuman powers to look after Phoebe.

'Here's a fancy nightie and robe for you to change into.'

He handed Bea a soft cotton bundle with a faded blue pattern that had clearly been through the wash many times. She thought of all the poor children who'd worn the gown before and dug her nails into her palms to stop herself crying.

'Any questions?' Dev looked from Phoebe to Bea.

'When can I have breakfast?' asked Phoebe quietly.

'Good question.' Dev high-fived Phoebe, and Bea detected a hint of a blush on her paler cheek. 'You'll be able to eat as soon as you wake up. Maybe something light at first, like a yoghurt, until you feel wide awake. Do you like yoghurt?'

'Strawberry yoghurt?'

'I'll see what I can do.' He winked and scribbled a note on his clipboard. 'Aunty Bea, any questions?'

Is there even the slightest chance she could choke on her own vomit while she's under? Can I have an anaesthetic, too? Because I really don't think I can bear the waiting. Who put me in charge? I'm not up to the job. I destroy things.

'No. I don't think so.'

'Good.' He bounced onto his heels and the soles of his rubber shoes squeaked on the floor. He moved again and his eyes flitted across the shiny linoleum. 'Did you hear that?'

Phoebe nodded. He scuffed his shoes again then dropped to his knees and searched under the bed. 'That might be Boris.'

'Who's Boris?' Phoebe rolled over the blue blanket to the side of the bed and peered underneath. Bea put out her arms to catch her, her heart thumping as the image of Phoebe's skull smashed on the floor swam in front of her eyes.

'My hamster,' he said. 'He lives on this corridor, but he only visits very special children.

'Boris the hamster?' said Bea, trying to keep the smile from her voice.

103

'I think it was your shoes making the noise,' said Phoebe seriously.

'Do you?' Dev dropped his head to his shoulder. 'Well, you keep an eye out for Boris, just in case. Okay? He's a cheeky chappy, and he's very good at hiding.'

Phoebe looked at Bea, who raised her eyebrows and forced a smile.

'Get yourself changed and I'll be along to collect you when Doctor Shah's ready. Shouldn't be long,' said Dev, clasping the clipboard to his chest and setting off for the door. Just when they thought he'd left, they heard a squeak from the corridor and his head appeared around the doorway, his eyes darted around the room, then he disappeared again, and they were alone.

Phoebe sat back up and Bea hurriedly grabbed the backpack in the shape of a mermaid's tail they'd packed after Phoebe's bath last night. 'What do you want to play with?' asked Bea, then slowed her voice down so she didn't sound manic. 'Koala?' She pulled the Beanie Boo from the bag and danced it along the blanket then up Phoebe's leg, tummy and chest. She wiggled it in the crook of her neck, and Phoebe giggled before becoming still and quiet.

'Do you think my birthmarks will go away this time?' She looked up at Bea. 'I think I'd like it if people didn't stare at me anymore.'

Bea swallowed hard. 'They'll get paler.' She kissed the top of her head and scrunched her eyes tight. She would do anything to take away the pain and sadness this tiny person had endured in her short life. 'I'm sorry,' she whispered silently into Phoebe's hair. 'I'm so, so sorry.'

* * *

104

Half an hour later, there was a squeaking sound outside the room. Phoebe's eyes widened and she pulled away from Bea to search the floor. 'Boris,' she hissed at Bea, who ignored the panic rising in her chest and pretended to look around the room, too.

Dev's head appeared followed by another squeak. He jumped inside. 'Is that what I think it is? Has Boris been here all along?' He scampered around the periphery of the small room, looking under the narrow drawers next to the bed and behind the blinds. He slapped his forehead. 'I've missed him again, haven't I?'

He sat down next to Phoebe, who gazed up at him adoringly. 'I tell you what. How about you come with me, and we'll get this laser business out of the way. Then, when you wake up, maybe Aunty Bea will have caught him?'

He looked at Bea, who ignored her lurching stomach and the urge to grip Phoebe's arm to stop her from leaving. She nodded. 'I'll do my best. No promises, mind. He seems to be a slippery customer, your Boris.'

'Come on then, trouble.' Dev nudged Phoebe's arm. 'Let's do this thing. Wait there.' He held his finger aloft and left the room, returning seconds later with a small wheelchair. He stood to the side and held out his arm. 'Your chariot awaits.'

Bea moved Phoebe's fringe aside and kissed her forehead, painfully aware of the big eyes searching her face. She took Phoebe's chin in her hand and said, 'I'll be right here when you get back.'

'And Boris?'

Bea laughed and patted Phoebe's arm as she felt the blood course more quickly through her veins. 'Love you to the moon and back,' she said.

'Love you, too,' said Phoebe, climbing off the bed and into the wheelchair. Dev turned it around and headed for the door, pausing to let Phoebe wave as he mouthed over her head, 'She's in good hands'. He gave her a thumbs up and Bea gripped on to the cold metal frame of the bed to stop herself from running after them.

Chapter Fourteen

Two hours later, Phoebe still wasn't back, and Bea's head was full of static electricity. Every thought stung and an endless procession of painful images and sounds assaulted her. She paced the room, trying to control her brooding, but couldn't stop the pictures of crash teams pumping on Phoebe's little chest and machines making long, low beeping sounds.

Opening the door of the room for the fortieth time, she scanned the corridor. A woman pushed a young boy in a wheelchair towards her. The fluorescent light shone on his naked scalp, his skin grey. She forced herself not to slam the door closed and shut her eyes. Instead, she directed her unruly features to smile at the heavy-lidded woman as she passed, and the woman forced herself to smile back.

At last, she heard Phoebe's voice and turned towards the sound.

There she was, sitting in the wheelchair halfway down the corridor, pushed by Dev, bright and chatting, as if she hadn't just been pumped full of drugs that, with one slip of the anaesthetist's hand, could have stopped her tiny heart from beating. Bea clung onto the door handle as relief weakened every muscle in her body. Her hands and feet felt heavy as the adrenaline pumped away. *Thank God*, her brain said on a loop. *Thank God, thank God.*

She almost winced at how swollen and red Phoebe's cheek was. The skin shone as though slicked in oil. Averting her eyes, she scanned the rest of her for signs that something had gone wrong, all the while trying to mould the smile on her face into something approaching normal.

'Hello!' She moved out of the way as Dev pushed the chair into the room. 'All okay?'

'Did you find Boris?' Phoebe's eyes looked hopeful, and Bea wished she'd been to a pet shop and bought a hamster.

'I'm afraid not. Oh, it's good to see your face. How did she get on?' she asked Dev, trying to read his expression as he helped Phoebe from the chair to the bed.

'It was a long job because there's quite a lot of skin to treat, but I think Doctor Shah is happy with how it went.'

Bea nodded quickly, hoping for more information, but Dev turned back to Phoebe. 'Remember what we talked about, Missy. You need to take it very easy for a while. No rough games and no direct sunshine for a few weeks. That skin's very fragile, like a butterfly's wings.' He mimed a butterfly's movement with his hands, flying around the room.

'Ouch,' said Phoebe and they both turned to her.

'What's up, poppet?' Bea asked, concerned.

'It hurts when I laugh.'

Dev moved close and examined her face. 'It will be a bit sore. It's likely to be bruised and bruises can hurt, can't they? But' – he raised his hand – 'you've had bruises before, right?'

Phoebe nodded.

'And what happens after a few days?'

'They get better.'

He high-fived her. 'Exactly. So your face is red and a bit bruised and swollen for now, but after a few days it will get better and you'll be able to see a difference.' He smiled at Phoebe. 'Any questions?'

'Do you have strawberry yoghurt?'

He laughed. 'On it. You deserve an apple juice as well. You did good, kid.'

Bea watched, aghast, as he turned and left the room. Surely he needed to take Phoebe's temperature, or blood pressure or something? She'd just had a general anaesthetic. Bea wasn't qualified to look after her so soon after her procedure. The relief she'd felt a few minutes ago was washed out by a new surge of panic. She opened the door, looking from left to right but the corridor was empty. She turned back to the bed, the knowledge that it was now her responsibility to take care of Phoebe entirely on her own ringing like an alarm bell in her ears.

* * *

Bea put two bowls of ice cream on the glass coffee table in the sitting room and offered a spoon to Phoebe. She took it, but her movements were slow, and her eyes had lost their sparkle. The buzzing in Bea's head got louder. She checked the size of Phoebe's pupils, the colour of her skin. Things looked alright, but she couldn't be certain. She put her hand on Phoebe's forehead. It was warm, but she wasn't clammy or hot.

'Okay?'

'Kind of.' She picked up the bowl and poked at the pink and brown mounds.

'Skin sore?'

'A bit.' She swirled the ice cream in the bowl, mixing it into a beige sludge.

Bea let some chocolate ice cream melt on her tongue before swallowing it and tracing its cold progress down her throat, then put the bowl down.

'Want to watch TV?'

Phoebe shook her head. There was definitely something wrong.

'You will tell me if you feel poorly, won't you?'

A tear dripped onto Phoebe's cheek. 'It's not that.'

Bea moved close to Phoebe, wrapping her arms around her shoulders gingerly, avoiding touching the treated skin. 'What is it, poppet?'

Tears flowed down her raw-looking cheeks and Bea felt paralysed. Should she dab them with a tissue?

Phoebe's lips parted in a gappy sob, her little body heaving under Bea's arm.

'What's the matter? You can tell me, sweetheart.'

She blinked wet eyelashes. 'I stood on my tiptoes and looked in the mirror when I went to the toilet.'

'Right.' Bea closed her eyes and breathed steadily.

'My face is worse.'

She twisted to look directly at her. 'It's not forever. Remember what Dev and Doctor Shah said? It will get better, like a bruise gets better. But it takes time.'

'But what if it doesn't?' A clear stream of mucus ran from her nose and mingled with her tears.

Bea cautiously dabbed the patches of clear skin with a tissue. 'It will. Honestly, darling, it will.'

'And if it stays like this, nobody will play with me or sit next to me in class.'

Bea wanted to squeeze her into a bear hug and take all the sadness and worry away. But she had to make sure she didn't break her fragile skin, and she couldn't make her fears disappear, because they both knew bad things could happen and life wasn't fair. She held her gently and let her cry, making shushing sounds and kissing the top of her head.

'Want to sleep in my bed with me tonight?' she asked. 'It's a big bed, and then you can wake me up if you feel sad or if you need some Calpol.'

Phoebe lifted herself away, her eyes brighter. 'Like a sleepover?'

'Like a sleepover.'

'I'd like that.'

Good, thought Bea. Now she'd be able to keep an eye on her all night.

'Finish your ice cream, then we'll get some moisturiser on you and watch a film. You're off school for a few days, so it doesn't matter if we stay up a bit later, does it?'

'Can we stay up 'til nine?'

'Nine o'clock?' Bea opened her mouth. 'That late?'

Phoebe nodded fast; her eyes hopeful.

'Alright then, but don't tell Grandma. She thinks bedtimes rules are actual laws.'

Phoebe pretended to zip her lips, picked up the mushy ice cream and pretended to unzip them again before slopping a spoonful into her mouth.

She hardly seemed to notice Bea smearing the moisturiser onto the swollen, red skin of her cheek and neck as she tried to see past Bea's oily fingers to the screen where, in the Disney fairy tale, all the beautiful characters sang and danced towards their happy endings, their skin perfect and blemish-free.

* * *

Six days later, Bea knew it was probably time for Phoebe to go back to sleeping in her own room, but she sometimes groaned in her sleep and Bea's heart leaped in her chest, prepared to see her limbs twitching and her eyes speeding from side to side under her thin eyelids. That hadn't happened so far, but Bea wanted to be there if it did.

When Bea turned over to see her scratching at the skin on her neck, she got an ice pack from the freezer, wrapped it in a tea towel and held it against the raw skin for a while, then smothered Phoebe in moisturiser before they both went back to sleep. She feared she wouldn't notice the scratching if Phoebe was in her own room.

* * *

'Could you drive me to Lorna's at two? I'm invited for afternoon tea,' said Joyce, calling on the phone the Wednesday after Phoebe's procedure.

Typical of Joyce's friends to invite her for afternoon tea. They probably made cucumber and dill sandwiches with the crusts cut off. Afternoon tea at Jan's was builder's tea with a jammy dodger if they were feeling flashy.

'Erm.' She tried to think of a reason that didn't mention Phoebe. She drew a blank.

'What?'

Bea took the phone away from her ear and pulled a face at the screen, then admitted, 'Phoebe's still at home.'

There was a pause, then a click, and five minutes later an impatient rapping at the door. Bea walked slowly down the hallway, feeling Gemma watching her from the photograph as always. She steeled herself and opened the door.

'Could I have my key back, by the way?' said Joyce, stepping inside. She was carrying a walking stick with a shiny silver handle. The rubber end clonked as she set off towards the kitchen. 'You borrowed it some time ago when you'd forgotten yours and never gave it back.'

'I'm not sure what I've done with it. I'll have to get another one cut,' she lied.

The tutting was audible from the other end of the hall. Bea followed her into the kitchen.

'Where is she?' Joyce turned and fixed Bea with her sharp eyes.

'Upstairs, playing with her dolls house.'

'At least she's not on one of those dreadful video games.' Her eyes flitted around the kitchen and Bea wished she'd cleared up the breakfast things straight away instead of leaving them out on the table. Phoebe had wanted a kitchen disco after breakfast, and that was more fun than wiping up crumbs.

'We're saving Roblox for after lunch.'

Joyce narrowed her eyes. 'Isn't she meant to be back at school by now? She hasn't had a seizure, has she?'

Bea bristled. 'No, but I'm still not sure her skin is healed enough for all that rough and tumble.'

'She's a six-year-old girl, not a prop forward. The teachers will ensure she doesn't do anything harmful.'

Bea marched into the hall, stopping at the foot of the stairs. 'Phoebe, could you come down here please?'

'I'm playing,' she shouted, and Bea glanced back at Joyce to see a predictably raised eyebrow. 'Now, please.'

There was a tumble of sound and Phoebe appeared at the top of the stairs. 'Koala was going to eat Mrs Pretty Feathers, so I was telling him off.'

'Grandma's here.' She kept her tone light but the change in Phoebe's face told her she knew what was expected of her. It was all she could do not to say *one, two, one, two* as Phoebe dutifully descended to present herself to commanding officer Grandma. Bea still couldn't draw her eyes away until she was safely off the bottom step.

She took Phoebe's hand and led her through to the kitchen where Joyce was sitting on one of the sofas in front of the bifold doors.

'Come here, child. Let me see you.' Phoebe trotted forwards and sat when Joyce patted the seat next to her. 'Raise your head.'

Phoebe lifted her pixie chin and allowed her grandmother to inspect the red, bumpy skin. 'It's itchy,' she said.

'Is it meant to look like that?' Joyce's nose wrinkled.

'She's had a significant procedure,' said Bea, trying to keep the exasperation out of her voice. 'It will be absolutely fine in a few days.' She turned to Phoebe. 'Why don't I give you a biscuit and you can go back and save Mrs Pretty Feathers?'

'Bye, Grandma.' She sprang up and took the biscuit Bea lifted from the packet in the cupboard, closing the door on the pile of crumbs accumulating inside.

'Is she taking that to her bedroom?' Judgement dripped from Joyce's words.

But Bea had some judgements of her own to make. 'Did you have to say that?'

'What?'

'"*Is it meant to look like that*?" In that voice?'

'What voice? I don't know what you're talking about.'

'She's self-conscious enough without you sneering at her.'

Joyce's mouth dropped open; red lipstick smeared on one of her greying teeth. 'I did not sneer.'

'You could have said how well it was healing.'

'It isn't.'

That was difficult to argue with. The bruising only seemed to have become worse, and the skin was red and rough where Phoebe clawed at it. But that wasn't the point. 'She doesn't need to know that.'

Joyce threw her head back. 'That's you all over, isn't it? Pamper them, protect them from the truth, let them get away with everything and hope for the best. That's not parenting, Beatrice. It's indulgence.'

Bea burned with rage. 'What is, in your book? Make them scared of you? Cut them off if they don't follow your instructions to the letter? Ruling by fear isn't parenting either. You didn't mother, you ran a sodding dictatorship.'

The two women glared at each other in silence, absorbing the shocks from the words that neither of them could take back.

Joyce rose to her feet, her knuckles whitening as she gripped the top of the cane.

Bea moved forwards to help her.

'No,' said Joyce, her voice wobbling.

'Sorry.' The heat was gone. Bea held out her hands, palm up. 'We've both said—'

'No.' Joyce walked unsteadily past her, along the hallway and out of the door.

Chapter Fifteen

Jan arrived that evening waving a bottle of Pinot Grigio and a bag of Doritos at Bea as she kicked off her trainers and left them by the door. Bea could have kissed her for agreeing to come over this evening. She needed to see a friend.

'I'll never get used to coming here,' Jan said. 'I feel like I should be hoovering the place, not sitting on a sofa that probably cost more than my car, sipping fancy wine.'

Bea took the bottle from her and checked the label. 'Fancy? You didn't need to go mad. It's my address that's changed, not me.'

Jan harrumphed. 'It's fancier than lager and lime. Anyway, that one got a very good write-up on the label at Lidl.'

'And I'm very grateful,' said Bea, hugging her friend.

'Hello, Mrs,' Jan said as Phoebe sauntered through from the kitchen. 'I thought you'd be in bed?'

'Aunty Bea lets me stay up 'til nine because I'm not going back to school.'

'Yet,' said Bea. 'Soon though.' She avoided Jan's eyes.

116

'Let's have a look how you're healing.' Jan beckoned Phoebe over and examined the red skin. 'You've been in the wars, haven't you? That'll be right as rain in no time, though. You're a little trooper.'

'You've never been so popular, have you?' Bea said to Phoebe, conscious that everyone seemed to be staring at her face. 'Everyone's impressed with how well you're doing.' Phoebe snuggled into Bea's side and she wrapped her arm around her shoulder. It felt good to have a little shadow again.

* * *

In the sitting room Bea was snug with Phoebe curled up next to her with her head resting on her stomach, playing a game on her phone, while Jan filled her in on the goings-on at Sweetingdale.

'Can you believe our Ciara's starting in the kitchen next week?' she said. 'I'm sorry she decided not to go to college, but it's her life, I suppose. The pay's shocking, but it'll be good experience and at least she'll be getting something while she works out what to do with her life.'

'That's what I said, now look at me.'

Jan seemed to take in the curtains and cushions, embroidered with hummingbirds, picking up the blue of the sofa in their wings. 'You look like you're doing alright.'

Bea glanced around, too. It wasn't her room, or even her taste. Everything matched, all neutrals with accents of colours and expensive fabrics. Nothing you could spill a cup of tea on and rub in with your finger to mask the stain. In her book it wasn't a home unless you could instantly tell people lived there.

Jan sipped her wine. 'And you've started that diploma course. That'll make a difference when you go back to work.'

Bea stroked Phoebe's hair absentmindedly. 'Yeah. I've made a good start with that. I'm quite proud of myself.'

'So you should be. You aced that first module.'

Bea relived the moment she'd opened the email with the grade for the first assignment. It felt good to see 'distinction' typed on a document with her name on it. She'd get back on track as soon as she was sure Phoebe was alright. 'That's on pause at the moment. You know . . .'

'I don't understand.' Jan shifted position again.

'With Phoebe being off school and everything.'

'She'll be back on Monday, though. Surely?' She looked at Phoebe. 'I bet you can't wait to see all your friends again.'

Bea patted Phoebe's bottom. 'Time for bed.'

'It's not nine. The clock on this says eight-fifty.' She pointed at the screen, pouting.

Bea caught Jan's look of surprise and lifted Phoebe upright. 'I said time for bed.'

'Am I sleeping in your bed again?'

As Jan's brow furrowed, Bea stood and tugged at Phoebe's hands. 'Say goodnight to Jan, and off we pop.'

'Sleep tight, sweetheart. Don't let the bedbugs bite.'

Phoebe sloped from the room and Bea followed. Over her shoulder she said, 'Won't be long. Stick the telly on if you like.'

* * *

When she eventually got Phoebe off to sleep, she looked at her watch and was mortified to see it was 9:45. She quickened her steps, rushing into the sitting room. 'I'm so sorry.'

Jan glanced up from her phone, mouth a straight line. The room was silent.

'Why didn't you put the TV on?'

'I couldn't work out how to use it.' She lifted one of the three remote controls by her side. 'I gave up. I wasn't expecting you to be that long.'

Bea grimaced. 'Yeah, sorry about that. I couldn't get her off.'

'I know she's only six, but surely it doesn't take an hour to brush her teeth and read a story.'

Bea's shoulders tightened. 'You've forgotten what it's like, having a little one.'

'I did have four.' Jan stretched out her short legs then rolled forwards in the seat and up to standing. 'I'd better get off. I'm on earlies.'

'Aw, don't go yet. We haven't had a proper catch-up.'

Jan viewed her, her head slightly on one side. 'I've been sitting here on my own for an hour.'

'I've said I'm sorry.'

'When did you say she's going back to school?'

Bea busied herself picking up the wine glasses and trying to lift the bottle at the same time. 'Soon.'

'Okay.' Jan took an audible breath. 'When's soon?'

'Oh, I don't know.' Bea brought her arms wide, slopping a splash of wine onto the floor. She tutted. 'She's been through a lot.'

'I'm not denying that, but don't you think it's all a bit much? Staying off school and sleeping in your bed?'

'I'm looking after her. That's my job.'

'She seemed alright to me.'

Bea marched towards the kitchen. 'And you're the expert?'

'I've got four bloody kids and none of them—' She stopped.

Bea turned around. 'None of them what? Go on. None

of them went off the rails? None of them found you so unbearable to live with that they disappeared into thin air?'

'I didn't—'

'Save it.' She flung open the door of the dishwasher and shoved the glasses inside. 'I'm just trying to get it right this time. Why can't anyone see that? I want to make sure whatever that little girl is going through, I'm here for her. I want her to know she's my priority and I won't let anything bad happen to her.'

The sound of Immy crying as Bea passed her bedroom door after they'd had another fierce argument flashed into her thoughts. She saw herself pause, hand raised to knock, but change her mind and carry on to her own room, closing the door behind her. What would have happened if she'd asked to be allowed in? Would Immy have let her sit on the edge of the bed, stroke her hair back from her face and soothe her? She'd never know.

'But nothing bad is happening to her. Not really. It's awful that she has to have that treatment, but she's got a better life than most. She doesn't want for anything. She's loved.' Jan's voice slowed. 'I'm more worried about you, to be honest. This isn't normal, Bea. You're on edge all the time.'

Bea gripped on to the work surface and watched her tears fall and pool on the granite. She felt Jan's hand on her back but didn't turn. 'I can't risk her being hurt again. Not after everything she's been through.'

'But wrapping her up in cotton wool isn't good for her either. You're treating her like she's made of glass. It's like you daren't take your eyes off her.'

She breathed in and out, feeling Jan's hand circling on her back. 'I'm doing my best.'

'I know, but—'

'I'm doing my best,' she shouted.

Jan's hand stopped moving and when she took it away Bea's skin felt cold. 'Okay.'

Bea pulled a tissue from her sleeve and blew her nose. Wiping her face dry with the back of her hand, she turned to face Jan. 'It's all I can do.'

'I know.' The sympathy on her face made Bea force back fresh sobs.

'Anyway . . .'

'Yep.' Jan walked towards the hall, dragging on her coat. 'See you soon, yes?'

'Soon. Yes.'

Jan hugged her for longer than usual, but when Bea closed the door, it was a relief to let the smile she'd been holding drop. All she wanted to do was go upstairs and climb in beside Phoebe and let the little girl's gentle breathing lull her to sleep.

Chapter Sixteen

'Daddy!'

Bea paused, the laundry she was holding hovering over Phoebe's drawers as she stilled to listen. She heard a man's voice downstairs and let out a sigh. Lord Ewan, back at the ancestral pile. She glanced around the untidy bedroom. The doll's house was open, a tiny table and chairs on the carpet next to a huge teddy bear. At least the bed was made. Only because Phoebe hadn't slept in it for over a week, but he didn't need to know that.

'Aunty Bea!' Phoebe shouted from downstairs. 'Daddy's here!'

She walked towards the stairs, trying to ignore the towel on the floor under the radiator and the duvet thrown back from her bed.

'I didn't know you were coming home,' she said, as Ewan leaned forward to air-kiss her. 'You should've said.'

'Last-minute decision.' Ewan's eyes flitted around the hall, landing on the shoes strewn across the floor. 'A meeting got cancelled, and I thought, why not?' He tucked Phoebe into his side. 'And I wanted to know how this little one was healing.'

'I'm doing good, aren't I?' Phoebe looked at Bea for confirmation.

'You are.'

'I thought you'd be at school, though.' Ewan peered at Phoebe with a knitted brow, and Bea knew the question was aimed at her.

'Like I said on Skype, I wanted to make sure she was fully recovered.'

'It's been nine days.'

'If you include the weekend.'

Ewan's lips drew back in a smile that didn't reach his eyes. Bea could imagine him using the same smile at work, just before he fired someone.

'I take it your mother rang you?'

'Sorry?'

She walked towards the kitchen so he couldn't see her eyes lifting skywards. 'Coffee?' She opened the cupboard, wishing she'd put the teabags in the jar Ewan used rather than plucking them from the packet. She remembered the biscuit crumbs in the next cupboard and made a mental note to clear them up as soon as Ewan went to another room. Although, looking around the kitchen, maybe that was the least of her problems.

Ewan paused in the doorway. She tensed. 'If I'd known you were coming back, I'd have cleared up. There doesn't seem much point when it's just the two of us.'

'Aunty Bea says, "A woman should never neglect her family for housework",' said Phoebe, mimicking Bea's northern vowels perfectly.

Ewan nodded. 'Really? I think the original quote was, "A man should never neglect his family for business".'

'And how is the job in New York?' asked Bea pointedly, and for once he had the grace to look sheepish. He asked for that. But this was Ewan's house, and when she tried to look at it through his eyes, it was pretty shambolic. 'Are you staying long?'

'Just the weekend.'

'Why don't you unpack, and I'll have a tidy? I'll have a coffee ready when you come down.' She didn't know why she was doing the Stepford Wives act. She was paid to take care of Phoebe, not polish the silver.

Phoebe followed Ewan out, twittering about kitchen discos, and staying up until nine o'clock. Bea laid her head against the cupboard door and was tempted to bang her forehead into the wood. She didn't. If she splattered blood everywhere, she'd only have more clearing up to do.

When Ewan talked to her and Phoebe over video, she'd steered the conversation in another direction when school came up. It was only a few extra days, so he'd better not make a fuss. She had every intention of taking her back to school on Monday. As long as her skin was okay.

* * *

When Ewan came back to the kitchen his eyes assessed the improvement and she silently challenged him to comment. He took the coffee she handed him and turned to Phoebe. 'I thought we could go for a day out with Grandma tomorrow. Give Aunty Bea a break.'

Phoebe's face fell. 'Can't Aunty Bea come?'

'Don't you want to have Daddy all to yourself?' said Bea.

Phoebe pouted. 'I do, but I want you to come as well.' She walked towards Bea and pulled up her arm, placing herself under it, tight to Bea's side. She knew she should peel herself free and felt Ewan's eyes on them both, but, surely, Phoebe's needs should come above hurting Ewan's feelings.

124

'I think Aunty Bea needs a break,' said Ewan. 'Let's go and see Grandma, let her know I'm back.'

Like she didn't summon you, thought Bea, feeling Phoebe clinging to her and moving closer. She took the fingers carefully from her arm and crouched down to look in her eyes. 'I'll be here when you get back. Go on. Go and see Grandma with Daddy.'

Phoebe let go and slunk towards Ewan, who took her hand in his and almost pulled her from the room, as the little girl stared over her shoulder at Bea with doleful eyes. When the door closed, the house seemed to double in size. So much empty space with only her to fill it. She wrapped her arms around herself, feeling acutely alone. It was a familiar feeling; one Phoebe had almost made her forget.

* * *

The following day, Bea said she had some diploma work to catch up on, so Phoebe reluctantly agreed to get into the car with Ewan and Joyce and go to the coast. It wasn't a lie. She had so much to do, it would take more than one day to catch up, but when she tried to read the chapter on Team Leadership in Adult Care, her mind kept wandering back to Phoebe.

She picked up her phone and opened Ewan's contact details. Should she text him a reminder to moisturise Phoebe's neck where the skin was still dry? She put the phone down. Earlier he'd snapped, 'She's my daughter, Bea. I do know how to take care of her.' And she'd closed her mouth and bitten her lip, so she didn't say anything more.

She peered out of the sitting room window, watching the trees across the road swaying. It was getting windy. The salt air at the coast might make Phoebe's skin even drier. She nibbled the cuticle at the base of her thumb nail and watched grey clouds scud across the sky. It looked like it might rain. The clouds were definitely darker. Should she call Ewan and suggest they came back? Phoebe's skin shouldn't get wet. It wouldn't do her any good to be out in the rain. She picked her phone up again and was about to dial when she heard a quiet knock at the door.

Chapter Seventeen

Bea's vision flickered. Her fingers couldn't let go of the cold door latch. Every part of her was frozen and it wasn't until the wind whipped her hair into her face that she remembered how to move.

'Mum,' Immy said quietly.

'Immy?' Her voice trembled. Her head spun.

'You okay?' Immy stepped forwards. Her daughter's hand on her arm felt like the only solid thing in the world.

She reached out and dragged Immy towards her, a ball of emotion gagging her. Head still spinning, she buried her face in Immy's hair. She drew back and let her go, staring at the woman in front of her who was once her little girl. 'I can't believe you're here.'

Tears rolled down both their faces. She looked up as drops of cold rain started to fall. 'Come in.' She stood aside but Immy shook her head. She was thin. Too thin. 'Come in, please.'

Immy didn't move. 'No, I—'

The rain was pelting now, and goosebumps raised the hairs on Bea's arms. She drank in her daughter, her hair was blonde now, framing a ghost-pale face, an inch of her natural brown at the roots. Her eyes skittered from Bea to her scuffed trainers and back again.

'You look—' Bea didn't know what to say next because the words that occurred to her were *ill, sick . . . like an addict.* Why had Immy turned up now, looking so unwell? She tried again, 'Are you . . . are you alright?'

She opened her mouth to speak but before she could, they heard the crunch of tyres on gravel and the black bonnet of Ewan's Range Rover appeared, orange indicator blinking a warning as it drew onto the drive.

Immy started and looked at Bea, her eyes fearful. Before Bea could stop her, she bolted away from the doorstep, sidestepping the car just as Ewan swung the door open, glaring at Immy, his face a mask of rage. His mouth moved, but Bea couldn't hear what he said through the pounding of blood in her ears. She leaped onto the gravel, ignoring the sting as the sharp stones bit into the soles of her feet and water drenched her socks. She ran towards the road, shouting Immy's name and skipping out of Ewan's way as he tried to block her.

Immy was pounding through the driving rain. She turned when Bea shouted but didn't stop and Bea chased her along the pavement until she could catch at Immy's wet sleeve.

'I shouldn't have come.'

'Yes. Yes, you should.'

'You saw his reaction.'

'Immy, please.'

They turned at the sound of Ewan shouting Bea's name.

128

'Meet me tomorrow. Walnut's Café on the high street at ten. Please?' Bea pleaded.

Immy nodded quickly, wrenched her arm free and ran.

* * *

'Phoebe, go to your room.' Ewan's voice was flint. Phoebe walked upstairs obediently, not looking at Bea, who stood near the door, rain-soaked and shivering. The photograph of Gemma watched her drip water onto the rug.

At the other end of the hall Ewan and Joyce stood like gargoyles guarding a church, faces snarled and contemptuous.

'Sorry to have interrupted your touching reunion,' said Ewan.

'It probably wasn't a reunion,' said Joyce. 'Has she been coming here all the time Ewan's been away? To this house?' She shifted and winced, leaning heavily on the cane.

'No,' said Bea, pushing her wet hair from her face, her fingers snagging on a knot and tugging at her scalp. The pain was welcome. She did it again.

'We're meant to believe that?'

'Believe what you like.' She was suddenly tired to her core. Immy had come back. She had seen her beautiful face again and might even be able to persuade her to come home. If she was given the time and if . . . She didn't want to think of the other ifs. But these two were trying to destroy any hope she might have.

All she wanted to do now was lie down next to Phoebe and sleep until tomorrow when she could see her girl again.

'That's it?' Ewan's voice rose. 'That's all you've got to say, after allowing *that girl* into my house.'

'She's got a name.' She walked along the hall and they parted, mouths gaping, as she entered the kitchen, picked up a towel and rubbed at her tangled hair.

'I can think of a few choice names for her.'

Bea stopped rubbing. The cold rainwater steamed on her skin as the heat flared inside her. 'Imogen.'

'Drunkard.'

She turned to face Ewan. 'Imogen.'

'It doesn't matter what we call her,' spat Joyce, limping towards the sofa and sitting down. 'The question is, what was she doing here?'

'You didn't give me a chance to find out.' Bea gesticulated to Ewan. 'You did your enraged widower act – and we all know it *is* an act.' She took perverse pleasure in his look of humiliation. 'Then she ran off.'

'Good riddance to bad rubbish,' said Joyce.

Bea turned to look at her. 'How can you say that about your own granddaughter?'

'Easily,' she said, eyes like slits. 'I remember what she did to my family.'

THEN

Chapter Eighteen

Twenty-Seven Years Ago

One of the shutters on the chateau's hallway windows banged open. Bea wrestled it closed, catching her knuckle on the wood. She swore, pausing to lick the blood from the broken skin before tackling the last window on the corridor. The wind battered against the shutter's slats and Bea marvelled at the speed a storm could pounce up from nowhere in this part of Southern France.

On her break from serving up tea and cake earlier in the day, Bea had spent an hour in the sandy cove basking in glorious sunshine. Now she shivered in her shorts and vest as the storm tried to break through the ancient walls.

She heard laughter from downstairs. Anna had sneaked in some of her university friends who were interrailing around Europe after their finals. Bea had liked Anna from the moment she met her in the kitchen on her first day here. Tall, with glossy blonde hair, Anna was ridiculously self-assured; posh but in an endearing, ditzy way, rather than snooty like some of the artists who were spending the summer at the chateau. They barely ever deigned to make eye contact with Bea.

Anna was working in the chateau's busy kitchen. It had been arranged by her well-connected father, who knew someone at the American Arts Foundation, the owners of the chateau. Bea had landed the job as cleaner and general dogsbody a week ago, after asking around the small town to see if anyone needed staff. She was trying to earn enough cash to move on to Chamonix, where she'd arranged to meet her college friends in a couple of weeks. Travelling around Europe after sixth form had been fun, but she envied the students who had the funds to travel without scrabbling around for a job to pay for the next leg.

One of the shutters blew open again and by the time Bea shoved it closed and secured it, goosebumps prickled her arms. She could smell wood burning in the huge fireplace in the library. It would be warm in there. She steeled herself to go and join the group of strangers.

'There you are,' Anna shouted when Bea pushed open the heavy oak door. 'I wondered where you'd got to.' Her words slurred and after a glance at the table full of half-drunk bottles, Bea raised her eyebrows at her friend. Candles flickered above the fireplace and on the table, making the room and its lounging inhabitants look like a beautifully lit painting. She could hear the storm swirling outside, but in the warm glow of the library with the hum of conversation, it felt like all was peaceful in the world.

'The residents left all these bottles unfinished,' said Anna, her eyes wide. 'And all these platters.' She shrugged then winked. The chateau's staff were allowed to finish off any of the wine and food the residents left, but from the feast of bread, cheese and cold meats on the low table, Bea imagined Anna had taken a bit of a liberty. She paused in the doorway, unsure of whether she should go straight up to bed. If she didn't join in, she couldn't be blamed if someone noticed the missing food and drink. It was alright for Anna; she could afford to lose her job. Bea needed the money.

'Introduce us, then,' a boy called to Anna. He was sitting on the floor, leaning against a battered leather footstool. His face flickered orange in the wavering candlelight.

Bea turned in his direction and she immediately knew she would stay. She took a step into the library. 'I'm Beatrice. Bea,' she said, holding his gaze.

'I'm Oliver. Oli,' said the boy, the corners of his eyes crinkling in a smile. 'It's very nice to meet you, Beatrice Bea. There's a space here. Come and sit down.' He patted the tapestried rug next to him and Bea couldn't have resisted the invitation if she'd wanted to. She was pulled like a magnet towards the dark-haired boy with the smiling eyes.

For the rest of the evening the others in the room were as irrelevant as the storm crashing outside. The only person Bea was aware of was Oli, and somehow she knew he felt the same.

* * *

On her break the next day, Bea sat on a towel on the sand in shorts and a bikini top, watching clouds change form over the sea.

'Beatrice Bea!'

She recognised Oli's voice and resisted the urge to lift the corner of the towel to hide her body. She didn't know why she felt so exposed, since she was the only woman in the cove who wasn't topless.

'Hi, Oli.' He sat down next to her and she examined him through the dark protective lenses of her sunglasses.

135

The stubble on his chin made him look older than he had in the candlelight last night, but his eyes had the same brightness, looking intensely green as he stared out to sea. 'You all packed up?' She tried to sound nonchalant, but when she'd learned last night that his group were planning to leave today and head back home via Paris, she'd inexplicably felt like crying.

'I'm not, actually.'

Her breath caught. 'No?'

'Thought I might stick around here for a bit.'

'Oh?' She didn't dare look at his face. She dug her toes into the sand and concentrated on the coolness of the hard, wet solidness underneath the shifting grains.

'Yeah. They're all starting jobs in a couple of weeks' – he gestured back towards where the chateau loomed over the cove – 'but my teacher training doesn't start until the end of September, so . . .' He trailed off. They watched the plump clouds flow across the horizon.

'Right.' She felt him shuffle closer to her.

'So—' His hand moved next to hers, their little fingers alongside each other making her stomach flip. 'Is that okay with you? I mean, if I stayed, could we hang out?'

She stayed completely still for a moment, then, in the bravest move she'd ever made, she hooked her little finger over his. She continued to watch the sky, and her toes remained buried in the damp sand, but the only thing she could sense was her finger, resting over his. He lifted his hand and for a moment, she froze, sure she'd made a shameful mistake, until his palm touched her cheek and turned her face towards his. Then his lips were on hers and she felt every nerve ending in her body come to life.

* * *

136

A week later, Oli waited for her at the kitchen door while she finished clearing up the residents' dinner things. The light was fading behind him, leaving a shimmer of orange on the horizon. 'Give up this job,' he said. 'Come and stay in the gîte with me. I've got a double room and money saved up. Then we can be on holiday properly.'

Bea kissed him. 'Not going to happen,' she said. There was literally nothing she'd like more, but she hadn't been brought up to leave a paying job to be looked after by someone else. 'What would I do if you got bored of me and I was left penniless on the streets of France?'

'Not going to happen,' he mimicked. 'Seriously, Bea. I've got one more week, then I have to go home. I want to spend every minute of it with you.'

'That's what I want, too, but I've promised my friends I'll meet them in the Alps. I don't like letting people down and I'll be working full time when I get back, so I should try to make the most of my freedom while I can.' Even as she said the words, she knew she didn't mean them. All she wanted was to be with Oli. Anything else seemed pointless.

They moved out of the way for a group of tanned teenagers carrying bottles of beer down the side of the chateau towards the beach. Oli watched them walk to the water's edge, then took her hands in his. 'You know, I love that you're going to work in an old people's home. I don't know anyone who wants to look after people for a living.'

'It's a *care home*.' She raised her chin. 'Not an old people's home. It's not that different to you wanting to teach. Some people would think you were bonkers to do that.' She kissed him again, breathing in his scent of coconut suntan lotion. 'And I'm just trying it out to see if I like it, and if I do, I'll do my training and I'll manage a whole chain of the best care homes in the country.'

'A noble ambition,' said Oli. He dropped his eyes to their intertwined hands. 'There are care homes all over the country, aren't there?'

Bea took a step closer. 'There are.' She held her breath.

'Because . . .' Oli looked up. 'This doesn't feel like a holiday romance to me.'

Bea swallowed, trying to contain the torrent of joy pushing up her throat. 'Or me.'

Oli moved closer, so that their foreheads were touching. 'So, I suppose it doesn't matter where we both go for the next couple of weeks, if . . .'

'If . . .?' She looked into his eyes, willing him to say what she felt in every sinew of her body; that she meant as much to him as he did to her. She had fallen so completely in love with Oli that the thought of separation caused her physical pain.

'If we're sure that, when we get home, we want to be together.'

'That is what I want,' she said. She wanted it more keenly than she'd ever wanted anything in her entire life. 'Do you think we can make it work?'

'I think we can,' said Oli, quietly. 'I see a future for us, Beatrice Bea. Let's spend this week planning the next couple of months.'

'Years,' she chanced, hoping he didn't recoil.

'Decades,' he said, then pulled her in tightly and whispered in her ear, 'a lifetime.'

* * *

Nerves about meeting Oli's family for the first time made Bea jittery. She tried to manifest calm, breathing deeply as she waited her turn behind the elderly people descending from the National Express coach one careful step at a time. Her stomach quivered when she spied Oli across the coach station concourse. His tan had faded in the months since they met in France, but he was still the most attractive man she'd ever seen.

She'd been distracted on the long journey from York by the woman in the next seat: a chatty seventy-four-year-old from Leeds called Petra. As the coach manoeuvred onto the M1 Petra had pulled a small photo album from her handbag, and by Leicester Forest services, Bea knew the names and faces of all of her grandchildren well enough to pick them out in a police line-up.

Petra reminded Bea of her own lovely grandma. Watching Petra's hand cling to the handrail as she lowered herself to the pavement, Bea allowed herself a few painful memories of her grandma's last days in hospital, then of standing alone after her funeral, feeling lost. She'd lived with her since her parents' ugly divorce and, when she died, Bea had felt the grief of an orphan.

That's partly why this trip was so important. She and Oli had decided to make their relationship official. Since Oli's family was still intact – two parents and a little brother at university – this was her opportunity to be part of a family again and she couldn't wait.

After ensuring Petra was safely on terra firma, Bea looked up and saw Oli bounding towards the coach, grinning. Her skin tingled with anticipation. The second she stepped down he took her in his arms and kissed her. The other passengers nudged each other and turned to watch them, letting out a collective *ahhhh*.

'I hope you're going to take care of her,' said Petra, interrupting their reunion.

Oli turned and flung his arm over Bea's shoulder. 'That's my plan.'

'Oli, Petra. Petra, Oliver James,' Bea introduced them, laughing when Oli took Petra's hand and kissed her lightly on the veiny skin.

Petra flushed, coyly pulling back her hand. 'Get away with you.' She smiled. 'Look after this one. She's a good 'un.' She squeezed Bea's arm. 'Thanks for keeping me company, pet.'

'You've made a friend for life there,' said Oli, throwing Bea's bag over his shoulder and leading her across the road to the car park.

'Good,' said Bea. 'That's my superpower: loving old ladies. I'm going to use it to charm your mum.'

Oli was quiet. He opened the boot of his old Fiesta and dropped Bea's bag inside.

'What?' Bea watched him, trying to work out what she'd said wrong.

'I'm just not sure my mother would consider herself an old lady.'

The hairs on Bea's arms bristled. 'God, not old, I meant . . . Sorry. I didn't mean to offend . . .'

Oli walked around to her. He took her face between his palms and kissed her. 'I know. It's just that my mum isn't like Petra.' He opened the passenger door for Bea. 'She might be a bit harder to . . .' He seemed to search for the right words before finally saying, 'Win over.'

'You underestimate my superpower,' Bea said, but the conviction had gone from her voice.

* * *

An hour later, she was sitting on a plush sofa in the most impressive house she'd ever been in, opposite a woman who had introduced herself as *Mrs James*. Oli's mother wore a tight plait wound around her scalp and seemed to assess Bea with eyes the colour and warmth of slate. Any hope of melting into the bosom of a new family slipped away when Bea saw herself through the gaze of this straight-backed woman.

Bea was not a superhero with magical love-powers. She was a foolish, unremarkable girl from the north. She was unworthy of this woman's son. *I don't care,* thought Bea. *Oli loves me and that is enough.* But the urge to run away was strong. It was only the warmth of Oli sitting next to her, relaxed and uncowed, that strengthened her resolve to persevere. She would win this woman over. And even if she didn't, it wouldn't matter as long as Oli was by her side.

Chapter Nineteen

Fourteen Years Ago

Joyce's face was flushed bright pink. It was the most animated Bea had ever seen her. She watched in surprise as her mother-in-law knelt down next to Immy and said something in her ear. The little girl nodded seriously.

'What's going on?' Bea whispered to Oli, who was sitting next to her on Joyce's Chesterfield sofa. 'Your mother is actually *kneeling*. I've never seen anything like it. What are those two up to?'

'Search me,' said Oli. 'I asked Immy and all she said was, "You'll have to wait and see".' He lisped as he said it, mimicking Immy's speech since she'd lost her two front teeth.

Bea chuckled and took another swig of mulled wine. If she'd had it her way they wouldn't have come to The Crescent on Christmas Eve. They'd be back tomorrow, so she would have preferred to spend tonight with just Immy and Oli. It was only Immy's insistence that she and Grandma had something special to show them that made them get in the car. Both she and Oli found Immy difficult to refuse. Looking at her now in her new tule dress with lacy pink tights and matching satin bow in her dark waves, Bea felt like the luckiest woman alive. With the soft lighting and stylish decorations, her husband next to her, she realised she was content with her life.

She squeezed Oli's hand and when he glanced down at her, she saw love and pride. It had been difficult for both of them to accept that the second baby they'd longed for wasn't likely to happen, not without asking Joyce to lend them the money for IVF. But they had each other and they had Immy. She was enough. More than enough. She was perfect.

Joyce stepped into the centre of the room and stood before her lavishly decorated Christmas tree. She straightened the hem of her red jacket and cleared her throat. 'Ladies and gentlemen,' she said, looking back with her finger over her mouth to shush a giggling Immy. 'Ladies and gentlemen,' she repeated, 'I would like to introduce to you, the most beautiful and talented six-year-old this country has ever produced.' Immy giggled again and Joyce's ruby lips twitched in a smile.

Bea loved to see this playful side of Joyce. It had only come out since Immy was born. Joyce made a balletic gesture with her right arm, holding it wide before saying, 'Please put your hands together for Imogen James, and her rendition of *A Visit from St Nicholas*, more commonly known as *The Night Before Christmas*, by Clement Clarke Moore.'

Bea put her hand over her mouth, willing the tears to wait as Immy stepped to her grandmother's side. Joyce kissed Immy on the top of her head, then retreated to sit at the edge of the nearest seat, leaning forwards, her fingers tightly clasped as Immy began to speak.

''Twas the night before Christmas, when all through the house, Not a creature was stirring, not even a mouse.'

Whenever the little girl faltered, she glanced across at Joyce, who was mouthing the words, her eyes focused on Immy, sparkling with pride. Bea was astonished that Immy had memorised the entire poem. Near the end, Immy gestured urgently for Joyce to join her in front of the Christmas tree and Joyce slid from her chair and held Immy's hand as they both said, 'Happy Christmas to all, and to all a good night!'

Bea and Oli leaped to their feet, clapping and whooping so loudly that Immy covered her ears as she bowed low, laughing.

'How did you learn all those words?' asked Bea, bundling Immy into a hug.

'Grandma and me did it. We started ages ago and it was secret!'

'Grandma and I,' said Joyce.

Bea resisted the urge to roll her eyes when she saw Oli standing with his mother, looking down at Immy, both their faces full of adoration.

'She's the brightest child I've ever known,' said Joyce.

'And that's a completely unbiased view!' Oli laughed.

'She'll do great things. Mark my words.' Joyce bent down to face Immy, who looked earnestly into her grandma's eyes. 'You are an extraordinary girl, Imogen. You did very well tonight.'

Immy grinned. 'I love you, Grandma.'

Joyce stiffened, blinked slowly then said, 'And I love you.' She closed her eyes and put her arms around Immy, as Bea and Oli looked across at each other, open mouthed at the words neither of them had ever heard Joyce say before.

Chapter Twenty

Seven Years Ago

'Sorry.' Bea shifted away from the door as the make-up artist squeezed into the already crammed hotel room carrying more luggage than Bea took on a two-week holiday. In reception she'd sneaked a peek at the price of the rooms and couldn't understand how a hotel could charge hundreds of pounds for such tiny spaces, or why anyone would choose to pay it. The word *boutique* appeared to be a magnet for people with more money than sense.

In her head, she calculated how many shifts she'd have to do at Sweetingdale to pay for one night in this luxury box. Too many. And the bed didn't look as comfortable as the soft old mattress she and Oli had slept on for the best part of two decades.

'Alright, Gem?' shouted the make-up artist to Bea's soon-to-be sister-in-law, who was having her hair styled by a mute and snooty hairdresser who probably charged extra for small talk.

'Hi, Larissa.'

Larissa blew a low whistle as she surveyed the suite. 'Geez, it's alright here, innit?'

'Only the best for the new Mrs James.' Gemma grinned. 'Bit of a change from the estate, isn't it?'

'Innit just?' Larissa plonked her cases on the bed and started to unpack palettes and brushes on the tapestried throw. Bea's fingers itched to grab a towel from the bathroom to put under the make-up. She made herself look away, focusing on Gemma's reflection in the dressing table mirror, brows knitted, watching intently as the hairdresser lifted a dark lock and wrapped it around the curler.

'Are the tendrils too thick?' Gemma asked, straight nose creasing at the sides. It was the most Bea had seen her face move all morning. She suspected Gemma might have frozen it with Botox but couldn't imagine why. She was only twenty-five, with perfect milky skin and cheekbones that softened into rosy apples when she smiled. And then there was the baby to think about. Could you have Botox when you were pregnant? Bea didn't know.

She caught her own face in the mirror behind Gemma's and almost laughed at how weathered her forty-year-old skin looked. It reminded her of the scene in *Snow White* where the wicked stepmother is about to give the poisoned apple to the beautiful young girl. She scrunched up her features and stuck out her chin to make herself witchy.

'What are you doing?' Gemma asked, catching Bea mid-grimace.

Bea relaxed her face and bit down on her bottom lip. 'Nothing.' She pointed to the soft curls framing Gemma's face. 'That looks lovely.'

'I'm not sure it looks right with my fringe.' She bounced the hair in her palm, moving her head from side to side. 'Do you really like it?'

Sometimes Gemma reminded her of a lost girl, always watchful, trying to fit in. Bea didn't know much about her background, but she knew enough to imagine how hard it must be to try to become an acceptable Mrs James. Acceptable to Joyce, at least. She'd been there herself. Squeezing Gemma's shoulder, she dropped her head to one side and nodded. There was gratitude in Gemma's eyes as she mouthed *thank you.*

A knock at the door broke the spell. Bea squeezed past the boxes of hair paraphernalia and opened it a crack, standing so her body shielded Gemma from prying eyes. Oli and Immy stood in the corridor and her breath caught at the sight of them, all dressed up for the wedding. 'You brush up alright, don't you?'

Oli pulled at his cuffs. 'You like it?'

'Even your mother has to be impressed with you in that suit.' She lifted the lapel and rubbed the soft material between her fingers. 'Hand stitched? Very nice.'

'Hmm, tasteful, but expensive enough for people to notice. That should meet with her approval.' He curled his lip. 'I'm glad Ewan insisted on paying.' They pulled the same awkward face, mirroring each other in a way they'd done for years.

She turned her attention to Immy, who stood with her shoulders rounded, as though trying to make herself invisible. 'Let's have a look at you.'

'Mum.' Immy drew the letters out to make the word a moan. The dimples at the corners of Immy's full lips turned down as green eyes flitted to meet hers momentarily, then returned to stare at the patterned carpet. Where had her bright, confident daughter gone? She still saw snatches, when Immy was on stage with her theatre group, or laughing with friends, but mostly, she was now this sullen girl with clenched fists and eyes always on the verge of rolling.

Bea had allowed her to choose her own outfit for the wedding, biting back her own concerns that it was too tight, too short. She was sure Immy felt exposed now, aware of her budding breasts and jutting hip bones, just visible beneath the duck-egg blue bandage dress. Bea could imagine Joyce scrutinising her, lips pinched tight. During the wedding planning, Joyce had suggested Immy wore a taffeta number and white satin gloves. Once upon a time, Immy would have worn what Joyce chose; anything to make her happy. But she'd grown less compliant with every teenage day and Immy was decidedly not a taffeta kind of girl now.

'You look amazing.' Bea tried to catch Immy's eye and failed. 'I'm so proud of my gorgeous family.'

'And we're proud of you. Aren't we?' Oli nudged Immy, who gave a brief smile. 'All ready in there?' Oli shouted through the doorway.

'Nearly,' Gemma yelled back. 'You can't come in though. I want to do the big reveal when I walk into the ballroom. I'd like you all to gasp really loudly when you see me. Okay?'

Oli laughed. 'We'll see what we can do. Everything's on track, so see you down there in an hour.' He leaned forwards to kiss Bea, and they lingered, lips pressed together, ignoring the derisive sigh from their daughter.

'See you down there.' She touched Immy's arm. 'You really do look beautiful.'

'Thanks, Mum. You do, too.'

There she was. Her girl. Bea smiled inwardly as she closed the door and turned back to the room.

'Bubbles for the bride-to-be!' Larissa held a flute of champagne out to Gemma.

'Erm,' Bea said.

'What?' Gemma's French polished nails clinked against the glass as she took it from Larissa.

'Well, should you be . . .?' She gestured to the glass.

'One won't hurt.' She took a sip and closed her eyes, a blissful look on her face. 'Why do you have to stop everything fun just because you're having a baby?'

Bea laughed. 'Not everything.'

'Name one good thing about being pregnant.'

'Getting a rich bloke to marry you!' shouted Larissa. They both turned to her, mouths open. She raised her glass and drank.

Bea could name a million good things about becoming a mother. From the second she'd seen the blue line on the pregnancy test she'd felt like a mum, and that was everything. Admittedly, she wasn't a huge fan of the giving birth bit; nobody in their right mind was. But Immy had been a cherub of a baby, a stubborn but characterful toddler and a bright, funny little girl. She couldn't deny the teenage years were proving more challenging, but Bea wouldn't change a thing. 'The baby.'

Gemma seemed to contemplate this for a second. A smile spread across her face. She put the flute down on the dressing table and stood, holding her hands out to Bea. 'I'm so glad I've got you to help me.'

'Don't be daft.' Bea ignored the hairdresser tutting as he held a can of hairspray aloft and waited.

'Honestly. You've been like a mum to me since I met Ewan. And since my mum isn't . . .' Gemma's lips trembled.

'I know, love.' Bea tried to hug her, but Gemma dipped away, pointing at her hair. 'You're part of the family now.' She smiled at the tiny bump just showing under the cream satin of the dress. 'And soon you'll have a husband *and* a baby. Incredible, isn't it?'

'I know!' Gemma sat back down and nodded to the hairdresser. She covered her face with her hands as he shook a fine mist around her head. 'A year ago, I was in a shared house with a crappy job, and now look at me!'

Larissa squealed like a tween at a concert. 'You've done alright for yourself, mate.' She lowered her voice and winked an eyelash the size of a moth's wing. 'I hope you didn't sign a pre-nup.'

'Do I look stupid?'

Bea turned to look to see if Gemma was serious, but her hands still covered her face and when she let them fall, Bea couldn't catch her eye.

Chapter Twenty-One

Four Years Ago

Bea and Oli raised their heads in unison when they heard the creak on the top stair. She glanced at his pale face to see if he was ready, but who could ever be prepared for what they had to do? The purple smudges under his eyes looked like the pretend make-up Immy used to love when she was a little girl. She wasn't a little girl anymore. And the shadows under Oli's eyes were partly there because they'd waited up for her for hours last night. At midnight, Bea had insisted Oli went to sleep while she continued to check her phone to see if Immy would reply to her messages. Eventually the sound of the front door opening and closing and the clumsy thud of feet on stairs allowed her to fall into a fitful sleep.

Now, they sat together at the kitchen table and tried not to watch the door as the footsteps neared.

Immy started when she noticed them. 'Why aren't you two at work?'

'Why aren't you at college?' Bea sniped back, then hated herself. This was not the time for an argument.

'Study period.' Immy shuffled past them in her oversized t-shirt, her long legs reminding Bea she wasn't a child who would simply do as she was told. As if she needed reminding of that. It was evident in every action, every word they exchanged.

She glanced across at Oli, whose head remained bowed, eyes on the brown film forming on his undrunk tea. She heard the kettle click on and the suction of the fridge door opening and the swoosh as it closed. 'You can't stay out and not tell us where you are.'

Immy gave an exaggerated sigh. 'I'm seventeen.'

'Old enough to reply to messages. Who were you with?' Bea didn't really need to ask. Immy was always with that arrogant posh boy these days – Zach. He reminded Bea of Ewan, but without the inbuilt fear of displeasing Joyce. A rebellious Ewan; what a thought.

'God, why don't you get me fitted with a tracker?' Immy poured boiling water into a mug and stirred it noisily. She turned towards them and sipped her drink. 'Dad, can you drive me to rehearsal tonight?'

Bea marvelled at her inability to read the room. Only a teenager could watch their parents sit in silence on a day they were meant to be at work and still only think of them as unpaid, slightly irritating staff.

'Sit down, love.'

Immy slumped. 'I really don't need another lecture. Honestly, sometimes I think you've forgotten what it's like to be young. Alright, I was out late and had a couple of drinks, but I'm here, aren't I? I'm safe. I'll go into college this afternoon. Nobody died.'

'Please sit down.'

When Immy dropped into the chair next to her, Bea could smell stale alcohol. She studied her daughter's face, taking in the bloodshot eyes and dull skin. 'How much did you have to drink last night?'

Immy shook her head and pushed the chair back, but Oli's voice was firm as he said, 'Sit down.'

Immy's expression changed from petulant to concerned. Her dad never spoke harshly. He was funny and firm but fair: the kind of teacher who even the tough kids at school spoke to when they bumped into him in town.

She sat back down and pulled the t-shirt over her knees. The gesture made her look painfully young. 'What's going on?'

Bea had read plenty of information about how to approach this moment. She'd watched recommended video clips. She'd even practised a rough script in her mind. But all of it fell out of her head as she watched her daughter's eyes widen.

'Seriously, you're worrying me now.' Immy's voice was quiet.

'Your dad's not well, love.'

Immy turned to Oli. 'What's up? Is it that bug going around school? Lewis couldn't get off the toilet, he said it was like—' When Oli didn't look up, she stopped abruptly then ducked her head down and searched his face with her eyes. 'Dad?'

She turned to Bea, but Bea couldn't meet her gaze. Instead, she watched the movement of her daughter's throat as Immy swallowed, before whispering, 'Mum, what's wrong?'

Immy lifted her feet onto the chair, pulling down the hem of her t-shirt and tucking it under her toes. She wrapped her arms around her legs as though she wanted to make herself smaller. Seeing the bony outline of toes against the stretched cotton reminded Bea of Immy's tiny infant feet straining against her baby grow as she kicked her legs in her Moses basket. Just seventeen short years ago, Bea and Oli had vowed to protect their precious girl from harm. Now it was down to Bea to say the words that would destroy what was left of her childhood.

Bea forced her eyes up to meet Immy's. 'I'm sorry, love. He's . . . he's got cancer.'

Immy's face crumpled. 'What?' She looked from Bea to Oli and Bea wanted to take the words back. More than that, she wanted them to be a lie, an awful, misjudged joke. But she couldn't. It was true. Oli had cancer. And it had spread.

'We got the test results back yesterday afternoon. We planned to tell you last night—'

Oli squeezed her leg under the table, and she bit her tongue.

Immy's bottom lip trembled. She covered her mouth and dug her teeth into the flesh beneath her thumb. When she took her hand away, the saliva trailed from her lip then snapped. 'Where is it? It's treatable, right? You'll have to have chemo and all that stuff, but you'll get better?' She was talking quickly now. 'Lexi's mum had it and she had a rough time, but she's okay now, and that man from the Post Office. He lost all of his hair and stuff, but he's back at work now.' She looked between the two of them, her face contorted, fat tears dropping onto the table.

'It started . . .'

'Started?'

'Yes.' Oli kept his voice steady. Bea didn't know how he did it. 'It started in the bowel, but I'm afraid it's spread to my liver.'

'Shit.' Immy rose and stood behind Oli, wrapping her

thin arms across his chest, and laying her head on his shoulder. He folded his arms around hers and his body rocked under her sobs.

'I'm sorry, Dad. I'm sorry I didn't come home last night. Please be okay.'

Bea had to look away. She pinched the skin on her thighs through her pyjama bottoms to stop herself from crying. The sight of the two people she loved most in the world in this much pain was too much to bear. 'We're going to fight it. The doctors have given us lots of options about what to do next and so that's one of the things we need to talk about, as a family.'

Immy nodded, sending cascades of tears onto Oli's t-shirt. She looked at her dad, who was smiling a reassuring smile, just as he had when they'd got home last night and Bea couldn't let go of his hand, as if holding on to him would tether him to her for good. 'But it's all going to be okay in the end. You're going to be alright, aren't you? Please be okay, Dad.'

'I'm going to do everything I can. I promise you that.'

But no more, thought Bea. *He can't promise more.* Because she'd been in the meeting with the oncologist, and she knew the tumours they'd found in Oli's bowel and liver were growing. She'd heard all the gaps in their gentle explanations.

The gaps where the words *definitely* and *future* should have been.

* * *

The positivity they'd felt after Oli's first round of chemo was well and truly gone after the sixth. The most recent scans had shown more tumours, and although nobody had said as much, the word *terminal* kept ambushing Bea's

155

thoughts. His body was reacting worse with every bout of poison and now he was struggling to eat.

'Believe me, I would if I could,' he said, pushing the plate of sausage and mash away. It was ten o'clock and this was the third time this evening Oli had attempted to eat more than a mouthful of his dinner.

Bea smiled. Her brave face had become a mask and now she felt her cheeks ache with the effort of pretending she was coping. 'Do you remember when Immy had flu when she was tiny? We were so worried about her not eating we put plates of sweets and crisps on the floor in every room to tempt her.'

Oli laughed weakly. 'Yeah. She must've been bad because Mum came around every day. Do you remember?'

Bea had forgotten that. Now she thought back, Joyce had been a godsend when Bea had been up all night, checking Immy's fever hadn't worsened. Bea would go to bed when her mother-in-law arrived and when she got up, she'd find Immy laying asleep in her grandmother's arms, her head resting on her shoulder, as Joyce stroked her hair and sang quietly into her ear.

'They were so close,' she said.

Oli rubbed his lower back and groaned. Bea wished she could absorb some of the pain he was going through.

'I think they'll make up when Immy's older,' Oli said. 'Remember, Mum's not used to teenage girls. I think Ewan and I were pretty straightforward growing up. I stayed under the radar and Ewan was too frightened to step out of line. I think one day they'll laugh about the fact that Mum's taken Immy's independent spirit as a personal affront. Those two are more alike than they think.'

Bea wasn't so sure. She looked at her watch and growled.

'Talking of independent spirit, that child was meant to be in half an hour ago.'

'You go up, I'll wait for her.'

'No. I'll stay up. Go on, get to bed.'

Oli laid his hand over hers. The skin on the back of his hand was grey and papery apart from the purple bruise with a red pinprick in its centre where a cannula had been removed. 'There's no point me trying to sleep yet. I'll only get the sweats and toss and turn if I go up now. I had a couple of hours when you were at work. Go on, up you go. You look knackered.'

'Charming!' Bea couldn't argue with him. The six a.m. starts at Sweetingdale, added to the fact she woke like clockwork at three every morning to begin her daily regime of worrying, meant she was shattered. She'd love to take some time off but was aware that things were likely to get worse before they got better, *if* they got better, so she needed to turn up while it was still possible. She tried not to think about what would happen when Oli was put on statutory sick pay, or worse. They were barely getting by as it was. 'Well, if you insist.' She squeezed his hand and stood, yawning. 'Don't let Immy off lightly when she gets in. She's getting lawless, that one. She needs taking in hand.'

'Yes, Captain.'

She shook her head and made her way up the stairs to bed.

* * *

The sound of retching woke Bea from a deep sleep. Oli's side of the bed was empty. She threw the duvet off, jumped to her feet and rushed to the landing. The light in the bathroom dazzled her and at first she couldn't make out what was going on. She'd expected to see Oli leaning over the toilet bowl, like he had regularly since the start of his treatment. Instead, Oli was standing, leaning over a crouching figure.

Bea blinked. When her eyes became accustomed to the light, she realised Oli was holding Immy's hair back as she vomited. 'What's going on?' She rubbed her eyes. The light was painfully bright.

'She's had a bit too much to drink,' said Oli, stroking Immy's back.

'For God's sake,' said Bea, as Immy retched again and a torrent of yellow liquid spilled from her mouth.

'A lot too much to drink,' said Oli.

'I don't feel well.' Immy's voice sounded too sweet and childlike to belong to a girl who'd drunk enough alcohol to create this tableau. She lifted her head and reached an arm out for the toilet roll. Oli leaned forwards to help and all of a sudden his eyes fluttered and his legs seemed to concertina beneath him. Bea leaped forwards but couldn't catch him before his head hit the edge of the bath and he fell, unconscious, to the floor.

* * *

Bea should never have allowed Joyce to railroad her into holding the wake at The Crescent. Oli felt like he'd escaped this house with all its stultifying dos and don'ts. And here she was, saying her last goodbye to him in a place he couldn't wait to get away from. She'd let him down.

A bang behind her made her spin around. Immy was leaning unsteadily against the kitchen door rubbing her elbow.

'Not today, Immy.' Bea gripped her wrist and whispered in her ear, 'Please, not today.' When she smelled the alcohol

158

on Immy's breath, her guts tightened. She'd told the waiting staff Ewan had hired not to serve alcoholic drinks to anyone who appeared underage. She hadn't specified Immy, but the only other under eighteen at the wake was two-year-old Phoebe, so she'd thought they'd work it out. Looking at her now, with mascara smudged under her bloodshot eyes, tall and slender in the fitted black suit she wore for sixth form, she could easily pass for eighteen.

She could easily have sneaked in her own alcohol, too. It wouldn't be the first time Immy had managed to get drunk when Bea wasn't even aware there was booze in the house.

Immy pulled her arm away. 'Don't worry, Mother. I'm not going to embarrass you in front of Grandma's la-di-da friends.'

'That's not what I'm worried about. I'm worried about you.'

'First time for everything.'

'That's not fair.' Her voice caught. 'We're going to have to address your drinking, Immy. You need help.'

'Help?' Immy laughed, but her chin puckered, followed by a hiccupping sob. 'Drinking is the help. I don't know how you're surviving this sober.'

This didn't seem like the right time to argue, especially since Bea herself would love nothing more than a pint of gin right now. She turned away, digging her nails into her palms. Glancing around the kitchen, she realised she hardly knew any of the people there. Jan had left to get back to the kids and all the remaining guests were strangers wearing expensive suits. The women standing in Joyce's kitchen wore heels and ornate up-dos. These weren't the teachers Oli worked with. There wasn't a scruffy jacket or untrimmed beard in sight. Why had she let Ewan and

Joyce make the arrangements? This was typical Joyce. Even her son's funeral was an excuse to show off how well connected she was.

Ewan walked past them and greeted a woman wearing a pillbox hat. They kissed on both cheeks and spoke to each other in cut-glass accents, which seemed an octave higher than necessary. Gemma was standing near the kitchen doors, Phoebe balanced on her hip, her beautiful face made ugly by the sneer she directed at her husband. Phoebe put her little hand up to her mother's mouth and Bea was astonished to see Gemma push it away. Gemma had been so careful with Phoebe since her seizures started, but today she looked exhausted. Bea supposed the strain of looking after a sick child might be getting to her. She would offer to help; just, not yet. Phoebe's bottom lip wobbled, and, despite her own grief, Bea felt the pull to go over to give Gemma a break.

In the moment Bea moved towards Gemma, Immy slumped back against the door, her head knocking loudly against the wood and all eyes seemed to turn in her direction. Bea took her arm and pulled her into the empty hallway. 'You need to sober up.'

Immy sat heavily on the bottom step with her head in her hands. 'I can't believe we left him there.'

Sitting next to her, the hollow in Bea's centre opened. She put her arm around Immy's shoulders and tried to soothe her.

'We left him there and now they're burning him. They're burning my daddy.' Her body shuddered under Bea's arm as the image of Oli, trapped in the coffin, engulfed in flames, blazed at the back of her eyes. No words came. The hollow feeling spread until she was simply a hole, cold, and empty and black. She wanted to comfort Immy, but the hole felt too big. She was gone, almost as completely as Oli was. There was nothing left of her to help herself. How could she find the strength to help their child when she was being swallowed by grief?

A high laugh came from the kitchen and Bea blinked at the extraordinary noise. It seemed so out of place and unfamiliar. She felt the heat of Immy next to her and the slowing of her shuddering breaths under her arm. They sat, still, consumed by emptiness, until the clack of heels on the parquet floor made Bea turn.

'What are you doing out here?' Gemma didn't wait for a reply, which was a relief because Bea didn't have one. She lifted Phoebe off her hip and thrust her towards Bea. 'Can you take her for a bit? She won't let me put her down.'

Phoebe's hands reached out for Bea, and she reluctantly lifted her arm from Immy's shoulder, feeling Immy shift away from her on the step and fold over herself. She couldn't think of a way of handing Phoebe back now her hands were around her tiny waist. There was comfort in the warm weight of her. 'Hello, little one.' She stroked her velvety skin. She didn't notice the vivid red of the birthmarks on her face and arm anymore. All she saw was Phoebe, adorable, perfect Phoebe. She glanced at Immy to see if she resented her cousin getting attention, today of all days, but her face was buried in her lap.

Gemma smiled quickly and mouthed *thanks* before scuttling away. Phoebe pulled at Bea's bottom lip and the hollow in Bea closed a little.

Immy raised her head from her knees and her face softened when Phoebe squealed with delight at the sight of her cousin. 'Hello, little legs.' She squeezed the plump flesh at the top of Phoebe's thigh, and she chortled and squealed.

'I remember when you were like this,' said Bea, bouncing Phoebe on her knee. 'You were the happiest baby I'd ever known.'

'What happened, eh?'

Bea glanced at her face to see if she was joking. Every word she said to Immy now needed to be assessed for possible explosive content. She was smiling. 'Shit happened.'

Immy's mouth grew wide in mock horror. 'Don't swear in front of the baby.'

Bea smiled. 'Sorry, Phoebe.'

'Shit really did happen though, didn't it?'

Bea glimpsed a tiny opening. Perhaps she could find a way of talking to Immy and really getting through, to start to mend the ruptured connection she always thought she'd have with her daughter. 'We'll get through it, together, if—'

'There you are.' Joyce's clipped voice made Phoebe jump in Bea's arms. She started to cry.

'Marjory Fellows said she saw you stumbling, Imogen. Surely that couldn't be the case? No one would be insensitive enough to get blind drunk at their own father's funeral.'

Immy stood. Bea's heart dropped when she wobbled. 'I'm not blind drunk.'

'You can't even stand up straight.' Joyce leaned forwards. 'I'm ashamed of you.'

'Nothing new there,' said Immy. 'You've been ashamed of me since I stopped being your little golden girl, haven't you?'

Joyce turned to Bea. 'You need to sort her out. So much for your libertarian parenting. This mess' – she gestured to Immy – 'is your doing.'

'This mess?' Immy shouted over Phoebe's crying. 'Nice way to talk about your granddaughter.'

'Don't you dare speak to us like that,' Bea said.

'This is my house and this is my son's funeral.' Joyce's voice wavered. 'I think I have every right to speak the truth as I see fit.'

Ewan appeared at her elbow. 'What's going on?' He looked at Immy then at Bea. 'I think she needs to go home.'

Bea struggled to stand, still holding Phoebe, who was wailing at the top of her lungs. 'I think it's time we both went home.' Maybe, she thought, if they left now, she could try to talk to Immy again, find that chink she saw before.

'Don't worry about me. My lift's here.' Immy walked unsteadily to the front door. When she opened it, car headlights shone in, making Bea shield her eyes.

'Immy, wait,' Bea pleaded.

'Nobody wants me here, Mum.' She stared into Bea's face and Bea felt the pain of a child who had gone through the worst year of their life and had no idea how to cope.

'I do,' she said. But Immy was already walking away.

* * *

The unmistakable sounds of the school orchestra tuning up made Bea smile as she and Jan crossed the reception and made for the hall. Every so often, over the discordant strains, the overture to *Jesus Christ Superstar* would be recognisable, before melting back into a cacophony of squeaking horns and rumbling bass notes.

'Hope it gets better than that,' said Jan, tugging on her arm and sniggering.

'They're really good, these productions, honest. And I'm not just saying that because Immy's Mary Magdalene.'

'Can't be worse than Ciara's last school show. One of

163

the chorus in *Fiddler on the Roof* was off his head on something and fell into the orchestra. Bloody hilarious.'

Bea tensed. She hadn't told Jan that Immy almost lost her part for turning up to the dress rehearsal with a half-drunk bottle of Smirnoff Ice in her bag. If it hadn't been so close to the performance, she was sure Immy would have been dropped from the cast.

Although, maybe not. It's amazing what a kid could get away with when their dad had just died.

She'd given Immy a real dressing down after that; played the *your father would be disappointed in you* card. It seemed to work. She'd behaved better since then. She was very quiet though, as though she'd drawn into herself. Bea hoped this production might help her feel better. Get some positive feedback for a change.

Bea nodded at the parents she vaguely knew as they took their seats, turning away when she discerned sympathy change the shape of their faces as they remembered she'd recently been widowed. She avoided catching anyone's eye for too long, aware how hard people found it to find the right words. They didn't know what to say and she didn't know how to react to whatever they came up with. Best to avoid conversation altogether.

Jan gripped her hand as the lights dimmed. The conductor raised her arms and the orchestra burst into the first powerful notes. As the show went on, Bea was grateful Jan was there. Truly she was. But she wished it was Oli sitting next to her. Like her, his heart would have swollen with the most intense pride when Immy sang 'I Don't Know How to Love Him'. The fact he was missing it was enough to split her insides in two.

Her girl was magnificent. Bea heard the pain of the last two years in her melodic voice. There was more depth of

164

feeling than she could bear to listen to. By the end of 'Could We Start Again Please' Bea was racked with sobs and the tissue Jan pressed into her hand was soaked.

She knew she didn't imagine the applause and cheers were louder for Immy than anyone else in the cast. The whole audience was on its feet. Whistles tore the air as Immy bowed low, her face glowing as she straightened and her eyes searched the crowd for Bea.

Their eyes met and Bea spluttered as she tried to grin through her tears and show her darling girl how proud she was of her, how she loved her beyond anything else in the world. Maybe this could be a new start for them. Without Oli, but at least together. She clapped until her palms stung. The warmth of Jan pushing up next to her, supporting her and clapping just as loudly, gave her the strength to feel hope.

After the final curtain, Bea stood to the side as the caretaker stacked the last of the chairs, loaded them onto a trolley and trundled them to the back of the hall. Immy was the last of the cast to appear through the door to the left of the stage. Bea opened her arms, and she ran into them, hugging her tightly. Bea closed her eyes and breathed in the sweet smell of deodorant and stage make-up.

'You were the star,' she whispered into Immy's hair. 'I am so very, very proud of you.'

'You liked it?'

'I loved it!' She took Immy's head in her hands and planted a kiss on her forehead. 'Come on. Jan's waiting for us in the car. She was blown away by you tonight. By all of you. Let's get a takeaway and I'll tell you all my favourite bits. Do you want pizza or Chinese? You choose.' She realised she was gabbling so paused before blurting, 'It was brilliant, love, really brilliant.'

Immy stared at the hall floor. Her feet shuffled and a feeling of doom gathered in Bea's chest.

'I'm not coming back right—'

There was a whistle from the doors leading on to reception. They both turned to see Zach gesturing Immy forwards.

'Oh,' said Bea, 'I was hoping . . .'

'I know, but . . .' She glanced at Zach then back to Bea. 'Don't be needy, Mum.'

Bea tensed. It felt like everything about Immy hardened when she saw Zach slouched against the wall, his leg bent, foot on the paintwork like he thought he was James Dean.

'I'm not.' In truth, needy was exactly how she felt. 'Go on then, off you go. Don't drink tonight, though, will you? You've got another performance tomorrow,' she added.

'I know,' Immy said defensively, and Bea wished she'd kept her mouth shut. She had every right to ask her underage daughter not to drink, but somehow Immy always made her feel like she was the one at fault.

'Have a good time.' The words sounded hollow now.

Immy smiled briefly and hurried towards Zach.

'Have you got your key?' Bea shouted after her. Immy threw her thumb in the air and skipped away, leaving Bea winded. She'd really thought she might be getting Immy back for a minute there. Not this time. She tried to keep the mounting desolation at bay by thinking, *soon; she'll come back to me soon.*

There was a quiet cough at the far side of the hall and when she glanced over the caretaker had his hand on the bank of light switches. She nodded an acknowledgement and went to find Jan to give her a lift back to her empty house.

* * *

166

Bea dabbed sweat from her top lip and tried to look cheerful as she waited for Gemma to open her front door. The sun's glare made her heavy eyelids even more desperate to close. As she heard the thump of footsteps in the hallway, she wished she'd told Gemma that she was too exhausted to look after Phoebe while she went to her art class today. Bea's alarm had gone off at five a.m., but despite her exhaustion, she was always awake before it beeped. The emptiness of the bed beside her was enough to keep her restless in the early hours of the morning.

'Hi, Bea.' Gemma's skin shone with dewy make-up. Phoebe sat on her hip, one small hand on Gemma's shoulder, the other shoved into her own mouth. 'Say hello to Aunty Bea, Phoebs.'

Phoebe reached for Bea. She leaned her body forwards and made a keening noise and when Bea lifted her into her arms, suddenly she didn't want to be anywhere else.

'Hello, poppet,' she said, kissing Phoebe's cheek, wet with saliva. 'Are you teething?'

'Do you think that's what it is?' Gemma's chin dimpled. 'She hasn't been herself this afternoon.'

Bea examined Phoebe's face. The skin outside the jagged lines of her birthmark was paler than usual. She followed Gemma into the sitting room and plucked a tissue from the box on the table to wipe Phoebe's wet mouth. 'This dribbling and fist chewing looks like teething to me.'

'I'm not sure I should leave her.'

Bea kneeled and tried to put Phoebe onto the brightly coloured mat on the floor, but she clung to her neck. 'That's not like you, is it?' She sat on the mat and let Phoebe nestle in her lap. 'We'll be fine. I can always call you, can't I? And Ewan will be back by seven, right?'

Gemma frowned. 'So he says.'

167

Bea stayed quiet. She didn't want to get into a conversation about Ewan. She had her own thoughts on how late he worked and how little he saw of his family, but she'd only ever shared them with Oli. And now Oli was gone, and she had nobody to talk to about Ewan and Gemma. Or about Immy's increasing defiance. Sometimes it felt like all those unsaid words blocked her throat and made it hard to swallow.

Phoebe reached for one of the plastic blocks scattered across the mat. She climbed from Bea's knee and crawled to get another, clonking them together, looking from her mother to her aunty, her eyes bright.

'Clever girl.' Bea clapped and Phoebe banged the blocks quicker, bouncing on her bottom gleefully. 'See, she's alright.'

Gemma smiled. 'Good,' she paused, 'because I really do need to go tonight.'

'Oh yeah?' Bea picked up two blocks and mimicked Phoebe's banging. 'You like that art class, don't you? It's good you've got something to break the days up. Toddlers are hard work at the best of times, and it hasn't been easy with this one, has it?'

'It's not just that.' Gemma's voice was quiet. 'There's something I wanted to talk to you about.'

'Sounds ominous.' Bea stiffened. She had enough to deal with without taking on anyone else's problems. She willed Gemma not to burden her with more.

The banging stopped abruptly, and Phoebe fell backwards onto the mat. Bea sprang onto all fours and felt Gemma lunge towards them as Phoebe's eyelids fluttered. Bea shifted out of her way, her hand rising to her throat as she watched, helpless as Phoebe's pupils moved from side to side and her arms and legs shot out in sharp spasms.

'It's okay, baby, Mummy's here.' Gemma turned to Bea. 'Time the fit, Bea.'

Bea jumped up and grabbed her phone from her bag. By the time she found the timer app Phoebe's limbs had stilled and her eyes were focused on Gemma, who was smiling through her tears and whispering soft words to her daughter as she lay limply in her arms.

* * *

Fifteen minutes later, Phoebe was asleep against Gemma's chest on the sofa. Gemma looked up at Bea. 'You might as well go. She can sleep for hours after a seizure. If she was going to have another one, she'd probably have had it by now, and that one was short, wasn't it?'

Bea nodded. 'Less than thirty seconds, I'd say.'

'I think she's alright. Could you pass me my phone and bring me a cold drink before you set off?'

'You sure?'

'I'm not leaving her now.' Her voice was firm.

Bea put a drink clinking with ice on the side table. 'Call me if you need anything, okay?'

'I will. Promise. Thanks, Bea.' Gemma looked down at her daughter's dark head with such tenderness, Bea felt like an intruder. She put the television on a low volume, kissed them both, and left.

* * *

Warm trickles ran from her armpits, down her sides as she pulled into the mini-market car park. The car's air conditioner had packed in at the start of the summer and it seemed to have collected every ray of sunshine between then and this early September heatwave to broil her alive. The blast of cold air when the shop door swished open

169

felt heavenly, until the moisture on her tunic chilled, making her hurry down the refrigerated aisle.

She threw a handful of bananas and some vegetables into a basket before finding the shelf with the reduced goods. She picked through the products near their sell-by dates and found two chicken Kiev at half price. Result. At the till, her eyes crept to the fridge full of wine and beer. A bottle of Cobra seemed to call out to her. She could taste the yeasty froth on her tongue. It was only four o'clock and Immy had a revision class tonight so wouldn't be home until six. Bea imagined herself sitting in the garden in the sunshine, drinking a cold lager. She deserved it after the day she'd had. Sod it. She slid the door of the fridge open and lifted the bottle from the shelf.

The boy at the till rang up the last of her shopping and Bea glanced at the total and opened her purse. She drew out a five-pound note and opened the compartment wide to find the other notes she knew were in there. She wiped her sweaty hand on her tunic and searched the purse again, but there was nothing but a few copper coins in the bottom. She rarely brought a debit card out these days because she didn't want to be tempted to spend over budget.

Lightheaded, she attempted a laugh. 'Sorry, I've forgotten my card.' She felt the eyes of the woman behind her in the queue boring into her back. 'I should have gone to the cashpoint. I've only got a fiver with me.' The words sounded like a lie, and she knew it. 'I'll put the beer back. Can you ring it up again? Sorry.'

The boy smiled sympathetically. 'Don't worry. I'll put it back in a bit.' He took the bananas and Kiev and ran them over the scanner as Bea did an Oscar-worthy performance of everything being fine. She winced with the shame of being pitied by a boy hardly old enough to shave.

* * *

At home, she changed into a t-shirt and shorts and sat on a garden chair in the fading sun. Tap water was no substitute for the beer. She took a sip and put it down on the unmown grass by her side. The sun made the tears in her eyes into prisms as she looked towards the fence where next door's Virginia creeper was turning red, reaching over to the ivy growing up her side, as though leaning to pull it up by the hand. Bea's fallen tears dried on her cheeks. She touched a finger to the streaks then put her finger in her mouth to taste the salt.

The sound of singing made her turn. She heaved herself from the chair, rubbing her eyes clear, and walked through the back door into the kitchen where Immy was standing in front of the open fridge door singing a song from *Jesus Christ Superstar*.

'I thought you had a revision session?'

Immy jumped. 'God, you frightened me. I thought you were looking after Phoebe.' She closed the fridge and flung her rucksack from her shoulder onto the table. There was a clank of glass.

'What's in there?'

'Why?' Immy stood with her feet apart, staring Bea down.

Bea grabbed the bag and opened the zip. Immy tried to wrestle it from her, but her movements were clumsy and slow. Two red caps sat on the top of a pair of glass bottles. Vodka, and not the cheap stuff either. 'Where did you get the money for this?'

'Wow.' Immy shoved her hand into the bag and dragged

out one of the bottles. Bea watched in dismay as she unscrewed the lid. 'That's your first question?'

'Put that down.' Bea felt every hair follicle on her arm stand to attention.

'Or what?'

'I'm in no mood for your games, Immy. Put that down right now and tell me where you got the money.'

When Immy lifted the bottle to her lips rage blurred Bea's vision. She wrenched the bottle from Immy's hand. Immy grabbed it back. It slipped from their fingers. Bea heard a smash as the bottle shattered on the floor, vodka splashing up her legs. Her arm flew out and before she could stop herself, she slapped Immy hard across her face.

Immy gasped. The accusation in her eyes as she lifted her hand to her mouth made the sting in Bea's own hand feel like a branding.

'You hit me!' The incredulity in Immy's voice made Bea's hand burn even more.

'I'm sorry, but I—'

Immy didn't wait to hear her apology. She marched into the hall and when the front door slammed shut Bea sank onto the floor among the vodka and the glass. The alcohol stung her nostrils, and even as she looked at her reddening palm, she wasn't sure she *was* sorry. All she truly knew was that every last thing in her life without Oli was too much to cope with alone.

Chapter Twenty-Two

Three Years Ago

The adrenaline coursing through Bea wouldn't let her sit in the chair next to the narrow bed in the Accident and Emergency triage room. She stood, holding Immy's trembling hand, trying to take in the enormity of what had happened that evening. Immy had been thoroughly checked over by the doctor and was lucky to have got away with only cuts and bruises. Thank God she'd been wearing a seatbelt. She was the only one who was.

Bea tried to regulate her breathing. The dried blood crusting on Immy's cheeks looked as though a child had splashed her with red-brown paint. Listening as the police interviewed Immy, she discovered it was Zach's blood, from when his head hit the windscreen and his face . . . how did Immy put it . . .? *Kind of exploded.*

The police officers left and now it was just the two of them, trying to absorb the reality of what had happened, in the tiny room that smelled of disinfectant. Immy let go of her hand and leaned over the grey paper kidney bowl on her lap. She retched up what was left in her stomach and the stench of vomit and alcohol made Bea's own stomach curdle.

The door opened and Ewan stood, ashen faced, his mouth hanging and eyes wild. 'Gemma's dead.'

Immy retched again. Bea covered her mouth. It couldn't be true. It was too horrific to be true.

Ewan's eyes fixed on Immy. 'Your boyfriend and my wife are dead. They're dead. What happened, Immy? How did this happen?'

Immy's breath was coming in short, staccato bursts. 'I'm sorry, I didn't know he would—' She leaned over and made a choking sound but there was nothing left to come out. 'I'm sorry.'

Ewan stepped forwards and Bea felt the need to turn, so her body was shielding Immy. The muscles in his jaw jumped and red circles formed below his cheekbones, vivid against the whiteness of his skin. 'What happened?'

Immy hiccupped as she spoke, 'I didn't expect him to—' She shook her head, as though trying to dislodge an image. 'I can't explain.'

'Try,' Ewan snarled. 'For the sake of my daughter. Tell me what happened.'

'It was my fault. It's all my fault.'

Bea's heart plummeted. 'No. You weren't driving. You tried to stop him.' She had to stop Immy saying anything more. This wasn't what she'd told the police. She'd said she tried to grab the wheel, but he'd gone mad and slammed his foot on the accelerator. 'It wasn't your fault.'

'When we saw Gemma's car, I told him I'd seen Gemma with a man in town, and he must've thought up the plan then.'

'What plan? I don't understand,' said Bea.

'Let her talk,' said Ewan.

Immy slapped at the wetness on her face. 'He told Gemma he wanted five thousand pounds not to tell you we'd seen her that night. He took pictures of her and the man on his phone and said he'd delete them if she gave him the money. But she laughed and he went mad. And then he started the car and—'

Bea examined Ewan's face, but his expression seemed to change so rapidly, she couldn't read it. There was no colour left in his cheeks and now his lips were pale, too. 'He asked her for money?'

Immy nodded, her falling tears staining the papery covering on the narrow bed with dark blue spots. 'But she said she was leaving anyway and the money didn't matter.' Her voice cracked. 'I don't know why he drove to that car park. It was dark and . . .'

The two red dots sprang up again on Ewan's face as he spoke. 'That's not the point, is it? You and your boyfriend were there.'

Bea put her hand on his arm but he shifted away. 'I'm so sorry, Ewan. I can't imagine how you're feeling. But you've got to understand that Immy didn't . . .' What didn't Immy? She tried to gather her thoughts. 'She would never have told Zach she'd seen Gemma if she thought he'd react like that.' She turned to her daughter, whose face was contorted with pain. 'Would you, love?'

Immy shook her head.

Ewan took another step forwards. His voice was hardly above a whisper as he pointed into Immy's face. 'But you did.' He breathed in and his lip curled. 'I can smell the alcohol from here. What else were you on? What had that psycho boyfriend of yours taken before he drove his car at my wife?'

175

Bea pushed his hand away. 'Ewan, I know you're hurting, we all are, but . . .'

'You told that monster she was having an affair. You were drinking and God knows what else, then you got in a car and . . .' His voice shattered as his mouth twisted and he let out a low groan.

Immy collapsed back on the bed and covered her face with her hands. 'I'm sorry. I'm so sorry. God, Phoebe. What will Phoebe . . .? Oh God, I'm so sorry.'

Ewan turned a rigid finger to Bea. 'Keep her away from me and my family. I don't want to see her face again. I won't ever be able to look at her again without . . .'

'That's not—' Bea started, but Ewan was already at the door. 'It wasn't . . .'

She turned back to Immy, who was rocking backwards and forwards, her hands still covering her face, gasping for breath, repeating, 'I'm sorry, I'm sorry, I'm sorry.'

NOW

Chapter Twenty-Three

Bea let the towel drop and glared across the kitchen at the rigid figures of Joyce and Ewan. They wore identical sneers and at that moment she despised them both.

'Immy had just lost her father when the accident happened. Have an ounce of sympathy. She's not the monster you make her out to be. She's just a girl who made mistakes.'

'She caused the death of my son.' Joyce fired the words individually, like bullets.

Bea shook her head. Joyce had never said this before. She'd said many cruel and bitter things, but not that. She must have dug deep to justify turning her back on the girl she doted on, but this was ludicrous. 'How can you say that?'

'Oliver would have had the strength to fight the cancer if Imogen wasn't so much trouble. And he fell when he was taking care of her – that was when his condition really started to deteriorate.'

'I was there; you weren't!' shouted Bea. 'Bowel cancer killed your son. The fall was just a terrible, terrible accident and Immy was punished enough by her own misplaced guilt. She doesn't need yours as well.'

Ewan snorted. 'Are you going to defend everything she did?'

He stood with his legs apart, hands on hips, making a wall of himself. Bea picked the towel up from the floor and wiped it over her face, but the tears kept coming. 'No . . . but she was as broken by Oli's death, just like the rest of us. More, in fact. And the accident that killed Gemma? That wasn't black and white, was it?'

Ewan turned away and she wanted to scream at him. Surely, even he had to accept that being a passenger in a car driven by someone who was high on drugs and entitlement didn't make you an accessory to murder. Yes, Immy had been stupid to even be involved with Zach and yes, Bea would regret until the end of her days that she hadn't been stricter with Immy, stepped in sooner and been a better mother. But he was acting as though Immy had driven the car into his wife herself. Why was he being so awful?

He turned back, finger pointing. 'I will not have her near my home, or Phoebe. I told you that before we made this arrangement, and I meant it.'

'But she came . . .' Bea had to make him understand. 'I'm her mother.'

'She is not part of my family,' said Ewan. 'You have to choose whether you want to be or not.'

Bea opened her arms wide. 'Ewan, surely you can see that this grudge—'

Joyce snorted. 'Grudge?'

'Whatever you want to call it, it's out of proportion. She's come back after three years. Hasn't she been punished enough? I'm begging you to try to find some forgiveness.'

She moved her head to catch his eye but he stared at the floor and a mass of fury burned up her throat. None of this was making any sense. 'What are you so scared of, Ewan? Why won't you even try to—'

Ewan's voice boomed into the room. 'If I discover that girl has been here again, our agreement is terminated and you will never see Phoebe again.'

Bea gasped. 'You can't be serious?'

'Try me.'

The air left her lungs, and she buried her face in the towel. The sound of Joyce's walking stick on the wooden floor mingled with the clattering rain on the glass doors and the names repeating in Bea's head: *Immy, Phoebe, Immy, Phoebe*.

Chapter Twenty-Four

'Sorry about last time you came around. I was—' Bea said when Jan opened her door.

'Forget about it.' She wrapped Bea in a bear hug.

'No, let me apologise. I was awful to you. I know you were just looking out for me. I should have listened.' She dropped her bag on the floor.

'I'm a wise old owl.' Jan winked, then sat her down at the kitchen table with a hot chocolate and a packet of digestives. 'Apology accepted. Now, tell me everything.'

Bea filled Jan in on Immy's sudden reappearance.

'Lord Ewan's surpassed himself this time,' Jan said. 'Imagine asking someone to choose between their own child and the one they're looking after?'

Bea didn't have to imagine it. When she'd told him she was going to stay at Jan's for the night, he'd said, 'Think carefully about what you do next. If you intend to let that girl back into your life, then you're choosing to walk away from my family.'

'*My* family!' said Jan when Bea told her. 'Who the feck does he think glues *his family* together? God, when I think of everything you've done for them.' She dipped a biscuit into her drink, swirled it around then held her hand under the soggy mass as she transferred it to her mouth. 'And she's no better, Lady Bloody Muck.' She chewed, then picked a piece of biscuit from her back teeth. 'Do you remember what she was like with Immy when she was little? Treated her as though she'd given birth to her herself. Nose in the air as if she was the one who'd taken her to drama classes and singing every week, as if it was down to her that her little princess was always the lead.'

'She wasn't always the lead.' Why did she feel she had to be modest about Immy's achievements, even now? It wasn't as if she hadn't fallen from her pedestal on her own.

'She bloody was. She was the most talented little girl I've ever seen on stage.' She dipped her biscuit again. It disintegrated and she used a teaspoon to retrieve the floating mush. 'Her Ladyship never treated Phoebe the same way. Poor kid.'

The thought of Phoebe waking up without her there made the inside of Bea's head prickle. What if she was worried she wasn't coming back, that she'd left her? Where would Ewan say she'd gone? She remembered Phoebe's face as she passed her on her way upstairs, unable to look her in the eye. That poor kid was brainwashed into believing her mother was murdered and Immy was a monster who was partly responsible for killing her.

Bea fantasised about one day telling Phoebe what had happened at the inquest into the accident. She had sat there, next to Ewan and Joyce, watching Ewan grow paler as Gemma's lover tearfully outlined their plans to start a new life together with Phoebe. Gemma had told him she'd married a wealthy older man and regretted it from the start. He said Gemma was the love of his life and she felt the same. They had everything to live for and Zach had taken that away. Whatever part Immy played, it was unintentional. Zach was the one who drove that car. But no one seemed to be able to see that, and eventually, Bea herself had taken on just as much guilt as if Immy had been the one behind the wheel – and in doing so, she'd betrayed her daughter just as much as the rest of them.

Bea blinked and found herself back in Jan's small kitchen. She didn't really want Phoebe to know her mother was unhappy with Ewan. She deserved to feel loved and secure, and if that meant believing Gemma was a perfect wife, then that was how it had to be. She just wished Immy didn't have to be the scapegoat.

'How did she look?' Jan said.

'Thin.'

'Do you think she's still drinking?'

'I don't know.' Bea was trying not to make assumptions about Immy's bony frame and gaunt face. But it was hard. 'She didn't look well. She looked poorly, you know?' Jan patted the back of her hand. 'I suppose I'll have more idea tomorrow.'

Jan nodded and they both turned at the sound of the door opening. Ciara's head appeared, her messy bun bobbing, almost as big as her skull. 'Room's ready. I'm going in with Juno. Night.'

'Thanks, Ciara,' said Bea, reddening at the thought of Ciara having to bunk up with her sixteen-year-old sister when Bea had a vast room at Ewan's she could be sleeping in. 'Sorry to turf you out.'

'No probs. Juno's got a new boyfriend, and she talks in her sleep, so you're doing me a favour. I'll have loads to blackmail her with by tomorrow.' She grinned before disappearing.

'Bless her,' said Bea, turning back to Jan. 'Hard to believe Immy was only a few months older than her when she left.'

'And now she's back . . .' Jan paused and stared down at the table.

'Go on.'

'Don't jump down my throat, but what if . . .'

'What if she wants money or something?' It wasn't as if Bea hadn't thought it herself. 'There's only one way to find out.'

They finished their drinks and went up to bed but Bea couldn't get comfortable on Ciara's thin mattress. When she did manage to fall into a light sleep, she dreamed of being in a small boat on a huge expanse of water. The voices of two children called for her to save them, but they were on opposite sides of the boat and whichever way she rowed, she would be leaving one to drown.

* * *

She woke before dawn, missing Phoebe's rhythmic breathing next to her. The faces on the posters on Ciara's walls turned from shadows of indistinguishable figures to bright images of pop stars. At least, she presumed they were pop stars. The androgynous characters in the pictures wore pantomime-thick make-up and eyelashes like cartoon donkeys, not like the grungy musicians she and Oli used to go and see in dingy clubs in the 90s. Immy used to laugh at their music taste, and they'd argue about the merits of guitar-based indie bands versus the rap and grime she started to listen to when she got together with Zach.

The arguments went from playful to angry when the

thump of the bass still pumped through the walls into the early hours when Oli was in bed, sweaty and drained from chemo. Immy didn't listen to reason. She was too busy shouting back. So, Bea had stopped trying to get through to her.

Looking back, she can see when she had stopped attempting to communicate. They were so angry with each other. It was all so raw. The pain of seeing Oli suffer and fade had consumed her, and it had seemed as though Immy was intentionally adding to the agony, being difficult and cruel. In hindsight, she could see that of course Immy was hurting, too. She was a child crying out for attention in the most ruinous way, but Bea hadn't been able to see past what seemed like selfishness and self-destruction.

Today was the start of making amends, she thought, as she snuck out of the house before Jan's brood woke up. She prayed Immy would turn up. All the way into town, she practised what she wanted to say to Immy, and she planned to start with *sorry*. She left her car near the park and walked around the lake in the centre, rephrasing her script in her head, knowing she'd forget every word when she saw Immy's beautiful face again.

Standing outside Walnuts Café, she breathed in through her nose and out through her mouth, trying to make her heart rate slow. She peered through the window from the pavement, past the laminated signs for meal deals, wondering if Immy might already be sitting there, at one of the pine tables, trying to choose between a flat white and a cappuccino. Bea imagined her looking up and beaming, showing those straight, white teeth, hard-won by endless trips to the orthodontist.

A woman with a pushchair struggled to pull the door from the inside and Bea leaped forward to hold it for her.

The woman looked harried as she offered numerous thanks and apologies and Bea smiled at the chocolate-smeared toddler who licked her chubby fingers, oblivious to her mother's stress. *And that's just the start of it,* thought Bea, stepping inside. *You've both got a rollercoaster ride ahead of you.*

And she'd give anything to do it all again.

Scanning the room, she saw Immy hadn't arrived yet, so she chose a seat facing the window and arranged herself on the hard chair. She stood and shook off her leather jacket, hanging it on the chair back. She picked up the laminated menu, but the list kept jumping around. Her heart rate wasn't slowing. She took her phone from her bag and checked the time. Ten o'clock on the nose. She kept her eyes fixed on the door. Would she come?

'What can I get you?'

Bea almost jumped off the chair.

'You alright?' The waitress looked amused.

Bea tried to smile. The shock of being brought out of her trance made tears spring behind her eyes. She stared at the menu, blinking rapidly. 'Fine, thanks. I'll have a latte, please.'

'Anything to eat?'

'I'm waiting for someone. I'll order food when she gets here.'

'No worries.' The waitress left and Bea glanced again at her phone. Ten past ten. She willed Immy to open the door. The minutes ticked on.

* * *

By ten thirty, Bea was biting the inside of her cheek to stop the sobs from coming. She scrolled through her phone, but the photographs on social media of people chinking glasses on birthdays or cuddled up with their pooches made her feel even worse. She didn't even have a bloody dog.

A blast of air ruffled her hair. Her heart pounded. Looking up at the door, she was crushed to see only a tall man with a sleek ginger dog walking close to his leg. The man lifted his head and she saw that it was Joyce's social worker, Eddie.

Eddie had a dog?

She shook the stupid thought from her head and noted the look of recognition on his face. His smile suggested he was pleased to see her, and for some reason that pleased her in turn.

'Hello, Bea,' he said, stepping towards her. 'Alright?' The dog moved in pace with him, as though attached to his knee by an invisible thread.

'Wotcha.' Why did she say that? She felt herself redden and dipped down to stroke the dog's shiny fur to hide her blushes. 'Who's this?'

'Maximilian Henry Lorimar the Third,' said Eddie cheerfully, as though they always had relaxed, convivial conversations. This man must take his job very seriously if he was so different outside work. Or maybe the dog had magical powers and could convert a grumpy middle-aged man into a smiling one. She should suggest he brought it along next time he saw Joyce.

She imagined Joyce's face when she found the dog panting on her doorstep, then couldn't remember what Eddie had said.

'Come again?' There she was, making an idiot of herself.

'Max.'

'Hello, Max.' The dog's tongue lolled and his brown eyes gazed at her so adoringly she wanted to bury her face in his neck. She had to get a grip.

'Can I get you another?' He gestured to the table. She glanced down at the latte she'd forgotten to drink. The foamy top congealed around the rim and dead, beige bubbles stuck to the top of the tall glass.

'No. Thanks.' She stirred the cold coffee. 'I'm waiting for someone.' She halted the spoon. 'My daughter.' It felt like a confession.

'I didn't know you had a daughter.'

'She's twenty-one.'

'Ah. Flown the nest then?' He tugged Max's lead gently and the dog resumed his position by his knee. 'I'll leave you to it. Good to see you.'

'You, too.' As simply as that, Eddie must've presumed her grown-up daughter was coming along for a casual coffee and a catch-up and given it no more thought.

How Bea wished that was the case. Instead, she watched Eddie order his takeaway coffee, Max never leaving his side. The waitress did a double-take when she handed over his paper cup. Bea watched her take in his Converse, dark Levi's and khaki bomber jacket and saw her smile become coquettish. A proprietorial feeling surprised her. He waved as he stepped out of the café and onto the pavement and she half wished she'd asked him to join her. She watched him walk past the window and when the end of Max's pointed tail disappeared from view a sob rose in her throat. It was ten forty-five.

She ordered another coffee.

* * *

Another half an hour went by. She tried to ignore the waitress whispering to the barista when a couple came in and couldn't find a free table so walked out without ordering. Her arms became too heavy to lift, so she gave

189

up pretending to drink the coffee and just stared at it as the bubbles slowly burst. By eleven-thirty, her legs were made of dense wood, and she had to snap the joints to force them to raise her from the chair. She put a ten-pound note on the table, not able to face the waitress, who knew, like she did, that Immy wasn't going to arrive.

Chapter Twenty-Five

Sitting alone in her car, Bea let the tears come. Her chest heaved. She let her lungs draw in air and throw it noisily back out into the bloody awful, unfair world. She leaned her forearms against the steering wheel and rested her head. The leather sleeves of her jacket turned shiny black from the liquid.

A tap on the window startled her. She lifted her head, imagining opening her mouth and aiming fire at any traffic warden who dared to interrupt her anguish. Through blurred eyes, a contorted orangey shape transformed into a dog. Blinking to clear her vision, she saw it was standing next to a very concerned-looking man. Shit. Eddie.

'You alright?' His muffled words steamed on the car window.

'I'm fine.' What a ridiculous thing to say. People who were fine managed to contain their snotty outbursts to the privacy of their own bathrooms. Oh God. She didn't even have her own bathroom. She dug her nails into her palms to stop another bout of sobs.

He made a winding motion with his hand then stopped.

He poked out his finger and mimed pressing something. 'Put the window down.'

She opened the car door because she couldn't think of anything else to do.

'That wasn't the right mime, was it?' he said. 'Winding down the window? When did we last wind down a car window?'

She shook her head; not confident she could speak without breaking down again.

'Walk?' he asked. Max's tail swooped back and forth, slapping against his jeans. Eddie nodded towards the dog. 'He thinks it's a good idea.'

'I don't know.' Bea rubbed under her eyes with a tissue, then the wet leather of her sleeves, sorry that shame couldn't be mopped up with a Kleenex, too. This was mortifying. What must he think of her? She glanced up at his face. His grey eyes were full of concern.

'Come on. I'm a good listener. I'm also quite good at walking in silence and listening to the birds when needed.'

Max stepped forwards and put his head on her lap, his tail swooshing from side to side. 'Can't say no to that, can I?' She patted his bony head then hoisted her tired body from the car. Every time she'd met Eddie, she'd come away feeling like he thought she was a complete loser. Now she'd confirmed she was unhinged by being caught wailing in a car like a dumped teenager, so she might as well let him see the full extent of her hopelessness. It wasn't like he had any respect for her to lose.

They meandered along the path around the still lake. Max gambolled towards the Canada geese, stopping abruptly and running back to Eddie's side whenever one turned in his direction.

'He's such a coward.' He scratched behind Max's ear.

'You're a big softy, aren't you, fella?' Max gazed up adoringly then galloped ahead.

After a few more paces, Eddie said, 'I take it the coffee didn't go well?'

'You could say that.'

In the middle of the lake a goose honked and reared up, its wings spanning wide, bringing Max scampering back.

'She didn't turn up. My daughter. Immy.'

'I'm sorry.'

They walked on and Bea imagined they must look like a couple who've just had an argument. Both serious faced, her with red, swollen eyes.

'I haven't seen her for three years. Or, at least, I hadn't, until last night.' The revelation brought shivers of hopelessness and she couldn't stop the sobs building and convulsing out of her. Surprised to feel Eddie's hand on her elbow, she allowed him to steer her towards a bench. He edged her down gently and sat next to her, his thigh warm next to hers. 'I think she's an alcoholic,' she admitted, for the first time, even to herself. 'She used to do the usual teenage drinking, you know, but after her dad died, it got worse.' She searched her pocket for the soggy tissue and blew her nose, not daring to look at Eddie's face.

'Most kids experiment with booze, in my experience.'

Of course, Eddie was a social worker. He must have seen all sorts. She carried on, the need to share overwhelming her peculiar desire for Eddie to think well of her, 'But when I saw her yesterday, she looked so thin. Her eyes were huge in her head. She looked really ill, you know?' She peeked at his face, and felt like he did know.

'And you're worried she's moved on to other stuff?'

She nodded, rolling the tissue in her fingers. 'I didn't want to jump to conclusions. I was going to try to work things out with her today, but . . .'

'But she didn't turn up.'

Max ambled over and sat at Bea's feet. She leaned forwards and stroked him from head to flank, the repetitive movement soothing her. 'And I have no idea how or where to find her.'

'Are you worried for her welfare?'

This sounded more like the official Eddie she was used to. 'Yes. I'm worried for her welfare.' She didn't hide the sarcasm, then saw confusion on his face and felt awful. 'I'm sorry.'

'S'alright. It's just that . . .' He paused and when she glanced up again, she saw he was wrestling with his thoughts.

'What?'

'Well, you said she's only twenty-one, is that right?'

Bea nodded.

'And you think she might be a vulnerable young adult?'

There he went with his professional phrasing again. She shifted her thigh away from his. She should remember he viewed her as a client, not a friend. Max nudged her hand with his head, and she resumed her stroking. 'Yes.'

'If you want, I could try to help you find her.'

'If I want?' Max jumped up at the tone of her voice. 'Yes, I do want that. I want that very much. God, really?'

Eddie put his hands out. 'Hold on. I can't make any promises.'

'Anything. Anything at all. Honestly, I'd be so grateful.'

A goose strutted towards them, and Max slid behind Eddie's legs. 'Come on, boy.' He clipped the lead onto the dog's collar and stood. Bea followed. 'I've been in this business for thirty years, so I've got a few contacts who might be able to do some digging. If you give me as much detail as you can, I'll see what I can find out.'

Bea's feet were light on the ground again. She felt dizzy from the extreme shifts in her emotions over the last twelve hours. Here was the lift she needed. It felt like Eddie had offered to return something she'd lost four years ago. She'd almost forgotten what it was like, but here it was, glittering like the sun shining on the lake.

Hope.

Chapter Twenty-Six

As she walked down the path towards the lake, she spotted
Eddie sitting on the same bench they'd talked on yesterday.
She looked around and under the bench but couldn't see
Max. She scanned the perimeter of the lake, but there was
no magic, ginger dog bounding away from the geese. This
didn't feel like a good sign. Anxiety quickened her strides.

'You don't mess about,' she said, approaching the bench.
'I'd prepared myself to wait for weeks.'

Eddie smiled, but she couldn't read his face.

'No Max?' She sat down and caught her breath.

Eddie scratched his head then tugged his left sideburn
down. 'Thought we could do without the distraction.'

Ah.

'Not good news, then?' She couldn't stop her fingers
from twirling around each other. She imagined she looked
like a witch from an old film. She put her palms together
but couldn't keep them still so went back to winding her
hands over each other.

'I'll let you decide.' Eddie took his rucksack from
between his feet and unzipped it. 'Don't jump to any

conclusions though. Remember, this is only one piece of the jigsaw. There's a whole story behind this we don't know anything about.' Bea's heart thumped in her chest. When he took out a sheet of paper it was all she could do to stop herself from snatching it from him.

'What's that?'

Eddie straightened out the sheet, then passed it to her. 'It was quick to find on the system because—' He pointed at the top of the sheet. 'That's her last known address.'

Bea focused on the neatly printed words and read *Langley Rehabilitation Centre, Carthing Road, Carthing*.

A mass clogged her throat. When she tried to speak, the words hit the lump and shattered into a grunt. The paper fell from her hand, fluttering onto the concrete. Eddie bent to pick it up, but it shifted on the wind, as though playing a game with him. She watched, too heavy to move, as he chased the paper, eventually catching the corner with his foot. He picked it up and returned to the bench.

'You alright?'

Sitting back, she was surprised the wooden slats didn't splinter under the new weight of her. She didn't know how to reply.

'It doesn't necessarily mean . . .' He trailed off.

But it did, didn't it? Immy was drinking regularly by sixteen, and God knows what else she was doing when she was with that bastard Zach. The post-mortem showed he was high on a cocktail of drugs when he drove his car into Gemma's, and Immy spent so much time with him back then.

Eddie could say what he liked about one piece of the jigsaw, but the picture looked pretty complete to Bea. When Immy came to Ewan's – was it only the day before yesterday? – she looked sick and withered. Like a poster girl for heroin addiction. Her last known address was a rehab centre. No amount of hope could stop the pieces coming together in Bea's head.

'It's the most likely explanation, though, isn't it?' she said.

Eddie was silent.

'Thanks for finding her.'

'I still think you should keep an open mind.' He leaned in to her: a kind, conciliatory gesture. His shoulder felt warm, and, exhausted, she closed her eyes and rested against him. 'There might be more to it.' She breathed in and smelled his Kouros, but it didn't take her back to her youth today. No smell was strong enough to lift her away from this stinging moment.

They sat in silence, the breeze tickling her hair against her face, and when she opened her eyes she watched the people passing by the bench, trying not to envy their carefree lives, because that's not real, is it? People looking at her now might see a middle-aged couple contentedly watching the world go by when really, she was in pain, and he was . . . God, she had no idea.

She sat up abruptly. 'Sorry.' She smoothed down her hair where it had ruffled against his polo shirt. 'You've done all this for me and I'm letting you comfort me like some kind of—' What? Princess? Damsel in distress? 'Pillock.' Where had that come from?

'You're not a pillock.' He smiled.

She'd never felt more like a pillock in all of her life. 'You must need to get back to your wife, or-or kids, or something.' She was stammering like a teenager.

'There's only Max, and he'll understand when I tell him I came to see the mad woman from yesterday.'

198

His eyes smiled but Bea felt the words like a spike. 'Sorry.' She stood and ran her fingers through her hair. She must look like she'd escaped an asylum; wild, with glazed over, red-rimmed eyes. 'Thanks again for that.' She gestured to the paper, still in his hand. 'I'll let you get on with your day.' She turned before he could see the colour rush to her face and when he called her name, she waved her hand behind her in a pathetic attempt at goodbye.

* * *

Later that day, she sat in the car on Ewan's drive, with her bag on the passenger seat, willing herself to get out and face them all. There was no choice now she knew the truth about Immy.

She replayed scenes of Immy standing on the landing in their old home, fists balled, face screwed up, shouting at Bea for not understanding her. Not listening. She said Bea judged her and her friends, that she didn't try to see things from her perspective. Maybe that was true. If she'd listened more closely to her angry girl, she might have been able to change what had happened. But in her memory, every time she tried to speak, Immy spat back a furious reply until it was better not to speak at all. The conflict was too constant, too hurtful.

Perhaps Immy would have responded differently if she'd known how Bea lay in bed craving her little girl. She might not have stormed off, slamming her door every time Bea asked her to put her washing away or go to bed at a decent time. If she knew that her mother smelled her pillow when she was out, to try to feel close to the girl who was all she had left after Oli died, would things have been different? The rift grew so vast neither of them knew how to cross it. Until Immy left and made the rift a chasm of miles.

Bea saw now that she hadn't only been grieving Oli in those hollow, dark times. She was grieving for her daughter, who was leaving her piece by tiny piece, and turning into a woman before Bea was ready. She saw that she had wanted Immy to stay needing her, to turn to her when she was suffering, to always be her safe place. Bea had mourned Immy then, and that pain surged through her again now. How long was she going to let it corrode her?

She opened the car and stepped onto the gravel. Crunching towards the front of the house, she dropped the door key back in her bag and knocked instead.

'Bea.' Ewan was wearing his weekend uniform of moleskin slacks and a shirt with tiny checks. His eyes scanned the driveway. Did he imagine she'd bring Immy here even if she had found her? 'You're back?'

'I am.' She forced herself to add, 'If that's okay?'

'Did you . . .?' He stopped and shifted his weight onto his other foot.

Bea stared down at his suede slippers and hated him. 'No. I don't know where she is.'

He opened the door then. She stepped in. It felt like a new contract had been drawn up between them and she'd signed it in Immy's blood.

'Aunty Bea!'

Bea's chest expanded at the sound of Phoebe's voice. She came tripping down the stairs and there she was, the only light to shine in all of this.

'Hello, poppet!' She knelt and took Phoebe in her arms. When she squeezed her, she felt her resist. Pulling back, she searched her face for signs that Joyce and Ewan had poisoned Phoebe against her while she was out of the house, but then noticed the real reason for her drawing back. 'Oh, sweetheart.'

The underside of Phoebe's jaw was a mass of blisters.

'It hurts,' said Phoebe, her bottom lip jutting out.

'It flared up overnight. We've put some cream on it, but it doesn't seem to be getting better.' Ewan crouched and inspected Phoebe's chin and neck. He turned to Bea. 'Any ideas?'

'I think I scratched it in the night.' Phoebe peeked under her fringe at Bea. 'I'm sorry.'

'Don't be sorry. I wasn't here to stop you, was I?' Guilt tightened her throat.

'You won't go again, will you?'

Bea avoided looking at Ewan. 'No, I won't go again.' She kissed Phoebe's forehead, scrunching her eyelids tight to stop the tears she could feel pooling.

Chapter Twenty-Seven

By the next morning, the blisters were filled with yellowy fluid and Phoebe couldn't sit still.

'I want to scratch it.'

Bea took her hands. 'You know why you can't, don't you? We don't want it to scar, poppet.'

Ewan stalked around the sitting room, rubbing the back of his head like a politician about to make the most important speech of his career. 'I should stay.'

Bea noted the word *should* and resented him more than ever. Why should she have to make him feel better about leaving his sick child?

'We'll be fine. If it's not better in the morning, I'll call Doctor Shah and see what she says.' She paused. 'I don't think she should be in school when it's like that. I'll email Mrs Andrews and get more work sent home.'

'Okay.'

She let her shoulders drop in relief.

Ewan crouched to speak to Phoebe, 'What do you think, Phoebs? Would you like Daddy to stay here until you get better?'

Bea hadn't expected him to ask that, and he went minutely up in her estimation. They both watched Phoebe chew over her response.

'Would Aunty Bea have to go away again if you stayed?'

Ouch. Bea couldn't help a surge of triumph at that, but it must sting Ewan to know any decision on him staying or going was dependent on Bea sticking around. 'I'm not going anywhere.' She watched indecision play on Ewan's face and, despite her judgement of him, was suddenly afraid he might cancel the car. That was the last thing she wanted. 'Seriously, we'll be fine.' She turned to Phoebe. 'Daddy can go back to work, can't he? Then, next time he's home, you can show him you're all better, can't you?'

Phoebe looked between the adults and Bea gave her a small nod of encouragement. 'Okay.'

There was a sharp knock at the door and Ewan left to answer it.

Phoebe shuffled closer to Bea on the sofa. 'It's good Daddy's going back. He said he's got a new friend called Camille who he wants to see tonight.'

'Camille?' She felt like a fool. Of course Ewan wanted to get back to his new life, leaving her to take care of his child. She wondered how much Ewan's indecision was just posturing. She was about to ask more but heard Joyce's voice in the hall.

'I don't want to stand in the rain like some kind of hawker,' she was saying as she shuffled into the room, followed by Ewan, who seemed somehow smaller in the shadow of his mother.

'Can you sort out a key for Mother?'

'No problem.' *It might take a while though*, Bea thought privately. *Maybe two years?*

'Is the other business dealt with?' Joyce looked from Ewan to Bea.

The other business? Wow. Bea bit down on the inside of her cheeks to stop the scream that was rising in her throat from escaping.

'All sorted,' Ewan muttered.

Words swam in Bea's head. It wasn't all sorted. Far from it. Immy was out there, somewhere, possibly suffering alone. Bea chomped her teeth together harder. Phoebe needed her now. She had to remain silent.

'Coffee, before the car comes?' Ewan asked Joyce.

'Earl Grey, please, Beatrice.'

She wanted to say that she didn't remember offering but found herself getting to her feet without argument and leaving the room to do their bidding.

* * *

Bea didn't join Joyce and Phoebe at the door to wave Ewan off. Closing her eyes with frustration, she heard Joyce's stick clomp along the hallway towards the kitchen after the door closed. She'd hoped she'd shuffle back to her own house and leave her and Phoebe to it.

'Could you take me to the surgery on Tuesday? I have an appointment at twelve.'

She stood in the doorway leaning heavily on the cane. Her wrist seemed fragile, and her knuckles were white with the effort.

'Take a seat.'

'I'm fine standing. Can you take me on Tuesday or not?'

Clearly the niceties had been withdrawn as a punishment. Punishment for what? Having a daughter of her own? 'I'll have to bring Phoebe, but I don't see why not. Is it your knees?'

Joyce turned unsteadily. 'Thank you.'

Bea noted the deflection. 'Let me help you home.' She stepped towards her, but Joyce banged her stick on the floor.

'I shall do perfectly well on my own.'

Bea stopped, unsure of what to do. Joyce was clearly not fine, but there was little she could do when the woman was being so hostile and defiant. She watched her limp along the hallway and unlatch the door, stepping gingerly onto the doorstep before pulling it closed behind her. When she was sure Joyce was at the end of the drive, she opened the door a sliver and peeked through the gap. Joyce turned right towards her house and Bea shoved her feet into her shoes and tiptoed as quietly as she could to the road, peering around the laurel bush, watching until Joyce turned safely into her drive.

Walking back to the house, she found Phoebe standing in the doorway, her little brow puckered. 'What are you doing out here?'

'I thought you were going away.'

'Oh, sweetheart. I told you; I'm not going anywhere. I was only making sure Grandma got home safe and sound.'

A six-year-old should never worry that those meant to care for her will desert her. What had she done to this poor child? She led her back inside and for the rest of the day Phoebe was like a warm and welcome limpet clinging tightly to her side.

* * *

'Why can't I sleep in your bed? My neck's itchy.' Phoebe lifted her hand to her throat and Bea caught it and kissed her fingers.

'It's time to get back to normal.' It was hard to fight

the battle when she was on the same side as the opponent but sleeping in the same bed as her six-year-old niece, however cosy and reassuring, probably wasn't ideal. As far as she was aware, Phoebe hadn't had another seizure, and Doctor Shah had said it was unlikely the epilepsy medication would have been affected beyond the procedure, so she needed to put her anxiety to one side and be the grown-up.

'I'm setting my alarm to wake me up every two hours to put your cream on and make sure you're alright.'

Reluctantly, Phoebe went to her own room and, after three more stories than usual, eventually fell asleep.

* * *

As promised, Bea dragged herself from bed every two hours, and the following morning, she was as groggy as she had been as a new mother. She remembered feeling an elemental connection with Immy, even then. When she fed her in the dead of night, it felt like they were the only two awake in the world. Immy's eyes would stare directly into hers as she suckled, one tiny hand resting on the top of Bea's breast, her milk flowing from her body into Immy's. She'd never felt more like an animal than when she was pregnant and breastfeeding. It felt primal and instinctive to care for her young.

It was an instinct she now had to fight.

* * *

The sound of Eddie's Lambretta buzzed outside, and Bea felt her spirits lifting as she opened the door and watched his thin face emerge from under his helmet.

'You must be sick of the sight of me,' she said.

'Not yet.' He paused in the doorway. 'How ya doing?'

She shrugged. 'Y'know.'

Phoebe bounced down the hall, then stopped at the sight of Eddie. She stood behind Bea, winding her hands around her legs.

Eddie crouched. 'You must be Phoebe?'

Phoebe's head poked out from behind Bea's thigh.

'I'm Eddie. I'm here to talk to Aunty Bea about your grandma.' He stood up, looking even taller than usual.

'I thought you said it's rude to talk about someone behind their back?' Phoebe's nose wrinkled and she watched Bea, who tried to keep a straight face.

'We're trying to help Grandma. We won't be saying anything mean about her.' *Although the temptation is strong.*

'Alright if I come in?' Eddie directed the question at Phoebe, who looked to Bea for confirmation, then nodded and let go of Bea's jeans.

* * *

'I'm not at school because my neck is sore. Look,' Phoebe informed Eddie, ten minutes later, apparently recovered from her shyness.

He examined Phoebe's neck and glanced at Bea. 'I'm no expert, but that looks like it might be infected.' He turned back to Phoebe. 'You're being very brave, aren't you?'

Bea handed him a steaming mug of tea. 'I spoke to her doctor at the birthmark clinic this morning and she said to carry on using the antibiotic cream, but if it's no better tomorrow, she'll call the burns unit in town and get her seen there.' She lifted Phoebe's chin. 'It's a bit better than last night, isn't it, poppet?'

'Aunty Bea put cream on it all night,' said Phoebe.

'All night?'

'Every few hours.' Bea pointed at the dark circles under her eyes. 'Thus.'

'You look fine to me.'

Bea's insides fluttered and she thought she noticed him redden, but when she looked again his face was its usual colour. She must have imagined it. She busied herself wiping up a drop of spilled milk and rinsing the cloth under the tap. 'Can you carry on with that book cover you were drawing for Mrs Andrews, please?' she said to Phoebe, who returned to the table and picked up her coloured pencils.

She ushered Eddie into the sitting room and closed the door. 'As I said on the phone, Joyce has a doctor's appointment tomorrow, but she won't tell me what it's for. I think she's having more trouble getting about than she's letting on.'

'Ewan emailed me over the weekend,' said Eddie, 'saying something similar.'

'She's a stubborn old goat.'

Eddie lifted an eyebrow.

'Well, she is. That house could be a death trap if she's struggling to move about – all those polished floors and that huge staircase. She'll kill herself rather than admit she's not coping.'

'I'll pop around to see her after I've drunk this. See if I can charm her into telling me what's going on.'

'Good luck with that.'

'I think you're underestimating my charm.'

'What charm?' She held her breath until she could see he knew she was joking.

Eddie laughed. 'Yeah, that's not really my skill set, is it?'

'Charm is overrated.' She looked down at her hands, hoping he didn't see her blush. She couldn't explain it, but this man had had more of an effect on her than anyone since Oli, although acknowledging that made her feel disloyal. The familiar sting of guilt soured the tea in her mouth and try as she might, she couldn't get rid of the taste.

Chapter Twenty-Eight

'I'm sorry I won't be able to take you to the surgery,' said Bea, standing on Joyce's doorstep, wondering why she hadn't been invited in. The end of November had brought icy winds and Bea's ears stung with the cold. Joyce hadn't allowed Eddie in on Monday, either, making him wait on the doorstep then telling him she had pressing matters to attend to. You couldn't help some people.

'It was the only appointment the burns clinic had available,' Bea explained. 'I've arranged a taxi for you. They know they have to wait until you've been seen.'

'That will cost an arm and a leg.' Joyce held the latch with one hand and the cane with the other, but still didn't look completely stable.

'I'll pay.'

'That's not the issue.'

Then what is? thought Bea, exasperated. She couldn't be in two places at once, and since one of the blisters under Phoebe's chin was weeping, she had to take the first appointment available to see a specialist. It wasn't her fault the appointment clashed with Joyce's trip to the doctor's. 'I need to get back. Phoebe's on her own.'

'On you go, then,' said Joyce, and closed the door in her face.

* * *

Bea was still seething when she pulled into the hospital car park. Joyce should want her to put Phoebe first. That's what adults were meant to do. And what she was paid for. She drove around the one-way system, praying to the god of car parking spaces to reveal a spot to her. Someone reversed out a few cars down and she thanked the gods, but they were just straightening up. Of course they were. She drove on.

With minutes to spare, Bea searched the board in the hospital reception for the burns unit. Second Floor. She pulled Phoebe towards the lifts and tapped her foot impatiently as they waited. The doors eventually opened to reveal a nurse pushing a man in a wheelchair with a drip dangling above. The nurse was kicking at something at the base of the chair. 'Sorry,' he said. 'The brake's stuck.'

Bea smiled tightly. 'No worries.'

The nurse carried on kicking at the brake as the man sat, his mouth hanging open, drool leaking down his stubbled chin. Bea hated herself for her impatience. The door spasmed into action and Bea leaped forwards to stop it from closing as the nurse released the brake and she almost collided with the man's bare knees. They halted abruptly on the threshold of the lift, the drip bag swinging above the man's head. The nurse and Bea did an apologetic dance, before managing to switch places.

'Want to press number two?' she said to Phoebe. She checked her watch then reminded herself hospital appointments rarely ran on time, so she could relax. Phoebe was seeing a specialist. It was all going to be okay.

* * *

'Nothing to be concerned about,' said the consultant fifteen minutes later, taking off his latex gloves and smiling at Phoebe. 'Just a little infection. I'll give you a stronger antibiotic cream. It should sort that out in a couple of days. Pop a pair of socks over your hands at night if you can't resist touching your chin.'

'Thank you. Thank you so much.' Relief made Bea light-headed, and she could have skipped back to the lifts.

'We'll have to get you some scratch mitts,' she teased Phoebe, 'like babies wear.'

'I'm not a baby,' said Phoebe indignantly. She followed Bea to the lift and waited while she tried to work out where to find the hospital pharmacy.

'The basement this time,' she said, thankful the lift was empty. 'Press minus one.'

The lift jolted, then swooshed briefly downwards, before stopping. The doors bounced open, and Bea gave a polite smile to the man waiting to get in.

Something caught her eye a few steps away in the foyer. A girl in a hoodie with bleached blonde hair was looking at the list of departments, exactly where Bea had been standing twenty minutes earlier. Bea's heart raced as she recognised the tilt of the head, the way she stood, one leg crossed in front of the other. Then she turned her gaunt face towards the lift and, as Bea opened her mouth to call her name, the aluminium door slid closed and the lift dropped, taking her heart with it.

She pressed the button to take them back to the ground floor, her finger bending backwards with the force. The button's orange surround illuminated but the lift kept falling. When the doors opened on the lower level, she grabbed Phoebe's hand and scoured the corridor for signs to the stairs.

'Why are we going back up?' Phoebe trailed behind her as she ran to the steps.

'Come on.'

'You're hurting me.' Phoebe pulled her hand from Bea's grasp and Bea grabbed her fingers again, willing her to keep up.

'This way.' Her breathing was heavy with the effort of pulling a wriggling Phoebe behind her up the stairs. She gripped her hand tighter. A couple tried to pass but there wasn't room for all of them. She didn't slow down, bumping her shoulder against the white wall and forging on, despite the woman tutting and Phoebe's protestations.

Her heart was thumping when she punched through the swing doors at the top of the stairwell. She searched the foyer, scanning every face, looking for a girl with blonde hair and dark roots. But she couldn't find her.

Phoebe was crying quietly by her side, and Immy was gone.

* * *

Back at Ewan's, Bea watched for the car bringing Joyce home. When it rushed past the end of Ewan's drive, she hurried Phoebe into her trainers and trotted down the road with her, singing as they went. The last thing she felt like doing was singing, but she was trying to make up for what had happened in the hospital. Phoebe's tears had brought her out of her trance and the guilt of causing them was acute.

Joyce opened the door when Bea knocked, but not wide enough to allow them in.

'How did it go at the doctor's?' said Bea. 'I picked up a message from Eddie. He said you've cancelled him twice now and when he popped around again you wouldn't let him in.'

'That man's becoming a pest, ringing all the time and calling without an appointment.'

'It's his job.'

'You can tell him I'm fine. I don't need his interference,' Joyce snapped. She peered down at Phoebe. 'How is your skin?'

Bea was pleased she remembered to ask, even if it was an obvious stab at distraction. 'All okay, thank goodness. Can we come in?'

'It's not a good time.'

When people said that it was usually because they were busy or had someone inside they didn't want you to see. Bea couldn't imagine what Joyce could possibly be busy doing since she now did all of the woman's cooking and washing. Perhaps she was hiding a man. Bea had a sudden image of Joyce astride an oily gigolo on a kitchen chair and almost laughed.

'I need a wee.' Phoebe jumped up and down.

'We'll just pop in for the toilet and leave you to it.'

Joyce pushed the door closed a fraction. 'You have plenty of toilets at home.'

'What's going on?'

Joyce gave an exaggerated sigh. 'I haven't had time to tidy up, what with appointments and everything.'

'That's why Eddie's been trying to see you. It's his job to arrange help with all the stuff you can't . . .' She wanted to say *manage* but knew that wouldn't go down well. 'The things you haven't got time to do yourself.'

'I don't want strangers in my home.'

Bea set her face in a smile, 'Let us in. I'll have a quick tidy around for you. Okay?'

Joyce seemed to consider the proposition and with a resigned breath, she opened the door. 'If you must.'

'What's that smell?' Phoebe's face scrunched and Bea was hit by the stench of rotting food.

Joyce tutted. 'I thought you needed the toilet.'

Phoebe kicked off her shoes and bounced through the kitchen to the toilet beside the utility room.

'I haven't had a chance to put the bins out.' Joyce leaned heavily on the stick as she walked in front of Bea. She was noticeably limping. There were leaflets and flyers scattered on the wooden floor. Bea stooped to gather them up.

There'd never been so much as a cup on a draining board in all the time Bea had known Joyce, so to see the disarray of her kitchen was enough to make her stop in the doorway, aghast. Dirty plates filled the sink. China cups with red lipstick smeared rims sat on every surface.

'Is this why you refused to let Eddie in?'

Joyce turned away without replying. Bea scanned the floor and found the root of the smell. A rubbish bag nestled by the wall was spilling its contents onto the floor. The top was tied closed. Bea dipped her head down and found a jagged hole torn in the bottom. 'Mice?'

'Possibly rats,' replied Joyce matter of factly, her head held high.

Bea wondered what it cost her to appear nonchalant. Her pride made her prefer living with rats over asking for help. 'Why didn't you say?' she asked, softly.

'You've been busy, haven't you?'

It was hard to stay sympathetic with Joyce for long. Bea might have known this would be her fault. She ran hot water into the sink. 'Ewan was home last weekend.'

Joyce flapped her arm and looked away. 'He has enough to worry about.'

Phoebe skipped into the room. 'Why is it messy in here?'

Bea remembered the blister under her chin and felt a surge of panic. 'Wash your hands, poppet.'

'I just did.'

Bea took her elbow and led her over to the sink, pulling her skinny arms so they were over the porcelain bowl. She squirted soap from the dispenser and rubbed it over her fingers before holding them under the tap.

'Oh, for goodness' sake. It's a bit of mess, not a nuclear fallout zone.'

'She has an open wound,' Bea snapped. 'If she scratches it with dirty fingers, God knows what will happen.'

'You're overreacting. It's an old house. All old houses have vermin at one time or another.'

'What's vermin?' said Phoebe, allowing Bea to rub soap between her fingers.

'Rats.' Joyce seemed to relish the word, as if not being afraid was some sort of show of strength.

Phoebe pulled her fingers from Bea's and squealed.

'Don't be dramatic,' Joyce snapped.

'I think that's a fairly normal response,' Bea growled. She opened the drawer where Joyce kept clean tea towels and checked for droppings before pulling one out and drying Phoebe's hands. 'I'm going to take you two back home, then I'll call pest control.'

'I can manage, thank you.'

But you can't, can you? thought Bea. 'I'm sure you can, but wouldn't you prefer to spend some time with Phoebe?' Joyce's lips were still tight. 'She needs to write about her dream house for school. Perhaps you could help her with that.' She walked towards the hall. Phoebe and Joyce followed.

'I'm going to have a slide instead of stairs and a swimming pool in my bedroom,' said Phoebe. 'What would you have in your perfect house?' She regarded Joyce earnestly.

Joyce's eyes misted. 'This is my perfect house,' she said, her voice softer than Bea had heard it in years. 'It always has been.'

'Don't you want a swimming pool?' asked Phoebe, pulling her trainers back on and dragging the Velcro fastenings tight.

'When the boys were small, that would have been nice, perhaps.'

Her mother-in-law's gaze swung around the wood-panelled hallway. Bea imagined her remembering Oli and Ewan careering around the house, young and boisterous. Or perhaps she was thinking of her own childhood, when her grandfather built this house. How did the wood smell when it was first nailed onto these walls? How grand it must have felt to a child.

'A slide instead of stairs might be useful now, too,' said Bea.

Joyce glared at her. 'I don't know what you're insinuating, but I'm perfectly happy with my staircase, thank you.'

'Fine. I still think you're going to have to stay with us until pest control have been.'

'Stop making a fuss. I've told you, I'm perfectly fine where I am.'

Bea raised her arms. 'Okay. Have it your way.' She turned to leave. 'Don't complain to me when you've got Bubonic plague.'

'Don't be childish.'

Bea took another step towards the door. 'Fine. But I wouldn't want a rat running across my face in the middle of the night.'

Joyce tutted. 'Reverse psychology. Very clever. Alright. But I'm coming straight home as soon as the little visitors have left.' She made for the door. 'You'll find my washbag under the sink.'

Bea sighed and trudged up the sweeping staircase to gather Joyce's things, saying words under her breath she imagined even the century-old wooden panels had never heard before.

* * *

By ten o'clock that night, Bea felt like she'd wrestled two toddlers into bed. Phoebe's blister had stopped weeping, but she was still angling to sleep in Bea's room. The thought of Joyce's reaction was enough to make her insist Phoebe went to sleep in her own bed, and after a while, she was drowsy enough not to argue any longer. Bea hated herself for still caring what that woman thought.

Joyce was in the room at the far end of the house but Bea could hear her snoring as she tiptoed downstairs with her folder of work. She'd been catching up with her studies and it was going better than she could have hoped. All of her assignments had been given distinctions so far, but one was still outstanding. She sank into the sofa cushions and opened the folder, contemplating making a coffee to try to stay awake.

There was the sound of footsteps on the gravel outside and the sensor light clicked on, shedding a yellow haze through the curtains. She stood and crossed to the window, heartbeat quickening. Opening the curtain minutely, she saw a thin figure standing near the front door. Whoever it was, they looked like they were trying to gather the courage to knock rather than ram the door down. The figure's arms wound around their middle, and they seemed to be rocking.

A second before the sensor light went out, she noticed the tilt of the head, the legs crossed over each other. She dropped the curtain and rushed to the front door. When she opened it, Immy was standing on the driveway, the hood of a grey sweatshirt pulled over her hair.

'Immy.' Her breath came quick and fast.

'Sorry I didn't come to the café. I—'

Bea glanced over her shoulder. She stepped outside, pulling the door to, imagining Joyce's reaction to seeing Immy on Ewan's doorstep. 'I've been worried about you. I saw you at the hospital. I tried to . . . The lift door closed and . . .'

Immy drew her arms tighter around her waist. Her eyes were hollows in the shadowy light.

'Why were you . . .' Before she could finish the sentence Immy staggered to the side and retched, holding her abdomen as her body convulsed.

'God. Immy.' Her instinct was to grab her and pull her in. But then she remembered the piece of paper with the address on it.

She tried to steady her voice, folding her fingers into her fists to stop herself from reaching out. 'Immy. Are you using drugs?'

Immy's head turned first, then her body. She straightened up and her lips parted, but no sound came out.

'Immy?'

'No. I . . .' Immy shook her head. She scrunched her eyes closed and sighed. 'I was going to ask if I could stay for a few days, but—'

Bea swallowed. This was the hardest thing she'd said to Immy since telling her about Oli's cancer. 'I need you to get clean. Then we can talk.' Tough love. That's what Immy needed now. It was for the best. For all of their sakes.

'Clean?'

'Off whatever it is making you . . .' She waved her arm towards where Immy had thrown up, although there was no vomit that she could make out. 'I can't . . .' She curled and uncurled her fingers, trying to find words to explain why her actions needed to go against what her heart and body were both screaming for. 'I need to think about Phoebe.'

Immy exhaled and nodded. 'Received and understood. You need to put Phoebe first, I get it.' She raised her arm in a weak salute and turned away.

Immy's understanding made the choice Bea was forced to make even more agonising. She stepped forwards, her arm reaching towards Immy of its own accord. 'Where will you go?' This was wrong. She should let her in. Sod Ewan and Joyce. Immy was her child.

But Phoebe. Hadn't she been through enough? Bea's heart ripped in two in her chest. How could she choose between her own lost, wayward daughter, and the little girl who now relied on her?

'Don't worry. I'll be fine. I've got a back-up plan.' She turned to look at Bea and the sensor sprang back to life, lighting up her sad face. 'I don't blame you,' she said. 'I'd do the same if I were you. I understand why you can't forgive me. I haven't forgiven myself either.'

'Immy,' Bea said. Her knees sagged and the name came out weakly, like she was deflating. Next time she said it, it was a whisper and Immy was already walking away.

Chapter Twenty-Nine

Lying in bed, the sound of Immy's retching replayed in Bea's head. What if she was sick and sleeping rough while Bea lay in this king-sized bed? Every time her limbs relaxed into the memory foam, guilt made her shift position. She didn't want to sleep. She didn't deserve to. She'd spent the last three years wishing she'd listened to Immy when she'd been able to, and the moment she was given another chance, she had reverted to her old self. And now Immy was gone again.

* * *

The next morning, she got Phoebe ready for school and served Joyce breakfast in bed on a tray. Her eyelids scratched across her eyeballs, but she had to keep going. This was the choice she'd made.

Joyce shuffled upright, her frame tiny in the enormous bed. Long plaits hung over her bony shoulders, making her look like a grey, shrivelled version of a child. 'I'm quite capable of making my own breakfast.'

'I thought it might be a treat.' She didn't add that the

221

longer Joyce spent in her bedroom the better. She was in no mood for her sniping this morning.

'Crumbs in the bed?'

'Suit yourself.' She plonked the tray on the end near her feet. Ignoring the coffee slopping into the saucer, she walked from the room.

* * *

At the school, the ache of loss intensified. She wanted to cling to Phoebe, or at least sit next to her in every lesson, shadow her at break and lunch to make sure she didn't scratch her sore skin. 'I've given your cream to the lady on reception,' she reminded her. 'And you can have some Calpol if it hurts. Kelly knows that. Okay?'

Phoebe nodded, hanging on to her hand. She gazed up at her imploringly, as if she knew all she had to do was ask and Bea would take her home. She would. In a heartbeat. Mrs Andrews came out of the classroom when the bell rang.

'It's lovely to have you back, Phoebe. We're making Christmas cards today. That will be fun, won't it?' She held her hand out to Phoebe and Bea forced herself to loosen her fingers. 'I know it's only the end of November, but I love getting ready for Christmas. It's nice to have something to look forward to, isn't it?' She smiled at Bea who nodded, despite no longer sharing the sentiment.

Sydney appeared behind Mrs Andrews. 'Phoebe!' she said. 'Come on. Want to sit next to me?'

Phoebe's hands slid from Bea's, and she took a couple of tentative steps towards the classroom.

'In you go,' said Mrs Andrews. She smiled a sympathetic smile at Bea. 'We'll look after her.'

'I hope so.' Bea knew that wasn't fair. There wasn't much a teacher could do to stop children being children.

But Phoebe was precious. Bea had given up a lot – her own daughter – to keep her safe and now she was handing her over to the care of people who hadn't invested so much. It didn't feel right.

'Have a good day,' said Mrs Andrews, and then she was turning and closing the door with Phoebe on the inside. Bea's breath fogged then disappeared as she looked at the space beside her. It was like a magic trick: she was breathing out dry ice, and when it cleared it left a gap where all the people she loved should be. Abracadabra. All alone again.

* * *

The pest control man was waiting for her outside Joyce's when she got back. He was wiry apart from a round belly protruding like a bowling ball stuffed under his company t-shirt. She took a deep breath in and tried to switch her mind away from how Phoebe was coping. Where Immy might be right now.

Joyce would have a conniption if she glimpsed the van with *Pest Exterminator* emblazoned on its side sitting in her drive for all the residents of The Crescent to see. That thought cheered her, slightly.

'Lovely old houses, these,' said the man, exposing sharp yellow teeth. He scratched his head under his baseball cap. 'Riddled with pests, though. Worse than a city tower block for rats.'

Bea imagined Joyce in a urine-stinking concrete stairwell. The image quickly changed to Immy. She shuddered. 'Let's try to get rid of the little blighters as quickly as possible, okay?'

'She staying with you, then?' He winked grotesquely and grinned, exposing the dark spaces where his back teeth should have been.

'How did you guess?' Bea opened the door. 'It will all be humane, won't it?'

'Do I look like a man who would hurt a poor innocent rodent?'

He looked like a man who might catch a rat and skin it alive with his pointy teeth, but Bea didn't think it prudent to say so. She pushed open the door, then sniffed. The smell seemed to have gone. Leading the man through to the kitchen, she smelled the air, then examined the floor. The rubbish bag had disappeared. She glanced around, noticing a smattering of brown pellets near the skirting board.

'Yep. Infested,' said the man.

'You alright here for a minute?' The man nodded and Bea retraced her steps to the front door. She went outside and around to the green wheelie bin, lifting the lid. The smell hit her straight away and she dropped the lid down with a bang. Try as she might, she couldn't remember taking the bag from the kitchen to the bin. While she lay awake last night, she'd chastised herself for not shifting it, thinking she'd foolishly left it for the rats to rifle through and scatter. All she'd wanted was to get the three of them out of there. Especially Phoebe. But here it was.

She must be going mad.

Back inside, she found the man on all fours examining the wooden frame of the doors leading to the garden. Without lifting his head, he said, 'I think I've found where they're getting in, so that's good.'

Bea followed to where he was pointing.

'See this hole here?'

There was a small gap where the wood had rotted.

'It's good news because I suspect the nest is outside, not under the floorboards or anywhere tricky.' He poked at the rotten wood with his finger and splinters came away and scattered on the tiles. 'I've got a mate who could patch this up. Want me to give him a ring? If he closes this and I set traps along the wall outside, and a couple in here, I think we can get your mother-in-law back in situ quick-smart.'

He straightened up and rolled his shoulders. 'Won't be cheap though.'

I'll act like a true James, she thought bitterly. *Throw money at the problem and make it go away.* 'Please, go ahead,' she said. 'Money is no object.'

He raised his eyebrows but didn't comment.

* * *

'You'll have to stay here for a few days, I'm afraid,' she said to Joyce when she got back to Ewan's.

Joyce let out an exaggerated sigh. 'If I must.'

From then on, she kept out of the way when Bea was home, so much so that Bea felt like she was hiding.

'Would you like to help us decorate the Christmas tree?' she asked on the second night when Joyce stood to leave the table straight after dinner.

'Yes, help us, Grandma!' squealed Phoebe, hopping from foot to foot.

'I'm happy with my book, thank you.' She said goodnight and limped from the room. Bea listened to her grunting with the effort of getting upstairs but didn't dare to offer help.

A man had delivered the tree that morning. Bea didn't even know there was a service where a perfectly sized, symmetrical tree could be ordered, delivered, and installed in your sitting room. She'd presumed at some stage she'd have to do what she and Oli did each year and go down to the local garden centre, tie a tree to the roof of the car, then hope for the best when it was released from the green netting when she got home.

They'd had some disasters over the years. Once, the tree was as wide as it was tall, and Oli had to trim back the branches so they could see the television. Another year the tree looked resplendent when they went to bed, but the next morning all the needles lay in a pile on the floor, the decorations hanging on dead, brown fronds.

'Looks like it's me and you, kiddo,' she said to Phoebe, who was twirling around in excitement. Opening the box of decorations Ewan had directed her to at the back of the understairs cupboard, she pulled out a laminated picture of a reindeer coloured in with random strokes of crayon. Her eyes stung.

Somewhere in the storage unit, she had a box of her own homemade decorations. Immy had made many over the years, presenting them like the treasures they were at the end of school days in long-gone, hopeful Decembers; back when Christmas was a fizzing, popping light beckoning them through cold winter days. Now Christmas was the dark thing, looming.

The thought of all those decorations sitting in an airless room made her lungs compress. She let Phoebe decorate this picture-perfect tree, pretending she preferred to watch while Phoebe placed baubles and strings of shimmering beads only as high as she could reach. Really, she couldn't bring herself to touch the colourful signs that Christmas was on its way.

Another Christmas without Immy, and this one felt worse even than the first one. Because this time, she'd had a choice.

* * *

Joyce's door frame was repaired two days later. Bea cleaned and disinfected the house and, when she was certain no more pellets were appearing, she helped Joyce settle back in.

'You never told me what the doctor said.' She opened Joyce's fridge and put the milk and butter she'd brought inside.

'He wants me to get checked for osteoporosis,' said Joyce, her voice full of disdain. 'As though knowing my bones are brittle is going to make them less so.' She tutted and limped into the sitting room.

Bea followed her. 'It's worth investigating.'

'I don't need to be prodded and poked to be told I'm getting old. I'm perfectly aware of that fact already.' She collapsed into her wingback chair and rested the stick against the arm.

'I just think—'

'I'd quite like to be left alone now, please.' Joyce cut her off. 'I would like a moment's peace.'

She was acting as though she'd had to sleep through raves at Ewan's house instead of the chatter and exuberance of a six-year-old. Admittedly, Phoebe had been livelier than usual since going back to school. She seemed to have a new energy now that Sydney had taken her under her wing. When she came back in the afternoons, she was less clingy. She didn't need Bea to be with her every minute. She hadn't asked to sleep in Bea's room, either. And although she knew that this was exactly how it should be, Bea felt bereft.

* * *

When Phoebe was in bed and all the clearing up was done, she called Jan and invited her to come around.

'You've got the house to yourself again?' said Jan,

227

handing over a bottle of wine and kicking off her shoes. She pulled a pair of fluffy slippers from her bag. 'I came prepared; it's cold enough for frostbite tonight. Wouldn't want to lose a toe.' She wiggled her toes inside her polka-dotted socks then shoved them in the slippers.

'Nice. Come through. Phoebe's already asleep.' She ignored Jan's raised eyebrow. Opening the fridge, she took out the bottle she'd started earlier, topped up her own glass and poured a fresh one for Jan.

'Drinking on your own? That's not like you.'

'I've gone wild,' she said, walking through to the sitting room. 'It's not like I've got any brain surgery to perform tomorrow.' She clinked her glass against Jan's. 'You on shift in the morning?'

'Nope.' Jan grinned. 'But I'll tell you who is.'

'Go on?' They flopped onto the couch.

'Our Ciara!' Jan tucked her chin back. 'She's on break-fasts! No more lying in bed 'til noon for that one.' She slapped a cushion and grinned.

'Is she getting on alright?'

'She loves it. I think this might be the making of her. The pay's rubbish, though.'

'Lynn not trying to get her to work for free yet?'

Jan chortled. 'Not yet. Give it time.' She dropped her voice. 'I tell you what, though; she reckons there's some-thing dodgy going on with that creepy Dave bloke.'

'Oh yeah?' Bea felt a pang to be back in the staffroom at Sweetingdale, gossiping with Jan, or sharing a cup of tea with Vera. Suddenly her life felt suffocatingly small.

'He's moved into the staff accommodation with Lynn, and people have said they've heard banging and shouting.'

Bea topped up Jan's glass. 'Couples argue, I suppose.'

'But Ciara says it's like he's running the place now.

Lynn's all like—' She dropped her lips in a downturned crescent moon and made her eyes doleful.

'Aww.' She remembered Lynn threatening her in the car park and the sympathy withered. 'Any more thefts?'

Jan almost spat out the gulp she'd just taken. She waved her index finger in the air. 'Yes! I can't believe I forgot to tell you. Mrs Prentice, on Marigold corridor – you know, the one with the eye patch.' She waited for Bea to nod. 'She's lost a gold watch, and she swears it's been stolen.'

Bea felt guilty to be pleased at the news. Mrs Prentice was a nice old lady, even if she did refuse to allow them to call her by her first name. 'Any suspects?'

'Our Ciara is certain it's Creepy Dave. He keeps popping up inside. He's not even supposed to be in communal areas, never mind the corridors.'

'Who's she going to complain to, though? Lynn?'

'Exactly.'

They sat in silence for a minute.

'You're coming to Vera's birthday lunch next week, aren't you?'

'I'm not sure I can face it.' She traced the embroidered hummingbird pattern on the cushion with her finger.

Jan turned to her. 'Oh, come on. Phoebe's back at school, Her Ladyship's returned to her own castle, you live on The Crescent and drive around in a Range Rover. What better way to rub Lynn's nose in it?'

'Immy came again.' Bea hadn't meant to say anything, but it just came out.

'Why didn't you say? Here's me blithering on. What happened?'

She put her glass on the coffee table and rolled her shoulders. 'She was sick.' She gestured towards the door. 'In the bush.' The scene rolled over in her head. 'Well, she retched, anyway. She was—' She scraped her fingers through her hair, tugging at the knots then releasing it to fall onto her neck. 'She was a mess. Drugs, possibly. I don't know. I think.'

'Oh, love.' Jan put her hand on Bea's, her thumb stroking the skin.

Bea blinked back tears. 'I sent her away.' Her voice broke. Jan shoved the cushion out of the way, pulling Bea into the softness of her chest, her warm, heavy arm wrapping her up and rocking her gently backwards and forwards.

'I sent her away. My own daughter. She was sick and I told her she couldn't stay.'

'You did what you thought was right,' Jan said, into her hair.

Her voice was quiet, but Bea could still detect the question underneath the statement. It sounded like she thought Bea had made the wrong choice. But it felt like a long time since she had made any choices that were truly her own.

Chapter Thirty

Bea wiped her damp palms on her trousers as she waited to be buzzed through the outside door at Sweetingdale. In reception, the familiar gaudy Christmas tree twinkled, the lights fighting their way through the heavy cloak of baubles and thick, silver tinsel. She'd dressed up for Vera's birthday party, but the black floaty top and skinny jeans made her feel out of place. She missed her maroon tunic. She knew where she was in that. Who she was.

Her stomach tightened as she was buzzed in by someone she didn't know. *More temps*, she thought. *Poor residents, never seeing the same face twice*. Walking along the corridor, she passed pictures of spitfire aeroplanes and classic cars, draped with the same thick strands of tinsel as the tree. She could feel the synthetic threads of it in her fingers. She was the one who'd draped it over the frames on the first of December for the last few years. Who'd done the job this year? Would she even know them? She lifted a piece that had come loose and hung it across a watercolour of an Aston Martin DB5.

The sound of big band music and chatter spilled into

the corridor as she approached the restaurant. It was called a restaurant in Sweetingdale. In a council-run care home, it would be a canteen, but not here, where there was nylon carpet instead of lino and you could order red or white wine with your meals. Somebody had stuck a 'Happy Birthday' banner above the double doors and the number '85' on each of the glass panes. Bea smiled through her nerves. She was glad someone was making a fuss for Vera.

Jan was the first to see her when she stepped into the crowded room. She bounded over and gave her a huge cuddle. When she let go, she stepped back and looked her up and down. 'Hello, Mrs *I Live on The Crescent*.'

Bea's skin prickled. 'God. Have I overdone it? I was nervous. Shit, I look like mutton, don't I?'

Jan's face crinkled. 'Are you having a laugh? You look amazing.'

Bea pointed at Jan's tunic. 'I'd rather be in one of those.'

'I'd swop, but I think I'm slimmer than you, so . . .' Jan shimmied, her breasts wobbling under her clothes.

'Stop it, you idiot.'

Bea was still laughing when Vera joined them. She held out the foil bag she'd brought holding the posh hand cream wrapped in silver paper. 'Happy birthday, gorgeous!'

Vera held out her arms and Bea leaned down to gently hug her. 'You really shouldn't have.' She put her mouth close to Bea's ear. 'I still get great joy from the last thing you bought for me.'

Bea furrowed her brow.

'The calendar.' Vera giggled.

'Oh. Right.' She pointed at the bag. 'Fewer naked men in there, I'm afraid.'

A deep voice rumbled behind her. 'Did I hear someone say naked men?'

232

Bea turned to see a tall man with slicked-back, greying hair, with a lascivious grin on his face. He shouted across the room, 'Lynn, did you hear that? This one's brought naked men to the party. You'd love that, wouldn't you?' He swigged from a bottle of lager.

Lynn sped towards them from the other side of the room. 'Bea,' she said. 'I'm surprised to see you here.'

'Ah, this is Bea, is it?' The man peered at her through narrowed eyes, the smile gone from his face.

'I asked her to come.' Vera's voice was curt. 'This,' she said, pointing to the man, her voice thick with disdain, 'is Dave. A friend of Lynn's.'

'Bit more than that.' Dave pulled Lynn towards him by the waist and nuzzled her neck. Lynn looked mortified, but when she tried to prise herself free his grip appeared to tighten.

'Good Lord,' Vera whispered under her breath. Bea was too astonished to say anything.

Vera took her elbow. 'Come and say hello to Kenny.' When they were at a safe distance, Vera spoke quietly. 'I'm no fan of that woman, as you know, but I'm beginning to think she might have bitten off more than she can chew with that one.'

Bea glanced over her shoulder to see Lynn try to take the bottle from Dave's hand. He snatched it away. The way his lip curled, and Lynn instantly dropped her arm, made her think Vera may be right.

Kenny was sitting on a checked armchair near the window. Bea approached him with a broad smile, but when he recognised her, he shifted his eyes away.

'Kenny?' She tried to catch his gaze, but his eyes kept flitting away. She bit her bottom lip, and scanned the room, assessing how many people here thought she was a thief. She bent down and brought her face to the same level as Kenny's. 'I didn't take that money, Kenny. I never would. I promise. I never would.' His mouth remained clamped closed, so she forced herself to stand and step away. She spied Mrs Prentice next to a buffet laid out along the serving hatch. She made her way towards her and was relieved to see her smile in recognition.

'Hello, dear. How are you?'

'Good, thank you.' She lowered her voice. 'Can I ask you something? It's a bit delicate. I heard your watch went missing recently and—'

'Bea.'

She turned to see Lynn standing very close. 'This is a party. Guests don't want to be reminded of difficult personal events.' She caught Mrs Prentice in her sharp gaze. 'I'm sorry, Mrs Prentice. Please, do go back to the buffet. The vol-au-vents are delicious.'

Lynn gripped Bea's elbow and led her away. 'Since you no longer work here, I think it's best you leave the sleuthing to those of us who do.'

Bea's shoulders tensed. 'You were the one who implicated me. Kenny can't even look me in the eye, so I think I have every right to find out what's actually going on.'

'You want to ruin Vera's birthday?'

Bea ignored the question. 'So, if things are still going missing and I'm not around, who's in the frame now?'

'As I said, this is Sweetingdale business. Not yours.'

She straightened her spine. 'When I finish my diploma, I will manage my own care home, and I'll do a damned better job of it than you do.'

She wasn't expecting Lynn to laugh. The sound was loud and ugly, and it made her throat tighten and her temples throb. It seemed like everyone in the place turned to watch her humiliation. Sweat dampened her armpits. The room was suddenly unbearably hot.

Lynn leaned in and said, 'You keep telling yourself that, love.' She turned and wandered away as if Bea was of no further interest. Half-formed, clever retorts occurred to her. She wanted to follow Lynn, grab her, swing her around and say something smart and pithy, loud enough for everyone to hear and be impressed. Instead, she stood perfectly still, radiating enough heat to singe passers-by, while everyone else chatted on, oblivious. She would show her. One day, she would make that woman eat her words. But for now, she needed to leave.

The door opened easily and the air in the corridor cooled her burning face. She wouldn't ordinarily leave without saying goodbye, but when she was out in the corridor, it seemed like the only option she could bear.

* * *

Bea and Phoebe made their daily trip down to Joyce's house with her dinner, the dish warming Bea's hands through her gloves. A frost sparkled on the road under the streetlights but when they arrived at Joyce's, the driveway and doorstep were clear of ice. Bea poked at scattered salt crystals with the toe of her boot.

'That was a good idea,' said Bea, when Joyce opened the door.

'What was?' She let them into the warm hallway.

Bea's skin stung with the change of temperature. 'Sprinkling salt on the drive and step. We nearly slid on black ice on the way here, didn't we?'

'It was funny,' said Phoebe.

Joyce appeared confused. 'I did no such thing.'

Bea opened the door and examined the threshold. Joyce

peered past her. There were definitely grains of white crystals peppering the step. 'Look.'

'Well, it wasn't my doing. Maybe it was that busybody chap.' She clicked her fingers, clearly annoyed that her memory failed to jump to attention.

'Eddie?'

'Yes. Him. Maybe that's part of his remit, to stop the biddies breaking their necks in inclement weather.'

'I'd be surprised; that sounds above and beyond.' Bea closed the door again and took Joyce's meal into the kitchen. 'And he's not a busybody. He's a social worker.' Joyce followed slowly. 'No more furry friends?'

'Not that I'm aware of.' She peered into the dish. 'What's this?'

'Gnocchi with ham hock.' Bea was experimenting more now Ewan wasn't around to be the concierge for Joyce's dinner requests.

'It's like a potato pasta thingy,' said Phoebe.

'I know what gnocchi is,' snapped Joyce and Phoebe's face fell. Joyce's face softened and she looked like she might apologise, but she shifted position and winced, her face hardening again.

'Clever girl,' said Bea. 'I didn't know any different types of pasta at your age.' Phoebe tried to smile but Bea could see she was winded. 'Come on, let's try to slip-slide our way home. See you tomorrow, Joyce.'

Joyce sat and turned her dinner over with a fork. 'Could you please check the doors into the garden are locked before you go? It's probably my imagination, but I've been hearing peculiar noises around the house.'

Bea tried to read Joyce's expression to see if she was worried. Her face was inscrutable. 'What kind of noises?'

'Like someone moving around.'

Bea checked the handle on the doors to the garden. They were locked. 'Has anything gone missing?'

'I don't think so.'

'And you've heard it more than once?'

'Over the last few days, yes.'

'Why didn't you say anything?'

Joyce dropped her fork on the dish. The clatter made Phoebe jump. 'I'm saying it now.'

Bea felt the muscles in her jaw contract as she clenched her teeth. 'Have you still got a key under the planter by the back door?'

'Yes. For emergencies.'

'I'll bring that in, just for now.' She put her hands up to stop Joyce from arguing and went out into the cold air to retrieve the hidden key.

Joyce tutted when she came back in. 'In my day you could leave the doors wide open. The youth of today have gone feral, that's the problem. No discipline.'

Her voice was tight and angry and she looked pointedly at Bea, who in that moment could have quite happily walked out and left her to her wretched life. Instead, she took a breath into the bottom of her lungs and said, 'If you like, you could stay with us again until . . .' Until what? God, that was an awful thought – Joyce living with her indefinitely.

Joyce scoffed. 'I asked you to check the locks, not treat me like a stray dog.'

Bea didn't say another word. She simply took Phoebe's hand and walked from the house.

Her breath fogging in front of her, Phoebe said, 'Why is Grandma always cross?'

'I don't know, poppet. I think her leg is hurting and that's making her grumpy.'

237

'I wasn't grumpy when my chin was sore.'

'That's because you're a very special little girl.'

She was. Her skin had healed, and the birthmarks were paler than they were before. She hadn't had another seizure. It had all been worthwhile.

But Bea knew that physical pain wasn't the only kind that could make the light go out in a person. What would happen to her in two years' time, when Ewan came back, and Phoebe was more independent? What about ten or twenty years on from that? She saw a terrifying future for herself as bleak as Joyce's – that of a bitter, angry old woman, alone and difficult to love.

Chapter Thirty-One

Eddie knocked on the door as Bea was reading *On a Tall, Tall Cliff* to Phoebe for about the hundredth time. She ran downstairs, stumbling slightly from the two glasses of wine she'd drunk to stave off the guilt of walking out on Joyce. She swung the door wide, her heart jumping a beat when she saw it was him.

'Oh, hello.' She put her hand to her hair, then realised she must look like someone who cared how they appeared so scratched her head instead. Great, now she looked like she had nits. 'Everything alright?' She checked her watch. 'Are you still working?'

'Yes. Late shift. Wanted to check on my favourite client.'

She couldn't work out what to do with her hands. She held them together in front of her but felt like a chorus member in a Gilbert O'Sullivan operetta. Eddie looked as confused as if she'd burst into a rendition of 'Modern Major General'.

'Joyce. I'm here to discuss Joyce.' He took a step back. 'Sorry. If it's not a good time I'll—' He swung his thumb backwards towards the road.

'No. No. Come in, it's freezing out there.' She wished the redness she could feel rising in her cheeks would bugger off. 'I was putting Phoebe to bed. Let me get you a drink. Are you allowed a beer on the job?' *On the job.* Had she really just said that?

'I'm clocking off soon, so a beer would be good. Thanks.'

She uncapped a bottle and handed it to him, then nipped upstairs to kiss Phoebe goodnight. She checked herself in the bathroom mirror before heading back down, stopping to pick dried pasta sauce off her chin.

Downstairs, she tried to appear calm and demure, although she knew she was neither of those things. Maybe more wine would help. She glugged cold Viognier into a glass and was tempted to roll it across her hot face before she drank it.

'Cheers.'

His bottle clinked against her glass.

'Oh, I meant to say thank you for salting Joyce's path.'

'Sorry? What?'

'You put the salt down to stop it being slippery?'

He shifted his lips to the side, the skin around his mouth creasing. 'Much as I would like to take credit for that, I can't. Wasn't me.'

She took another drink and noticed half the glass was already gone. 'Strange. I wonder who it was, then.'

'Search me.'

She imagined doing just that. She opened the fridge so he couldn't see her colour rise again and topped up her glass. This time she did hold it against her cheek for a couple of blissful seconds. 'Must be a neighbour. Can't think who, though. They're all a bit up their own arses around here.'

She saw surprise flit across Eddie's face and could have kicked herself. 'Sorry. That was crass.'

'I've heard worse,' said Eddie. 'I work with geriatrics. You ought to hear what an old fella with a UTI can come up with before the antibiotics kick in. It would make your ears bleed.'

'Well, I'm glad I'm not as bad as an octogenarian with a bladder infection.'

Eddie laughed and dropped his head. 'I know how to flatter a girl.'

A girl? She took another drink.

'Joyce has moved back home, then? After the vermin invasion?'

'She did. Although she told me tonight that she's hearing noises. If I didn't know better, I'd think she was angling to move back in here.'

Eddie surveyed the kitchen. 'It's probably a more mobility-friendly place, and the company must seem attractive.'

Bea took another drink. Did Eddie just call her company attractive? While his attention seemed to be on the layout of the room, she found herself noticing the muscles on his forearm and his long, slim fingers wrapped around the bottle. His nails were neat squares and she suddenly wanted to feel the soft skin of his palms.

Was it the cold wine that made her shiver, or the thought of Eddie's hand, cold from the bottle neck, touching her skin? She forced herself to think of her mother-in-law. 'She's probably getting used to the sounds of the old place again. Old houses have a language of their own, don't they?' That was quite profound. She congratulated herself by draining her glass. 'Another?'

Eddie swallowed what was left of his lager. 'Why not? The scooter's in the garage, so I came on the bus.'

She uncapped his beer and twisted the screw top off a new bottle of wine. 'I never did give you a ride on my bike, did I?' She sniggered. 'Sorry. That wasn't meant to be an innuendo.'

His lips parted like he was about to say something, but he stopped and put the bottle to his mouth. She dragged her eyes away but could only force them as far as his Adam's apple, moving in his neck as he swallowed. She imagined the liquid flowing down into his chest, then lower. Her vision blurred.

'Come through.' She needed to sit down. She was light-headed and the wooziness felt like a warm blanket. In an act of daring in the sitting room, she sat next to him when he took a seat on the smaller of the two sofas. He didn't look horrified, so she leaned her elbow on the seat back and angled herself towards him, acutely aware of her foot being close enough to touch his calf if she gave a little kick. Should she give a little kick?

'Where's Max?' It was a stupid question. Where did she think he was, at the supermarket? Down the pub with his doggie mates? An image of a painting bounced into her head: dogs in waistcoats around a pool table, holding pints and smoking cigars. She giggled.

'What?'

'He's probably out playing pool.'

'Eh?'

She shook her head. She needed to get a grip. 'Sorry. I'm talking rubbish.' She pointed at the half-empty glass on the coffee table. 'This wine Ewan gets delivered must be stronger than the plonk I used to get at Lidl.'

'I'm more of a beer man.' She watched him take another

swig and this time she kept her eyes on his mouth, wet around the rim of the bottle. She wanted to taste his cool lips, dip her tongue into his mouth and feel his stubble graze her chin.

Without warning, he leaned forwards and started to lift himself from the sofa. 'I should—'

Panic gripped her. She put her hand on his arm more firmly than she intended. He slumped back down. 'You don't have to go, do you?' Suddenly the thought of being alone was horrifying.

She shifted closer to him, trying to recreate the feeling of being moments away from having his mouth on hers. 'Don't go.'

He stared into her eyes, and she felt a connection, like he really, really saw her. Moving her face towards his, she could smell his Kouros and it stirred something deep inside her. She put her hand on his thigh and his warmth moved up her arm and through her body. Her lips moved towards his and she closed her eyes.

The material of his jeans shifted under her hand, and she toppled forwards. When she opened her eyes, Eddie was standing in front of the sofa, looking down at her. 'Sorry . . . I need to . . . Er . . . Thanks for the drinks. I, er, Max is on his own.' He gave a brief wave before leaving the room. The front door banged closed before Bea could register how she felt.

To stop herself howling, she curled into a ball, moving backwards and forwards with her arms wrapped around her calves, trying to rock away the shame.

* * *

When Bea rolled over in bed, she could just about distinguish the shadowy figure of Phoebe. Her hands were pulling at her arm. Bea's head pounded and when she opened her mouth to speak, the words scraped along her dry tongue. 'What's wrong?'

'Somebody's banging on the door and there's lights outside.'

Bea tried to blink moisture across her scratchy eyes. She heard a knock downstairs and her heart leaped to attention. 'Okay.' She squeezed Phoebe's hand. 'It's alright. I'm up now.' It didn't feel alright. Knocks on the door in the middle of the night were never alright.

The cold air nipped at her skin, making all the hairs on her body stand on end. She rushed down the stairs, cursing the alarm beeping before she pressed in the code. A blue light brightened then fell away, before shining in through the glass panes next to the door. Her heart jumped in her chest. Not again.

A frowning police officer was standing on the doorstep when she opened the door. The thumping in her chest spread throughout her body when he said, 'Beatrice James?'

'Yes?' She looked out to the road where a police car was parked across her drive, a blue light circling on its roof.

'I'm afraid there's been an incident at the home of Joyce James. She told the paramedics she's your mother-in-law?'

Joyce? Not Immy. Joyce. Bea squinted against the lights, still groggy with sleep. 'What sort of incident?'

'We can't be sure exactly what happened, yet, but Mrs James has sustained some injuries.'

'Injuries?' Bea's hands trembled as she dragged her dressing gown cord tighter. 'Is she alright?'

'The paramedics are taking her to the hospital now.'

'Aunty Bea? What's happening?'

Bea peered around at Phoebe, cowering halfway down the stairs. 'Just a second, poppet.' She turned back to the policeman. 'What happened? Did she fall?'

He looked beyond her at Phoebe, then lowered his voice. 'There was an intruder at the scene. They've been arrested.'

Oh no! She said she'd heard noises and Bea had dismissed her. It must have been a burglar casing the place. God knows what they could have done to her. What they had done to her.

Over the policeman's shoulder she detected movement. A woman officer was leading someone in handcuffs towards the car. She opened the door and put her hand on the head of the person she was ushering into the back seat. The person turned towards the house as the blue light swished around to illuminate gaunt, hollowed-out cheeks. Their eyes met for a moment before the face Bea knew better than her own disappeared into the car.

Chapter Thirty-Two

Jan arrived fifteen minutes after Bea called her. Bea left her to look after Phoebe, trying to reassure the terrified girl that Grandma would be alright, with no idea if that was even true.

When the taxi dropped Bea off outside the A&E Department, she was paralysed with fear. What if she went inside and found Joyce had died? What if her daughter was responsible for the death of yet another member of her own family? Really, properly responsible, this time. The wine roiled in her belly. Sweat burst through her pores and she bent over, saliva filling her mouth, bile pushing up her throat. She pulled herself up straight and forced her feet to walk her into the building, blinking against the painful brightness.

Tapping her toes on the linoleum floor, she waited for the receptionist to locate Joyce. Her throat was now too dry to swallow and her breaths came out in quick bursts, burning with stale alcohol. She was sure the receptionist would smell it on her. She turned away, seeing the exact spot she had spied Immy through the closing lift door.

Why hadn't she tried harder to get through to her? Why was she always forced to choose between protecting Immy or Phoebe?

Oh, Immy. What could possibly have led to her breaking into her grandmother's house? She must have been looking for money to buy drugs, or things to steal and sell. God. But to hurt her? How could her perfect little girl have sunk so low? Where had she gone so wrong as a mother that her daughter was capable of something like this?

The receptionist looked up through tired eyes. 'She's been taken to ICU. Level Four.'

Bea nodded her thanks and walked through the empty space towards the lifts, swiping her flowing tears with the back of her hand. The clock above the lift told her it was 12:45 a.m.

The lift doors opened onto a quiet corridor. She followed the signs hanging from the ceiling to the Intensive Care Unit and pressed the buzzer on the wall. The door clicked and she pushed it open onto another corridor with a nurse's station halfway along. Her boots squeaked on the polished floor. A nurse in blue scrubs smiled. 'Hi.'

'I'm looking for Joyce James. She was brought in by ambulance.' Her eyes were drawn to the room to her right. She could see one bed flanked by a bank of monitors on each side. A nurse with a face mask was reading the screen and pressing buttons next to bright lines, which rose and dipped in colourful patterns.

She turned back to see the nurse reading through a list on a clipboard. 'Can I have your name, please?' Bea found her soft Irish accent reassuring.

'Bea James. I'm her daughter-in-law.'

'Could you follow me? I'll take you through to the family room and we can talk there.'

Bea swallowed. She'd seen this in films. They took you somewhere private to tell you bad news. She followed the nurse into a small room off the corridor and sat where she was directed as the blood pounded on her eardrums.

The nurse sat beside her, and Bea shuddered, remembering her mortifying behaviour with Eddie earlier. 'Your mother-in-law has been taken to theatre for emergency surgery.'

She covered her mouth to stifle her sobs. 'She's not dead?' It came out muffled through her hands.

The nurse smiled gently. 'She has a broken hip. That's what they're working on now. There's a risk she's suffered more injuries after a fall like that, but we'll be able to tell you more after the operation.'

The nurse handed her a tissue from the box on the table. Bea blew her nose, taking another to wipe her face. 'Fall?' She blew her nose again. 'I didn't really hear what the police said.' She thought back to when the policeman spoke to her after she watched Immy being driven away, his words distorting like a tape stuck in a machine.

'From what the police told us, it looks like she was found at the bottom of the stairs. An intruder was arrested at the scene, but that's all we know for now.'

A fall – or a push? A sob escaped Bea and the nurse's head dropped to the side in sympathy Bea didn't deserve. She couldn't tell this, sweet, compassionate woman the intruder was her own daughter. That she was probably high on God knows what and had caused her own grandmother to break her hip. Maybe worse.

'When will I be able to see her?'

'It'll be a while yet, I'm afraid. The best thing you can do is to go home and try to get some rest. I'll call you when she's out of surgery and let you know how it's gone. Okay?'

Bea nodded, sniffing back more tears. She closed her eyes as she recited her phone number and when the nurse left the room, she stood, her shaking legs only just strong enough to take her weight. A new wave of horror engulfed her when she realised what she needed to do next. Ewan. She had to tell Ewan what Immy had done.

* * *

It didn't seem right to wake Ewan when she wouldn't know how Joyce was until after she came out of surgery. She would wait until the morning. By then, hopefully, she would have something concrete to tell him about the operation. She called Jan from reception, told her what she knew and asked her if she could stay the night with Phoebe.

She walked out of the building into the darkness where the icy air caught at the back of her throat. Once off of the hospital grounds, the roads became quiet, except for the occasional car with high beams glaring, moving fast because there was nobody around to see. Her footsteps crunched on the frosty pavement. She shoved her tingling fingers into her coat pockets and wished she'd remembered her gloves.

By the time she reached her old house, her feet and hands were numb with cold. She stood at the end of the driveway and stared at the brick walls that had once encapsulated her small, perfectly formed family. The orange streetlight glinted on a rope of fairy lights pinned around the door. She thought they must look pretty when they were switched on and wished she'd thought of putting Christmas lights around the door when Immy was little. She would have liked that. Would more little kindnesses like that have stopped them from arriving here?

Shivering, she ran through the Christmases Immy had spent in that house. They had been happy, hadn't they? For the most part. She was sure they had. She remembered carol singing and board games, putting out sherry in front of the electric fire for Father Christmas and a carrot for Rudolf. She could almost feel Oli and Immy next to her at that window, looking up into the dark sky on Christmas Eve, trying to see if they could spot the sleigh overhead.

There was the year Oli sliced his finger open when he used a Stanley knife to open whatever plastic gubbins Immy had asked Santa for. That wasn't the best year, especially since Joyce refused to wait for them while Oli had stitches and served up Christmas dinner at one p.m., because that was when they always ate it. Heaven forbid she should miss the Queen's speech. Her majesty was much more important than her own son's bloody digit. Bea's teeth rattled with the cold. This was not the time to be remembering Joyce's misdemeanours.

The year after Oli died, the last Christmas before Immy left, they hadn't gone to Joyce's. Immy had refused and wouldn't tell Bea why, so they sat and pushed dry turkey around their plates until Immy stormed up to her room when Bea told her she was selfish, spoiling Phoebe's Christmas by stopping them from going. Immy snarled something about Gemma being the selfish one, which Bea hadn't understood at the time. She hadn't understood so much of what her daughter did by then.

She understood it even less now.

Her nose ran. She wiped it and the raw skin above her lip stung. She'd been crying for so long she was surprised she had any liquid left in her. She looked at her phone to check the time and the picture of Phoebe grinned out at her, guileless and innocent. Her fingertips were white against the cold casing. She'd be no good to Phoebe if she got pneumonia. Taking one last look at the home where she'd made so many mistakes, she forced her numb feet to walk back towards The Crescent, to take care of Phoebe. To try to pay a debt that could never be paid.

Chapter Thirty-Three

Bea cradled a mug of coffee between her palms, certain she'd never be warm again. Ewan's house was silent, with Jan and Phoebe asleep upstairs, but Bea couldn't bear the thought of closing her eyes. There were too many images behind her eyelids grappling with each other to torture her. So she stayed awake and watched the blackness turn to grey through the bifold doors.

The Irish nurse called at seven-thirty to say Joyce's operation had gone as well as could be expected, but they were keeping her in the ICU for now. Able to breathe to the bottom of her lungs again, Bea braced herself and called Ewan.

'Immy's done what?' Ewan shouted, his voice gruff with sleep.

'We don't know exactly,' Bea tried.

'But my mother has a broken hip and your daughter's been arrested?'

Bea balanced her forehead on her hand, leaning on the table for support. 'Yes.'

'Fuck, Bea. Fuck! Is she planning to kill us all? Is that

what she's come back for? Is this some mad revenge plot because she's been wronged, or something?'

Bea took the phone away from her ear and swiped the tears from her cheek and the phone screen with her sleeve as Ewan's voice ranted tinnily from the speaker. But even through her shock and exhaustion, questions surfaced like bubbles. Why was he talking about revenge? Why would Immy feel wronged? It didn't make sense. In his worry and anger, she thought, Ewan must be confused.

When he finally seemed to fall silent, she brought the phone back up to her ear. 'Let's concentrate on Joyce for now. We can deal with the rest later.'

'I'll let you know what flight I'm on,' said Ewan before he ended the call.

His voice was still ringing in her ears when her phone buzzed with an unknown number five minutes later.

'Beatrice James?'

'Yes.'

'Can you confirm you are the mother of Imogen James?'

Her skin crawled with shame. The things Ewan had sworn down the phone about Immy were still circulating in her head, along with new questions of her own.

'Who's speaking please?' She leaned her elbows on the dining table, cursing herself for picking up. She prayed it wasn't a journalist. They'd doorstepped her for days after Gemma and Zach died. Even when Immy wasn't charged, they still hovered on the pavement, making them prisoners whether she was guilty or not.

'I'm Sergeant Gifford calling from Belmoat custody suite. Imogen James is being released pending further investigation. She gave your name and address. Said she'd be staying with you. That right?'

Bea gasped.

'Mrs James?'

'I'm here.' Although that didn't feel strictly true. She felt like she was floating outside herself in some kind of surreal fever dream.

'You'll need to fill in some paperwork when you pick her up. Ask for me at the front desk. Sergeant Gifford.'

'Okay.' She said it automatically and when the sergeant said goodbye and hung up, she found herself staring at the fridge door, wondering if she was delirious.

She jumped when she felt Jan's hand on her shoulder. 'God!'

'Sorry, thought you'd heard me.' She flicked the switch on the kettle, and it growled into action. 'Is Ewan coming back, then?'

'What?'

Jan peered at her over her glasses. 'Ewan. Will he be coming back today?'

'Oh. Erm—' She tried to remember what he'd said but her mind was doing scattered hurdles, jumping from one train of thought to another.

'You need a strong coffee.' The kettle seemed to sigh when she switched it off. She stood in front of the machine. 'How the hell do you work this contraption?'

'I need to pick Immy up.'

Jan spun around. 'What?'

'That was the police station, the custody suite. They're releasing her. She said she was staying here.'

Jan flopped in the chair next to her. 'I don't think Ewan will be too happy about that.'

Bea pieced together what Ewan said on the phone. He was going to get on a flight and come home. As soon as he could. She turned to Jan. 'He's setting off soon.' Her head flipped through different scenarios. She found one that could work, but it was a long shot. 'I'm going to ask you something, but you've got to say no if—'

'What?'

'If you don't . . . I mean, I'll completely understand if—'

'You want to know if Immy can stay at mine?'

Bea nodded. 'I know it's a big ask, with everything that's gone on.'

If Jan had any trepidation, she didn't show it. 'Alright.'

Before Bea could thank her, they heard Phoebe humming as she came down the stairs. Jan said quickly, 'I'll come with you to collect her when we've dropped the little one at school.' She squeezed Bea's arms. 'We'll sort it together. It'll be okay.'

* * *

A cocktail of adrenaline and guilt pushed through Bea's veins as she watched Phoebe skip off towards her classroom with Sydney. She was about to betray her niece and her family. But if that's what it took to see Immy again, then so be it.

* * *

Bea couldn't take her eyes off Immy as she was led from behind a solid door by Sergeant Gifford. Both she and Jan stood up from the chairs they'd perched on since filling in the forms. Jan agreed to put her house as Immy's address. Bea hadn't dared ask about how her friend felt, allowing someone like Immy into her home, to stay with her own four precious children.

'I owe you, you know that,' she said to Jan, as Immy walked towards them.

'You'd do the same for me.'

255

'I would, but I want you to know how much this means to me.'

She squeezed Jan's hand, then her fingers twitched to reach out for Immy, her face a thinner version of the one she'd kissed a million times. Older and careworn but familiar enough to bring a lump to her throat.

'Is Grandma alright?'

Bea's chest burned. 'What do you think? They found her at the bottom of the stairs.' The tears dried. Maybe she should have refused to come. What a ridiculous question after what she'd done. Of course Joyce wasn't alright.

'Oh God.' Immy covered her mouth and Bea had to look away.

Jan stepped forwards and took Immy's elbow. 'Your grandma's had an operation to fix her hip, but she's still very poorly. Come on.'

Immy walked with Jan, but her head turned back towards Bea. 'Mum.'

'Your mum's coming with us. Don't worry.'

Bea followed them out through the glass doors of the custody suite in a daze of conflicting emotions: fury tangled with love. When Immy stopped, holding her stomach, and leaning over like she might be about to be sick, she forced her eyes away. She and Jan exchanged worried glances as they waited for Immy to straighten up and get into the back seat.

They sat in silence in the car. Whenever Bea was tempted to turn her head to look at Immy, she remembered the beeping monitors she'd seen next to the bed in the ICU and imagined Joyce hooked up to a morphine drip. She must be in terrible pain. The irony of sympathising with Joyce over Immy after the last three years felt cruel. Immy didn't speak either.

As they pulled into Jan's driveway, Ciara emerged from the door at the side of the house. When Immy stepped from the back of the car Ciara's face lit up. 'Hello, stranger!'

Bea watched as Ciara embraced Immy then stood back to look at her. 'You look like shit.'

'Thanks.'

'Seriously, mate. Every time I think of running away, I'm going to remember the state of you and go back to my own bed.' She laughed at her own joke. 'Anyway, some of us have work to go to. Catch ya later, yeah?'

Immy nodded and Ciara tramped off down the drive.

'Never been great at reading the room, that one,' Jan said, opening the door to the kitchen. It smelled of burned toast and instant coffee, and Bea wondered how anything could be homely and normal today.

Jan gestured for them both to sit, and filled the kettle. Bea couldn't bring herself to look at Immy. Her thoughts churned. She put her hands flat on the table to try to steady herself. No sleep, a hangover, a hospitalisation, and an arrest. What a night. Now the prodigal daughter was sitting next to her, and it all seemed like a surreal dream.

Jan placed steaming mugs in front of each of them, then sat in a chair at the opposite side of the table. 'Right. I'll be mediator,' she said. 'I've got a couple of questions first, though, since you're going to be staying in my house, I need some things clearing up.'

Immy nodded.

'First off: are you on drugs?'

Immy slumped back; her eyes didn't leave the table. 'No.'

Bea watched her face. She looked so sad, but she didn't

look like she was lying, but then, would she be able to tell anymore? Could she ever?

'I don't mean to be harsh, my love, but you would say that, wouldn't you?' Jan's voice was soft. 'It's just, I've got a house full of teenagers here, and so you'll see why I need to be careful.'

'I haven't taken anything I haven't been prescribed since the day I left Belmoat.' She rubbed her forehead. 'I did have a drink problem when I left here. I went to a hostel and spent about four months in a state.'

Bea felt her bottom lip quiver. She looked at Immy's grey-tinged skin, her cheeks hollowed under her cheekbones. She said, 'So that's why you were you living at an addiction centre, then?' It came out cold.

'No.' Immy closed her eyes. 'Is that why you think I'm on drugs? I stopped drinking before that. There was a woman, Livvy, she was at the hostel with me. She . . .' Immy's voice cracked, 'She died. She was in the next bunk to me, and we were sort of friends, but she was on more than just booze and she overdosed. It was kind of a wake-up call, you know? After that, I got a lot of help from the youth workers, got sober.'

'That's when you went to rehab?' Jan asked.

'I was never in rehab. Honestly, I worked there, as a cleaner at first. Accommodation came with the job because I did shifts.'

Bea swallowed. 'That sounds very convenient.'

'Convenient?' Immy gasped. 'Do you think I wanted to be there instead of at home? When I knew I could stay sober, I came back.'

'Here?' Bea felt the world slow down.

'To our house, but then I saw you come out of the door carrying Phoebe. You were both laughing about something,

258

and I thought . . . well, I thought if you could be happy after what happened, I couldn't be the one to mess it up again. That didn't seem fair, so I went back to the centre and stayed until . . . until now.'

'You went back to the rehab centre instead of coming home?' Bea couldn't take it all in.

'To work,' Immy emphasised. 'Call them. Look them up on your phone so you can see I'm not giving you a number for a friend or anything dodgy.' She turned to Jan when Bea didn't move. 'Go on, Jan, look them up.' She gave the address Bea remembered from Eddie's piece of paper.

Jan glanced at Bea, then picked up her phone and typed in the name of the centre in Carthing.

They watched her press the screen then hold the phone to her ear. 'Hello. Yes, I wonder if you can help me.' She bit the skin by the side of her thumb nail. 'I was wondering if you could confirm that someone called Imogen James worked there?' She glanced up. 'She's a family friend, I'm helping her write her CV.' She shrugged and Bea saw a tiny smile on Immy's face. 'Yes. Right. Okay. Thank you. I will.'

She clicked off the call and placed the phone slowly down on the table. 'Adele said to say hello.' She carefully wrapped her hands around her mug. 'She also said to say good luck with the baby.'

Bea's mug jumped in her hands. Hot coffee burned her fingers. 'Baby?'

Immy's face brightened. 'This wasn't how I meant for you to find out, but yeah, I'm twenty weeks pregnant.'

Bea wiped her hands on her jeans. 'You've been drinking when you're carrying a child?'

Immy's face dropped. 'What? No.'

Bea was too angry to listen, She knew she was acting exactly as she had when Immy was a petulant teenager, but she couldn't help herself. She stood, the chair legs scraping on the floor, 'You can do what you want to your own body, but—'

'Mum.' Immy stood and tried to take Bea's shoulders. Bea shook her off.

'How could you?'

'Mum. Listen!' Immy pleaded.

'Sit down. The pair of you,' Jan yelled over them. 'This is my house, and we will talk in a civilised fashion.'

Bea rearranged her chair at the table with trembling hands. She sat. Immy did the same.

Jan spoke slowly and deliberately, 'Bea, I'm sorry, I didn't make it clear before you flew off the handle. That Adele I spoke to said Immy *was* working there. She definitely wasn't in rehab.'

Bea blinked. She tried to get her thoughts in order. 'You worked there?'

'I'm not lying to you. I haven't had a drink for two years.' She caught Bea's eyes flitting over her haggard appearance. 'I've had uncontrollable morning sickness since the start. That's why I was retching outside Uncle Ewan's and why I was at the hospital. I've got to have regular check-ups, to make sure everything's alright with the baby.'

Bea burst into sobs. 'And you tried to come home before?'

Immy took her hand and gripped it. 'I always wanted to come home. I missed you so much. I just didn't think I deserved to. I was sure everybody blamed me as much as I blamed myself after Dad's fall. He got so much worse after that.'

Bea returned the grip on her hand and reached for the

other. 'That wasn't your fault. The treatment had stopped working. What happened afterwards wasn't because he hit his head. It was the cancer that killed him. I don't blame you. I never have.'

Immy's eyes searched her face. 'Really?'

Bea smiled through her tears. 'Really. And you're having a baby?'

Immy nodded, tears now flowing down her cheeks.

'I'm going to be a grandma? Oh my God, Immy. You've got a little baby in there?' She held her hand towards Immy's tummy. 'Wow. I can't get my head around this. Who's the father?' Bea's phone dinged. She jumped. 'God, I'm all over the place.' She glanced at the screen and went cold. 'It's your Uncle Ewan. He's on the plane already.' She turned to Immy, her colour draining away. 'What happened at Grandma's?'

'It was awful,' said Immy, her eyes filling with fresh liquid. 'After I came to see you that night, I went to Grandma's and looked in through the window. She looked like she was crying.'

Bea's face contorted in disbelief. 'Joyce?'

'I saw her trying to boil the kettle, but she didn't seem to be able to lift it. She was limping really badly.'

'Okay.'

'I was worried about her, so, instead of going to the Travelodge like I planned, I broke into the room over the garage so I could keep an eye on her. I knew she wouldn't want to see me, so it seemed like a good idea to stay behind the scenes.'

All at once, things began to fall into place. 'Did you take her rubbish out and put salt on the path?'

'Yeah. I did bits and bobs. The key was still under the big planter, so it was easy to get in.'

Bea spoke quietly. 'What happened last night?'

A tear hung on Immy's eyelash, dropping onto her cheek when she blinked. 'I was checking on her before I turned in and there was clattering and a scream and then I heard this awful moaning.' She wiped her face with her sleeve and carried on. 'The key wasn't under the planter, so I tried all the doors, but they were locked, so I smashed the glass in the kitchen door and found her at the bottom of the stairs, all bent, so I called an ambulance.'

'Why did the police arrest you?' Jan asked.

'Because she was screaming at me to stay away and calling me a murderer when the paramedics arrived. I suppose, when they found the smashed glass in the kitchen, they had to call the police.'

'I didn't stop them taking you away.' The words almost strangled her. 'I'm so sorry.'

Immy picked at her nail, then said quietly, 'Will you start believing me now?'

'I will. I'm so sorry, love.'

Jan sniffed loudly and Bea shook herself out of the trance where only she and Immy existed. 'I fantasise about having my kids arrested on a daily basis,' said Jan, chortling, but when they both turned to look at her, her face was wet with tears, too.

'Can I come home, Mum?'

Bea was too choked to answer, but she nodded and tried not to wonder where their *home* could possibly be.

Chapter Thirty-Four

Bea dug her nails into her palms. She'd planned to say many things to Joyce, but seeing her here, so tiny in the hospital bed, she couldn't make the words come.

'There's someone standing in the corridor who would like to see you,' was all she could muster?

'Imogen?'

'Yes. Can I bring her in?'

Joyce closed her eyes and nodded minutely.

Bea felt washed through with relief. She squeezed Joyce's hand before walking back towards where Immy hovered nervously, out of sight of the private room Ewan had arranged. Her shoulders visibly lowered when Bea smiled and beckoned her forwards. She followed Bea into the room and stood at the foot of the bed, fingers tapping on the white metal frame.

'I'm told you saved my life,' said Joyce.

'Least I could do.'

Joyce tutted. 'Don't be glib.'

There she was: the old Joyce. How easy it was to slip back into familiar ways, even after years of separation.

263

Bea found it hard to take her eyes from Immy's face. In it, she saw Oli's green eyes and the set of his stubborn jaw, teeth clamped together. Turning towards the bed, she noticed the same look on Joyce's face. These two weren't as different as they thought.

'You've told the police Immy didn't break in?' Bea poured water from the plastic jug by Joyce's bedside into a flimsy cup.

'Strictly speaking, she did.' She took the cup from Bea with an unsteady hand and held it up to her lips.

'Don't be glib,' Bea said, enjoying her new-found confidence. 'And, strictly speaking, if she hadn't, you'd have got hyperthermia and wouldn't be here now.'

Joyce handed the cup back to Bea. Her frailness was shocking, like watching a magnificent tree lose all its leaves overnight.

'I told them.'

The tight fist in Bea's abdomen unfurled.

'Are you in a lot of pain?' Immy moved closer to the bed and Bea willed Joyce to look at her, but her eyes, small without their line of dark kohl, stayed fixed on the blue blanket covering her.

'One of those things is morphine, I think.' She gestured to the bags hanging next to the bed with lines leading to cannulas taped to the back of her veiny hand. 'It helps.'

'Speaking of drugs . . .' Bea knew it was a clumsy segue, but she wanted to let Joyce know her beliefs about Immy were unfounded. She was interrupted when the door to the room opened and Ewan appeared. He halted, his lip curling as he caught sight of Immy.

'What the hell are you doing here?' he snarled, then turned to Bea. 'How could you let her near my mother again after everything she's done?' Bea felt spit land on

264

her face as he pointed at Immy and shouted, 'Get out. Get away from my family!'

'Ewan, stop it,' Bea's voice was lost under Ewan's shouts. Immy backed towards the door, her face crumpled, hands raised to cover her ears.

'Joyce, tell him!' But Joyce's eyes were closed and Immy had reached the door and all she could do was try to protect her daughter. An explosion of rage burst inside her. 'Your mother would be dead if it wasn't for Immy.'

Ewan's face screwed up. He turned to Joyce, but before he could say anything else, Bea did what she should have done years ago and turned her back on Ewan and Joyce and went to take care of her child.

* * *

'I'm so sorry,' she said, when she found Immy at the end of the corridor, tears streaming down her face. She threw her arms around her and pulled her into a hug, breathing in the smell of her hair. 'I'm sorry.'

Immy held her tightly for a moment then pulled back. 'You don't need to be sorry. God, there's too much to unpick in a hospital corridor. Let's get a drink.'

She sounded so adult. Bea ached that she'd had to do so much growing up on her own.

* * *

They snaked through the warren of pale blue passageways, staying close to each other. Immy's shoulder touched hers as they walked. It felt natural and right. When they found the café, Immy sat on a plastic chair while Bea bought drinks. She kept looking over her shoulder as she queued to make sure Immy was still there. It felt like falling in love. Losing her again was unimaginable.

'Decaf,' said Bea when she put the coffee on the table in front of Immy. She put two sachets of sugar next to the cup. 'Still two?'

'I don't have sugar anymore. Weaned myself off.'

Immy used to take sugar and now she didn't, and the time in between was lost, and she would never be able to get it back. Immy put her hand to her mouth and swallowed and Bea recognised she was quelling the nausea she'd mistaken for drunkenness. God, she was a terrible mother.

'You going to be sick?'

'No. I don't think so. It's getting better every day, but I still get the odd pukey wave.'

'*Pukey Wave*. Good name for a band.' Bea tried to laugh, but it caught on the lump in her throat. 'I should have listened,' she said, but the tears came, and she found herself spluttering. She glanced around, mortified, but no one was looking their way. A hospital café must witness more difficult conversations than most. The couple on the next table huddled together, speaking urgently, their fingers tightly intertwined, and it was hard not to imagine that their words were equally full of pain. She wiped her eyes and turned back to Immy. 'Before, when you were younger, you know, I'm sorry I didn't try harder to understand what was going on with you.'

'You had your hands full with Dad and I was a nightmare. I can't believe I used to say I hated you.' She scrunched her eyes closed and shook her head. 'Obviously that wasn't true. I was an awful teenager. It was un—'

'But you needed me, and I wasn't—'

'Mum. None of this is your fault.'

Bea blinked. 'But it was.'

'No.'

266

'But what you wrote in your letter . . .'

Immy gave a short laugh and squeezed her hand. 'I can't exactly remember what I wrote, but I'm pretty sure it was the result of hormones and teenage angst.'

Bea could remember exactly what it said. Every last word. 'You told me I didn't listen, and, looking back, I think you're right. I nearly didn't listen earlier today, even. I haven't changed, apparently.'

Leaning forwards, Immy took Bea's other hand and held both tightly. 'It was easier to blame you than think about what was really going on in my messed-up head.' Her eyes searched Bea's face. 'If I didn't say it, you couldn't listen, could you? I guess I wanted you to be a mind-reader or something. I was angry you couldn't see past the front I was putting up.'

'I should have.' Bea stopped. 'I'm listening now. Tell me.'

Immy released her hands, took a drink of her coffee and seemed to consider for a moment. She put the cup down and placed her fingers on the edge of the table. 'I was angry. I was mad at Dad for getting sick and dying, at you for not being able to make him get better. I hated myself for . . .' Her voice wobbled. 'The stuff with Zach. That should have been a phase. First love, and all that. When I realised what a dick he was, I should have got over my little rebellion and moved on, but I suppose I was intent on showing you I didn't need you . . .' She sniffed and fumbled in her pocket. Bea took a tissue from her bag and handed it to her.

Immy blew her nose. 'But I did need you. Pushing you away only hurt me. And back then, I hated Grandma thinking badly of me. She was always so disappointed in me.'

'I'm sure she—' Bea stopped when she saw Immy's raised eyebrow.

'She wanted a perfect little girl. I was always trying not to disappoint her, but nothing seemed to come up to her standards. Especially not when I grew out of being cute and compliant. Then, after what happened . . .' She swallowed. 'After Zach killed Gemma.' She let her head fall into her hands. 'I tried to stop him. I tried to grab the wheel. I didn't know he'd taken tabs as well as other stuff. It was like he thought it was a video game or something.'

'It's alright.' Bea stroked her back. 'It's okay.'

'It's not, and it never will be. If I hadn't told him about Gemma's affair, none of it would've happened, so it was down to me. I sort of wanted to be punished. I couldn't bear how I'd let everyone down.'

'I'm sorry. I should have known. I should have listened.'

'It's not your fault, Mum.' Immy's eyes bored into Bea's. 'That's the most important thing I want you to understand. You did nothing but love me and support me. You did everything you could to get through to me, but I was too full of self-pity and grief to accept it. I knew I didn't deserve you to still love me the way you did. That's partly why I left. I couldn't bear being loved so much when I loathed myself.' She put her hand on her stomach. 'If I can be half the mum to this one that you were to me . . .'

Bea leaned forwards, folding her weeping child into her, trying to absorb some of the shockwaves, to quiet her sobs and make her know she was there, would always be there, that she would do everything in her power to stop her pain. Because that's what mothers do. That's what she had always tried to do. She may not have always got it right, but she had tried her very best to be a good mother to Immy. And Immy knew that.

Chapter Thirty-Five

Jan must have been waiting for them when they arrived back at her house, because she flung the door wide before Bea had a chance to knock.

'How's she doing?'

'Not bad, considering. Until Ewan turned up.'

'Ah.'

'Yep. Fireworks.'

'You can't really blame him,' said Immy. Bea rubbed her back through her coat and bit her tongue.

'You'll never guess what.' Jan's fingers danced in front of her. She pushed her glasses up her nose and grinned. 'Terry and Paula next door are setting off on their Christmas trip tomorrow.'

'Okay?' Bea put her bag on the floor and sat down. After the drama of the last few days, she felt like she could sleep for a week. 'That's nice.'

'They always go to Malta for a month over Christmas.'

'Lucky them.' Immy slumped into the chair next to her. Bea remembered how draining being pregnant was. She couldn't believe Immy had gone through the last few months alone. She cut off the thought. She wasn't going to do that. Her days of beating herself up were over. It was time to look to the future.

'They've got two cats. They're like Paula's babies. She loves those cats.'

Bea looked at her. 'Right.' Why were the neighbours' cats making Jan giddy? Cats usually made her sneeze, not wet her knickers. Although the two weren't mutually exclusive at their age.

'And she hates putting them in the cattery, but Terry says he's got to have a month away every winter because of his arthritis.' She danced a jig in her slippers.

'Have you been at the Christmas sherry? Why on earth are you so excited about cats and Terry's arthritis?'

'Because I had a word with them, and they said you can house sit while they're away as long as you look after the bloody cats!'

Bea's eyes sprang wide. 'What?'

'Next door. You can stay there while they're away. The two of you.'

Immy bounced out of her seat and threw her arms around Jan. 'You absolute legend!' She turned to Bea. 'That's amazing, isn't it, Mum? We can stay there until we get organised.'

'It is. It is amazing.'

Jan's brows knitted. 'Tell your face that, then.'

'It's just that—'

'Phoebe?' said Immy.

'Yep. What about our little Phoebe?'

* * *

The phone call with Ewan was brief and terse. 'I'm taking Phoebe to New York for a week before Christmas. My girlfriend, Camille, is keen to meet her,' he said. 'She's between jobs, so can look after Phoebe while I'm at work.'

Bea tried to stop herself from imagining what this Camille was like. The clip where Mrs Merton says to Debbie McGee, *'So Debbie, what first attracted you to the millionaire Paul Daniels?'* played in her head.

'So, you'll go and see Mother every day?' he asked, and Bea finally understood why he was being so civil after his outburst at the hospital. She was still useful.

'Of course.'

'And you're staying at Jan's?'

'Her neighbours said we can house sit. You know, Terry and Paula, you met them at—'

'Right. Well, I need to get along, get things ready. I'm taking Phoebe to the hospital before we leave tomorrow, around nine.'

Bea knew what that meant. 'We'll go in the afternoon.'

There was a pause, then Ewan breathed deeply. 'And if you put your key back through the letterbox when you've cleared out your things, that would be great.'

Great? She swallowed. 'Will do.' That was it then. 'Can I have a quick word with Phoebe?'

'Sorry, she's upstairs, packing her things. Another time, perhaps.'

'Okay. Another time. Bye.'

She imagined Phoebe in her room, trying to cram all of her Beanie Boos into a case. She bet Ewan was leaving her to pack on her own. He would have no idea that, left to her own devices, Phoebe would probably only pack toys and swimming costumes. She'd take her Peter Rabbit t-shirt because it was her favourite, but no jumpers because she would have no idea what the weather would be like in New York in December.

271

Should she call Ewan back to remind him to pack her scarf and gloves. Would he make sure she had enough moisturiser and remember not to let her use bubble bath? She held her finger over the button, but she let the screen go black. She had no choice but to let him parent his own daughter. He'd asked her to collect her things. Their agreement was at an end. He didn't want her to take care of Phoebe anymore.

* * *

Bea hooked her arm through Immy's as they walked the hospital corridors, unsure if she was trying to transfer strength to her or find some herself. She wondered if she'd still choose to visit Joyce if she hadn't fallen, after everything she'd put them through. Immy was determined to see her though, so Bea hadn't had to make that choice. She glanced over as they neared Joyce's room and Immy must have sensed her eyes on her. She turned and smiled nervously. Bea squeezed her arm. 'You alright?'

'Yeah. I'm determined to fix things. Too much time's been wasted.' She looked towards the door of the room. 'We never know when things are going to change, do we? So, I'm not going to leave things to fester anymore.'

Bea nodded, wondering when her rebellious daughter had turned into this wise old sage. She pushed the door open and paused. A man sitting on the chair next to the bed turned his head towards her.

Eddie.

The image of him standing in Ewan's sitting room after she'd tried to kiss him, burned the inside of her eyes. Sweat ran under her arms and she felt it soak into her bra strap. She opened her arms at the elbow but realised too late that she was flapping like a chicken. Why did she always act like a muppet when this man was around?

'Bea.' There was a hint of colour on Eddie's face, but his smile was wide and welcoming. 'Is this Immy?' He stood and walked over to them and shook Immy's hand. 'I've heard a lot about you.'

'Oh, God,' said Immy. 'It's not all true. I promise you.' She sucked in a breath. 'Well, it is, but I'm a reformed character these days. Honest, Guv'.' She wrinkled her nose, looking at each of them to see if it was too soon for humour.

'Your grandma was telling me about the time you played Matilda. Apparently, you were West End standard.'

Bea felt her face contort in response to this second surprise. 'Really?' Of all the things Bea might expect Joyce to disclose after the last three years, a glowing appraisal of Immy's musical theatre skills was the last. The iceberg that was her mother-in-law appeared to be melting.

'Yes, really. Isn't that right, Joyce?'

Joyce was propped higher on the pillows today, wearing full make-up. When Bea looked over at her she raised her chin and said, 'It was an extraordinary performance in a child so young.' Her lips twitched. 'But then, the role suited you, didn't it, Imogen?'

'Precocious brat?' Immy walked towards the bed and sat on the end. Bea waited for Joyce to complain, but she stared at Immy with an unreadable expression on her face. At least she could look at her now.

'Quite.' Joyce turned to Eddie, patting some brochures that lay on the blue covers beside her. 'Thank you for these, Eddie. I'm going to give it some thought.'

'What are those?' asked Bea, when she recovered her composure enough to speak.

'I'll let Joyce tell you all about that.' Eddie dragged on his bomber jacket. He lifted his crash helmet from the floor and flung his rucksack over his shoulder. It looked like he couldn't wait to get away. The sweat cooled on Bea's back. 'Nice to meet you, Immy.' He nodded at Bea. 'See ya. Bye, all.' And with that he left the room.

Feigning nonchalance at the encounter, Bea picked a shiny brochure from the top of the pile. She recognised the building on the front. 'Sweetingdale? What's this doing here?'

'I asked your friend to bring them in.'

'He's not my—' She stopped. She didn't need to explain or defend herself. These two hadn't witnessed the unholy show she'd made of herself, thank God. 'Why?'

'Because I'm looking for new investment opportunities,' snapped Joyce. She sighed. 'Because, as I'm sure you're fully aware, I'm not managing as well as I would like at home, so I'm considering my options.'

'Gosh.' Bea didn't know what to say. She never thought Joyce would consider moving into a care home. 'If you need any advice?'

'Yes, yes. It's only a thought, so let's not get carried away.' She turned to Immy, 'So, then, young lady, what brings you back into our lives after all these years?'

'I thought it was about time I tried to make amends.'

'I see.'

'And I needed my mum.'

She looked across at Bea and Bea's knees weakened with love. She sat in the chair Eddie had left empty.

'And I'm pregnant.'

'Good Lord.'

Bea straightened her back. 'Do not judge her, Joyce.'

'She's only twenty-one!' She turned to Immy. 'Is there no trouble you won't get yourself into?'

Bea stood. 'Come on, Immy. We don't need this. Let's

go.' She glared at Joyce. 'I haven't seen my daughter for three years because of you and your bloody son. I let you blame her for everything, when really, I should have seen that she was suffering. She was a teenager who had to watch her father die.'

Joyce looked away and fury boiled over in Bea.

'Her father – who, incidentally, couldn't wait to get out of your clutches. And thank God he did. My daughter was brought up with love and compassion, not fear, like your boys. She might have gone off the rails, but she is bright and clever and brave. She had the courage to face her part in what happened and to walk away rather than causing us any more pain. She went off to God knows where and suffered on her own, while you and Ewan manipulated me into thinking she didn't deserve to be part of this family.'

She drew a deep breath, relishing the feeling of finally speaking all the words she'd been holding back for so long. 'And what kind of family is this? It's not the one I lived in with Oli, where we talked and laughed and loved each other unconditionally. There's always a condition with you lot. Do as I say, or everything will be withdrawn. Ewan is threatening to take Phoebe away because I didn't follow his instructions. Phoebe is just a little girl. And she loves me. I love her and she loves me but winning a point in this awful family tennis match where you're the bloody umpire, is all you've taught him to care about.'

She pointed a shaking finger at Joyce. 'Well, I've had enough. I want to live in a family where we all want the best for each other, and since that's not how you and Ewan operate, then I choose to walk away.'

She took a step towards the door, then turned back once more. 'Where is he, this perfect son of yours, by the way? Where is he when you're laid up in hospital with a broken hip? Who was there for you the night you fell? Who was looking out for you?' She pointed at Immy. 'She was. Who's here now when he's off gallivanting with some new girlfriend in America?' Bea jabbed her forefinger into her own chest. 'Muggins here. Me. I'm the one picking up the pieces. Well, enough. Come on, Immy.' She marched towards the door, but Immy stood still, looking between the two of them. 'Immy.'

'Grandma?' Immy's voice was quietly pleading.

Bea's chest was rising and falling with the exertion of her speech. She forced herself to take one last look at Joyce and her lungs deflated when she saw tears rolling down her face.

'Don't turn on the waterworks now you're worried no one will be here to do your bidding.' But her voice had lost its conviction.

'Mum.' Immy's tone made Bea fall silent. She took a tissue from the box on the table and passed it to Joyce, who dabbed at her eyes.

Black kohl smeared the tissue and when Joyce eventually focused on Bea, her eyes were small and pale again. 'That was quite the speech.'

'It seems I've been saving it up.'

Joyce folded the tissue and pressed it against her eyes. She held her hand out and Immy passed another tissue. 'Regretfully, I'm finding it hard to disagree with most of your points.'

That wasn't what Bea expected her to say. The fury coursing through her dissipated and suddenly she felt immensely sad and tired.

Joyce stared into her eyes. 'You've got a good heart, Beatrice, an unusually good one, and one, I fear, my youngest son and I may have taken advantage of.' She patted the wooden arm of the chair and Bea dutifully sat. Some things didn't change.

Joyce looked across at Immy, who was still perched nervously on the mattress. 'So, I'm to become a great-grand-mother?'

Immy nodded, her hand instinctively resting on her stomach.

'May I ask who the father is?'

'It's none of your business,' said Bea, although she was desperate to know.

'It's alright,' said Immy. 'But don't freak out.'

Bea's mouth went dry. God, not more drama. Her mind flashed through scenarios, each one worse than the last.

'He's someone you'll recognise.'

Bea and Joyce exchanged confused looks. They hadn't seen Immy for three years. Who on earth did they all have in common except Ewan? Bea felt nauseous. She almost didn't want to ask, 'Who?'

'Jude Valley.'

Bea knew the name but couldn't exactly place it.

'*The* Jude Valley?' asked Joyce.

'Who's *the* Jude Valley?' Bea was watching Joyce's face as her jaw dropped open. She seemed uncharacteristically lost for words.

'He's the presenter of that antiques show Grandma likes. Turns out his brother died of a drugs overdose when he was a teenager, so he's a patron of the rehabilitation centre where I worked. He used to come in for the board meetings and we started seeing each other.'

'Good Lord.' Joyce's eyes were still wide.

'Anyway, I thought we were keeping it all quiet because he was a board member and I was the receptionist, but . . .'

'He didn't?' Bea growled.

'What? No!' Immy shook her head vigorously. 'Nothing like that. He's a nice bloke, he didn't force me into anything. I thought we were in a proper relationship, but—'

'He's . . .?' Bea prompted, realising where this was headed.

Immy nodded.

'What?' Joyce's eyes darted between them.

'Married?' said Bea.

Immy nodded again.

'The swine!' said Joyce.

'I'm sorry, love.' Bea moved around the bed and wrapped her arms around Immy.

'It's alright. I was upset when I first found out what an unfaithful shit he was, but he was never going to be the love of my life, and . . .'

'Does his wife know?'

'Yeah.' Immy grimaced. 'She knew he'd had affairs before, but when she found out I was pregnant, she left him. He tried to come crawling back to me, but that's not the kind of man I want to share my life with. Just wish I'd known before.'

'Has he accepted . . . you know?' Bea patted Immy's stomach and felt instantly protective when she found it hard under her hand.

'Yep. He's not trying to pretend he's not the father or anything. He's actually kind of excited about it. He's not a bad man. Just one that can't keep it in his trousers. He's been nagging to meet you, actually.'

'Goodness,' said Joyce. 'You know he graduated from Cambridge a year early, with a first-class honours degree? The youngest antiques expert ever hired by that show. Handsome devil – and descended from aristocracy, too.'

'Grandma!' Immy shook her head. 'He's a thirty-year-old serial philanderer.'

'A well-bred, intelligent one, though.'

'Your value system is seriously skewed,' said Bea, trying to get her head around this new, unexpected information. 'I can see you're feeling better.' She winked and Joyce smiled back. 'I'm going to leave you two here to catch up while I move my stuff out of Ewan's.' She sighed. 'All change.'

'He'll come to his senses,' said Joyce.

'He'd better, because I'm sure Phoebe will be missing me as much as I miss her.'

'I'll make sure he comes around.'

And if anyone could make sure of that, it was Joyce. On her way out, Bea glanced back from the doorway to see Immy move into the seat beside Joyce and reach across to take her grandmother's hand. Joyce gazed at Immy in a way Bea recognised, but hadn't seen for many, many years. There was warmth in her eyes. There was love.

Chapter Thirty-Six

The sound of the gravel under her tyres as she drove up Ewan's drive made her feel unexpectedly sad. She'd got used to the noise. It had told her she was home for the last few months. And now she wasn't. She parked in front of the house in the spot she'd got used to seeing as her own. Inside the house she switched off the alarm, then lifted the picture of Gemma in the frame and studied her face.

She remembered her wedding day, and the way she'd shuddered when Gemma said she hadn't been stupid enough to sign a pre-nup. She was a girl, really. Silly and naïve, maybe, but she had no idea what she was really letting herself in for with Ewan as a husband and Joyce living on the same street. Ewan was forty when they got married. What was lacking in him that he needed to be with someone so much younger than he was? Maybe he needed to be in control in one of his relationships? Perhaps Joyce's parenting had been even more destructive than she thought.

Gemma's chin resting on Phoebe's shoulder broke her heart for both of them. Putting the picture down, she trudged upstairs. She walked past her bedroom, *the guest bedroom* she corrected herself, and went into Phoebe's. The room was a mess. The open drawers with clothes tumbling out confirmed that Phoebe at least had a hand in her own packing.

Bea lifted a pink pyjama top from the floor next to the bed. She folded it and then brought it to her nose and breathed in. The scent was unmistakably Phoebe. She closed her eyes. How could it be that now the hole left by Immy was filled, a new, Phoebe-sized one had to be gouged out of her? It was raw, its edges jagged and stinging. This wasn't fair on either of them.

She forced herself to put the pyjama top down and resolved not to tidy the room. Let Ewan try to do it, although she doubted he had a clue which drawer her pyjamas went in. The craft chest next to Phoebe's bed was open, colouring books and boxes of felt tips scattered on the carpet in front. Even when she felt like fun Aunty Bea, she'd avoided this chest, full to the brim with paints, glue and tubes of sparkles. Now the opportunity was gone, she wished she'd said yes every time Phoebe wanted to do painting and sticking. She peered inside and noticed what looked like old school exercise books piled at the bottom, vaguely remembering what Phoebe had said about her finding Mummy's story books in the chest. The thought of Phoebe holding on to Gemma's things made her close her eyes. She stepped over the colouring books and tins of fuzzy felt and left the room.

The guest room door was closed. She pushed down on the handle and stepped inside, winded to see the duvet still thrown back as she had left it. She kneeled and dragged out the cases she'd stowed under the bed, unzipped the biggest and flung it on top. Something white on the pillow on the far side of the bed caught her eye. Leaving the case gaping, she walked around the bed and lifted the piece of paper from where it rested against the white cotton. A note, written in Phoebe's round letters.

> *Dear Aunty Bea*
> *I miss you and I love you. Pleese come home sune.*
> *Love from*
> *Phoebe*
> *xxx*

Bea slumped on the bed, unable to take her eyes from the childish handwriting. She held it to her mouth, the paper crinkling with each breath as her tears discoloured the edge. She took it away from her face and closed her eyes. The only completely innocent person in all of this was Phoebe, and the fact she was hurting sliced into Bea's heart.

When she opened her eyes, she spotted an exercise book like the ones in the bottom of Phoebe's craft box on the carpet next to the bed. A blue and yellow striped pencil lay next to it, as though Phoebe had been disturbed when she was writing the note for Bea, dropped it, and run from the room.

Bea picked up the book and it fell open at the back. A scrappy edge of paper matched the torn edge of the note. She flicked to the front of the book. On the first page she was surprised to see writing. The handwriting was rounded like Phoebe's, but neater, the letters small and perfect. Bea started to read.

> *The counsellor told me to write a journal. I can't see how it will help, but it's worth a try, so here goes. I'm supposed to write about how I'm feeling. She*

wants to find out what's causing my 'anxiety and low mood'. I don't know why they can't just call it depression. Low mood sounds like I'm a teenager sulking because my mum won't get me a new top.

But I know exactly why I'm anxious and depressed and I don't think I can bear to say it out loud to anyone.

I'm a moron. I did a stupid thing and now I'm being punished.

Bea blinked. She closed the book and stared at the front cover. Other than a square box with black printed lines, there was no title, but it was clearly Gemma's diary. She remembered Phoebe telling her about finding Mummy's stories as they walked home from Joyce's house months ago. This must be what she meant. Bea's heart thumped in her chest. She should put it back. Back where? She held it in her hand for a moment, then, heart racing quicker, opened it and read on.

When I was growing up, I envied people like Ewan, living on roads like The Crescent, with their high-paying jobs and fancy cars. I thought because they had everything they needed, they must be happy. Who wouldn't be happy when they didn't have to worry about money all the time?

Turns out, people are just people, with messy, complicated lives, whatever road they live on. Who knew? Not stupid little me.

I should have seen the signs at the start and run a mile. The first time I saw Ewan and Joyce together, him watching for her approval all the time, I should have gone back to the estate. I wish I'd noticed that

Oli was the only really happy one out of the lot, and that's because he turned his back on it all.

I can't believe the way they talk about Bea, as though having a Yorkshire accent and swearing a bit makes her less than them. She's the best of the lot and at least she's not scared to be herself. She's the kind of mum I wish I'd had, the kind that sees when you're not yourself and asks about your day. I don't think anyone's ever hugged me as much as Bea does. If you make her laugh, she gives you a squeeze, if you're sad, she'll pull you in for a cuddle.

Bea wiped away the tears dripping onto the paper and read on.

I can see how much Immy loves her mum, but she's a mess since her dad died and she's giving Bea a hard time. I wish she'd get away from that idiot boyfriend. It's like she's under his spell.

I've seen him following me when I'm out. Ewan doesn't know I've seen the messages on his phone telling Zach where he thinks I'm going. I checked yesterday and they've all been deleted, so maybe he's given up paying him to spy on me.

Bea reread the neat handwriting. Ewan knew Gemma was having an affair? If that was true, then Immy hadn't told Zach. *Ewan* was the one who told Zach? Acid began to bubble in Bea's stomach.

I tried to end it with Sam when I found out Ewan knew about us. I cried for three days. None of this is fair on Phoebe. Sam says he wants her to live with us when I get the nerve to leave, but I know Ewan won't let her go without a fight, even though he never spends any time with her. He's got no idea what it's really like, watching your baby girl twenty-four hours a day in case she has a seizure.

I think the anxiety really started the first time Phoebe had a fit. Watching her little arms and legs spasm and not being able to stop it. I hated putting her through all those tests while the doctors tried to find out how much damage the birthmarks had done to her brain.

It's a miracle, really, how well she's doing, now they've got the medication right. Apparently, the laser treatment will take the redness on her face right down too. Not that it matters. She's beautiful to me. Always has been, always will be.

I just can't shake the fear though. Sometimes I see her hand jerk and I think it's happening again. It's like I'm stuck on high alert. I'm so tired all the time. Ewan seems to think that now she's stopped fitting, it's all okay. He goes to work and gets on with his life as though the world isn't always about to collapse.

Sam helps. He says he gets it, but he can't, not really. He does see the real me though, and he still loves me. Ewan only notices me if his mother wants a lift to her Bridge club or we've run out of loo roll.

I want to talk to Bea, but then I'll have to admit I married Ewan for all the wrong reasons. When she's lost her lovely Oli, it seems cruel to say I've got my husband, but I don't want him. And with Immy giving her a hard time, I don't want to pile all my stuff on her, too. I hope Immy kicks Zach into touch. She's worth more. Ha! Listen to me pretending I know what other people should do when I've made such a mess of my life.

I should never have married Ewan, but at least he gave me Phoebe. I'll tell him after I've seen Sam tonight.

Bea stared at the page, reading the last line over and over again. It seemed incomprehensible that hours after Gemma wrote this, she was dead.

And, if you followed the logic used to blame Immy, her death was not Immy's fault, it was Ewan's. And he had known that all along.

THEN

Chapter Thirty-Seven

Four Years Ago

Zach leaned across and pulled the handle to open the car door as Immy staggered down the drive, away from the noise and bustle of her father's wake. He'd been annoyed when she called. He was playing Call of Duty and she'd thrown him off his game. Now he saw her, he was glad he'd come. She clearly needed someone to take care of her.

Immy was always telling him how distracted her mum was since her dad got sick. It was like she didn't know Immy still existed. That's why she spent so much time at his house instead of at home. He felt sorry for her. That's partly why Immy was perfect for him: they both had parents who'd let them down. She needed him and it felt validating to be needed, especially by someone as good as Immy.

'Alright?'

Immy flopped onto the passenger seat, looking rough. 'Not really. I wish you'd been there.'

Zach had been relieved when Immy told him her mum wouldn't allow him to come after she overheard him calling her a bitch. 'Yeah. It's not fair on you. Sorry, babe.'

He peered past her to the doorway of her gran's massive old house to see if he could spot Ewan. Ewan was a prick, like Zach's dad and all of his friends who worked in the city, but at least he didn't treat him like he was a moron. He'd been really interested in his photography project last time Immy had forced Zach to go to one of their tedious family meals. Zach was working hard on manipulating night-time photos and his technology teacher was impressed with how he could improve grainy footage using an American programme he'd found. His dad said taking pictures in the dark was creepy, but Ewan seemed to get what he was trying to do. One day he might tell him about his big plan for starting a tech company. He might even ask him to invest, give him some start-up capital.

Craning his neck, he could only see the silhouette of Immy's mum, standing with that little kid with the red cheek on her hip. He didn't know whether to wave. He wasn't usually bothered, but you had to act differently at funerals, didn't you? He raised his arm, but she didn't respond, and he felt stupid. She was watching Immy with this soppy look on her face, like a dog who wants to be allowed on the sofa.

He could smell the alcohol fumes coming off Immy and her head was lolling as though it wasn't fully attached to her body. She used to be a right laugh when she was drunk, all giggly and affectionate. These days she was quiet and moody. He missed the old Immy. He pushed the gearstick into reverse and pulled out of the drive, trying not to look at Immy's mum as the headlights high-lighted her crying face.

It was embarrassing. Parents weren't supposed to cry. His dad hadn't even cried when Grandma died. He was probably too busy calculating how much he was going to make on her house. Zach had only cried about missing his grandma in his room when he was on his own. He used his pillow to muffle the sound. The memory of that made his throat tight. He put his hand on Immy's leg and squeezed.

The sight of Immy's mum, all devastated like that, made him wonder if his parents had any feelings at all. They didn't seem to. They were like moaning machines. One of these days, after listening to his dad bore on about whatever he thought Zach had done wrong this time and watching his mum nodding her head, all pious and snooty, he'd tell his mum about all the women his dad was shagging behind her back. How perfectly self-righteous would she be then? The sick thing was, his dad knew he knew, but he acted like it was some kind of in-joke, some dad-son bonding crap.

Alright, Zach might have got off with a few girls behind Immy's back, but when you were married and had kids it was different. You didn't do that shit then. He looked across at Immy and wondered if he should tell her about Grandma and the pillow, that he knew how she felt. But he couldn't think of the right words. He clicked on the indicator and turned out of The Crescent.

'Where do you want to go? We can't go back to mine. My mum's got her book group. House is full of menopausal feminists. I'm surprised I got out with both bollocks.' He laughed and glanced across at Immy again, but her face was stone. She never laughed at his jokes anymore. 'Yours? Nobody's in there.'

He glanced across and saw tears streaming down her

face. To be fair, that was probably insensitive. 'Sorry, I didn't . . . I'll just drive around for a bit.'

Immy nodded and he pressed his foot harder on the pedal. He wished he'd had a smoke before he came out. He didn't have his stuff with him and Immy would only give him a hard time anyway. She was always going on about how much he smoked, even though everyone smoked weed these days, and everyone knew it was less harmful than alcohol, anyway, which made her a bit of a hypocrite, didn't it? God knows what she'd do if she knew about the tabs he'd got off Tristan in year thirteen. She'd do her nut.

'Slow down.'

He saw how pale Immy's face was and lifted his foot. 'You're not going to be sick, are you? Immy? Please don't throw up in my car.' He turned into a car park on the left and parked across two bays, resentful he couldn't do a handbrake turn if she was going to vom. This deserted car park would be perfect for it. 'Come on, out if you're going to throw up.'

Immy opened the door and climbed out. She stood, hunched over, holding on to the door. He turned off the engine and walked in front of the bonnet to join her just as she spewed the contents of her stomach onto the tarmac.

He jumped back but splashes of yellow liquid splattered his new white trainers. 'For fuck's sake!' He grabbed a discarded McDonald's napkin from the door pocket and scrubbed at the bile stain, but that only rubbed it in. 'For fuck's sake.' He'd paid a fortune for these trainers. Now he'd have to beg his mum to clean them.

'Sorry.' Immy wiped the back of her hand across her mouth. She looked at him and something in the way her pink-tinged eyes searched his face made the fury that was always inside him subside.

'It's alright.'

She made him want to be a better person. She always did that. It was one of the reasons he didn't break it off when she stopped being fun. Immy was good and being with her made him feel like some of the slime from his dad and the shitty rich kids he hung around with at school was washed away.

He stepped around the mess on the ground and took her in his arms. 'It's alright.' She felt small against his chest and when her body shuddered against his he felt his own eyes sting.

Chapter Thirty-Eight

Three Years Ago

Zach tugged at the neck of his designer t-shirt. He couldn't stop his jaw from pushing his teeth together and his fingers twitched. It was annoying. He wanted to look fierce when he met up with Ewan, not like a jittery kid. He needed Ewan to see him as an equal, or he'd never take his business idea seriously when he was ready to launch. Things hadn't been going as well as he'd hoped. His dad had laughed when he'd told him about the tech he wanted to invest in, told him to go to university like everyone else, or get a job to earn the capital he wanted.

He pulled the small bag of powder from his pocket, licked his index finger and stuck it inside. He rubbed the powder on his gums then sucked his finger clean. It tasted rank and made his tongue and the back of his throat numb, but he needed a quick bump.

Checking his Apple Watch, he saw Ewan was ten minutes late. No respect, like all the others. Did he even want to go into business with someone who didn't respect him? He went through the list in his head of all the people who treated him like some rich, posh kid, starting with the self-important teachers at that stuck-up school. They acted like gods, but he knew how much his dad paid in fees every term. He went on about it enough. He paid their wages. Who did they think they were, treating him as if they were his superiors? They'd learn.

He was sick of people treating him like a kid. If his parents hadn't gone off their nuts and cut off his allowance when they found a tiny bit of coke in his room, he wouldn't have to do the stuff he did now. His knee jiggled. There was a smear of dirt on the dashboard of the Golf. He rubbed at it with his finger. When it wouldn't shift, he slapped it with the palm of his hand.

Fucking car. It was an embarrassment. All of his friends' parents bought them decent cars, at least something with a proper badge. Not like this piece of shit. His hand stung now, and Ewan still wasn't here. What did he want, anyway? He'd only met Ewan a few times with Immy, at crappy family parties where that old bag who insisted on being called 'Mrs James' looked down her nose at him.

Ewan's wife was well fit though. He was punching above his weight there.

The bump was kicking in and he felt his heart lift in his chest and pump against his ribcage. Maybe Ewan had been thinking about the tech Zach had shown him. Maybe he understood Zach's vision, even without him explaining it. He could be coming here to suggest they went into partnership. Zach wasn't going in fifty-fifty, even if Ewan was bringing all the money onboard. He wasn't giving half his company away that easily.

Headlights rose over the brow of the hill and a black Range Rover came to a stop next to his car. Zach breathed in through his nose and a glob of coke dislodged and dropped into his throat. He could taste the chemical bleachiness of it when he swallowed. He waited for Ewan to get out and walk around to him before he opened his door. It helped him feel like he was in charge.

When he stood, he was glad he towered over Ewan. He might play the big man with his money and fancy car, but he was still a short arse.

'Zach.'

Ewan looked in his eyes but, when Zach refused to look away, he shifted his gaze to his old-man shiny shoes. Why did old men wear such crappy shoes? Did they think that polishing their shoes made them like army sergeants or something? He was always going to wear trainers, even when he ran a multi-million-pound tech company. And he'd let all of his employees wear trainers. None of this shiny shoe bollocks. Ewan would look so out of place when he came in for meetings with his dated shoes.

'What's up, man? You gonna tell me what all this is about?' Zach's heart beat faster. Was this the moment someone told him they'd seen his true potential? 'It's not every day that a bloke DMs me on Insta and asks to meet up.' He gave a nervous laugh and coughed to try to cover it.

'It's a delicate matter,' said Ewan. He glanced over his shoulder like he was worried the feds were tracking him. 'I wouldn't want any of this getting back to Immy.'

'Oh yeah?' Zach tried to work out why Immy would be involved in their business. 'This about money?'

Ewan shuffled his feet on the tarmac. 'In a way. I was hoping you could do some, erm, surveillance, for me.'

'Surveillance?' This wasn't what he was hoping for. He wished his heart would slow down. He needed to think.

'I know you're an expert with, you know.' Ewan waved his hands around. 'Photography and night vision . . . that sort of thing. I want you to find some evidence of . . .' He looked over his shoulder again.

Ah, now he got it. The wife was playing away. Of course she was. This wasn't what he wanted, but he could make it work. Ewan had seen he was an expert, that was a good start. And if he did this for him, then he would owe him, wouldn't he? He couldn't do it for free though. Nobody respected people who gave things away for free. 'It will cost you.'

Ewan's face hardened. He dug into his pocket and pulled out a wallet stuffed with notes. 'Naturally. It goes without saying that I need you to be discreet. You can't let Immy know anything about this. I want you to follow my wife and photograph her with anyone she spends time with.' He pulled a wad of twenty-pound notes out of the wallet. 'Here's two hundred.'

'You want me to lie to my girlfriend about this?' Zach dropped his head to one side and pursed his lips.

'Three hundred.' Ewan rolled his eyes and counted out more notes. 'That's it.' He spat the last 't'.

Zach held out his hand and took the notes. They felt slippery and new. 'No problem.'

'She's going out tonight at seven, to see her *friend* from her art class.'

'Gotcha.' He eyed the money. 'Just proof that her and this friend are . . .?'

'That should be enough to stop her trying to take everything I've got.'

'Man, that must be hard, finding out she's cheating, then having to hand over half your money.'

'And house, and daughter.'

Even Zach knew the order of that was wrong. 'I feel for you, man.' He imagined how he'd feel if Immy cheated on him. Their relationship wasn't setting him on fire, exactly, but he liked having a pretty girl like Immy to rely on. She was a good girl. It would be humiliating if she went off with someone else and he was the last to know. He felt the muscles in his cheeks tensing. His teeth ground together as he imagined everyone laughing at him behind his back. 'You must want to kill her.'

'Yep,' Ewan said, matter of factly, then snapped his wallet closed and shoved it in the inside pocket of his suit. He glared at Zach. 'If you tell anyone about this, I'll deny everything.'

'You can count on me.' He took a step closer to Ewan. 'When I've done this, I'd like to talk to you about a business idea.'

'Business?' Ewan scrunched his face.

'Yeah.'

Ewan shrugged and climbed into the Range Rover. 'Let's just get this unpleasantness out of the way first, shall we?'

That wasn't a no. When Ewan pulled away, Zach counted the money. His buzz added to the edgy anticipation. This wasn't what he'd hoped for, but it would do for now. This was the easiest money he'd ever made, and he had just come up with a plan to make ten times more.

* * *

Immy was whining again about some argument she'd had with her mum and Zach was trying but failing to listen. He hadn't slept more than three hours a night for days and he was finding it hard to concentrate.

'I feel bad for saying I hate her again,' Immy said, 'but she just winds me up all the time. It's like she's watching, waiting for me to do something wrong so she can have a go at me. Honestly, she needs to back off and get a life of her own. It's like I'm the only thing in her life and it's her mission to make me as miserable as she is.' She took a swig from her glass. 'And she wants us to go to family counselling. How mad's that? Like I'm going to sit there and tell a stranger how I'm feeling. I don't even tell her when—'

'I'm off for a slash.' She was mid-sentence and the look she gave him when he stood up made his heart drop. He didn't know how she still managed to make him feel stuff. He'd successfully put up a solid wall in front of his parents' disappointment. Nothing they said could get through it. Now they'd cut off his money altogether, he was even less interested in what they had to say.

But, somehow, Immy could still look at him with those big eyes and make him feel like the shit he knew he was, or, on the rare occasion he tried to be better, she could make him feel like a god. When he got what he needed, he'd make life good for her, for both of them. She deserved that. He sploshed more Raspberry Absolut in her glass and kissed her on the lips before leaving his bedroom.

When he got to the toilet, he took the little plastic bag with six small triangular-shaped pills nestled in the bottom from his pocket. He preferred coke, but Molly was cheaper. He put one on his tongue, stuck his head under the cold tap, slurped the water and swallowed. Wiping water from his chin, he cursed Immy for being so straight. She didn't know how much he needed this stuff right now. It was the only thing stopping his head from imploding. Anyway, after she begged him not to take coke, he'd promised her he'd stopped. He wasn't lying, was he? He wasn't taking coke. He planned to stop taking everything when the business was up and running, but while he was still in the planning stages, he needed the focus the tabs and speed gave him.

He shrugged his shoulders as he looked in the mirror and tugged at his white t-shirt, straightening the creases. He peered at his reflection. There was no denying his pupils were enormous, but Immy wasn't going to notice. She was throwing back the vodka tonight. His phone buzzed in his pocket. He took it out and forced his eyes to focus on the Snapchat message.

I've tracked her phone to here. Do what we agreed.

Underneath was a screenshot of a map with a red arrow. Zach enlarged the screen with his fingers and recognised the car park of a local woodland trail. His cheeks burned at the terseness of Ewan's message. He'd tried to get pictures of Gemma with the man Ewan thought she was seeing but hadn't managed to get one incriminating shot so far. He thought he'd got one good one, but the technology let him down. He'd tried everything, but it still looked like a big shadow, not two people kissing. He needed a recognisable picture to prove to Ewan what he could do. He was worried about that. His plans relied on being able to make images clear enough. That way he could sell his skills to security companies, maybe even the police and the government. In his head, the whole world would need him one day. He'd be a hero.

In the last message Ewan had said he wanted his money back. There was no way that was happening, not least because Zach had spent the lot. He had too much riding on this. He hadn't applied to university, and he wasn't about to get some dead-end job. He needed money to start his business, then his life would really begin. Instead of wasting time sleeping, he spent hours working with the programmes, trying to find a way around the problems, but he kept coming up blank. When he was the boss, he'd pay people to solve this shit. It was all in the business plan he'd drawn up and revised a million times in his bedroom as the sun surprised him by rising before he'd even closed his eyes.

'Let's go out,' he said, when he came back into the room. He could hear his parents' TV through the wall, and it was setting him on edge. His heart was pumping harder and the urgency to be on the move set his fingers twitching.

'I can't be bothered.'

'I'll go on my own then.' He dragged a hoodie from the wardrobe and pulled it over his head.

Immy sat up on the bed. 'You can't leave me here with your parents.'

'Your choice.' He was buzzing now, and the room was too small and too hot. He took the hoodie off again. 'Come on.' He moved to the bed and buried his head in her hair, breathing in her apple shampoo, then biting her earlobe. 'Don't be boring.'

Immy giggled. 'Get off.' She pushed him, but she was smiling, and he was flooded with love for her. His brain conjured an image of the two of them sitting by a pool, overlooking the sea, cocktails in their hands. He would make that happen for them. Tonight was the first step.

Necking back the vodka in her glass, Immy groaned, but followed him out of the room and down the stairs.

'You can't be serious?' Immy said, when he stuck the key in the car lock. 'You're not going to drive? I thought we were going for a walk?'

'Come on, Immy.' He rolled his shoulders and clicked his neck from left to right. 'I can't have you on my back as well as everyone else. All I hear is what I can't fucking do. I thought you were on my side. You know what, get in the car or don't. I don't care.' He flung open the door and shoved the key in the ignition, not looking at Immy when she slumped in the seat next to him.

He knew exactly where he was going, even though the roads seemed windier than usual. Immy sat silently in the passenger seat, and he wished she'd stayed at home. She was bringing him down. He turned right into the lane leading to the car park, where he saw a soft-top BMW parked at the far end next to the wall. He switched off his headlights but kept driving up the dimly lit lane.

Immy sat up a little straighter. 'Where are we going?'

'Just up here.'

She leaned forwards. 'That looks like Gemma's car.'

'Does it now?' Zach smiled inwardly, his heart pumping faster.

Immy put her hand on his forearm. 'Stop, Zach, stop.'

'Why?'

'If Gemma's here . . .'

Zach turned to her, 'What?'

'It's just that' – Immy squirmed in her seat – 'I think Gemma might be seeing someone. I saw her with a man in town and they looked pretty cosy. I was going to tell Mum, but I haven't yet.'

Excitement whooshed through Zach. This was it, the chance he needed. 'Let's find out then.'

'No. I don't want to. Not like this. I'll talk to Mum and work out what to do.'

Zach accelerated and screeched to a halt at a right angle to Gemma's car, close to the driver's door, blocking her in.

'What are you doing?' Immy yelled. She grabbed at his hand on the steering wheel but he shook her off. She'd thank him one day, when she saw why he had to do all this. It wasn't pretty, but you didn't get ahead by being a coward. He wasn't the one cheating either. Gemma was like his dad. She deserved everything she got.

He put the headlights on full beam, only pausing for a second when he saw Gemma's face lit up like a terrified death mask. He took out his phone and started to take pictures of her trying to open the car door, but she was barricaded in by Zach's bumper. A man's face was blinking against the bright light in the passenger seat. Zach carried on snapping as the man started to open the passenger door. Gemma, seeming to recognise Zach and Immy, turned and held his arm to stop him moving.

Zach threw his door open and leaped from the car, elation fizzing through him. Those pictures would be bright and clear. 'Who's been a naughty girl then?' he yelled, as Gemma opened the window.

'What the hell are you doing?' She looked behind him. 'Immy? What in God's name is going on?'

He felt Immy by his side and heard her shouting. He ignored her. 'I've got a proposal for you.' He held his phone up to Gemma, then waited as she whispered something to the confused-looking man sitting next to her. 'I'll delete all of these pictures for five grand.'

'What are you talking about?' Gemma looked at Immy. 'What's going on? Immy?'

Immy shook her head. Tears and snot ran down her face. She was really killing his buzz now.

'Five thousand pounds and hubby doesn't need to know about your grubby little secret.'

'Oh, piss off, Zach.' Gemma didn't look sorry. She

303

didn't even look nervous. Her face twisted in a sneer. 'Don't interfere in things you don't understand. Go home to your PlayStation and stop trying to be the big man.'

He held the phone out for her to see. 'One click and that's your divorce settlement fucked.'

A sound came out of her mouth that it took him a moment to process. She was laughing. Her head was thrown back on the leather headrest, and she was actually fucking laughing. 'I mean it.' His voice sounded like a spoiled child. Heat rushed into his face.

'Do what you like. I'm leaving Ewan anyway and couldn't give a toss about the money. I've tried being rich and, you know what? It doesn't make you happy, so click away, kid.'

She was laughing and shaking her head as though he was some kind of toddler throwing a tantrum in the supermarket aisle. Humiliation flooded his veins. His heart jumped in his chest and his mouth went dry. He marched back to the car, the sound of Gemma's laughing taunting every step. Immy was shouting, running towards the car. She jumped in and slammed the door. She was screaming as she did up her seatbelt, but the words didn't penetrate the wall of anger in his head. He turned the key in the ignition and slammed the gearstick into reverse.

He'd show her who was a child. He was sick of nobody treating him with respect. He'd had enough of everyone else taking charge of his life. He'd had plans for that money. He'd already spent some of it on the Molly in his pocket, and now he wouldn't be able to pay his debts or start his business, and it was that bitch's fault.

He heard the tyres screeching underneath as he backed up as fast as he could. Immy was screaming. His heart beat faster as he pushed the gear stick into first and blood pounded in his ears, adding to the revving of the engine as he smashed his foot onto the accelerator and the car leaped forwards, throwing his head back against the head-rest. He felt like he was flying, the thrilling smell of burning tyres, the fear on Gemma's face lit up as the headlights careered towards the driver's side of her car. The sound of metal on metal, the splinter of glass as his head hit the windscreen, the . . .

NOW

Chapter Thirty-Nine

Bea stormed into the hospital room, shaking from head to toe. 'Did you know?'

'Shh.' Immy put her finger to her lips. She pointed at Joyce, whose head lolled back on the pillows, mouth agape. She was snoring gently, and it was all Bea could do to stop from dragging a pillow out from under her and pressing it against her face.

'Joyce,' Bea shouted. 'Wake up, Joyce. I need to talk to you.'

The old woman's eyelids fluttered open. She peered around the room as though trying to get her bearings.

'Mum, what's going on?' Immy put her hand on Joyce's arm and Bea felt new fury at her trying to protect Joyce after everything she and Ewan had done.

'Did. You. Know?'

'Know what?' Joyce winced as she struggled to get more upright.

'The truth about what happened to Gemma.'

'What are you talking about?'

'That Ewan was paying Zach to follow Gemma?'

'When?'

'Before the crash.'

'Why would he do that?' Joyce looked confused.

'Because he knew she was having an affair and he wanted Zach to get evidence.'

Immy shook her head. 'No, that's not right. I told Zach about Gemma. That's why—'

She stopped speaking when Bea slapped the exercise book on the bed. 'Read that.'

Immy picked up the book and started to read. Bea watched her face change from confusion to anguish as she turned each page. 'I can't believe—'

'What is it?' Joyce was fully awake now. 'Pass my glasses. They're . . .' Her eyes flitted around all the surfaces in the room. 'Where are my blasted reading glasses? What is that you're reading?'

'It's Gemma's diary, or a journal, or something.' Immy closed the front cover, but finding no title, opened it again on the rounded words.

'Well, what does it say?'

Immy squinted from Joyce to her mother. 'It says it was Ewan who told Zach about her affair. He got him to follow her. He was the one who told him where to find her that night.'

Joyce's hand shook as she took the exercise book from Immy.

'It never occurred to me to ask Zach why we went up to the trail. He said he wanted a drive. I presumed he'd been restless because of the drugs, and it was just an awful coincidence that we saw Gemma's car.' She was trembling now, too. 'It wasn't my fault, was it, Mum? It wasn't my fault.'

Bea gathered Immy in her arms and rocked backwards

and forwards, all the while watching Joyce read the words which proved they'd turned their backs on Bea's innocent daughter because of lies told by her wicked son.

* * *

'Do you think it was pride that made Ewan lie?' asked Jan, when Bea and Immy got home from the hospital and explained what had happened. 'Or shame maybe?'

'God knows,' said Bea. 'I don't suppose he thought for a minute Zach would go on to kill anyone. I mean, what made him do it?' She tucked a strand of hair behind Immy's ear. The poor kid looked exhausted.

'Male privilege and toxic masculinity,' Immy said, her voice heavy.

'Eh?' said Bea and Jan in unison.

'Seriously. I've thought about it a lot. Zach was always going on about nobody respecting him, as though he deserved to be treated like he could walk on water or something, for no reason at all. It's the kind of elitist bullshit Ewan believes in, too. When Zach didn't get what he thought he deserved, he was like a little kid throwing a tantrum. Add a bloodstream full of narcotics, and you've got the makings of a right nutter. If we were in America, he'd be the kind of kid who did a school shooting.'

'God.' Jan pulled her lips back. 'You really have thought it through.'

'You don't work in a rehab centre without picking up a few tips. I'm planning to do a psychology degree when this one's old enough.' She patted her stomach. 'I'm so sorry I didn't see what Zach was capable of. If I hadn't brought him into our lives . . .'

'Oh no, missy,' Bea said. 'I'm not letting you do that. You've been cleared. I'm not letting you take responsibility

311

for any of it. Zach was the one behind the wheel, but Ewan was the one behind Zach. And he's not going to get away with pretending he's the injured party for one second more.'

* * *

Bea clapped her gloved hands together, but it did nothing to restore the feeling in her fingers. A boy rode past on a scooter, the bobble on the top of his hat bouncing like a ping pong ball every time he slapped his foot on the path to propel him forwards. His parents picked up their pace to follow him, their breath fogging as they said a quick *hello* on their way past. Everyone said hello on Christmas Eve. It was like a holiday from the social norm of putting your head down and getting through the day. Bea liked it. It reminded her of growing up in a village in Yorkshire when everyone greeted each other, even without the fuel of mince pies and half a bottle of Bailey's.

Despite the good cheer radiating from everyone else in the park, she felt murderous. It was six days since she'd found Gemma's diary and Ewan had only just got back from New York. She was sure Joyce would have filled him in, and bitten a chunk off him, if her reaction was anything to go by, but Bea refused to speak to him on the phone. She wanted to look the bastard in the eye.

Now, she approached the bench where they'd arranged to meet and there he was. She wanted to tear into him, ripping at the expensive ski jacket he was wearing, gouging the flesh from his bones with her nails. Instead, she breathed deeply, like Immy instructed, and made her way towards where he was leaning forwards with his elbows on his knees, staring across the misty lake. He lifted his gaze when he heard her footsteps. He raised his eyebrows. Was that all he had? Acid churned in her belly.

'Bea.'

She sat next to him and stared out at the lake. The thin film of ice that had formed overnight was cracked and jagged. Leaves and slurry collected at its edges. Bea thought it couldn't look more different from the frozen lakes she'd seen in films, where the ice was like a mirror and people in dress coats and top hats ice skated on its shimmering surface.

But life wasn't like a film. In real life, stupid boys did awful things and uncles betrayed their nieces to save their own pathetic skin.

She turned to look at Ewan. His ears were red at the tips. She was glad he was freezing. 'Why did you do it?'

He shook his head. 'I don't know.'

A sound like a roar flooded her ears. She balled her fists to stop herself from lashing out at him. 'My child left for three fucking years.' She measured the words carefully to make sure he felt the weight of each one. 'Because you made us all believe she was responsible for the death of two people.'

'I know.' He ran white fingers through his hair. 'I know you won't believe me, but I didn't . . .'

'Didn't what? Mean to put all the blame on her? That's a lie, and you know it.'

'I didn't think she'd leave. I was embarrassed about getting a kid to do my dirty work instead of confronting Gemma about the affair. I suppose blaming Imogen was easier than facing up to my part in what happened, but, honestly, I didn't think she'd leave.'

His lips trembled and Bea had to look away. She would not allow him to make her feel anything but fury. A heron stood tall on the little island in the middle of the lake and she watched it stretch out its magnificent wings. It seemed

313

to shudder, then fold back in on itself, as though suddenly feeling the cold.

'You could have come clean after she'd gone. You saw the letter. I remember showing it to you. You knew the state I was in and you knew it was the guilt that made her go.'

'It seemed too late then.'

'Bollocks. You wanted to save your own skin. If she stayed away, there was no way of anyone finding out about your connection to Zach. That's why you carried on trying to poison us all against her.'

His gaze dropped to the ground.

She wiggled her toes inside her biker boots to try to get the blood flowing. 'Three years. Can you imagine not seeing Phoebe for three years?' She remembered this wasn't a fair comparison. She loved Phoebe more than he did. He only loved himself.

His lip jutted out and he shook his head again. 'That's what I was afraid of, I suppose, at the start, when I asked Zach to follow Gemma. I knew she'd get custody. I could see how it would pan out. I'd have her for weekends, the odd holiday, but she wouldn't be my little girl anymore. Not really.' He turned to Bea. 'I promise you, on Phoebe's life, I had no idea he was going to do what he did. I wanted to have ammunition for divorce proceedings, that's all. I just wanted to be in the best position I could when it came to custody. I promise, that's all I wanted.'

'So why didn't you admit it at the inquest? Why pretend Immy was the one who told Zach about the affair? Why would you let a grieving teenager carry that guilt?'

'I wasn't thinking straight. It was all such a mess; Oli dying, then Gemma—'

'Are you really going to try to use Oli's death as your

defence?' she snarled. Her spit landed on his cheek and she silently dared him to wipe it away. He didn't. 'Oli would be ashamed of you. You did that to his daughter while she was grieving. You let her think she'd caused two deaths when she was trying to cope with losing her own dad.'

Ewan dropped his head into his hands, and she sat still as his body juddered.

'You're not even a good dad.' She wanted the words to slice through him. 'If you really started all this so you didn't lose Phoebe, you failed. You were a shit husband. You're a shit father, a shit brother, a shit son and fucking devastating uncle.'

It felt good, like some of the corrosive that burned her insides was vomited out in those words. 'I hate you.'

He tipped his head to the side and peered at her through bloodshot eyes. 'I don't blame you.'

'Good.'

But the fire inside was going out and the cold was seeping in. It was all too sad.

'I'm going to make it up to you,' he said. 'And to Immy.'

She huffed out a breath and watched it cloud, then disappear. 'Oh yeah? How exactly do you make up for lost years, for all that pain?' When she turned to him, he looked broken, and she was glad. 'You've taken so much from us. You made us believe we were bad people when we were really just trying to do our best. That kind of damage can't be mended by, I don't know . . .' She cast her eyes around the park trying to find the right words. She noticed a woman wearing a long camel coat and pointed. 'A nice coat, or a meal out. It's become part of our history, our sense of who we are.'

'Then I'll try to rebuild it. Make it better.'

Bea shook her head. He didn't get it.

'Look,' he said. 'I've made massive mistakes. I got caught up in the wrong stuff. I wanted to make as much money as Dad, so Mum would think I was a success at something.'

'Your mum? Do you know how you sound?'

He went quiet. 'I know. I lost sight of what was important. Making amends will help me as much as anything.' He searched her face, imploring her with his eyes. 'I need to do better.'

'I won't argue with that.'

'Let me start tomorrow. Christmas day is a good time to start to try to make up for things.' He smiled weakly. 'Worked for Scrooge.'

Bea refused to smile back. 'Hmm.'

'Come over in the morning? Watch Phoebe open her presents. Meet Camille?'

She'd forgotten about Camille. 'I don't know.' It felt too soon. She wanted to make him suffer. But the thought of watching Phoebe open her presents was tempting. She did deserve that.

'Ask Immy. Let me try. Please?'

'I'm not making any promises.'

'I understand.' He shivered. 'I mean it. I owe it to Oli and to all of you to put things right. I also need a coffee before I freeze to death. Although,' he snorted out a brief laugh, 'that might be the best solution.'

Bea tutted. 'Yeah, that's what Phoebe needs: another dead parent.'

'Sorry. You're right. That's the last self-pitying thing you'll hear from me. Can I get you a drink? Something warm?'

'No. I'm going to sit here for a minute.'

Ewan stood. 'Okay. I mean it, Bea. I will do everything in my power to make up for what I've done. I want to be better, especially for Phoebe. I've already started to make plans. Come tomorrow. It's a good day for new beginnings.'

He squeezed her shoulder and walked away, almost tripping over an orange dog in a padded blue coat trotting towards the bench. The dog ogled her and did a little skip. It bounded forwards, feet skittering to a stop by her knees. It gazed up with expectant brown eyes then put its paw on her knee.

'Hello, Max.' She rubbed his bony head and looked up as she heard Eddie whistle and call his name. He came over, looking cosy in a military-style wool coat and beanie hat, wisps of sideburn escaping near his ears.

'Ah, it's you.' His grin suggested that was a good thing. 'You like this bench, don't you? You're always here.'

For some reason, seeing his face made her want to cry. She couldn't trust herself to talk.

'What are you doing sitting here in this weather?' He sat down beside her and rubbed at Max's rump. 'You must be freezing.'

'Long story,' she managed, and attempted to smile.

'Okay.' He took a ball from his pocket and threw it along the path, and they watched Max bounce after it, bringing it back, wiry tail wagging in delight. Eddie threw the ball again. 'How's Joyce?'

'She's doing well, thanks.' Bea and Immy visited every day, and every day Joyce had grown a little stronger. The way she looked at Immy was exactly how she had when Immy was a child. Her face lit up as soon as she entered the room. 'I think she's considering going to Sweetingdale to recuperate, actually.' Bea had asked Jan whether she

317

thought Joyce convalescing at Sweetingdale was a good idea, since Lynn was still in charge. Jan had promised to look out for her, and they both agreed that if anyone was a match for Lynn, it was Joyce.

'I hope she does,' said Eddie.

'Ha. You can't wait to get rid of us?'

'No, that's not what—' He seemed flustered. 'Anyway.' He stood and took the ball from Max's mouth and put it back in his pocket. 'I'd better . . .' He flapped his arm towards the path. 'Good to see you, Bea. Merry Christmas.'

'Merry Christmas.'

She watched him walk away, Max looking up at him as he trotted alongside, and realised she felt better for just a few minutes in his company. Sweetingdale, with Jan there to watch over her, was probably a good idea while Joyce got back to full strength, but it would be a shame she wouldn't see Eddie anymore if she did move in there.

Unfortunately, it didn't seem like Eddie felt the same way.

Chapter Forty

She turned the key in the ignition and the engine juddered back to life. Bea felt the heater's tepid air and watched a crescent of clear glass grow up the misted windscreen. She turned her head back towards their old house. 'I'm sorry I couldn't hold on to this place.'

Immy sighed. 'Maybe it's a good thing. I've got loads of brilliant memories of that house, but there are some really sad ones, too. Now, wherever we are, we can start afresh.'

Bea nodded slowly. 'I hope the people who live there now don't see us. They'll think we're stalkers or something.'

'Stalking our old life,' Immy said wistfully, leaning over from the passenger seat to get a better view.

Bea shivered. 'I wish we could go back. I'd do a lot of things differently.'

The lights on the front of the house illuminated the door they'd spent half their lives opening and closing.

'You weren't the problem.'

The trouble with guilt, thought Bea, is that, once you've let it in, it's in your system, part of you. It runs through

319

your arteries, narrowing the passages, stopping your blood from flowing the way it did before. Hers had built up for so long; she didn't know how to clear it out. That didn't mean she wouldn't try. 'If you say so.'

'I've got my scan next week. Will you come?'

Bea turned, almost colliding with Immy's head. 'Try and stop me.' Immy's eyes were full of concern. 'What's the matter? You're not worried about the baby?'

'What if it's a girl?' Immy's voice wavered, 'What if it's like me?'

'I hope it is like you. Exactly like you.' Bea squeezed her knee with her cold hand.

'Teenage me?'

Bea dipped her head. 'Yeah, I won't pretend that bit's easy.' She held her hands over the heater, letting the hot air burn her fingertips. She drew them away. 'But you'll – we'll – muddle through. We know what we might be up against now, all those hormones and brain changes. Forearmed, and all that.' She smiled at Immy, who didn't look convinced. 'And you were dealing with losing your dad. We shouldn't underestimate the impact of that.'

They both looked at the house. Bea imagined the family inside, harassed but cheerful parents trying to get excited children ready for bed on Christmas Eve.

'He was a good dad, wasn't he?'

'The best.'

The lights around the door glowed brighter, then dipped. Bea imagined them as a coded signal from Oli, letting them know he was still with them. Oli would have told her she was being silly, but the truth was, Bea saw him everywhere; a stranger clapping a friend on the back in greeting the way Oli always did, the rumble of a low voice in a crowd.

320

'That's why I don't get Ewan.'

Bea's imaginings whooshed away like a popped balloon. 'Can you believe they were even related?'

'But it's sad, isn't it? Dad loved being part of the family. He was always there for me, involved in every discussion, telling me off when I was out of order, cuddling me, always at my shows. All of it. Ewan never seemed to be there for Phoebe. He always seemed to be at work, or if he was at home, he'd be fussing around Grandma.'

'He still isn't there for Phoebe.'

'That's really sad, isn't it?'

Bea tutted. 'It's his choice.'

'But he's missing out as well as her. Imagine having to always be in charge, always having to be right. It must be exhausting, and I don't think it helps anyone.' She folded her arms. 'That's my tinpot psychoanalysis, anyway.'

Bea laughed. 'When did you turn into a therapist?' She shook her head. 'I can't forgive him for what he did to you.'

'I think I can.' Immy rubbed at her nose with the back of her hand. 'Maybe not forgive but I'm going to try to accept what he did, and the way things turned out. I want to, anyway. I can't do anything to change it, can I, so if I come to terms with it, even if I don't exactly forgive him, then I can move on. I saw a lot of angry people at the rehab centre, and I don't want to be like that. I'd rather try to let it go.' She shifted to peer towards the house again and Bea felt her warm breath. 'I think we should go tomorrow.'

'Really?'

'It's not about him, is it?' Immy laid her hand on her tummy. 'It's about Phoebe. She's gone through too much for a kid that age and, from what you've said, she's still just as gorgeous as she was.'

'She's a very special girl.'

'Then, let's make it alright for her. I'd like to have a proper relationship with her. I want her and my baby to grow up together. That way, we'll all have each other when things are rough.'

'Wow.'

'What?'

Bea searched for the words, 'That's very mature.' She looked into Immy's eyes and felt Oli with them. He lived on through their beautiful, wise, kind girl.

The heating cut out and the temperature dropped. 'Shall we go?'

Immy nodded. 'I am mature,' she said over the noise of the engine re-starting and the heater kicking back in. 'But I still get a stocking, right? I'll never be too grown-up for a stocking.'

'You'll still get a stocking,' said Bea, her heart full to bursting. She took one last look at the house with the lights around the door, released the handbrake and set off towards their future.

* * *

She woke in Terry and Paula's house on Christmas morning with a fizzing feeling inside. She could hear Immy moving around the kitchen and the smell of coffee drifted up the stairs. It seemed too good to be true; Immy with her, having breakfast with her best friend, then going to open presents with Phoebe. After she'd fed the cats.

They could hear the festivities at Jan's before they crossed the path and reached the side door. The radio blasted out 'So here it is, Merry Christmas' through the open window. Steam obscured the glass and when Bea pushed open the door, the heat from the room hit her like getting off a plane in a hot country.

'How are you feeling about seeing Lord Ewan?' Jan asked Immy, after she'd squeezed them both and forced them to accept croissants and steaming mugs of tea.

'Bricking it,' said Immy, dusting pastry crumbs from her chin. 'Can't wait to see Phoebe though.'

'He better have his tail tucked firmly between his thighs.' Jan wagged her finger.

'He texted this picture first thing.' Bea took out her phone and held up the picture of Phoebe in a red Santa hat and pyjamas, waving.

'Aww, bless her little heart.' Jan took the phone and scrutinised the picture. 'Those birthmarks are much paler, aren't they?'

'I couldn't believe it when I saw her,' said Immy. 'I reckon they'll almost disappear with the next treatment.'

Bea took the phone back and examined the screen. They were right. She didn't really notice Phoebe's birthmarks when she looked at her these days, but when she concentrated, she could see they were pink when they had been livid red.

'You sure she wants to see me?' said Immy, rubbing her tummy. It was protruding very slightly under her t-shirt. She hadn't been sick for the best part of a week and Bea was convinced her mothering was a healing influence, even though she knew being firmly in her second trimester was probably the more likely factor.

'That's what Ewan says. He messaged last night to say he's told her he was wrong when he thought you'd been unkind to her mummy and you are the only cousin she has, so she should make the most of you. Apparently, she's very excited to see you.' She clicked onto her messages, showing them a trail of texts from Ewan. 'He's been quite the phone pest since yesterday. He seems to mean what he said, at least.'

'I should think so, too,' said Jan, shoving half a croissant into her mouth. 'Now you two go and say hello to the ones that are up, and shout up to our Ciara, will you? She's making Christmas dinner at Sweetingdale. God help them all!'

* * *

Bea's stomach quivered as she parked in front of Ewan's house. She put her hand over Immy's. 'You ready?'

'I feel a bit sick.'

Bea pointed to the bush to the right of the house. 'There's your usual vom bush. Crack on.'

Immy laughed and shook her head. 'I can't believe we're already joking about that.'

Bea shrugged and Immy laughed harder.

On the doorstep, she put the bag of presents down and held her daughter's hand. She had to let go swiftly when Phoebe threw the door open and leaped into her arms. 'Aunty Bea. I missed you!' Bea lifted her, wrapping arms under her bottom as the little girl clung onto her neck and buried her head in her hair.

'Merry Christmas,' she said, halfway between laughing and crying. She breathed in the strawberry shampoo and felt the perfect weight of Phoebe in her arms. 'I've missed you so much, my darling, darling girl.'

'Hello, Phoebe. Can I join in?' Immy asked, softly.

Phoebe raised her head slowly and observed her cousin, then smiled and nodded and Bea felt Immy's arms fold around them both and it was a feeling so perfect she didn't ever want it to end.

'Bea.' Ewan was standing in the hallway and Bea was immediately irritated. Why did he always say her name instead of saying hello?

'Immy.' There he went again.

'Ewan.' She matched his formal tone.

Go Immy, Bea thought. Play him at his own game. The lack of the word 'uncle' went without comment, but she was sure they all felt it. He'd lost the right to that title.

'Thank you for coming. It's very gracious of you.' He focused on Immy. 'Especially you, Immy. I know it can't be easy and I appreciate I have a lot of work to do to deserve . . . Well, anyway . . . Come in.' He stood aside. 'Come in.'

Phoebe made no attempt to get down, so Bea carried her into the house, followed by Immy, as Ewan grabbed the bag. The house smelled of fresh ground coffee and mulled wine spices. When they reached the kitchen, a stranger was sitting at the table. She stood and for a moment, Bea was lost for words. Her tall, lean frame and short, blunt brown fringe made it look like Gemma's ghost was visiting from Christmas past.

'Bonjour, hello!' said the woman.

Bea closed her mouth and tried to make it smile. She loosened her arms to let Phoebe down, but Phoebe gripped her around the neck, so she stayed where she was and said, 'Hi. I'm Bea and this' – she turned her body towards Immy – 'is Imogen.'

'Immy,' said Immy, and walked forwards with her hand outstretched.

'I've heard so much about you,' said the not-Gemma woman in a thick French accent. She held Immy's hand in both of hers and shook it vigorously. When she let go Immy turned to Bea, one eyebrow cocked, and Bea read her mind. God, she'd missed her. A growl of fury at all the time Ewan had stolen from them rumbled inside her, but Phoebe's head resting on her shoulder made her ignore it. For today, at least.

'Come on then, let's open these presents,' Ewan shouted from the sitting room. They traipsed through, Bea's teeth gritting when she spied the magnificent tree in the corner looking different to how she'd left it. All the homemade decorations seemed to have disappeared and the baubles Phoebe had hung on the bottom branches had all been distributed evenly from the top down.

'Camille spoiled our tree,' whispered Phoebe in Bea's ear. 'She took everything off and put it back all wrong.'

Bea grimaced at Phoebe and set her down on the carpet. 'What do you want to open first?' She kneeled and patted the bag of things she'd brought. 'Silly old Santa dropped these off with me. He must've known I was coming to see you today.'

Phoebe eyed her with suspicion. Bea picked a brightly coloured present from the top of the pile and soon Phoebe was ripping off the paper. 'A Horrid Henry game!' she squealed, throwing her arms around Bea again and kissing her loudly on the cheek.

'Open this one from Camille,' said Ewan. 'It's come all the way from New York.'

Phoebe struggled with the pink ribbon tied in an elaborate bow. Bea put her hands under her knees to stop herself from helping. Eventually, Phoebe got inside the paper and opened the lid of the box. Bea could tell she was forcing herself to look pleased when she opened the layers of white tissue paper and pulled out a pale pink cashmere cardigan. 'That's beautiful. Let me feel it?' Phoebe handed it to her. 'Oh, that's lovely.' She rubbed it over the back of her hand and then on Phoebe's cheek as she giggled.

'What do you say to Camille?' coaxed Ewan.

'Thank you,' said Phoebe mechanically and leaped on the next present from Bea's stack.

As Phoebe tore through the last of her stocking fillers, Ewan picked his way through the discarded paper towards them with two envelopes in his hand. He held the first one out to Immy. 'From Camille and me.'

Joint presents, already? thought Bea incredulously. *Joint mortgage next.* She tried to push her catty side down but failed, silently adding, *as if this Camille would be with him if he needed a mortgage.*

'I haven't bought—' Immy looked embarrassed.

'God, really, there's no need,' said Ewan. 'This is only part reparation for . . .' He licked his lips. 'Anyway, I hope it's useful.'

Immy peeled back the lip of the envelope and plucked out a voucher for a baby supplies shop in town. 'Wow! I can't . . . This is too much.'

'I disagree.' He handed the other, bigger envelope to Bea. 'Don't try to argue with me on this one. Mother and I both think it's the least I can do.'

'What is it?' Bea put her hands back under her knees. 'Open it.'

'I don't want your money Ewan.'

'It's not money, not exactly. It's a lease. On this house.'

'What?' That didn't make any sense at all.

'You gave up a lot to come and live here and I know we didn't make it easy for you to say no.'

'You can say that again.' Her mind went back to the dinner with Ewan and Joyce that felt more like an ambush.

'And we agreed that you'd live here for two years.'

'Yes, well, things—'

There was no stopping him. 'And I know you and Immy need somewhere to live, so it only seems right that you have a tenancy agreement for the remainder of the time we agreed, rent-free, of course, which means I can't chuck you out if things don't go my way.'

'I can just—'

'And,' he cut her off again, 'I have taken on board what you said about being a better father to my lovely little girl.' He scooped Phoebe up and kissed her cheeks, 'So Camille and I have talked' – he took Camille's hand – 'and decided Phoebe should come and live with us in the States.'

Bea froze. Immy looked from Bea to Ewan and back again, her face a mask of horror.

Phoebe let out a howl.

Chapter Forty-One

'You can't be serious?' Bea said over the noise of Phoebe's crying. 'Have you even asked her what she wants?' She took Phoebe from him and let her cry into her hair.

'She's six.' There was genuine confusion on Ewan's face, and anger rose in Bea's throat.

'She's still a human being.' She held the back of Phoebe's head and shushed her. She tried to gather her thoughts.

'But you said . . .' Ewan scratched the back of his head, looking between the women as if he could find the right thing to say in one of their faces.

'I said you needed to be a better father.'

'That's what I'm trying to do.'

Camille came to his side and snaked an arm around his waist. 'Shush, baby.'

Bea huffed. If anyone needed comforting now, it wasn't Ewan. 'Being a better father means putting your child first, not moving her to a different country without consulting or preparing her, just to fit in with your new life.' She watched as Camille stood on her tiptoes and kissed Ewan's neck and the gesture seemed so out of place with the soundtrack of Phoebe's wailing that Bea couldn't believe what she was seeing.

'I know you two are in love and all that, but there's a bigger picture, you know?' Her voice was slick with sarcasm, but Camille's innocent face suggested it hadn't translated.

'Let's have breakfast and talk about this civilly.' Ewan's voice was business-like and, once again, Bea wanted to punch him.

'We've eaten.'

'Please, Bea, we have so many pastries. You must try the chausson aux pommes,' said Camille, unwinding herself from Ewan's neck and smiling obsequiously.

Bea glanced down at the child in her arms. She couldn't leave the poor thing alone with these two idiots on Christmas morning. 'I'll have a coffee.' She marched through to the kitchen and saw the table festooned with enough pastries to serve the Foreign Legion. She sat, picking up a pain aux raisin and took a bite, ignoring the flakes of pastry floating to the floor.

Ewan held out his hand for Phoebe, but she ignored him and hid her face in Bea's neck. Bea wrapped her arms around her and when Phoebe leaned back, slotting her body into Bea's, it felt like coming home. Immy sat next to them and stroked Phoebe's hand. Rage bubbled inside Bea. This is what she had dreamed about, and now bloody Ewan was going to spoil everything again.

'It's alright, poppet,' she whispered into Phoebe's ear and the little girl snuggled in closer. She turned back to Ewan, 'What are your actual plans?'

His mouth twitched. He looked from her to Camille and back again. 'There's nothing firm yet, but—' He was interrupted by Camille wrapping her arms around him again. The woman was like a bloody python.

330

'So, you can rethink?'

'I, erm . . .'

Phoebe withdrew her face from Bea's neck and looked at her father.

'If Phoebe doesn't want to come to America, perhaps she could stay here, in this house, with you, Bea?' Camille gave a Gallic shrug as though this wasn't a particularly important matter.

'Well, no.' Ewan flushed and stepped away from Camille. She wobbled, then regained her balance and switched on the coffee machine, her face registering mild annoyance. 'Phoebe will be living w-with me,' he stuttered. 'With us.' He gestured to Camille, who was humming aggressively as she frothed milk in a small silver jug. 'I'll find an international school in New York.'

'No!' Phoebe shouted so loudly it hurt Bea's ears. She looked at Bea imploringly, fat tears chasing each other down her cheeks. 'Aunty Bea, no!'

'Let me talk to Daddy,' said Bea. 'Okay?'

'Immy.' She pulled Phoebe's arms away from her neck. 'Why don't you take Phoebe upstairs and play the Horrid Henry game with her for a few minutes while I talk to these two?'

'Let's take the chocolates.' Immy picked up a bowl of Quality Streets from the middle of the table and winked at Phoebe, whose sobs slowed.

Phoebe stood facing Ewan, with her feet wide, fists on her hips. 'I'm not leaving Aunty Bea or my school, or my friends,' she hiccupped, 'because I love them.' Her chin crumpled and she sniffed dramatically before following Immy from the room.

Listening for Phoebe's bedroom door closing, Bea turned to Ewan. 'Have you learned nothing from all of this?'

He looked utterly confused. 'I'm only doing what you told me to do. You said . . .'

Bea shook her head. 'I said she needed her dad.'

'Here I am!' He flung his arms wide.

'With your new girlfriend and new priorities, none of which seem to be your daughter's happiness.'

Camille shrugged again. 'I don't see the problem. Phoebe wants to stay here, she can stay here, *non?*'

'And you can shut up,' Bea couldn't help herself.

Camille tutted and headed through to the utility room, slamming the door behind her.

'You can't speak to *my* guest like that in *my* house,' Ewan said.

'That tells me all I need to know about that fucking envelope, doesn't it?' Bea marched into the sitting room and picked up the lease from the table, bringing it back into the kitchen and thrusting it at Ewan. 'Your house. Your money. That's all you care about, isn't it? You can pretend you're changing your plans for the sake of Phoebe, but really, it's a salve for your guilty conscience while you go off to New York and live happily ever after with your new teen bride.'

'Camille is twenty-six.'

'You are fifty, you sad old man. What the hell do you think she's doing with you?'

'Say what you like about me but leave Camille out of it. We are in love, and we're going to get married.' Ewan flung open the door of the utility. 'Aren't we, Camille?'

Bea was sure Camille would have liked to have answered, but she seemed a bit busy with the rolled up twenty-pound note and the line of white powder she was snorting off the draining board.

* * *

332

An hour later, Camille left in a taxi. She tried to take a small, intricately wrapped box from under the tree, but Ewan snatched it out of her hands before she flounced out, slamming the door behind her.

Now, he sat at the kitchen table with his head in his hands. 'She completely fooled me.'

Bea almost felt sorry for him, then she remembered his diatribes about drugs when he'd talked about Immy and all pity dissipated. 'Yeah, it was all her fault. Nothing to do with your pride, arrogance, greed and libido.' She remembered what Immy had said. 'And your male privilege and toxic masculinity.'

'Don't sugar-coat it.'

'I won't.' She made him a coffee and sat next to him in silence. The sounds of giggling from upstairs made them both look up. 'Do you know who her best friend is?'

Ewan shook his head. 'I didn't know she had one. She's never been very happy at that school. That's one of the reasons I thought she wouldn't mind moving.'

'If you'd asked her, she would have told you things have changed a lot since you've been away.'

He glanced up with sad eyes. 'Who's her best friend?'

'A girl called Sydney.'

'Sydney?'

'Yep. They greet each other like long-lost relatives every morning. She doesn't look back when I drop her off anymore.'

'I didn't know.'

'No.' She couldn't be sure he'd remember now she'd told him, either. 'If you stop chasing superficial things to make yourself feel young and successful, you might be able to see you have the makings of a pretty good life already.'

333

Ewan shifted in his chair to face her. 'I thought I was supposed to be the clever one.'

'There are different kinds of clever.'

'So I gather.' He paused and examined her face. 'Admittedly, it's taken a while, but I can see why my brother was so happy with you.'

Bea swallowed. 'We were happy with each other.'

'Come on then, oh sage one.' Ewan squeezed her hand. 'Let's tell Phoebe she's not going anywhere. Then we can all go and wish my mother a merry Christmas.'

'Do we have to?' Bea groaned.

'You know you love her really.'

And the funny thing was, she realised he was right.

Chapter Forty-Two

'You've split up?' said Joyce three days later, as Ewan rolled the wheelchair along the corridor at Sweetingdale. 'Already?'

He'd asked Bea to keep the news and the circumstances to herself over Christmas, but now Joyce was comfortably ensconced in the best room Sweetingdale had to offer, he was sharing a sanitised version with his mother. Bea walked more quickly to catch what they were saying. 'But you said she was *the one.*'

'Yes, but it turned out we weren't compatible, after all.'

That's the story, is it? thought Bea. A little part of her wanted to tell Joyce what a poor choice Ewan had really made; how he'd been thrown off his high horse so inelegantly that he was lying in the mud staring up at its underbelly.

'In future, I've decided not to date anyone more than five years younger than me.' He paused. 'Seven at the most.'

Bea rolled her eyes behind his back.

'And they need to get Phoebe's seal of approval before anything gets serious.'

That made her smile.

'Where is Phoebe?' Joyce twisted to try to see behind them where Immy and Phoebe were trying to walk and do a clapping game at the same time.

Phoebe skipped forwards. 'Here I am.'

Joyce reached out for her hand and Bea detected a sparkle in Joyce's eye. Maybe, at last, she was letting Phoebe in.

They arrived at Joyce's room at the end of Primrose corridor. Phoebe ran inside and jumped on the bed. 'This is really comfy, Grandma.'

'Glad to hear it. I might be here for some time.'

Bea crossed the room to the patio doors and scanned the garden. Kenny was walking along the path and his face lit up when he recognised her. He waved. She waved back. That was a turnaround since she last saw him. 'Are you thinking of staying?'

'It's very tempting, since I've never been so popular.' Joyce's voice was unusually giddy. 'Everyone seems to have heard I'm related to you, and they've welcomed me with open arms. I'm overrun with offers of Bridge partners and Scrabble companions. There's never a dull moment.' She rubbed her hands together. 'And the food . . . well!'

'Ciara's doing a good job, is she?'

'She's splendid. They have a nice Rioja in the restaurant, and there's no shortage of people to chat to. I should have done this years ago.'

Immy and Phoebe sat on the bed and continued to clap their hands together in a complicated rhythm. Immy patted Phoebe's foot, reminding her to move her shoes off the covers. Phoebe dutifully dropped her legs over the side and Bea's breath caught as she remembered her daughter would be parenting her own child soon.

Joyce crooked her finger for Bea to come closer. 'I have a suggestion, now Ewan has decided to relocate back home.'

'Oh yes?'

The light was dancing in Joyce's eyes. 'Now I'm settled in here, my house is empty, so if you and Imogen—'

Bea flung her arms in the air. 'Will you lot stop trying to give me your bloody houses!' She turned to Immy. 'When will our family realise we can look after ourselves? Joyce, I'm a big girl now. I'll get another job and when I do, we'll manage just fine, thank you very much.' She realised she'd said *our family* and meant it. She tucked the warm feeling that gave her away to take out and enjoy later.

'I'm afraid you don't have much choice about it,' said Ewan. 'Mother and I have agreed that if you and Immy don't live in the house, then I'll rent it out to the bank for the foreign fund managers and put the money in your account anyway. I have your bank details, so you can't stop me.'

Bea flushed but didn't have time to formulate a reply because there was a knock at the door. Ewan opened it. 'Hello. Thanks for coming. I think we're ready to sign her off.'

'No problem.'

Bea recognised Eddie's voice and spun around to see him standing in the doorway with his bike helmet tucked under his arm. 'Hi.'

'Eddie, good to see you,' said Joyce, and Bea watched Eddie's eyebrows lift.

'Looks like this place suits you,' he said, scanning the room.

'Well, come in then. I believe you have some forms for us to sign to allow me to live my own life again?'

He stepped forwards and put his helmet by the door.

'If you mean, releasing you from our care, then yes.' He swirled his rucksack off his shoulder and rummaged inside, pulling out a folder of notes. 'Good to see you again, Immy.' He smiled over at her. 'Hope they're treating you like the legend you are after saving your gran's life?'

Of all the things he could have said in front of Ewan, this was the one he chose. Bea could have kissed him.

Immy's hand went to her stomach and her smile made her face shine. 'I don't know about that.'

'He's right,' said Joyce. 'We are very fortunate you came back when you did. Well, at all, really.' She gave Ewan a scorching glare.

To stop herself from blubbing in front of Eddie again, Bea forced herself to lift her chin and say, 'Papers?'

'Yes. All here somewhere.' He shuffled through the notes. 'Although we can't finish the whole process today because there's no manager on.'

'Lynn not around?' Bea thought about it and realised she hadn't seen Lynn since the first day they moved Joyce in. She and Creepy Dave were in the restaurant the first evening, but she hadn't set eyes on them since.

'Didn't I tell you?' said Joyce. 'I saw that unpleasant man taking a purse from someone's bag a couple of days ago. I called out in the restaurant when it happened and a dear old man by the name of Kenny made a citizen's arrest, on my instructions, naturally. That cultured lady down the corridor, Vera, called the police there and then. It was all terribly exciting because when they arrived the residents insisted they searched their staff accommodation and they found all manner of illicit contraband belonging to the people living here.'

Bea's mouth fell open. 'And you didn't think to tell me about this?'

338

Jan's distinctive laugh came from the doorway. 'You've heard the good news then?'

'I can't believe you didn't ring me!'

Jan plucked a jug of water from the trolley she'd been pushing and weaved through the now crowded room to put it on Joyce's bedside table, stopping to plonk a kiss on top of Phoebe's head. 'There was a little something I wanted to sort out first.'

Eddie was nodding and grinning from ear to ear. 'I had a word, too.'

'What are you two on about? You're talking in riddles.'

Jan walked over to Eddie, reached up and hooked her arm through his. 'The owners are in a right state, now Lynn's had her marching orders.'

'I can imagine,' said Bea. 'Between Christmas and New Year, too. Nightmare.'

'They need somebody quick-smart to fill in. Somebody who the residents like, who knows the place and how it runs.'

'Someone who's on course for a distinction in their management diploma,' Eddie said, with an even wider grin.

'Someone who wouldn't mind moving into the manager's two-bed flat,' Jan added.

'Really?' Immy was by her side, gripping her elbow. 'What did they say?'

Bea scoped every face in the room, too terrified to speak in case she'd misunderstood what was happening.

'They are waiting in the manager's office to speak to your mum, right now.'

The grip on her arm got tighter and when she turned Immy's eyes shone with excitement. 'Do you want it, Mum?'

339

Did she want it? To come back to a place she'd loved working? To be in charge of getting it right for people she loved, like Vera and Joyce? To have somewhere for her and Immy to live that wasn't anywhere near the bloody Crescent?

'I'm not prepared.' Sweat tingled in her armpits. She looked down at her jeans and shirt. 'I can't go like this.'

'They need you more than you need them, Bea,' said Eddie. 'Plus, your cheerleading team has already done the groundwork.'

Ewan cleared his throat. 'When I interview, what I'm looking for most is—'

'Shut up, Ewan,' said Joyce. 'Bea is quite capable of handling this herself.'

Was she? She overheard voices in the corridor and poked her head out of the door. Vera was the first face she glimpsed. Her cheeks crinkled in a smile, and she gave her a double thumbs up. Kenny stood behind her, waving, and behind him other friendly faces hovered, all looking at her with hopeful eyes.

'They're waiting,' said Jan, giving her a not too gentle nudge.

'Am I doing this?' Bea asked her family.

'Yes!'

As she turned into the corridor, the residents parted for her to walk through them, flanked on either side by Eddie and Jan. They then closed the gap and trailed behind, their shuffling footsteps and thumping sticks giving her confidence to put one foot in front of the other. She made out Phoebe's excited chatter and the squeaking wheels of Joyce's wheelchair amongst the encouraging murmurs. Her heart filled to bursting and as she neared the manager's office, she was reminded of a euphoric dream she'd had once where she could fly.

She looked behind her at the faces of the people in her life. Her daughter, grown into an incredible young woman; the bump of Bea's grandchild rounding out her middle. She glanced at Phoebe, riding on the back of Joyce's wheelchair, her arms draped over the old lady's shoulders. Even Ewan was grinning like a loon, nodding his head as though trying to transfer some of his confidence to her.

'Go on then,' Jan said, but she was nudging Eddie this time.

Eddie glanced behind him, then back at Bea. He lowered his head and whispered, 'When you've finished in there' – he nodded towards the door – 'I should have the papers signed off, so I'm not involved in your family's care anymore, professionally, I mean.'

'Get on with it,' whispered Jan.

Eddie gave her a harassed glare, then turned his attention back to Bea. 'So, I was wondering whether you'd give me that ride you promised?'

Jan sniggered. 'Filthy bugger.'

'On your motorbike,' Eddie said, stifling a laugh. 'Then maybe we could go for dinner?'

'I will,' said Bea. 'I'd love to.' She knocked on the door. 'Just let me get the job of my dreams first.'

The door opened. Bea put her shoulders back and walked inside.

The End

Acknowledgements

It takes a village to raise a book-baby.

First, I'd like to thank my brilliant Literary-Doula and agent, Laura Williams, for her enthusiasm and support throughout. Next, the midwives, Avon Editors extraordinaire, Thorne Ryan and Elisha Lundin. Thank you for trusting me to be part of the Avon family, for making me push hard at the end and ensuring the manuscript had ten fingers and ten toes when it went out into the world.

Thank you to my mentor and friend, Kerry Fisher, who has spent years guiding me through the whole book-parenting process. I will be forever grateful.

I'd like to thank the book's favourite aunties, the early readers, whose encouragement and advice was invaluable: Jodi Rilot, Emma Warburton, Hannah Maynard, Ruth Rutter, Heather Moore, Tracey Cullens and Emma Buxton. What would I do without you?

As in life, so many of the most supportive and vital members of the community are other mothers, so I would like to thank those with book-babies of their own who have given their time, wisdom and unwavering support during the years of learning and rejection which inevitably come with the process of birthing a book. To the Chislehurst Writing Group, Suzy Oldfield and Nichola Ibe. Thank you. I love you both.

To the Writers Beers and Cliterati: Callie Langridge, Susie Lynes, Emma Robinson, Claire McGlasson, Clarissa Angus, Emelie Olsson, Bev Thomas and Kate Riordan, you are inspiring, incredible women and spending time with you has been a highlight of this whole, bonkers experience.

Rowan Coleman, Laura Pearson (The Literary Cupid), Nikki Smith, Annie Lyons and Clare Pooley, thank you for cheering me on and putting my work forward. Women who lift as they climb are the very best.

To Deb and Drew Royston, thank you for being so open about what it's like to live with physical challenges, and for showing me that, with a sparkling personality like Drew's and a mother as strong and loving as Deb, a disability is only ever a small part of the story. Also, many thanks to Marie Cavalier, Chair of Sturge Weber UK. For more information, and to donate, please visit www.sturgeweber.org.uk.

Finally, to my own family, John, Eva and Isla. Thank you for giving me the time and space to bring this book to life. Thank you for believing in me, supporting me and for being just as excited as I am about the members of our family who only live in my head. You are my world.

Now this book is out in the wild, I'm nervous because it will have to fend for itself. But it has you, the reader, so I'm sure it's in safe hands. If you enjoy it, I'd be very grateful if you could review and recommend. Thank you for reading right to the end. You are lovely.